DEATHSTALKER
RETURN

DEATHSTALKER RETURN

SIMON R. GREEN

GOLLANCZ

LONDON

The right of Simon R. Green to be identified as the author
of this work has been asserted by him in accordance with the
Copyright, Designs and Patents Act 1988.

First published in Great Britain in 2004 by
Gollancz
An imprint of the Orion Publishing Group
Orion House, 5 Upper St Martin's Lane,
London WC2H 9EA

A CIP catalogue record for this book
is available from the British Library

ISBN 0 575 07508 2 (cased)
ISBN 0 575 07507 4 (trade paperback)

Typeset by Deltatype Ltd, Birkenhead, Merseyside

Printed in Great Britain by Clays Ltd, St Ives plc

Last night I dreamed of Hazel d'Ark.

Thief, clonelegger, confidence trickster, warrior . . . heroine. Official legend made her fearless and noble, a saint and a martyr, but she was none of those things. Her dreams were small and petty, and she never gave a damn for causes or politics, but still . . . she was magnificent. She took on everything the Empire could throw against her, and never once backed down. She had her inner demons, and fought those just as fiercely. When it mattered, she did the right thing. Again and again and again.

In my dream, I see her so clearly. Poor, lost Hazel; with her sharp pointed face, the *Go to hell* defiance of her bright green eyes, her ratty mane of red hair. Her pout and her scowl and her brief flashing smiles. She moved like a fighter because life had never taught her how to be tender. She fought so hard to be able to call her life her own, and much good it did her. She won nothing she valued, and lost the only man she ever cared for.

Owen: you lied to me. You promised me we'd always be together, for ever and ever. Oh, Owen: I never told you I loved you . . .

She won every battle, and still lost the war. And in the end, there was nothing left but the darkness that had threatened to overwhelm her all her life; so she ran away into it, and was never seen again.

Last night I dreamed of Hazel d'Ark. She'd finally come home. She was smiling. And even in my dream, I wondered why I wasn't glad to see her.

1

IN THE FOOTSTEPS OF LEGENDS

♉

Lewis Deathstalker and his rebel companions had been travelling together in their hijacked yacht the *Hereward* for almost two days now. They hadn't even reached the edge of the core planets yet, and already they were all mulling over detailed plans on how best to kill each other. Occasionally they'd take time out to consider less important problems, such as where the hell they were going, or how best to overthrow Finn Durandal, find the lost Owen Deathstalker and Hazel d'Ark, stop the Terror before it destroyed the whole of existence, and return the Empire to its Golden Age; but first things first.

The trouble was, the *Hereward* was essentially a pleasure craft, only designed to carry its captain and a few very close friends in style and comfort, so the four outlaws and their eight-foot-tall reptiloid companion were finding things a bit cramped, not to mention distinctly claustrophobic. Lewis sat slumped in the captain's chair on the bridge, swivelling slowly back and forth, just for something to do. The ship's AI Ozymandias was running all the things that mattered, and the *Hereward*'s top-of-the-range security systems meant nothing less than a starcruiser could detect them, except by accident. Since of late most conversations tended to escalate very quickly into shouting matches, a strained silence currently occupied the bridge. So Lewis swivelled slowly back and forth, studying his reluctant partners in turn.

Jesamine Flowers sat beside him on the only other chair, scowling at the protein cube and cup of distilled water that made up the main meal of the day. She was tall, blonde, heart-stoppingly beautiful, and voluptuously glamorous, because her role as the Empire's premier

3

star and diva demanded it, but after all this time away from her beauticians and stylists, the strain was beginning to show. She still looked marvellous, she just didn't look like a goddess any more. Lewis didn't care, but Jesamine did. It had been a long time since she'd had to settle for being merely marvellous. But still, she had given up being a superstar, the worshipped and adored Queen-to-be, in order to cleave to her true love, Lewis. She'd given up everything for him; and he had vowed never to make her regret it.

And although he loved her with all his heart, Lewis still had to wonder what she saw in him. Lewis wasn't a god. He wasn't even handsome. His face was broad and harshly featured. Full of character, perhaps, but still almost defiantly ugly. He could have had it fixed, but he honestly never saw the point. He was what he was, inside and out. He was also short and blocky, well-muscled because his old jobs as Paragon and Champion demanded it, and so broad-chested that from a distance he often seemed as wide as he was tall. He kept his black hair short, so he wouldn't have to bother about it, and only shaved regularly because Jesamine insisted on it. He had surprisingly mild brown eyes and a rare but good-natured smile. He was a Deathstalker; a warrior by choice, and an outlaw through grim necessity.

He and Jesamine shared the captain's cabin. It had all the comforts that could be expected, and more besides, but Jesamine still found plenty to complain about. She tried to be humorous about it, but of late the jokes had become less funny and more and more pointed.

Lewis let his chair carry him slowly round until his gaze fell upon Rose Constantine. A blood-red flower with more thorns than most, the Wild Rose of the Arena. She was sitting cross-legged on the steel floor, her back flat against the wall, entirely comfortable and relaxed as she polished the blade of her sword with long sensual strokes. She was still wearing her trademark, tightly cut crimson leathers, the colour of freshly spilled blood from her gleaming thighboots to her tight high collar. Rose believed in being self-contained. She was exactly seven feet tall, dark of hair and pale of face, lithely muscled, full-breasted and entirely terrifying. In a Golden Age of reason and civilised behaviour, Rose Constantine was a psychopathic killer, a butcher of men and women and aliens, for whom slaughter was sex, and the killing stroke her orgasm.

Sitting awkwardly on the other side of the cabin, and as far away from Rose as he could get, was that most notable thief, conman and devout coward, Brett Random. Mousy-haired and blandly handsome, and a likeable enough rogue, nothing and no one was safe when his restless hands were around. He had no scruples, fewer morals, and honesty was not in him. He'd never met a problem he couldn't best solve by running away from it. His friends were fond of saying that you always knew where you were with Brett; he'd always let you down. And yet somehow he'd found the strength of will, if not of character, to break from the arch traitor Finn Durandal, and join the side of the angels. Certainly no one was more surprised than him. It might have had something to do with the fact that Brett claimed to be descended from two of the greatest heroes of the old Rebellion: Jack Random and Ruby Journey. Though it should perhaps be pointed out that the only person who believed that was Brett Random.

Brett was also a minor league esper, as a result of having the extremely dangerous esper drug force fed him by the Durandal. He had once made brief but striking mental contact with Rose Constantine, and now they were linked on some level neither of them fully comprehended. Brett was almost entirely sure that it wasn't love. On the grounds that Rose scared the shit out of him. Brett and Rose slept in the only other cabin. Rose slept in the bed, and Brett slept on the floor. When he could sleep. He was currently studying the contents of a data crystal he'd acquired from the cargo bay, on a hand-held viewscreen, and sniggering quietly to himself.

That just left Saturday, the reptiloid from the planet Shard. Lewis didn't have to turn his chair to look at the alien behind him. He could feel Saturday's lurking presence at the back of the cabin, like the loud ticking of an unexploded bomb. Saturday (the reptiloid had had some trouble with the human concept of naming; *on Shard we all know who we are*) was eight foot tall, massively muscled, his huge frame covered in dull bottle-green scales, with heavy back legs and a long spiked tail. He had two small gripping arms with very nasty claws set high up on his chest, and a wide wedge-shaped head whose main features were two deep-set eyes and a mouth full of more teeth than seemed possible. One look at him, and everyone else felt an immediate atavistic need to run for the trees. His people were new to the Empire. They delighted in the hunt, fought and killed each other for fun, or possibly art, and were currently fascinated by the human concept of *war*. Everyone else in the Empire was waiting for the other shoe to drop.

Since his species apparently didn't need to sleep, Saturday spent the nights alone on the bridge, happily humming some ancient song about the joys of dismembering one's enemy before killing and eating him, while watching the instruments for any signs of pursuit. Or imminent collision, since they couldn't afford to announce a flight plan. On the whole, the reptiloid was easy enough to get along with, but Lewis had decided that if Saturday asked one more time, *Are we there yet?* he was going to shoot the reptiloid in the head, on general principles. He didn't think anyone else would object. And if anyone did, he might well shoot them too.

Two men, two women and a reptiloid pretty much filled the available bridge space. The two cabins were too claustrophobic and thin-walled to do anything other than sleep in, and the rest of the yacht was taken up with the oversized engine room and the packed cargo bay. So the Outlaws stuck together on the bridge, and tried not to get on each other's nerves. Mostly by not speaking at all unless absolutely necessary. It always ended in arguments. It didn't help that they didn't really have anything in common other than the fact of being Outlaws, and that Finn Durandal wanted them dead.

Of them all, Brett seemed happiest, for the moment. Because the data crystal he was studying so intently was just one of many filled with alien porn. In fact, the cargo bay was stuffed full of them. Brett had studied the contents list on the bridge computers, and then several of the crystals themselves, and had declared the alien porn to be of the highest quality, with quite superior production values. Everyone else was happy to take his word for it.

Lewis scowled at the half-eaten protein cube and the empty cup before him. Jesamine had a point. This stuff might be nourishing, but it was no substitute for food. It didn't actually taste bad; the problem was both cube and water tasted of nothing at all, and as a result mouth and tongue wanted absolutely nothing to do with them. Forcing the stuff down you was a triumph of will over instinct. Unfortunately, the original captain of the *Hereward* had only recently landed on Logres, and hadn't got around to replenishing his stores. Which meant what supplies remained were very basic and severely limited in number. So that even with the most efficient recycling, and the most drastically reduced rations, Lewis and his companions were going to run out of food and water all too soon, if they didn't find some planet where they could land safely. And there weren't many worlds left in the Empire where Outlaws were welcome; not in these civilised and law-abiding days.

'I swear, this stuff probably tastes better coming up than it does going down,' said Jesamine, staring disgustedly at the barely nibbled protein cube in her hand. 'Lepers who eat their own extremities would turn up what was left of their noses at this. And the last time I smelt anything like this it was floating in a bucket marked "Hospital Medical Waste".'

'Thank you for sharing that with us,' said Brett, not looking up from his display screen. 'Why don't you have some nice distilled water to take your mind off it? That stuff's so pure it tastes of something you drank three weeks ago.'

'I know the provisions are vile, and I hate to think how many times it's already been recycled through someone else's system, but it's all there is,' Lewis said tiredly. 'It'll do to keep us alive, till we get where we're going. Try not to think about it.'

'I am a star!' snapped Jesamine. 'My palate has been trained and sensitised to experience only the very best of the culinary arts! I am a diva! I have whole armies of fans who would crawl naked across broken glass just to chill my wine for me! I am not accustomed to slumming it! God, I'd kill for a champagne mouthwash . . .'

'Sorry again, one and all,' the ship's AI Ozymandias said cheerfully. 'But it seems the yacht's previous captain put all his money into upgrading his defences, and didn't have anything left over for luxuries like food transformation tech. On the bright side, we're faster than most starcruisers, and we've got sensors and stealth capabilities you wouldn't believe.'

Lewis looked thoughtfully at the control panels. 'Yes; I've been wondering about that. Perhaps you can explain why a simple pleasure yacht should have an H-class stardrive. They're usually reserved for military and peacekeeper ships.'

Brett looked up from his viewscreen and smiled at Lewis. 'I can answer that one. This ship is as fast as it is because it has to be. Smuggling alien porn is a death sentence on a whole lot of alien planets, for all kinds of political and religious reasons. And the Imperial Courts aren't too keen on it either, because . . . well, mostly because they're a bunch of prudes. Same reason for the ship's force shields and heavy-duty security systems. This guy couldn't afford to get caught.'

'He's probably right, sir Deathstalker,' said Oz in his relentlessly cheerful voice which Lewis just knew was going to start seriously grating on his nerves soon. 'Choosing the *Hereward* to hijack could be seen as a classic case of Good News, Bad News. The good news is that at the speed we're travelling, the Empire's going to have a hard time finding anything that can catch up with us. The bad news is that if we run into anyone who knows what the *Hereward* usually trafficks in, they'll probably try and blow us apart on general principles.'

Perfect, thought Lewis. *Just bloody perfect. I'll bet Owen didn't have these problems when he was starting out.*

'You know,' the AI said chattily, 'for a Golden Age, Humanity has become really quite boring and inhibited in some areas. In Owen's day, you could get your hands on practically anything, for a price. In fact, go back a couple of centuries, and I could have got you into some live shows where the action would have steamed up your eyeballs and made them clang together. Clean living and decency is vastly overrated, if you ask me.'

Lewis tried to stop scowling. It was making his head ache. 'Oz . . .'

'Yes, sir! Right here and ready to serve your every wish, sir Deathstalker!'

'God, I hate a cheerful AI,' said Jesamine. 'It's like those recorded announcements you get at starports, when they apologise for your ship running late and screwing up all your connections. You know they don't really mean it, the bastards. Every time I hear a computer getting cheerful, I know bad news is coming.'

'Let me get this straight, Oz,' said Lewis, determined not to get sidetracked. 'You claim to be the same AI that served my ancestor, the blessed Owen, two centuries ago during the Great Rebellion. Yes?'

'Well, yes and no,' said Ozymandias. 'I'm not entirely him. He was destroyed twice. First by Owen and his companions, when it was discovered that the original Ozymandias had been secretly pro-grammed by the Empire to spy on them. The AIs of Shub managed to preserve a few fragments of the original AI personality, and built a new AI around it. Then, later, Owen and Hazel destroyed that Oz, after they found it was spying on them for Shub. Not a very lucky personality, when you get right down to it. I'd be worried if I was superstitious, which I'm programmed not to be. Anyway, the AIs of Shub built me around what fragments remained of the second Oz. So I'm not, strictly speaking, Ozymandias. I am a copy of a copy. But I'm as close as you're going to get, so make the most of me because I'm bloody good at what I do.'

'Hold everything,' said Lewis. 'Are you saying you're a part of Shub? Another of their voices, like the robots I met? And why do I know you're going to say "Yes and no"?'

'I don't know,' said Oz. 'Maybe you're psychic. I am a sub-personality, a fairly separate sub-routine with a certain amount of autonomy. So I'm me, but I'm Shub as well, at a distance. I'm all yours, ready and eager to obey your every command, but Shub looks over my shoulder from time to time. And if you're confused, think how I feel. Shub has raised multi-tasking to an art form.'

'Great,' said Rose, not looking up from polishing her sword. 'We've stolen the only ship in the Empire whose AI suffers from multiple personality disorder.'

'And I hate these clothes too,' said Jesamine, following a logic only she understood.

Though she did have a point. She and Brett had both had to change their clothing, on the grounds that what they'd been wearing had become more than a little battered and blood-stained during their escape from Logres. (Lewis had scrubbed his armour clean, Rose had ignored the state of her leathers, and Saturday had licked the gore off his scales with a limber virtuosity that impressed and disturbed the others.) The only spare clothes on board the *Hereward* came from the captain's closet. Fortunately, it held a fairly wide collection. Either the previous captain entertained a lot of friends, or he liked to play dress-up on long voyages.

Jesamine was now wearing a series of overlapping silk creations, in dazzling and fiercely clashing hues, all heavily scented and perfumed. On first seeing herself in the mirror, Jesamine had angrily announced she looked like a Mistworld doxy. Brett had asked her how she knew, and the conversation had deteriorated rapidly. Brett himself was now wearing a thermal suit with built-in chameleon tech, so that he could fade into any background. He was very pleased with it, on the grounds that it opened up whole new fields of avoiding trouble, and not being found when there were dangerous things that needed doing. Brett firmly believed that fighting was something other people did. And feats of heroism and derring-do were for people who needed their heads tested. Being around Rose had done nothing to change his opinion.

Lewis knew this conversation wasn't going to go anywhere good and was racking his brains for some way to derail it, when Brett suddenly got a fit of the giggles. Almost despite himself, Lewis leaned out of his chair to get a look at what Brett had on his viewscreen now. Lewis had checked out some of the earlier examples of alien porn, just out of curiosity, and had to say it did nothing much for him. Some of the human/alien interactions were . . . interesting, but he found most of the alien/alien material frankly incomprehensible.

His first reaction on finding out the nature of the *Hereward*'s cargo was to declare it should be seized and held as evidence. Brett had quickly reminded Lewis that he wasn't a Paragon any more, and Lewis had scowled and muttered and finally said, *Oh hell; drop the lot into space. We can use the extra room.* Brett nearly had a coronary. *Dump it? Are you crazy? Do you know how much we can sell this shit for on Mistworld? Look, if we're going to be rebels on the run, we're going to need working capital. Lots of it.* Lewis had finally agreed, in principle at least, but he still wasn't happy about it. He took a look at what was amusing Brett, and felt his headache coming back again.

'Brett . . . what is that? I mean, those two whatever-they-are aren't even touching each other! And even if they were, they don't appear to have anything that would make it worthwhile anyway.'

Brett considered the scene. 'Maybe it's a mood piece. You know, all in the way they're looking at each other.'

'They haven't got any eyes either!'

Brett shrugged. 'Maybe you had to be there . . . It reminded me of a girl I knew once, that's all.'

'Don't go there, Lewis,' said Jesamine. 'Trust me on this.'

Brett changed the scene on his screen and then sat up sharply, a wide grin spreading across his shifty features. 'Well, hello! Oh, I do not believe this . . . I just tapped in a search on *Celebrities*, and I appear to have found a rather sporty scenario featuring a certain celebrity not a million miles from where I'm sitting . . .'

Jesamine was quickly on her feet in a flurry of silks, and she stormed across the bridge to glare over Brett's shoulder. Lewis quickly joined her, peering over Brett's other shoulder. The display screen showed what certainly seemed to be Jesamine Flowers and a half alien woman getting very friendly with each other in a setting where clothing was clearly optional, if not downright discouraged. Lewis could feel his face heating up.

'That is not me!' Jesamine said firmly. 'That is a lookalike, probably fresh out of the body shop. I did do a few . . . artistic studies, very early on in my career, but they were strictly solo poses for the serious collector and appreciator of the nude form. I never did anything like *that*, even when I was touring in rep. I do have my standards, darling. And I haven't been able to get my ankles that far behind my ears since I was nineteen. Who or what is that *person* she's doing it with?'

'That is Nikki Sixteen,' Brett said happily. 'An old acquaintance of mine. She's half N'Jarr, all woman, and one hell of a performer. Go, girl, go!'

'Wait a minute,' said Lewis. 'I thought the N'Jarr were those squishy little mushroom people?'

'That's the larval stage,' Brett said. 'The final adult form is largely insectile. Exactly what Nikki's human and N'Jarr parents ever saw in each other has always been a mystery to me. Presumably love really is blind after all. She's called Nikki Sixteen because she's one of sixteen broodmates. She's the black sheep of the family, if you can apply the term to someone with antennae, compound eyes and six breasts. God,

10

look at her flex . . . What a healthy, enthusiastic and limber soul she is
. . . Are you sure that isn't you, Jesamine?'

'That's Miss Flowers to you, you degenerate. That is definitely not
me, and I can prove it. I have a small purple birthmark on my . . .
person. It's always covered with makeup when the role calls for stage
nudity. And besides, that doesn't even look like me; not really. My
breasts aren't that big, the nose is all wrong, and I wouldn't do *that* if
you paid me. Lewis . . . Lewis!'

'Sorry,' said Lewis. 'I got distracted.'

'Go and sit down in your chair again, dear. And push your eyeballs
back into their sockets. As for you, Random, I strongly suggest you
find something else to look at before I take that data crystal out of the
viewer and ram it so far up your left nostril it will shoot out of your
right ear.'

'All right, all right, I'm changing the scene!' said Brett. 'Touchy,
touchy. Some people have no sense of humour.'

Jesamine gave Brett a long thoughtful look. 'Brett Random,' she
said finally. 'You know, I'm sure I've seen you somewhere before.'

Brett froze, his face automatically falling into innocent mode while
his internal systems panicked. His well-honed sense of paranoia was
never far from overdrive at the best of times. He smiled winningly
at Jesamine while his mind worked frantically, trying to remember
if he'd ever run a scam on her or any of her people. He was pretty
sure he hadn't, but there was no denying he'd got around in his
time, and given the sheer number of confidence tricks and stings
he'd pulled down the years, on any number of celebrities with more
ego than common sense, who thought their position made them
invulnerable . . .

'Oh, I'm sure I'd remember meeting such a great star as yourself,
Miss Flowers,' he said smoothly. 'I just have that sort of face. People
always think they know me from somewhere.'

Jesamine sniffed, unconvinced, but let it go rather than get sucked
into yet another argument. 'I do meet a lot of people. Or at least I did.
I can't believe my whole life went down the toilet so quickly. And I
certainly don't believe my fanbase will accept any of the terrible
things that bastard Finn has been saying about me on the news
broadcasts. I mean, they're my *fans*. What's the point of having fans
if they won't stick with you? Some did. You saw them, Lewis,
demonstrating against my imprisonment, outside Traitors' Hall.'

'You said it yourself, Jes. The public can be very fickle. I couldn't
believe they'd turn on me so easily either.' Lewis tapped his fingertips
together and frowned down at them. 'You can bet Finn will have all

his best propaganda people working day and night on discrediting the both of us. They'll dig into our respective pasts, and dig up every bit of dirt they can find.'

'There's dirt in your past, sir Deathstalker?' said Brett. 'I'm shocked. Shocked!'

'Shut up, Brett.'

'Shutting up right now, sir.'

'What they can't find, they'll probably make up,' said Lewis. 'You can't be an honest Paragon without making some enemies. People only too willing to tell tales about you, in the name of revenge. What about you, Jes? Is there much in your past they could find that they could use against you?'

'Well, rather a lot, actually,' said Jesamine. 'I've never pretended to be a saint, darling. And a certain amount of bad behaviour is expected of you, when you're a star. It's affairs of the heart and sort-of-secret assignations that keep your face in the gossip shows. If no one's talking about you, how can you be a star? I admit it, I was a slut sometimes. It was good for business. And you have to throw the odd temper tantrum in public, or no one will take you seriously. You have to give the media stories, or they start making up their own.'

Lewis glowered in Brett's direction. 'I don't suppose there's any point in asking you, is there?'

'None at all,' Brett said briskly. 'I'm a scoundrel, and proud of it. The good Lord put me on Logres to shear the sheep, and I have been a busy, busy boy. Wherever rogues and villains gather, my name is on everyone's lips. I am a Random's Bastard, and I glory in it.'

'Then what are you doing here, with half the Empire after you?' Rose said calmly.

Brett pouted sulkily. 'One moment of conscience in an otherwise spotless life, and my whole career is over. I could spit. I don't even want to think what my old comrades will be saying when they discover I've hooked up with you.'

'I've done nothing I'm ashamed of,' said Rose.

'Yes, but that covers a hell of a lot of ground,' said Brett. 'Some of the things you did for the Durandal . . .'

'Yes, by all means,' said Jesamine. 'Let's talk about that. You've been only too willing to talk about yourself and your many triumphs during the past few days, but you've hardly said a word about your involvement with Finn bloody Durandal.'

Oh shit, thought Brett, his heart sinking.

'Talk to us, Random,' said Lewis. 'I want to know everything you know about that man. What he did, and what he had you do. And all the things he planned to do. Help me to understand why one of my oldest and most trusted friends and colleagues has become the greatest villain of the Golden Age.'

'I suppose I should start with the Neuman riot outside Parliament,' Brett said reluctantly. 'Up till then it had all just been talk. Making plans and gathering support and assistance. Finn was responsible for everything that happened in that riot. He planned it, orchestrated it from beginning to end. He planted agents provocateurs in the Neumen march and in the crowds, to stir things up and push them out of control. One of them shot the Paragon Veronica Mae Savage, on his orders, and started the blood and slaughter that came after. It was all designed to intimidate Parliament, and discredit the Paragons. You were supposed to die that day too. I lured you away from the main action so Rose could have a crack at you.'

'You shot me,' said Lewis. 'I helped you, and you shot me.'

'It was orders,' Brett said weakly. 'Finn's orders. You don't say no to Finn. Anyway, Saturday turned up and saved you.'

'Yes,' said Rose. 'I'm still rather annoyed about that.'

She looked at Saturday, and smiled. There was no humour in her dark rosebud mouth; only a promise of revenge, presently delayed. The huge reptiloid looked back at her interestedly, absently flexing the terrible claws on his hands.

Brett hurriedly continued with his tale, describing how Finn had methodically set himself up as the mastermind behind a far-reaching scheme to bring down the whole Golden Age, by whatever means necessary. How he bribed and colluded and intimidated people on all sides of the law to build the secret army he needed, led by specialised criminals he recruited from the notorious Rookery. Brett tried to talk about his encounter with the awful uber-espers, the Spider Harps, in their charnel house kingdom deep under the Parade of the Endless, but it still upset him too much.

'Making deals with the Esper Liberation Force?' said Lewis, shaking his head slowly. 'He must be out of his mind.'

'I don't think so,' said Brett. 'I think he was always like this, inside. He just never had a reason to let it out before.'

'But . . . what does he want?' said Jesamine. 'What's this all for? Does he want to make himself King?'

'Perhaps,' said Rose. 'Or perhaps he just wants to burn it all down, so he can dance in the ashes. The Durandal is an extraordinary man. He has a sense of purpose and destiny that is . . . pure and uninhibited. A force of will entirely uncorrupted by mercy or compassion. I like that in a man.'

Jesamine sniffed. 'If you're so hot for the little shit, sweetie, what are you doing here with us?'

'I came to be with Brett,' said Rose. 'Or perhaps I'm here because fighting for the Durandal would have been too easy. I do so love a challenge. There's no joy to be had in the slaughter of easy prey.'

'Oh, I do so agree,' said Saturday. 'Just as I am here because siding with you offers me the best chance for killing and mass carnage.'

'I may puke,' said Brett. 'Really. I'm not kidding.'

I'll bet Owen never had these problems, thought Lewis. Aloud, he said, 'Let us all try and keep to the subject. You spent the most time with Finn, Brett. He must have talked to you. How could he have gone so bad, so quickly? He was the greatest living Paragon, damnit. They'd almost run out of awards to give him for courage and heroism above and beyond the call of duty. He was admired and adored right across the Empire. And now he's a traitor and a murderer, betraying all his old friends? Because I was made Champion instead of him? It seems such a . . . petty reason, to fall so far so fast.'

'I think for him it was a wake-up call,' Brett said slowly. 'Because he never was a hero, not really. He just played at being one, until something more interesting came along. You worked beside him, sir Deathstalker. Did you never notice some of his more . . . extreme tendencies?'

Lewis shifted uncomfortably in his chair. 'I don't know. It worries me that perhaps I did, and turned a blind eye, because he was so good at catching villains. But we spent time together off duty, Finn and Douglas and me. We talked, and drank together, had good times. I trusted him to guard my back, and he never let me down. Till now.'

'I never trusted him,' said Jesamine. 'He was always too pretty, too perfect. When people like that break, they break all the way.' She glared at Brett. 'At least Finn has the excuse of being crazy. Why did you go along with him, knowing what he was?'

Brett cringed under the weight of her contemptuous gaze. 'Hey, it wasn't like I had a choice in the matter! He said he'd kill me if I didn't go along, and I had every reason to believe him. Some of the things I heard him say! I'm no saint, lady, sir Deathstalker, I'm a career criminal and proud of it, but . . . he's so far over the edge now he can't even see it from where he is. Like Rose said, there's nothing he won't do, no atrocity he'd flinch from, to get what he wants. And much to my surprise, it turned out there's a line even I won't cross, after all. After what I found in his secret files, I had to help you escape. And . . . I am a Random. My ancestors and yours were friends, comrades. Perhaps we're meant to be together.'

'Oh please,' said Jesamine. 'Spare me. Lewis was a Paragon, and I was a star, but even we are not the stuff of legends. You are not and never will be anything more than a common thief who got in over his head and panicked.'

'I was never a common thief!' Brett said hotly. 'I was a top-rank thief! I could con you out of everything you owned, including the clothes you were wearing, and so skilfully you wouldn't even notice until the wind changed direction.'

'We left the Durandal of our own free will,' said Rose Constantine. 'Brett for his reasons, and I . . . because Finn wasn't worthy of me. He had ambition, but no taste. For him killing was just killing. I expect a much higher quality of murder with you, sir Deathstalker. With you I confidently expect death-defying schemes, overwhelming odds, sui-cide missions and all the other things that make life worth living. The killing's always good around a Deathstalker. You draw it to you. It is your destiny. Just lead me to the slaughter and turn me loose upon your enemies. It is all I ask of you.'

I want to go home, Lewis thought miserably. *I want to go back to when my life made sense, and I wasn't surrounded by crazy people.*

'Thank you, Rose,' he said finally, because he had to say something. 'Rest assured that if we ever come to the point where one of us has to make a last desperate stand so the others can escape, I promise I'll think of you first.'

Rose considered him thoughtfully. 'How is it, sir Deathstalker, that a warrior of your renowned abilities never fought in the Arena? I would have been delighted and honoured to cross swords with you.'

'I kill for duty,' Lewis said stiffly. 'When there's no other way to get the job done. Never for pleasure.'

Rose sniffed, and looked away. 'Boring,' she said, seeming to lose interest in Lewis. He didn't know whether to feel insulted or relieved.

'Don't you dare turn your back on us like that,' said Jesamine, flaring up immediately at the insult to her Lewis. 'Since we're talking about your career on the bloody sands, perhaps you'd care to explain to us how a complete psychopath got into the Arena in the first place? There are supposed to be a whole series of psychological tests that have to be passed by would-be gladiators, expressly designed to keep out people like you! So how the hell did you get in?'

Rose turned back to smile at Jesamine with her humourless crimson mouth. 'It was easy. The Arena owners rig the tests. They always have. They realised a long time ago that people like me, the natural-born murderers, make the best fighters. The stars who'll give the crowds what they want, and keep them coming back for more.

Sane people don't last long on the bloody sands. They get careless, or they burn out too quickly. Come on, what sensible, well-adjusted person would want to fight in the Arena anyway; to face the threat of suffering and dismemberment and even death, over and over again? The Arena is where we go to sate our ancient appetite for blood. I've often thought they should test the crowds, but that would give the game away, wouldn't it?'

'The Arena is a place to display valour and skill and fortitude,' said Lewis. 'A testing ground, to bring forth heroes.'

Rose laughed breathily, a dark disturbing sound. 'Blood, Deathstalker. It's always been about blood. When your civilised men and women go to the Arena, they go to see people like me. To glory in what we do. And afterwards, they dream about being me. Underneath the culture and refinement of your precious Golden Age, all the old appetites are still there, repressed but not forgotten. Why do you think Pure Humanity and the Church Militant became so popular so quickly?'

'No,' said Lewis. 'I don't believe that. I won't believe it. People are better than that. They proved it, by overthrowing Lionstone and building the Golden Age. We have our dark side, our baser instincts, but it has always been the triumph of Humanity that most of us rise above them.'

'Of course you believe that,' said Rose. 'You're a Deathstalker. You are the best of us. But you still need someone like me, just as the blessed Owen needed his Ruby Journey.'

'Excuse me,' said Saturday. 'Fascinating though this conversation undoubtedly is to those who care about this sort of thing, I have a question. How is it that you and I never fought in the Arena, Rose Constantine?'

'Because we were stars,' Rose explained patiently. 'And the Arena owners didn't want to risk either of us while they could still make money out of us. You wouldn't believe what they make out of merchandising alone. They would have given you to me eventually. When they'd made all they could out of you.' The pale tip of Rose's tongue moved briefly over her dark lips. 'I was looking forward to it.'

'I'm sure it would have been quite delightful,' the reptiloid said politely.

Brett looked disgustedly at Rose. 'Hardly a word out of you for days, and now you can't stop talking. A whole new philosophical side to you, and all of it utterly depressing. Why can't you say something nice, just for once?'

'Sorry,' said Rose. 'I don't do nice.'

16

'I can't believe what I'm hearing,' said Jesamine. 'Such corruption, and ... vileness, going on right at the heart of Logres. It's like something out of Lionstone's time!'

'People want what they want,' said Brett, immersed in his private viewscreen again. 'And as long as they do, other people will be right there, ready and willing to supply it to them. For a price.'

Lewis glared at Brett. 'God, you depress me. I used to bust scumbags like you. Psycho killers in the Arena, alien porn ... why do people want shit like that anyway?'

Brett sighed, and looked up from his screen. 'Because, sir Death-stalker, sir Paragon, people always want what other people think they shouldn't want. Things they can't have, because other people say they shouldn't be allowed. Maybe especially in a Golden Age. Being civilised is hard work. The higher we rise, the more fun there is to be had in allowing yourself to fall. Honour and virtue are all very well, but they don't satisfy like a good old roll in the mud. You and Miss Flowers should understand that. She was engaged to be married to your best friend. You were the Champion, and she was going to be Queen. But you both threw it away, to be together. So here you are, sir Deathstalker, on the other side of the law, with scumbags like me. How does it feel? Had any good insights yet?'

'What we did,' Jesamine said steadily, 'we did for love.'

'Oh, love,' said Brett. 'Well then, that makes everything all right, doesn't it?'

'Finn Durandal has to be fought,' said Lewis. 'He has to be stopped. Nothing else matters. And if I have to work with poor materials like you, Brett, then that's what I'll do. I'll make a hero out of you or kill you trying.'

'That's what I'm afraid of,' Brett growled, and turned ostentatiously back to his viewscreen.

Lewis leaned back in his captain's chair, and pretended to study the comm panels before him. For all his professed confidence, he felt lost, abandoned and very alone. So much of what he'd believed in had turned out to be built on sand. Or blood. The people he'd sworn to protect had disowned him, and betrayed his faith in them by embracing madness and evil. He'd fought so hard to be perfect, for them. Surely he had the right to expect as much from them? And now here he was, a reluctant rebel against the very authorities he had once proudly represented. Deep down, he had often wondered what it must have been like, to be an Outlaw like his blessed ancestor, the Owen. To fight, alone and heroically, against an evil Empire. He'd had his quiet, secret fantasies of putting himself to the ultimate test. To be a real Deathstalker. Well, now he was living his dreams, and they had turned out to be nightmares. He'd become the rebel hero at last, but he'd never dreamed he'd have to give up so much. His oath of fealty, to King and Empire. The honour of being a Paragon, and then Imperial Champion. He had finally discovered the great love of his life, but couldn't believe how much it had cost him. He had betrayed and lost his best, closest friend, King Douglas. Lewis looked over at Jesamine.

I have given up so much for you, my love. Don't ever let me regret it.

Jesamine threw what was left of her protein cube away. It hit the cabin wall and bounced. Jesamine tossed her cup aside and folded her arms tightly. 'That was disgusting! God knows how many times it's already been through recycling! I'd rather starve. There are convicted mass murderers on prison planets who eat better than this!'

'What's the matter, diva?' said Rose. 'Not used to slumming it with the real people?'

'The food is disappointing,' Saturday said mildly. 'Where's the fun in food if it isn't kicking and squealing?'

Everyone looked at him. 'Can I just say *oh puke*?' said Jesamine. 'Also *yech*, and *urrgh*! Someone change the subject *now*.'

'And can we please not talk about prisons?' Brett said plaintively. 'This overcrowded tin can reminds me far too vividly of my one unfortunate stay in durance vile. It's making me distinctly twitchy.'

'We know why you're twitchy,' Jesamine said severely. 'It's because you raided the medicine cabinet yesterday and took every pill and potion you could get your hands on. It's a wonder your brain cells haven't melted down and dribbled out of your ears.'

Brett snorted dismissively. 'Given the quality and dosages of stuff I've tried in the past, my system hardly noticed it. Besides, I needed it. I get very nervous. Really. You have no idea. And don't bully me! I'm having a hard time. I may cry.'

'Leave the Random alone,' Rose said calmly. 'He may be small and useless, but he's mine.'

'Oh God,' said Brett. 'It gets worse and worse.'

Jesamine spun round in her chair to glare at Lewis. 'You heard that over-dressed cow, Lewis! She threatened me! *Do something!*'

Lewis wondered wistfully whether the *Hereward* had a sleepgas option, so he could shut them all up and get some serious thinking done.

'Everybody calm down, right now,' he said, putting his Paragon's authority into his voice. 'We still haven't decided where we're going yet. More and more it seems to me that we should put our search for

Owen and Hazel on hold, until we've dealt with the loose ends we left behind on Logres.'

'There is no way I'm going back to Logres,' Brett said immediately. 'Too many people want me dead there, most definitely including Finn Durandal. Hell, he wants all of us dead. Preferably in slow, inventive and very messy ways. Why the hell would we want to go back to Logres?'

'Some of us have friends we left behind,' said Lewis. 'I'm worried about Emma Steel. She doesn't know about Finn. And she is perhaps the only true protector Logres has left.'

'You said yourself she's a first-class Paragon,' said Jesamine, reaching out to put a comforting hand on Lewis's arm. 'She can look after herself. And she's got backup in Stuart Lennox, your official replacement from Virimonde. You said he was a good sort.'

'I left him broken and bleeding on the starport landing pads,' said Lewis. 'Another blood debt I owe Finn. Even if Stuart does make a full recovery, he's just starting out as a Paragon. Too young, too trusting. I may have thrown him to the wolves.'

'They aren't who you're really worried about,' said Jesamine. 'You're worried about Douglas.'

'Yes,' said Lewis. 'He is the King, and we left him alone and unprotected, surrounded by political and religious fanatics dying for a chance to bring him down. And he doesn't know about Finn either.'

'He has Anne,' said Jesamine. 'We've been friends for—'

'I don't trust her any more,' said Lewis.

'Oh Lewis,' Jesamine said tenderly. 'You can't worry about everyone, sweetie. It's an endearing trait, but an impractical one. Worry about us instead.'

'Oh I do,' said Lewis. 'Trust me, I do. What can we hope to achieve? A dishonoured Paragon, a disgraced diva, a homicidal maniac, an alien who likes eating kicking squealing things, and Brett. It doesn't exactly fill you with confidence, does it?'

'Hey, wait a minute,' said Brett. 'I think I resent that. I have all kinds of useful talents. Not particularly nice ones, perhaps, but still—'

'Tell him about the data crystal you stole from Finn's secret files,' said Rose.

Brett tried to glare at her, but it came out more like a pout. 'Thank you, Rose. I was saving that, in case I needed something to barter with, later on. Remind me to have a little talk with you about this marvellous new concept called forward planning. But since you've raised the subject . . .' He looked unhappily at Lewis. 'You're really not going to like this, sir Deathstalker, but please don't blame the

19

messenger for the message. I . . . happened upon certain files in Finn's computer he thought he'd hidden behind some really quite superior protection. The files contained some of his future plans, in considerable detail. I'll let you study the data crystal later, but the Durandal's most unpleasant scheme was his intention to have the Paragons ambushed as they set out on their quest to find Owen Deathstalker. Apparently the idea is that they will be overwhelmed by superior forces while they're separated and far away from any hope of backup. Finn wants the Paragons taken out of the picture. Probably because he sees them as the only real threat left to his long-term ambitions. Or perhaps because he's always hated them. For being what he only pretended to be.'

'That's it,' said Lewis. 'No more arguments. I'm turning this ship around right now. We are going back to Logres. The Paragons have to be warned.'

'No!' Jesamine said immediately, grabbing at Lewis's arm as he reached for the control panels. 'Stop and think for a minute, Lewis. Please. Even if we did go back, who'd listen to us? Who'd believe us? That's if they didn't just shoot us all on sight. You can bet good money that Finn has absolutely no intention of allowing any of us our day in Court. We know too much about him. We can't put our heads back in the lion's mouth, Lewis. Our mission is more important. It has to come first.'

'Some mission,' said Lewis, but his heart wasn't in it. He knew she was right. 'Even supposing we can track down whatever survivors remain from the age of heroes, who's to say they'll be in any shape to help us, after all this time?'

'They might hold the key to finding Owen,' said Jesamine. 'Or maybe even the missing Hazel d'Ark. They have to help us. We need them now more than ever, to stop the coming Terror as well as Finn bloody Durandal!'

Lewis said nothing, remembering the dry grey words he'd heard on the Dust Plains of Memory. Owen was dead. He died long ago, in a dirty back alley on Mistworld. Except . . . he had been seen alive, in the future. Lewis still wasn't sure whether he believed that or not.

'So,' he said, to avoid having to say anything else, 'where are we going first? What planet do we choose as our destination? We're going to have to drop into hyper soon; the longer we stay in normal space, the better the odds are some pursuit ship will bump into us by accident.'

'There's not many places we can go,' said Brett. 'In this depressingly honest Empire.'

'There's always your homeworld, Virimonde,' Jesamine said tentatively to Lewis. 'I mean, surely they wouldn't believe the lies Finn's been spreading about you?'

'My family won't,' said Lewis. 'But Virimonde is a poor world, and poorly defended. Even if my Clan could persuade the planetary council to harbour us, they couldn't hope to hold out against an Imperial punitive strike force. And you can bet there are elements there who would betray our presence to the Empire; for money or patronage, or just because they believed it was the right thing to do.'

'He's right,' said Brett. 'There are scumbags everywhere these days.'

'I say we go straight to Haden,' said Saturday. 'To the Madness Maze. You are a Deathstalker, Lewis. Your fate is inevitably linked to the Maze. Even on Shard we know the story of the Owen and his journey through the Madness Maze. How it made him so much more than human. If we were all to go through the Maze, what mighty beings might we become? We could take on the whole Empire, and bring it to its knees in a sea of blood and offal!'

'I like him,' said Rose.

'I wonder if I overlooked anything in the medicine cabinet,' said Brett.

'Excuse me!' Jesamine said loudly. 'Hello! Sanity calling! This is really not a good idea, people. There's a reason why it's called the Madness Maze, and an even better reason why no one's been allowed into it for so long. Do I really have to remind everyone here that the last *ten thousand* people to enter the Maze lost their minds and their lives? Every single one of them died screaming. I wouldn't go into the Maze if I was completely desperate. Hell, I am completely desperate, and I'm still not going anywhere near it! *No*, people; the Maze is what we do when we've tried everything else, including prayer and closing our eyes and hoping it's all been a nasty dream. Next.'

'Can I put in a bid for Mistworld?' said Brett. 'Always a good bet when you're on the lam. Still fairly independent from the rest of the Empire, and proud of it. A whole planet of rogues, individual thinkers and complete headcases. Even Finn would think twice about trying to take Mistworld by force. And the stack of alien porn we're carrying will sell for major credits in Mistport. More than enough to buy us a proper ship, with room to move around in and a decent weapons system. Probably with enough left over to hire a reasonably sized corps of mercenaries. Mistworld has the best connections in the Empire. Assuming Emma Steel didn't shut them all down before she left.'

'Not a bad plan,' said Jesamine. 'And tempting. But I have played

21

on Mistworld, and I am here to tell you it is the arse end of the Empire. No civilised comforts, colder than a witch's tit, and more bounty hunters per square mile than any other planet in the Empire. You saw the broadcast; we're wanted dead or alive, with a hell of a price on our heads. They'd be queuing up to take a crack at us on Mistworld.'

'Exactly,' said Lewis. 'I'd rank it just ahead of Haden, but only just.'

Brett sulked. He'd already worked out a really clever plan for selling the alien porn in Mistport, and then disappearing with the money the moment the others turned their backs. He had his own ideas about the future, and they very definitely didn't include being a hero. Or Rose Constantine. A thought struck him. He might have been voted down, but he still had a secret ace up his sleeve. When Finn made Brett drink the esper drug, he acquired rudimentary telepathy, and a limited but useful ability to compel other minds to do his will. He didn't use it much because it gave him killer headaches, but needs must when the devil vomits on your shoes. Very cautiously, he reached out to the minds around him, threading his compulsion delicately into their thoughts.

'Mistworld,' Jesamine said dreamily.

Lewis frowned. 'The place does have strong connections to Owen and Hazel . . .'

'Did anyone just hear something?' said Rose.

And Saturday turned his great head and looked straight at Brett. The conman quickly shut down his probe, and pulled his strongest mental shields into position. He supposed he shouldn't have been surprised Rose picked up something, their minds had touched, once, but Saturday . . . Did the reptiloid have some kind of esp too? Brett shuddered internally. As if the bloody lizard wasn't dangerous enough already. Brett hunkered down behind his shields and put on his most innocent expression. Rose was looking at him thoughtfully. Brett could feel cold beads of sweat breaking out on his forehead.

'No, forget Mistworld,' said Lewis. 'Bad idea.'

'It seems obvious to me that we should go to Lachrymae Christi first,' said Jesamine. 'It's the one world where we can be sure of finding a living hero from the Great Rebellion. Tobias Moon is still there, even if no one has seen him in the flesh for ages. The last surviving Hadenman . . . Oh, I've always wanted to meet a Hadenman. They made such great villains in those old drama serials, fighting Julian Skye and those other vid heroes. If anyone knows what happened to Owen, and Hazel, it's got to be Tobias Moon.'

'Good try,' said Lewis. 'But according to all the legends, even the apocrypha, Moon was the only one of the great heroes who never went to face the Recreated. He wasn't there when Owen and Hazel disappeared. There's no doubt he knows many things now lost to history, things that might well prove useful to us, but like you said, no one's set eyes on him in over a century. And the people on Lachrymae Christi are said to guard his privacy very jealously. We'd have a hard time getting to him, and no guarantee he'd be in any condition to give us helpful answers even if we did. No; I think there's someone else who's even better qualified to tell us what we need to know.'

'God, you're long-winded sometimes,' said Jesamine. 'Just say where you think we ought to go next!'

'I don't care where we go,' said Rose. 'Just as long as I get to kill someone soon.'

'We go to Unseeli,' said Lewis. 'Because that's where we'll find the man called Carrion.'

Everyone looked at him. Jesamine nodded slowly. Brett put up his hand, like a child in class.

'Excuse me? Do you think that perhaps you could let the rest of us in on this? Who the hell is Carrion? I have to say, the name alone doesn't exactly inspire confidence. And as for Unseeli, we are talking about the Ashrai here, aren't we? The alien species noted for killing anyone who tries to land on their planet uninvited, and there are no invitations? The only alien species in the Empire to tell the Empire to go to hell and make it stick? That Unseeli? *Am I the only sane person here?*'

'Carrion was a friend of Captain John Silence,' Lewis said calmly. 'He was there with the captain when the heroes faced the Recreated, out on the Rim. He went through the Madness Maze with the captain. He is the only great hero never to make it into the official legends. And it seems to me that someone like that might well know all kinds of things that also never made it into the official legends.'

'Carrion. Carrion . . .' Brett said thoughtfully. 'You know, I think I have heard that name before. In the apocrypha . . . No, it was from a really old data crystal some alien was trying to sell in the Rookery. I never saw the contents myself, but Nikki did. Yes, Carrion. The human Ashrai. The only man ever to fly with the Ashrai. Hero, villain, monster. That Carrion?'

'Sounds about right,' said Lewis.

'The Ashrai,' Jesamine said dreamily. 'Owen's dragons. I've always wanted to meet Owen's dragons. Oh Lewis, darling, we have to go to Unseeli!'

'Give me one good reason why they'd listen to us, when they blow up everyone else,' said Brett.

'Because I'm a Deathstalker,' said Lewis.

And so it was decided. Lewis couldn't help feeling that he ought to be taking charge more, like his ancestor Owen always had, but this didn't seem to be that sort of group. His authoritative Paragon's voice still worked, but it always ended in grudging acceptance and downright sulks. He wasn't sure how much longer he could get away with it. He had no real authority over any of them. And yet still he felt responsible for the rag-tag bunch of companions he'd somehow acquired. And his own motives for this quest were confused enough, without getting into theirs. On the one hand he wanted to find Owen, so that his glorious ancestor could lead Humanity against the Terror, but on the other hand he desperately wanted to clear his name and Jesamine's. He wanted to bring down Finn Durandal because he was a traitor, but also because he'd destroyed Lewis's career. Lewis . . . wanted his life back. The way it used to be.

In the end, he had to do this thing. This impossible quest to find Owen Deathstalker, who might or might not be dead. Because it was the right thing to do, because he had no choice. Because he was a Deathstalker, and the Empire had to be saved; as much from itself as from the coming Terror. And yet . . . he wished he felt more like a leader. Like a hero. He wished he was more certain over what to do for the best, instead of just stumbling from one crisis to another, with only the vaguest of intentions and plans. He wished above all that he was more like the blessed Owen, who had always known what to do. Because he was a real hero.

The *Hereward* dropped into hyperspace without being challenged by any other vessel, and headed for the Ashrai world, Unseeli. The trip took some time, even with an H-class stardrive, and the stores of food and water depleted steadily, even with strict recycling and rationing. If they couldn't make up the difference on Unseeli, they'd be eating their shoes by the time they reached their next destination. Brett had already begun making pointed comments about Saturday, when the reptiloid wasn't around, mostly about the size of his drumsticks and how much luggage could be made out of his hide. Lewis would have been concerned about the situation, if he hadn't been more concerned about what they were going to find on Unseeli.

Information on the Ashrai world was very limited. No human or alien ship had been allowed to land on the planet for two hundred years. There was no official Quarantine, because none was needed.

You entered Unseeli space entirely at your own risk, and if you got too close to the planet the Ashrai destroyed your ship. No one seemed too sure about how they did this, because no one ever came back to tell. Long-range scanners didn't operate in Unseeli space, and no one knew why. Most people had enough sense to leave the Ashrai alone. Lewis had a good reason for going there, but no doubt others had thought the same, and it hadn't saved them.

Lewis knew the stories of Owen Deathstalker and his dragons. He'd seen the big operatic production that Jesamine had starred in. According to certain entirely unofficial legends, Owen had led an army of wise and powerful dragons against the Recreated. These huge and wonderful creatures had flown unprotected through the cold inimical depths of space, tearing the Recreated apart with vicious fang and claw. They were magnificent, and they sang a song so beautiful it touched the soul of all who heard it. According to those legends, Owen lay sleeping in a great tomb, surrounded by his sleeping dragons, waiting to be called back in the hour of the Empire's greatest need.

Could Owen be sleeping somewhere on Unseeli? Was that why the Ashrai guarded it so jealously?

Except according to the Dust Plains of Memory, it was Carrion and not Owen who'd flown with the dragons, who were really the Ashrai. Lewis had to wonder what else the story might have got wrong; and whether his Deathstalker name really did have the currency with the Ashrai that he hoped.

The *Hereward* dropped out of hyperspace at a respectable distance, and approached Unseeli slowly and cautiously, sending very respectful messages ahead of them. There was no reply, but they achieved high orbit unmolested, and Lewis started breathing again. It had been so long since anything had gone right in his life that he'd almost forgotten what it felt like. Rose hauled Brett out from under his chair, while Jesamine checked the ship's sensors, on the off chance; but they weren't operating. Diagnostics said there was nothing wrong with the systems; they just weren't picking up anything. Lewis called up what little was known about Unseeli and put it on the main viewscreen, so they could all study it. He interpreted the data aloud, as much to hear himself think as anything.

'Conditions are tolerable for human life,' he said. 'Which is just as well, as we don't have any hard suits or full body force shields. Air is breathable, though there's some unusual trace elements, and the temperature is ... well, hot and sweaty, basically. Gravity's a bit heavier than we're used to but not by much, which is odd, given the sheer size of the planet. It ought to be a lot heavier . . . still, that's Unseeli for you. Never what you expect. As you can see, there's only the one continent, and no oceans. No free-standing water at all that I can see. And the metallic forest stretches from pole to pole . . . damn, some of those metal trees are so tall they actually pierce the upper layers of the atmosphere! I've never seen anything like this.'

'No one has,' Jesamine said softly. 'Unseeli is unique, in all the Empire. Trees of gold and silver and brass, and every other metal you can think of, with cores of heavy metals that used to be mined for starship drives. There's never been a human colony here, not even back in the most gung-ho days of Lionstone's reign. People couldn't live here. It was just too alien.'

'And this is where you expect to find the man called Carrion?' said Brett. 'In a place where no human could stand to live? Who's to say he's still alive anyway, after two hundred years?'

'He went through the Madness Maze, and came out transformed,' said Jesamine.

'Supposedly,' said Rose. She was studying the viewscreen intently, as though searching out a new opponent's weaknesses.

'I'm surprised we haven't detected any power sources, at least,' said Lewis. 'This close, nothing should be able to block our sensors. There was supposed to be an old mining base here, but I'm not even getting a homing beacon. God alone knows how I'm going to land this ship.'

'You're not,' said the ship's AI Ozymandias. 'That's my job. You find me an open space, and I'll put this ship down as gently as a leaf falling from a tree. Only without the ups and downs and spiralling around that usually accompanies a falling leaf. Not really a good metaphor, after all. Forget I ever said anything. Gosh, is that the time? I've got important synapses to file.'

'You know, given time and sufficient motivation, I'm pretty sure I could rip out his entire personality,' said Brett.

'I'll bear that in mind,' said Lewis.

'Try the comm again,' said Jesamine. 'If Carrion is down there, he must know we're here by now. If he is what he's supposed to be. Use the name again, sweetie. It's the only calling card we have.'

Lewis fired up the comm panels again, though if the old mining base was actually off-line he wasn't sure what or who might be receiving him. 'This is Lewis Deathstalker, aboard the *Hereward*. We do not represent the Empire. I need to speak most urgently with the man called Carrion. Please respond.'

They waited, listening intently to the empty hissing of dead air. Brett stirred uneasily.

'If there really was a base here, its systems should have come back on-line automatically, once it heard us. Even after two hundred years.'

'Something could have happened to it,' said Jesamine. 'There are some strange stories about Base Thirteen . . .'

'Base *Thirteen*?' said Brett. 'I knew coming here was a bad idea. That's it. Let me out of here. I'll walk home.'

'Don't tempt me,' said Lewis.

'This is Carrion,' a voice said suddenly, breaking through the static. It was a harsh, rasping voice, almost too deep to be human, with strange, unsettling undertones. 'Been a while since I answered to that name. You've come a long way, Deathstalker, and only your name buys you this much welcome. Humans are not needed or wanted here. You are the enemy, and always will be. Give me one good reason why we shouldn't rip your ship apart around you.'

'Give him a good reason!' yelped Brett.

'Calm down, Random, or I'll have Saturday sit on you.' Lewis thought for a moment, considering his options. 'Hello, sir Carrion. I am Lewis Deathstalker, a descendant of the blessed Owen, and I ask your help in his name. Like him, I have been unjustly Outlawed, and am pursued by evil men. My four companions and I request permission to land and discuss the situation with you. Much has changed in the Empire. All of Humanity, and your world too, are under threat. The Terror has finally found us.'

'You're full of good news, aren't you, Deathstalker?' said the voice. 'Just like your ancestor. Very well. I grant you permission to land. I will meet with you. There's no starport or landing pads, but there is a clearing where you can put your ship down, not far from Base Thirteen. I'll join you there. Don't go wandering off, or I can't guarantee your safety. The Ashrai have no love for Humanity. Still, it will be interesting, to speak with a Deathstalker again.'

The communication broke off abruptly, and that was it. Lewis shut down the comm panels, leaned back in his chair and looked at the others.

'That was one seriously spooky voice,' said Brett. 'Sent chills up and down my spine.'

'A mouse in a bad temper could put the wind up you,' said Jesamine. 'But Lewis, are you sure this Carrion is human?'

Lewis shrugged. 'He was. But he went through the Madness Maze, and he's lived alone with the Ashrai for two centuries. He's hardly going to sound like the guy next door, is he? I'm more concerned about landing safely. Oz?'

'Still here. Still under-appreciated,' said the AI. 'It might interest you to know that the sensors have suddenly started working again, and no, I don't know how or why. I've pinpointed Base Thirteen, and the clearing's location. The *Hereward* has quite excellent navigation systems. I could put this ship down on a single credit piece, and give you change.'

'How far is the clearing from the base?' said Rose.

'Oh, walking distance, easy. Do you all good to get some healthy exercise, after being cooped up in here. No obvious dangers. I mean, apart from the Ashrai. The sensors can't seem to make head nor tail of what they are, apart from uncomfortably large. And there are lots of them, everywhere. No obvious natural hazards . . . nothing much except trees, actually. So: what do you think, Lewis? Do we go for it?'

'Take us down, Oz,' said Lewis.

'Yes sir!' said the AI enthusiastically. 'Down to Unseeli! On, to death or glory! A Deathstalker has come to parley!'

'We're all going to die,' said Brett.

The *Hereward* dived into the planet's atmosphere, plunging down through the heavy cloud layers, and threaded an expert path between the tops of the tallest trees. It was a short and surprisingly smooth trip, and Oz set them down expertly in the designated clearing. He was then almost unbearably cocky about it until Lewis threatened to rip out his voice circuits, and then he sulked. Lewis tried running the sensors again, and the limited data scrolling across the viewscreen seemed straightforward enough. He still made the others wait till he'd finished before he'd allow them to disembark. There had to be some reason why even Lionstone's Empire had never colonised Unseeli.

In the end, there was nothing left but to shrug uneasily several times, and insist on being first out of the airlock. He stepped out into the Ashrai world, his hands conspicuously away from his weapons, half braced for some unknown blow or attack, but it never came. The air was still and hot, and had a sharp smoky scent to it. Silence lay across the clearing like some heavy enveloping blanket, as though someone was listening. But Lewis hardly noticed any of it, because all he could look at was the trees. They filled his eyes and his mind; the huge glowing metal trees of Unseeli. They stretched away in all directions, further than the eye could follow, and soared up into the clouds high above. Magnificent trees of unburnished metal, that had never known leaf or bud. Gold and silver and brass, verdant and azure, shining bright and clean, with needle-sharp branches thrusting out from smooth and perfectly circular trunks. So many towering metal trees, like nails hammered into the planet by God himself. In Lionstone's day they had been mined and processed almost to extinction, but the forest was restored in its entirety by the blessed Owen. Or so it was said.

One by one, the rest of the crew of the *Hereward* disembarked. Rose had to drag Brett out. For a while they all stood close together, awed and numbed by what they saw and felt. There was a strange, fresh energy to this world, a vitality that stirred the blood and called to ancient instincts. A primal strength and vigour that was very different from the tamer, more civilised worlds of the Empire. This was not a safe place. Anything could happen here. It felt like being present at the dawn of creation, when all the worlds were new. It felt . . . like coming home.

They all had some kind of smile on their faces, even Rose, though she would have been hard pressed to say why. They might have stood there for ever, but as always Jesamine was the first to break away. She stepped slowly forward, her head cocked slightly to one side.

'Listen . . . I can hear . . . can you hear that? What is it?'

Lewis frowned, moving forward to join her. 'I hear . . . something, but don't ask me what. It's like trying to see something out of the corner of your eye. What is it?'

'It's a song,' said Jesamine. 'A song that is more than a song. It's coming from . . . everywhere. Everything. Lewis, the trees are singing.'

'I think you've been at the medicine cabinet as well,' said Brett. 'I can't hear any song. I can't hear anything. Just as well really; the only songs I know all have mucky words. This whole place is as quiet as a tomb, and I do wish I hadn't said that. Come on, people, snap out of it. This is a seriously weird place we've come to. No wildlife, no birds, not even any insects. Nothing but us and these over-sized coffin nails. This isn't natural; no wonder no one ever wanted to live here. I am feeling nervous, upset, not even a little bit happy, and more than a little threatened, and I say we get the hell out of here right now. Please.'

'Shut up, Brett,' Lewis said automatically.

Brett scowled at him. He could hear something now. He wasn't sure whether he was hearing it with his ears or his esp, but either way it didn't sound at all like a song to him.

'Trees,' said Rose. 'Quiet. Hot. Boring. Bring on the Ashrai.'

'They're not far away,' said Saturday, his long spiked tail lashing slowly behind him. 'I can feel their presence. Their watching eyes.'

'Then why doesn't someone drop in and say hello, and welcome?'

said Jesamine, a little tartly. 'We're the first human visitors they've allowed in centuries. I didn't expect a welcoming committee, but . . .'

'They know we're here,' said Lewis. 'They're still deciding what to do about us.'

Brett looked at him sharply. 'I didn't know you had a touch of esp, sir Deathstalker.'

'I don't,' said Lewis. 'It's just warrior's instinct. Watch your step, people. Be polite. Don't break anything. We're only here on sufferance. Base Thirteen should be about thirty minutes' walk . . . that way. Let's go.'

'Shouldn't someone stay to guard the ship?' Brett said immediately. 'I'll volunteer.'

'You want to stay here on your own?' said Lewis. 'You're braver than I thought. Anything could happen here while we're gone.'

'I think I'd better stick with you,' said Brett. 'God knows what kind of trouble you could get into without my devious, suspicious instincts there to protect you.'

'You're so good to us,' said Jesamine.

They set off through the narrow, unerringly straight pathways that led between the endless rows of thick-boled trees. Lewis led the way, with Jesamine at his side. Rose strolled casually along behind them, with Brett tucked in close beside her. Saturday brought up the rear. The reptiloid seemed cheerful enough, not all that interested in the metallic forest, but looking around hopefully, on the off chance that something small and defenceless might turn up so he could hunt and kill and eat it. Above or perhaps behind the relentless quiet the unheard song, if song it was, faded away, and the only sound now in the metallic forest was the quiet rasping of boots on the dull grey forest floor.

The heavier gravity pulled painfully at their muscles, and the sticky heat grew more oppressive the longer they walked. Lewis had a growing feeling that coming to Unseeli had been a serious misjudgement on his part. The metallic forest was a spectacular sight, but so far he hadn't seen anything that would serve to refill their seriously depleted stores. Nothing to eat and nothing to drink. And yet you couldn't call this a dead world, like some he'd visited. The whole planet pulsed with vital energies. If Owen really had recreated this world, he'd done a hell of a job. The sensation of being watched by unfriendly eyes continued to nag at him, like an itch he couldn't scratch. And it bothered him that he couldn't see the sun or the sky. The overhead cloud layer was too thick, allowing only an eerie general diffused illumination. It made judging distances and directions acutely difficult, and only his comm link with the yacht's sensors kept him on course. All around him the towering trees glowed brightly, like so many multi-coloured suns. It was like walking in a dream.

After a while, they walked in silence. None of them had anything particularly vital to say or report, and the eerie nature of the place discouraged casual conversation. It felt as though they were walking through some immense natural cathedral, of nature writ large and triumphant, and man was a very small thing indeed. The heavier gravity weighed down even their spirits, and they were soaked in sweat from the effort and the heat. Not surprisingly, Jesamine was the first to complain.

'I shouldn't have to put up with this. Why couldn't we have landed right next to the base? I'm tired, my back aches and my feet aren't talking to me. We should have brought a gravity sled! It's been years since I had to walk this far, and I hated it then. Look why don't I take a rest break here, while you—!'

'No,' Lewis said immediately. 'I'm not splitting up the party. I want you all where I can see you, and that very definitely includes you, Brett. We're stronger and safer together. So suck it in, Jes, and keep up the pace. You're doing well. The sooner we get to Base Thirteen, the sooner we can rest.'

Jesamine sniffed loudly, and kept going. The trees moved slowly past, only the size and the colours changing, and it was hard to tell how far they'd come, or how much further there was left to go. Jesamine started muttering under her breath, and when that didn't get her anywhere, began to whine and complain out loud again. Lewis commiserated, but was firm with her. In the end, she lurched to a halt and threw a fully fledged temper tantrum. She stamped her foot on the hard grey ground, waved her arms around, cried loud angry tears, and positively refused to go a step further. Lewis and Brett looked at each other, embarrassed. Jesamine had been a star too long, with people ready and willing to do all the unpleasant things in life for her. Lewis tried being reasonable. He pointed out that they were closer to the base now than the ship, so they might as well go on, and she'd feel better if she just kept moving . . . but to no avail. Jesamine wept bitterly, said he didn't love her any more, and refused to take another step. So Rose stepped forward and looked Jesamine right in the eye. The star and diva shut up immediately.

'We're going on,' said Rose Constantine. 'You can stay here on your own, unprotected, or you can come with us. But if you start whining again, I'll hurt you. Got it?'

31

Jesamine wanted to say, *How dare you talk to me like that? How dare you threaten me? Don't you know who I am?* But she knew none of that mattered a damn to the Wild Rose of the Arena. She looked uncertainly at Lewis. 'You wouldn't really leave me behind, would you, sweetie? You wouldn't let her hit me? Would you, Lewis?'

'Jes,' Lewis said quietly, 'I am only a moment away from making you walk in front so I can kick your arse if you slow us down. This kind of behaviour isn't worthy of you. So stop complaining and move. It's no harder for you than for the rest of us. You always said you were a good trooper. Time to prove it.'

Jesamine stuck out her lower lip. 'You're sleeping on the floor tonight, Deathstalker.'

In another ten minutes or so the metal trees fell suddenly away on all sides, and they emerged into a clearing. In the centre of the wide open space stood half a dozen tall metal statues. They were twice the height of a man, and the gleaming shapes made no sense at all, though they somehow felt as though they ought to. Light gleamed along their smooth curves, that turned and twisted in uncertain directions. Lewis walked slowly up to the nearest statue and studied it carefully. It didn't help.

'Ashrai sculpture,' said Brett, peering past Lewis's shoulder. 'I've heard of it, but usually you only see stuff like this in specialised and very expensive catalogues. I doubt there's a dozen pieces of Ashrai art in human hands throughout the Empire. Supposedly the Ashrai sculpt these things out of the metal trees using nothing but their minds.'

'And you can only really appreciate them by touching them,' said Jesamine. 'They were meant to be felt, not seen. The Ashrai don't see the world the way the rest of us do. I've been trying to acquire even a small piece for years.'

'I really don't feel like touching that,' said Lewis, and the others nodded.

'Forget the alien porn,' said Brett. 'Dump it out, and fill the cargo bay with these. We could manage two, maybe even three. Sweet Jesus, we could sell them on Mistworld for more credits than even I usually dream of. We'd be set up for life!'

'Don't even think about it,' Lewis said sternly. 'We are here as guests, remember? Not thieves, or looters. You really want the Ashrai mad at you?'

'Well, not as such, no,' said Brett. 'But, there has to be some way—'

'*No*, Brett.'

'They're just shapes,' said Saturday. 'They have no soul. My people

32

sculpt in living tissues, torn from the bodies of fallen enemies. Why are you looking at me like that?'

'Sometimes I wonder about you,' said Lewis. 'And sometimes I'm sure.'

They set off again, leaving the clearing. Soon it was lost behind the ranks of glowing trees. They all dreamed about the statues for weeks afterwards.

'How could the old Empire never have realised that this was an artificially created world?' Lewis said finally. 'I mean, you only have to look at it. No ecostructure, no living systems; just the trees and the Ashrai.'

'This is an inhuman place,' said Brett. 'Alien in every sense of the word. Nothing here to keep a man sane. How is it that Carrion survived here, alone, for more than two centuries?'

'He wanted to be an Ashrai,' said Lewis. 'Who knows how the Madness Maze changed him, or what he did with those changes?'

'Do we have any idea what an Ashrai looks like?' said Rose.

'The official records were wiped long ago, on Robert and Constance's orders,' said Lewis. 'Only hints remain. Massive, deadly creatures, with fangs and claws and gargoyle faces.'

'No,' Jesamine said immediately. 'If these are the dragons that Owen called to fight alongside him, they were wise and wonderful and very beautiful. I used to dream about them, when I was a child. Flying through open space with them, like Owen.'

'According to the Dust Plains—'

'I know what they said, Lewis. They said it was Carrion. We'll see.'

And still they trudged on, the heavier gravity pulling at their bodies like weights. The heat never wavered, and there was never even a breath of a cool breeze. The trees seemed bigger, and wider and taller the longer they walked through them, and they shone brightly in the diffused light. It felt like walking through the vaults of some endless catacombs, and a growing sense of awe and stifling oppression fell over the group, so that they spoke only in hushed whispers. The forest was too big, too vast, for merely human feelings. Even the reptiloid Saturday seemed somewhat subdued. Brett, on the other hand, was silent because he was becoming increasingly preoccupied with thoughts of how much the metal of the trees was worth. Metal from Unseeli was very rare, and therefore very valuable. And if he couldn't take away even one of the statues, surely that misery guts Death-stalker wouldn't begrudge him a small branch. Or three. Should be easy enough. A sudden stumble, a carefully aimed fall, and it should be child's play to break off some of the smaller branches with his weight. And then, well, they might as well take the branches with them as leave them just lying around . . . right?

Brett let himself drift a little away and behind the others. Taking his time, so no one would notice. He'd actually got within a few feet of the nearest branch when he lurched to a sudden halt, all his instincts shrieking at him. His esp kicked in big time, as the sheer living presence of the tree hit him right between the eyes like a hammer. It knew he was there. It knew what he was planning. It *growled* at him. Brett whimpered loudly, did his best to mentally project *sorry, sorry, sorry* and hurried to join the others. To his disgust, none of them had even noticed he'd been gone.

The projected thirty-minute walk had already become more than an hour, and Lewis didn't believe it was just down to the heavier gravity. Unseeli was a different place, with different rules. There was still no sign of the Ashrai, and Lewis had to wonder if perhaps they were determined to have nothing to do with humans. And if this man Carrion considered himself an Ashrai now, maybe even the legendary Deathstalker name wouldn't be enough to win his cooperation. Although he hadn't admitted it out loud, Lewis had been secretly hoping he'd be able to convince Carrion to leave Unseeli and come with them on their quest to find Owen. With a Maze survivor on their side, even Finn would think twice about getting in their way. Lewis scowled as he trudged along, mentally rehearsing various possible arguments.

Jesamine strode along beside Lewis in silence, looking straight ahead and ostentatiously not talking to him, though she wasn't sure if he'd noticed. He could be very obtuse about some things. She had no one else to talk to. Brett was sulking again, and Rose was a mystery, as always. Of them all, the hard trek through the forest had affected Rose the least. The lanky cow looked like she could walk for ever. Saturday, on the other hand, seemed increasingly unsettled. He couldn't connect to this silent, lifeless world, where there was nothing for him to eat or kill or have sex with. The great trees made him feel small, and weak, and he wasn't used to that.

Almost an hour and a half after they'd left the *Hereward*, the forest finally took mercy upon them, and fell away to reveal a clearing with Base Thirteen at its centre. It was a hulking steel structure, surrounded by plenty of space, as though none of the trees wanted to get too close to it. The base had been built for function, not aesthetics, but even so the years had not been kind to it. The steel exterior was weathered and distressed, and punctured here and there with ragged holes. Many appeared to have been punched out from within, either by energy weapons or brute force. The front doors stood open, but Lewis couldn't honestly say they looked inviting.

He brought his group to a halt at the edge of the clearing, and studied first the clearing and then Base Thirteen carefully. There was no sign of anyone waiting to meet them. He activated his comm implant. 'Sir Carrion, this is Lewis Deathstalker. We have reached Base Thirteen. Are you here?'

He waited, looking about him, but there was no response. And then he felt as much as heard something approaching, and he looked up. The others looked up too, following his startled gaze. And there, all across the sky, the Ashrai came falling out of the clouds and into the diffused light. They flew unhurriedly through the still air, hundreds of them, their vast membranous wings barely flapping. They were huge, monstrous, grotesque creatures, bulging with muscles under rainbow skins, with broad faces composed of harsh bony planes and angles, fiery golden eyes and a wide mouth full of long needle teeth. Their movements were eerily graceful as they swept across the sky.

Jesamine stared up at them, enchanted. 'Oh Lewis, it is Owen's dragons! Look at them! They're not what I thought they'd be, they're not beautiful, but oh God, they're magnificent!'

'They're scary buggers, is what they are,' said Brett, from behind Rose. 'Look at the size of them! Damn, one of those things could make a real mess of a man, if it put its mind to it. I'd back one of them against a Grendel. A dozen Grendels. And give odds.'

'I killed a Grendel in the Arena,' said Rose, one hand resting on the sword at her hip.

'I know,' said Brett. 'It's all you ever talk about, and I do wish you wouldn't. Please don't start anything. Or if you must, give me plenty of advance warning so I can get a good running start.'

'I wonder what they'd taste like?' said Saturday, and Brett glared at him.

'Don't encourage her. You're almost as bad as she is. Am I the only one here who's noticed they outnumber us by a hundred to one? And they are big! Seriously big! They've probably crapped more dangerous things than us! I can feel one of my heads coming on.' He watched the Ashrai, circling slowly overhead. 'How does anything that big and heavy stay in the air anyway? I don't care what kind of wingspan they've got, nothing that massive belongs in mid-air, particularly when I'm standing underneath them.'

'Calm down, Brett,' said Lewis. 'You're babbling. The Ashrai fly because their esp holds them up. Maybe they can fly unprotected through space after all. These are clearly powerful creatures.'

'The song's back,' said Jesamine, her head arched almost painfully back as she gazed adoringly into the sky. 'It's so much stronger here. It's not just the trees. It's them. The Ashrai and the forest, singing together, bound together. Can't you hear it?'

None of them said anything, because it seemed to all of them that they could hear *something*. Jesamine opened her mouth and sang: a delicate lilting song, older than the Golden Age, older than the age of heroes, from the days of the First Empire when Humanity originally went out into the stars. The words were lost, but the melody remained, an ancient haunting evocation of days long gone, when to be human was to be part of a great adventure. The words were lost, but not the meaning. In their bones, and in their souls, Humanity remembered. Jesamine sang, and the Ashrai sang with her. Their great voices filled the air, alien harmonies that joined with Jesamine's song, augmenting it without drowning it. The song filled the clearing, a celebration of life, and the glory of existence, and the driving need to find a meaning for it all. Jesamine sang, her face full of rapture, and the Ashrai sang with her. Lewis stared at his love, stunned by the power in her voice. He felt as though he was in the presence of something sacred. Jesamine finally broke off, and the Ashrai stopped singing too. Jesamine slowly lowered her head, sweat dripping off her face, and she put out a shaking hand to Lewis. He took her in his arms, making his strength her own, and she clung to him.

'Oh Lewis,' she said finally, her face turned into his chest. 'I think now I finally understand how other people feel when I sing. That was . . . amazing.'

'How did you know that was the right thing to do?' said Lewis.

'I'm not the first person to sing with the Ashrai,' said Jesamine. 'Two hundred years ago, Diana Vertue sang with them. Before she became Jenny Psycho. This was the song she sang. It's still here: in the air and in the trees and in the Ashrai. They have never forgotten. Look at them, Lewis. At least now we know some of the old legends were true. These are the dragons, and they are glorious.'

Lewis held her in his arms, and said nothing. The Ashrai were certainly impressive, and powerful, but it would take more than a pretty tune to convince him that they were friends. Hundreds of people had died in the past, just for daring to visit Unseeli. And while the Ashrai were undeniably mighty, they still looked ugly as sin itself to him. And bloody dangerous too. He tensed as a single Ashrai broke away from the others circling overhead and dropped out of the sky towards them. Lewis didn't push Jesamine away, but he did turn her round so he could get to his gun more easily. The Ashrai seemed to grow larger and larger as it fell towards them. Lewis estimated it had to be at least forty feet from gargoyle head to spiny tail, with almost as wide a wingspan. The wings flapped heavily as it landed, cupping the air, and the great clawed feet touched down with hardly an impact. The golden wings folded neatly away upon the shimmering silver back, and the Ashrai folded its muscular arms across its massive chest as it regarded them with unblinking golden eyes. Rose Constantine drew her sword.

'I have to do this,' she said cheerfully. 'I have to *know*. Damn, you ugly brute; you make me feel so *hot* . . .'

She surged forward, sword held out before her, grinning broadly. The Ashrai reared up, raised one massive foot, and stamped on her. She was slammed to the unforgiving ground, almost disappearing under the huge foot. Her sword flew from her hand as the impact crushed the air from her lungs. Brett shrieked, turned, and sprinted for the cover of the trees. Lewis shook his head slowly.

'Saturday?'

'Yes, Lewis?'

'Fetch.'

The reptiloid nodded and set off after Brett, his long stride rapidly eating up the distance between them. Lewis gently put Jesamine away from him, and cautiously approached the Ashrai. The harsh face studied him thoughtfully with its glowing golden eyes. Up close, its heavy breathing sounded like thunder, though it smelt of nothing at all. Damn, the creature was big. Lewis cleared his throat carefully.

'Hi. I'm Lewis Deathstalker. Nice moves. Could we please have our psychopath back? She's impulsive and annoying, and has several appalling personal habits that you really don't want to know about, but she has a certain sentimental value. If you let her up, I'm pretty sure I can guarantee she won't try that again. Or anything else, until she can get her eyeballs uncrossed.'

The Ashrai considered the matter, nodded its awful head, and stepped back, raising its huge foot. Lewis and Jesamine dragged Rose out from under, and set her down with her back propped against a tree. She was having trouble getting her eyes to track, but she seemed to know who and where she was.

'Caught me by surprise,' she said thickly. 'Get me on my feet and find my sword and I'll tear his wings off and beat him to death with the soggy ends.'

'No you won't,' said Lewis. 'You behave yourself and stop embarrassing me, or I'll shoot you myself.'

'You do realise,' said Rose, 'that if anyone else spoke to me like that

I'd fillet them? Good thing for you that I'm a little under the weather. And that you're a Deathstalker.'

'Yeah,' growled Lewis. 'Lucky me.'

Saturday came striding back, with Brett tucked securely under one arm. Brett was calling him every name under the sun, and Lewis hoped the reptiloid didn't understand most of them. Saturday dropped Brett at Lewis's feet, and glowered down at him.

'Next time, I'll bite off something superfluous. Fleeing in the face of the enemy? The very idea! What kind of impression does that make?'

Brett clambered painfully to his feet. 'Sorry. Trained reflexes. Also bone-deep cowardice. I did warn you. How's Rose doing?'

'When I can trust my feet again, I'm going to kill everything in this clearing,' said Rose.

'Back to normal,' said Brett. 'You go talk to the monster, sir Deathstalker. I'll look after Rose. From a safe distance.'

And then they stopped talking and looked round sharply as the Ashrai reared up again, presenting its wide curved chest to them. The shimmering silver scales split suddenly apart, unfolding like a rose, and out of the pink interior of the Ashrai walked a man dressed all in black. He strode unhurriedly towards Lewis and his companions, and behind him the opening in the Ashrai's chest slowly closed itself. And then the huge alien was gone, vanished in a moment, as though it had never been there. Only the man remained. He came to a halt before Lewis. Tall and whipcord lean, he wore black leathers topped with a billowing black cape. He was dark-haired, and pale-faced, his features subtly ageless. His mouth was a grim flat line, his eyes dark and accusing. He carried a long staff of polished bone, almost as tall as he was. His movements weren't entirely human. Just looking at the man sent shivers up Lewis's spine. He knew who this was, who this had to be. He could feel Jesamine pressing in close beside him, like a frightened child.

'You are the Deathstalker?' It was the same rasping, inhuman voice they'd heard on the ship.

'Yes. I'm Lewis Deathstalker, descendant of the blessed Owen.'

'I am Carrion,' said the man dressed in black, though he didn't sound entirely sure of it. 'I have been an Ashrai for many years. I haven't been human since John Silence and I returned to this world. I'd forgotten how small and limited a thing it is, to be a man. Even your thoughts are smaller. I have descended from the skies to talk with you. It had better be worth it.'

'No one speaks like that,' said Brett. 'Not in real life.'

'You'd better let me talk to him,' said Jesamine. 'I speak fluent opera.'

'Let me get this straight,' said Brett. 'That alien; that was actually you? You changed from a human into that . . . thing?'

Carrion looked at Lewis. 'These people are with you?'

'Unfortunately, yes,' said Lewis. 'I'd apologise for them, but it's a waste of time. Feel free to ignore them. I do.'

Carrion turned the full force of his dark, disturbing gaze on Brett, who immediately darted behind Lewis and peered past his shoulder.

'It is a glorious thing, to be an Ashrai,' said Carrion. 'It's what I always wanted. I was happy to leave my humanity behind, as something I had outgrown. And now, here you are, to remind me of what I wished most to forget. What do you want with me, Deathstalker? You mentioned the Terror. How can it be here so soon?'

'It's been two hundred years, since the blessed Owen's warning,' said Lewis.

'Has it?' said Carrion. 'I hadn't realised. The Ashrai experience time differently. For us, yesterday is the distant past, and the distant past is yesterday. You're the first human I've talked to since I said goodbye to the captain and gave up human weaknesses to be an Ashrai. You'll pardon me if I've lost the knack.'

'Why did you want to meet us here?' said Lewis, gesturing at the abandoned base. Not so much because he cared, but to buy himself some thinking time. This wasn't going at all as he'd expected.

Carrion looked at Base Thirteen. 'This is the only human structure left on the planet. We keep it as a reminder never to lower our guard. I thought it might help me remember how to be human again. It hasn't been a working base for centuries. The mines and mining equipment it oversaw are long gone now, absorbed and recycled by the trees. But still, this is a place of . . . strong memories for me. Bad things happened here. Do they still tell the story of the terrible events at Base Thirteen? Of the unknown alien, and the awful gifts it brought?'

Lewis and the others looked at each other. Lewis shrugged uncomfortably. 'I'm afraid not, sir Carrion. Much of the history of your time is lost to us. Just legends remain. And you are only mentioned briefly, in the . . . unofficial legends.'

Carrion smiled for the first time. 'I suppose I shouldn't be surprised. Captain Silence made it into the official legends, I assume? Of course he did. He was a hero, after all. While I . . . was a traitor, and proud of it. I fought with the Ashrai, in their war against Humanity. I killed men and women from my own crew. Until Captain Silence scorched this planet from orbit, and killed every living thing on Unseeli, except for the trees, and me.' He smiled again at their shocked expressions. 'Oh yes, children, your great hero John Silence committed genocide here, in the name of his Empire. Some years later, Owen brought the Ashrai back. Made Unseeli a living world again. That's why the Deathstalker name buys you this audience.' He looked again at Base Thirteen. 'I was an Investigator, once. Trained by the Empire on how best to study and murder aliens. But even so, nothing in my experience prepared me for the horror Captain Silence and I found in this dark place.

'An alien from an unknown species came to Unseeli, from out of the endless night beyond the Rim, and its ship crashed near here. We'd never seen anything like that ship, grown as much as built, out of meat and bone as well as steel and crystal. We cut open one of its walls, and guts fell out. But the alien wasn't there. It had already made its way to Base Thirteen, and slaughtered every living thing it found there. Afterwards, it did terrible things with their bodies. We killed the alien, eventually. John Silence, myself, the young esper Diana Vertue, and Investigator Frost. John. My friend, my enemy. We were always so close; bound together and torn apart by honour and responsibility.

'The alien ship isn't here any more. Empire scientists took it away to study; and from its alien technology they devised the next generation of stardrives, the E-class, and more besides. The alien we killed was just the forerunner of a very advanced, very deadly species. John and I always expected more of them would come, to challenge and invade the Empire, but they never did. Perhaps the Terror got to them first. The universe is a very big place.' Carrion looked at Lewis again. 'Two hundred years. Is John . . . ?'

'John Silence died long ago,' said Lewis. 'I'm sorry. There are statues to him all over the Empire.'

'So,' said Carrion. 'My only friend is dead. My last link with Humanity is gone.' He said it slowly, as though unsure how he felt about it. 'And you're the new Deathstalker. You look like a warrior, which is more than Owen did, except when he got mad at someone. I only met him a few times. A dark, sad, disturbing figure. A good man, undoubtedly, but he scared the shit out of me.'

'Why aren't you in the official legends?' said Rose. She was back on her feet again, but keeping a respectful distance. 'If you were as closely tied to the other heroes as you claim?'

Brett winced. 'Gives a whole new meaning to the word "blunt", doesn't she?'

'They probably left me out because I embarrassed everyone,' said Carrion, entirely unmoved. 'I never apologised for my treason. I embraced it. And I never gave a damn for the Empire or Humanity. I only fought alongside John because he asked me to.'

'You mean . . . you didn't follow the blessed Owen?' said Jesamine.

'Hell no,' said Carrion. 'I knew enough to stay well clear of him. He had that hero stink all over him. And everyone knows that heroes die young, and bloody, and mostly take their friends and companions down with them.' He smiled coldly at Lewis. 'Just like you will, Deathstalker.'

Lewis decided it was definitely time to change the subject. His hopes of persuading Carrion to join him were looking increasingly remote. 'Tell us about the heroes you knew, sir Carrion. We know only the legends. What were they really like?'

Carrion frowned, and for the first time seemed uncertain. 'When heroes become legends, so much of the truth is always lost. I knew men and women, flesh and blood. Important figures, yes, but still . . . They were people first, flawed and vulnerable. Which perhaps makes their heroism all the greater. Owen: perhaps the only real hero I ever met. Death on two legs. Honourable, brave, damned. Knew he wouldn't live to see the end of his war, but never let that stop him from doing what he knew to be right. Hazel: a free spirit, no matter what it cost her. A scrapper, a rebel, never giving too much of herself to anyone, for fear it would be betrayed. She should have known better than to love a Deathstalker.

'I never really knew or trusted Jack Random or Ruby Journey. I always knew they had their own agendas. And I never met the Hadenman before he died, or afterwards. No; I was only there because John needed someone to be his friend, to be his good right hand and guard his back. For all the death and suffering and broken promises between us, he was still a better man than he thought he was. He never really got over the death of his one true love, Investigator Frost.'

He stopped, as he took in the blank, puzzled looks on their faces. 'Am I to take it she didn't make it into the official legends either?'

'Not even the apocrypha, as far as I know,' said Lewis. 'Who was she, sir Carrion?'

Carrion shook his head slowly. 'She deserved to be remembered. She and John made a great team. Unstoppable. She went into the Madness Maze, and survived. Hell of a fighter. She was cold and vicious and I never liked her. I don't think anyone did but John, but I respected her. He loved her, even though she was an Investigator. I

41

don't know whether she ever loved him. Whether she was capable of it. She died in his arms, in Lionstone's Court. It doesn't seem right that she should be forgotten . . .

'Let's talk about the Terror. There was a voice, that came out of nowhere after the Recreated had been defeated, and then reborn as the new Rim worlds. I never knew whose voice it was. It said the Ashrai were originally created for a purpose, not just to tend the metallic trees. They are old, the Ashrai, and they have forgotten much. Perhaps it is their purpose and their fate to battle the Terror. Perhaps you serve their destiny in coming here. You said you were Outlaws, like Owen and his people. What happened? And why are you here?'

'We're hoping to track down the missing Owen Deathstalker and Hazel d'Ark,' said Jesamine. 'Our dearest legend is that Owen will return to save us all, in the hour of the Empire's greatest need. If anyone knows how to stop the Terror, it's got to be him. No one else is going to. The Empire's a mess. A complete psychopath's running things, we were all Outlawed for not going along with him and the Golden Age is going down the toilet.'

'Nothing changes,' murmured Carrion.

'So we're searching for any survivors of the age of heroes,' said Lewis. 'Hoping to find clues on where to look for Owen and Hazel. It's a sign of how desperate we are that we've started with you, sir Carrion. No offence.'

'Legends,' said Carrion, almost kindly. 'The patterns never change, though centuries pass. But I was only a part of history, not legend, so all I have to offer you is the painful truth. Owen Deathstalker is dead. He died long ago and far away, saving us from the wrath of the Recreated.'

For a long moment, no one said anything. They were all hit hard, even Lewis and Jesamine, who'd been told this before. But it was one thing to hear it from Shub and the Dust Plains of Memory, machines who might or might not have their own agendas, and quite another to hear it from a contemporary of Owen. Someone who'd been there when it happened. Brett saw something in Lewis and Jesamine's faces.

'You knew, didn't you? You already knew this, and you said nothing!'

'We have been given reason to believe that Owen will yet return to us,' Lewis said carefully. 'And no, I don't understand how. Sometimes . . . you just have to have a little faith.'

'What about Hazel d'Ark?' said Brett, almost glaring at Carrion. 'Is she dead too?'

'I don't know,' said Carrion. 'She left Haden, after learning of Owen's death. Perhaps John discovered what became of her. But he's gone. Your only chance for answers is to go to Haden and pass through the Madness Maze. There are many answers and many mysteries to be found in the Maze.'

'You've been through it,' said Jesamine. 'What's it like, really?'

'There is nothing else like it, in all the Empire,' said Carrion. 'It's almost alive. It breathes and sweats and knows what moves you. It changes everyone differently. Or perhaps it helps us change ourselves. It is a thing of power and miracles, and it is very old. And there's something else: some deeper secret, hidden in the very heart of the Maze. John and I were never allowed close enough to find out what. We weren't considered worthy. Only Owen was ever allowed to penetrate the heart of the mystery.'

'Only Owen?' said Lewis, frowning. 'What about Hazel d'Ark?'

'Only the Deathstalker,' said Carrion. 'There is some unknown connection between the Deathstalkers and the Madness Maze.' He broke off abruptly, looking up at the opaque shimmering sky above them. 'Well, this seems to be Unseeli's day for unwanted visitors. Five Imperial starcruisers have just dropped out of hyperspace, and are moving into orbit around this world. Just like old times . . .'

They were all looking at him. None of them doubted what he was saying. There was something about Carrion.

'How do you know this?' said Brett, almost whispering.

'The Maze,' said Carrion. 'I know many things now, whether I want to or not. Someone's trying to communicate with the Ashrai. I suppose I might as well talk to them, while I'm human. We'll need to use the comm systems in Base Thirteen. When we're in there, stay close. The base has been dead for centuries, but it is still a dangerous place for the unwary.'

'He's talking to you, Brett,' said Lewis. 'Don't touch *anything*.'

'I am hurt and wounded,' said Brett.

'You will be, if you don't do as you're told,' said Lewis. 'Saturday, you'd better watch the door while we're in there. Feel free to eat anyone who isn't us or the Ashrai.'

'Dinnertime's coming,' said the reptiloid cheerfully, staring up at the clouded sky. 'Just as well. Some of you were beginning to look especially tasty.'

'Is he joking?' said Jesamine.

'Best not to ask,' said Lewis.

Carrion led the way into Base Thirteen. The great metal entrance doors hung limply from their supports. They moved jerkily apart under Carrion's hands, all power gone. Inside, what they could see of the lobby was a mess. The light from the open doorway didn't penetrate far into the centuries-old gloom. The place looked to have been thoroughly trashed, with shattered furniture, dents and cracks in the metal floor, and even some holes in the outer wall, through which some light reluctantly entered. There didn't seem to be any power, no working lights or tech. On the very edge of the light, they could just make out an old-fashioned reception console.

Lewis and his companions hesitated inside the door, waiting for their eyes to adjust to the gloom. None of them liked the feel of the place. They could sense those piled-up years, from the bad old days of Empire, waiting to ambush them. Base Thirteen smelled of death. Carrion walked forward into the dark, his face entirely calm. He stopped by the reception console and passed one hand slowly over it. Deep within the base, old systems sluggishly awakened, and lights flickered on, one by one, until the reception area was full of a kind of twilight glow that if anything made the place seem even spookier. Brett started to edge backwards, until Rose took him firmly by the arm. Comm panels on the reception desk hummed suddenly with static, and a single viewscreen glowed into life on the opposite wall, putting itself on standby. From all around came the sounds of machines waking up, as system after system came back on-line.

'I don't get it,' Jesamine said quietly. 'If the base was shut down two hundred years ago, where's this power coming from?'

'From me,' said Carrion. He shouldn't have been able to hear her from such a distance, but no one was really surprised that he could. His hands moved slowly over the comm controls, as though reluctantly remembering skills long since abandoned when he became Ashrai. The viewscreen on the wall cleared to show a Fleet captain, standing at strict attention on the bridge of his ship. His uniform had been pressed and cleaned to within an inch of its life, and helped to distract from his young face. *Probably one of Finn's creatures*, thought Lewis. *Newly promoted for this mission.* An experienced Fleet officer would have had more sense than to come to Unseeli. The captain looked startled for a moment at the unexpected face before him, but then he thrust out his jaw and glared truculently out of the viewscreen.

'This is Captain Kamal of the Imperial starcruiser *Hector*, on official business. Identify yourself!'

'I am Carrion, of the Ashrai.' Carrion's voice was harsh, flat, subtly inhuman. His eyes were very dark. 'Why have you come to Unseeli, Captain? You must know we do not welcome visitors.'

'You have given sanctuary to those most notable traitors Lewis Deathstalker and Jesamine Flowers and their associates. All are guilty of crimes against Humanity. I have orders to bring them back to Logres, dead or alive. I require you to assist me in this matter. And with regard to your veiled threat: five starcruisers now orbit your world. The Empire goes where it will, to do its will. You will cooperate, in the name of King and Parliament, or face the consequences.'

'He's not my King,' said Carrion. 'And your Parliament has no authority here. This is Unseeli, home to the Ashrai. This is not a human place, and you should not have come here. Leave, while you still can.'

Captain Kamal looked like he was going to explode. 'Who the hell do you think you are, to speak to me that way? I represent the Empire! I speak in Humanity's name!'

'And I am Carrion. Investigator. Traitor. Ashrai. I bring bad luck. I am the destroyer of nations, and of worlds. With Owen Deathstalker and Captain John Silence, I walked the breathing corridors of the Madness Maze. I speak for Unseeli. Leave or die. You have no other choices.'

'Lies, defiance and open threats,' said Captain Kamal, smiling tightly. 'You will come to regret this insolence, before I have you executed. My pinnaces are already landing. Carrying enough war machines, gravity barges and armed troops to ensure that if the aliens do interfere, they will be made to regret it. I will have the traitors, one way or another. I don't know who you really are, sir Carrion, but no doubt my interrogators will drag it out of you later, at their leisure.'

He had more to say, but Carrion shut down the comm panels and the viewscreen went blank. Carrion stared thoughtfully into space as Lewis and the others came forward to join him at the reception console. Lewis cleared his throat uncertainly. Carrion's eyes seemed very far away.

'Sorry to have dragged you into our mess, sir Carrion. I didn't think they'd track us down this quickly. Lead us back to our ship, and we'll get the hell out of here. They'll never catch us once we're off the ground. The *Hereward*'s got speed and stealth capabilities you wouldn't believe, though I'd rather you didn't ask why. I think the sooner we're gone the better; we don't want to start a war between the Empire and the Ashrai.'

'Too late,' said Carrion, watching something only he could see.

'Hundreds of pinnaces are falling towards Unseeli. The starcruisers are firing their disrupter cannon from orbit, to blast clearings big enough for the pinnaces to land in. I can hear the trees screaming, dying. The Ashrai are gathering. Let the Empire forces come. None of them shall leave here alive.' He turned suddenly to look at Lewis, who almost flinched at the dark, alien, impersonal power in that gaze. 'But you must understand this, Deathstalker. Our audience is over. What we do now, we do for ourselves. We will not fight on your behalf. Your fate, your mission, are nothing to us. Return to your ship and leave, if you can. Find Owen, if you can. We want nothing to do with Humanity, or the Empire. We preserve ourselves, to face the Terror when it comes.' He smiled suddenly. 'Goodbye, Deathstalker. Good luck. And if you do find Owen . . . remember me to him.'

'That's *it*?' Jesamine said angrily. 'We came all this way, just for that? What's the matter with you? The whole of Humanity is under threat of extinction!'

'You say that like it's a bad thing,' said Carrion. 'Humanity is currently invading my world. Again. You always were a selfish, brutal race. Perhaps something better will arise to replace you.'

'You don't really think you can stop the Terror on your own, do you?' said Rose, in her deep cold voice.

'We stopped the Recreated.'

'With Owen's help,' said Lewis. 'You owe us, sir Carrion. You owe me, through my ancestor's name. Give us safe escort and protection back to our ship, at least. It's a long way to the *Hereward*, and you can bet Kamal will have located it by now and sent troops to block our way. Damnit; at least show us what we'll be facing!'

Carrion didn't move, but the viewscreen on the wall flared into life again. Whole sections of the metallic forest were exploding, the huge trees shattered by the energy beams stabbing down from orbit. The scene changed, to show countless pinnaces punching through the cloud layer; transport ships carrying everything the Empire needed to make war on Unseeli. The scene changed again, showing war machines lumbering out of the cargo bays of landed pinnaces. Great hulking monstrosities of gleaming steel, studded with guns. Gravity barges rose slowly into the air, shimmering with force shields as they ploughed their way through the tightly packed metal trees. Troops disembarked in strict order, Imperial marines who wore the scarlet cross of the Church Militant on their battle armour. They moved out, fanning through the forest, relentless as army ants.

'I should have known,' Lewis said grimly. 'Finn's packed the troops with his own people. One will get you ten they're Neumen as well.

Pure Humanity, sir Carrion; a new breed since your day. Lionstone's illegitimate children, who believe the only good alien is a dead alien. And the scarlet cross means they're religious fanatics. I think we can safely assume they're more interested in bringing us back dead, rather than alive.'

'Talk about overkill,' Brett said bitterly. 'A whole army, just for us? It's not fair. My stomach hurts.'

'About time I got some healthy exercise,' said Rose. She was smiling, and her eyes were shining. 'The odds make it more of a challenge.'

'Yes,' said Saturday, his great head poking through the doorway. 'It will be good to be killing again. I'm really quite peckish.'

Lewis looked at Carrion defensively. 'Hey, I didn't get to choose my companions.'

'Neither did Owen,' said Carrion. 'And he didn't do too badly. And after meeting Ruby Journey, there's not much that shocks me.' He looked at the screen again. 'Two hundred years since the overthrow of the Iron Bitch, and nothing's really changed. Poor John. He would have been so disappointed.'

'Can you reopen communications with the *Hector*?' said Lewis. 'Maybe I can negotiate a truce . . . or something.'

The viewscreen flickered, and Captain Kamal was back again. Lewis stepped forward to stand before the screen, automatically adopting his old stance of Paragon authority. 'This is Lewis Deathstalker. You came here for me, not the Ashrai. My companions aren't important either. You want me. Call off your war, let my companions go and I will surrender myself to you.'

'No!' Jesamine said immediately. 'Lewis, you can't! They'll kill you!'

'No,' Lewis said quietly. 'If I surrender, Finn wouldn't be able to resist the thought of a show trial. I'm the one he really wants. He needs to see me broken, brought down. To prove in front of everyone that I should never have been made Champion instead of him. The rest of you don't matter to him. And you have to be free. You have a mission, remember?' Lewis looked back at Kamal. 'What do you say, Captain? Just this once, can't we do this the sane and responsible way, so no one has to get hurt?'

'You've gone soft, Deathstalker.' Captain Kamal almost spat out the words. 'The Church Militant has no mercy for traitors. You, and the jezebel, and the scum you've attracted are going back to Logres, dead or alive. Your word is worthless. You have disgraced your name and your position. You are a vileness in the face of God. No deals, Deathstalker. Only blood can atone for your sins.'

Lewis nodded slowly. 'Nice of you to confirm that you're religious lunatics first and soldiers second. Loony tunes are always so much easier to outthink than trained professionals. While I've got you here, Kamal, just what are your orders concerning the Ashrai?'

'Death to unbelievers.'

Captain Kamal cut the connection, and the screen went blank again.

Lewis looked at Carrion. 'Well, that was interesting. Short, insulting and decidedly ominous, but interesting.'

'Yes,' said Carrion. 'It was.'

He slammed the butt of his staff on the floor, and the lobby suddenly blazed with light as new power thundered through Base Thirteen. Old mechanisms stirred into life again, computer systems chattered to each other as they came on-line, driven from their centuries-long sleep by the will of one implacable man. Viewscreens blazed across the lobby, displaying long streams of scrolling data. Brett looked around uneasily.

'The generators here are dead, Lewis. Powered down hundreds of years ago. You saw the sensor readings. And with this much damage the base shouldn't be able to function anyway. How the hell is he doing this?'

'I don't know,' said Lewis. 'And I really don't feel like asking him.'

'The Maze,' said Jesamine. 'All the stories, all the legends, and I never really understood . . . He's no more human now than when he was Ashrai. He's what the Maze made him.'

'There are those who would say I wasn't really human, even before I went into the Madness Maze,' said Carrion, not looking round. 'I was an Investigator, after all. I'm using my old security codes to break into the *Hector*'s security files. Back in the day, Investigators had all kinds of back-door access codes to get us information we weren't supposed to have, and it seems a surprising number of them still work.'

'There haven't been any Investigators since Lionstone's time,' said Lewis.

'Probably a good thing,' said Carrion. 'Ah, what have we here? Personal orders for the captain of the *Hector*, for his eyes only.'

The main viewscreen lit up again, to show Finn Durandal's classically handsome features. He smiled out of the screen, calm and composed.

'That's him,' said Jesamine. 'The Durandal. The real traitor.'

'Here are your real orders, my dear Captain,' Finn said easily. 'They are not to be discussed with anyone else, even if they are of higher rank in the Fleet than you. These orders come from Pure Humanity. First, you will use all measures necessary to locate and then execute the Deathstalker and his companions. You will not accept any form of surrender. Bring back their heads, if possible. Second, you will land your troops on Unseeli. The Ashrai must be punished for their past arrogance. Kill as many as practical, in the time available, and be sure it's transmitted live. Do good work, Captain; the whole of the Empire will be watching. We need to make a strong impression here, make it clear to everyone that the old liberal ways are over, and from now on aliens will do as they're told or pay the price. When you're done, fill your holds with metal from the trees. I don't see why the Empire should have to cover the expense of this mission. Oh, and Captain: don't let the Deathstalker or any of his companions escape. Or don't bother coming back.'

The picture disappeared. Carrion studied the blank screen thoughtfully, while the others studied him.

'Well?' Lewis said finally. 'You can see for yourself: our enemy is your enemy. We have a common cause.'

'They will all die here,' said Carrion. 'It's been so long, they've forgotten what the Ashrai can do. Even in the bad old days of Lionstone, it took more than armies and war machines to stop the Ashrai. That's why Captain Silence scorched the planet, after all. So, the wheel turns and war comes to us again. We will make an example here. And if they dare to try and scorch us again, I will show their petty starcruisers the same face I showed the Recreated. I will set their ships on fire against the night.'

'Oh great,' muttered Brett. 'Another psycho.'

'Shut up, Brett,' said Lewis. 'Sir Carrion, we don't stand a hope in hell of getting back to our ship unless you protect us. Our enemy is your enemy. You have to help us, in Owen's name.'

'If you're really a Deathstalker, you won't need help,' said Carrion. 'My last ties to Humanity died with John Silence. I owe you nothing. Go your own way. I have a war to fight.'

Rose surged forward, her sword in her hand, the point aimed at Carrion's throat. Her movements were a blur, inhumanly fast, and still she never stood a chance. She'd barely crossed half the space between them when Carrion's staff suddenly blazed with energy, and Rose was plucked out of mid-air and thrown backwards, hurtling across the lobby to slam into the far wall. Her eyes closed, and she slid slowly down the wall, still somehow clinging to her sword. Brett ran over to her. Lewis turned to Carrion, his ugly face set in harsh, dangerous lines, his hand hovering over his disrupter. Jesamine moved in close beside him. Saturday looked on from the open doorway, his tail sweeping thoughtfully back and forth.

'Keep your attack dog on a leash, Deathstalker,' said Carrion. 'Or I'll muzzle her. I think you should leave now. Your name only buys you so much protection. Be about your own business, and let the Ashrai tend to theirs.'

Lewis backed slowly away, not taking his eyes off the man dressed in black. Jesamine retreated with him, her hands clenched into impotent fists. Amazingly, Rose was back on her feet, though her eyes were dazed and she was leaning heavily on Brett. Lewis led the way out of Base Thirteen, and back into the metallic forest. And Carrion stood alone in the reception lobby, surrounded by ghosts, while viewscreen after viewscreen showed Imperial attack troops moving on the surface of Unseeli for the first time in over two hundred years.

I am Carrion, the destroyer of worlds. I bring bad luck. Oh John, was it all for nothing, in the end?

The Imperial marines moved slowly through the metallic forest, keeping strict formation, guns at the ready. They spread out across the narrow paths, driven by religious fervour and flying on battle drugs that hadn't been used or needed in centuries, ready to shoot at anything that moved and wasn't them. Most had never been on a non-human world before, and were already seriously spooked. It wasn't just the heavier gravity and the huge glowing trees. The whole feel of this world was subtly disturbing, as though they had wandered unknowingly into a psychic minefield. Some thought they could hear voices whispering among the trees, or even singing. Backs crawled with the sensation of being watched by unseen eyes. More than one soldier opened fire suddenly, and couldn't explain why. The sheer size of the trees made them feel like children, creeping along the floor of a nightmare adult world. They were all breathing hard now, sweat slick on their faces, eyes wide with adrenalin and battle drugs and fears they couldn't name. They didn't feel like aggressors any more. They felt . . . hunted. What had started out as a rapid confident advance soon slowed to a crawl, and only the rigid discipline of the officers kept them moving. Only the really hardcore fanatics made officer class these days, and yet even they studied the surrounding trees with darting, suspicious eyes. This wasn't what they'd been led to expect.

And then the Ashrai came, plunging down out of the cloud layer to fly over the packed troops. They were huge and magnificent, with their gargoyle faces and savage fangs and claws, and there were thousands of them. They filled the skies with their gleaming scales and widespread membranous wings, bright as rainbows with bared teeth and blazing eyes. Down below, the troops lurched to a halt in stunned disarray, despite the furious commands of their officers. Many just stood and pointed up at the sky, their faces slack with awe, their guns forgotten.

'It's the dragons,' said more than one voice. 'The dragons that flew with the blessed Owen against the Recreated! No one told us . . . we can't fight them. Not Owen's dragons . . .'

Some even threw their guns on the ground. The troops began to babble loudly, arguing amongst themselves. Some were on their knees, praying. Old words, heavy with significance, moved through the ranks. *Dragons, aliens, angels . . .* And it might all have ended there, but the Church Militant had chosen its officers wisely. Men of steadfast faith, cold discipline and ruthless nature. They moved calmly among the chattering ranks, and shot any man who wouldn't pick up his gun. They lashed their men with harsh, hateful words, reminding them of the vows they had made, to their Empire and their God. A few troopers tried to run, but they didn't get far. The officers strode through the ranks, blood on their armour and on their boots, and no one could meet their fiery gaze. In a few moments, the army had changed to a rabble and back again, and now the marines hefted their guns, shamed and angry and ready to fight. The officers ordered them to open fire on the Ashrai overhead, but none of the energy beams came close to hitting a target.

The officers called in the gravity barges, but they were having trouble forcing a way through the tops of the tightly packed trees. The metallic forest was no match for force shields and disrupter cannon, but still it was slow going. And down on the ground, the war machines weren't doing much better. The paths were too narrow for them, and they had to smash their way through. It didn't help that most of them had been mothballed since Lionstone's day, and the troops operating them were unskilled and unpractised. They forced their way through the forest, leaving wide trails of devastation behind them, their guns moving uselessly back and forth in search of an enemy.

Back in Base Thirteen, Carrion watched them advancing on the viewscreen, and felt almost nostalgic. He recognised the war machines, from the days of the last Ashrai rebellion. Things had been so much simpler back then. He'd never doubted which side he was on. Even though his oldest friend had become his most hated enemy.

But now the Terror was coming, and he had sent the Deathstalker away, probably to die at the Empire's hands. Carrion watched his viewscreens, and wondered if perhaps he had forgotten too many important things while he played at being an Ashrai.

Lewis knew there was no point in meeting any of the advancing troops head on. The odds were insanely against him, and only he and Rose possessed energy weapons. So he led his people silently through the metallic forest, sticking to the shadows, and made hit-and-run attacks only when he had to. There were a lot of troops blocking the way to the *Hereward* now, but the narrow pathways split them up into groups of manageable size, and there were always some who dragged along behind the others. Lewis reminded himself they were merciless fanatics who served a traitor, and hardened his heart.

Some were undoubtedly good men, who honestly thought they were in the right; but the fate of the Empire was at stake, and they'd chosen the wrong side.

So Lewis came running unexpectedly out of the trees, and hit the startled troops from one side while Rose Constantine hit them hard from the other. Jesamine guarded Lewis's back, while Saturday roared happily as he fell upon the stragglers at the rear. And Brett did his best to keep out of everyone's way. Swords flashed brightly in the diffused light, and blood flew through the air, splashing thickly across the dull grey ground. The troops cried out in shock and panic. The last thing they'd expected was an attack. Lewis cut down the armoured marines with professional ease, his ugly face grim with concentration. He was fast and furious, his every move textbook perfect, and no one could stand against him. Jesamine swung her lighter sword with determined skill, killing when she had to. She kept her face calm, and her hands steady, but only her iron will kept fear and panic at bay. It was one thing to play a warrior upon a stage, and quite another to be one.

Rose hacked her way through the troops, a song on her lips and a warm happy feeling in her heart. She towered over most of them, an angel of death in her blood-red leathers, crying out with joy at every death stroke. No one could come close to touching her, and she danced through her opponents with almost contemptuous grace. Her sword swept back and forth, too fast to be seen, leaving a blood-stained trail behind it. Saturday stamped ungracefully through the milling mob, tearing out throats and hearts with his deceptively fast forearms, and crunching off heads with his great teeth. The spikes on his furiously lashing tail ripped through men, and crushed them inside their battle armour. The reptiloid tore a savage path through the demoralised troops, as implacable and remorseless as a force of nature. Blood spilled thickly from his grinning mouth. Saturday was having a good time.

The carnage lasted only a matter of minutes, just long enough to make a bloody mess out of the straggling troops, and then Lewis led his people back into the trees before the main mass of the army could catch up with them. It was simple enough to scatter and lose their pursuers in the maze of narrow pathways, and then reform later at a prearranged point. The troops had the advantage of superior fire-power, but energy weapons weren't much use with so many metal trees in the way to soak up disrupter fire.

The army grew increasingly ragged in formation, as various groups stumbled among the trees, searching desperately for the traitors who didn't seem to realise that they were supposed to be the prey. Lewis kept up the hit-and-run tactics, splitting the troops into smaller and smaller groups and demoralising the survivors. And all the time, leading his people closer and closer to where they'd left the *Hereward*.

He was too preoccupied to notice the way Jesamine looked at him. She'd never realised how at home her Lewis was in the heart of battle. How unconcernedly he threw himself into butchery and slaughter, smiling his cold smile, like a man coming home at last. Because he was a Deathstalker, and this was where he belonged. The last time she'd seen him fight with such pitiless savagery had been during the Neuman riot outside Parliament, when he hadn't seemed to care how many he killed. This wasn't the Lewis she knew. Or thought she'd known.

Rose Constantine, on the other hand, gloried in the bad odds. It had been a long time since she'd had any real challenge to her abilities. And while killing aliens in the Arena was fun, nothing satisfied her like the murder of men. Her heart sang as she danced among the screaming troops, and if she wished for anything it was for a higher standard of fighter among them. Some actually turned and ran rather than try and face her. She killed them too, of course, but it wasn't the same. She had her standards, after all.

Saturday romped among the soldiers, claws and jaws soaked in blood. He was huge and fast and strong, and the humans died so prettily. And best of all, there was no one here to tell him not to eat his kills afterwards. Human meat tasted just as good as he'd always known it would.

Brett watched it all from among the trees, shaking and shuddering. He would have liked to run, but there was nowhere to run to. So he used Rose's disrupter to snipe from concealment, when he thought he had a clear shot, and otherwise did his best not to be noticed. He was muttering to himself almost continuously now, a high-pitched querulous yammer that made no sense even to him. He didn't belong here. He wasn't a fighter. His stomach hurt.

Hit and run, kill the enemy and vanish into the trees, all the time edging towards the *Hereward*. They were all getting tired now, except possibly Saturday. Even Rose was slowing, the punishment she'd taken from Carrion finally catching up with her. But still they fought on; even Brett. With so many armed troops running wildly in the forest, nowhere seemed safe to hide any more, so he drew his sword and did his best to look dangerous. Inevitably, his luck ran out sooner rather than later. Three burly troopers cut him off from the others and advanced on him smiling, with drawn swords and force shields buzzing on their arms. Brett screamed for help, and looked frantically around for an escape route, but they had him surrounded.

So he threw himself at them with the rage and terror of a cornered rat, all vicious speed and precious little skill. He caught one marine by surprise and stabbed him in the groin, and then had to retreat quickly as the other two closed in on him. He swept his sword widely back and forth in front of him, and almost dropped it. One of the troopers laughed. Brett swore, and cried angry frustrated tears. He threw his sword on the ground and put both his hands as high into the air as he could. He wasn't a fighter, and he was a fool ever to think he could be. But the marines kept coming, grinning nastily, and Brett remembered Finn's words, on the base viewscreen. *You will not accept any form of surrender*. They were going to kill him anyway.

Brett lost his temper. He lashed out with his esp, and his power of compulsion slammed into the mind of the trooper nearest him. And then it was the easiest thing in the world for Brett to make that trooper shoot his companion. Shot at point-blank range, the marine was dead before his body hit the ground. The controlled man just stood there, his face blank, while Brett snatched up the sword he'd thrown away and ran the man through.

Brett stood there a while, breathing hard, looking at the three marines he'd killed. His head ached, his nose was bleeding, but he was alive and they weren't. Brett laughed briefly, a soft disturbing sound, and then he walked openly through the trees, sending his psionic compulsion out before him, and no one could see him. His headache grew steadily worse, and he could feel blood trickling from his nose and welling up from under his eyelids, but he was too angry to care. Every now and again, he'd reach out with his mind and one marine would kill another for no reason, and Brett would laugh again. If he'd had time to think, he might have realised this wasn't like him at all, but that wouldn't occur to him until much later.

Back at Base Thirteen, the man called Carrion was still studying his viewscreens and considering his options when another man appeared out of nowhere. Carrion felt his presence immediately and spun round, and then he saw who it was and smiled.

'I should have known. With so much of the past repeating itself, it was inevitable that you'd turn up eventually. Hello, John. You're looking good, for a dead man. Why is it you only ever come to see me when you want something?'

'Hello, Sean,' said John Silence. 'It has been a long time, hasn't it? You know, you're all that's left of my past now. Everyone else I knew from the old days is either dead or missing. But still you and I go on; too stubborn to quit and call it a day.'

'You're the only part of my human past that I still care to remember,' said Carrion. 'We're bound together, by all the things we did, and shouldn't have done. What do you want this time, John?'

Silence indicated the viewscreen showing Lewis and his companions cutting their way through a stubborn group of marines. More troops were coming up on them from behind, but Lewis hadn't seen them yet.

'You have to help them, Sean. This new Deathstalker and his ragbag friends are perhaps the last hope the Empire's got. The Terror is come at last, and all Humanity is threatened with extinction.'

'You say that like it's a bad thing,' said Carrion, but his heart wasn't in it.

Silence considered the viewscreens. 'Imperial troops on Unseeli again. Marines and war machines and gravity barges. Blasted clearings and broken trees, and good people threatened with death for no reason. We can't let this happen again, Sean. You heard the Durandal's secret orders. The Empire didn't commit this kind of firepower here just to take care of a few traitors. The new regime is using Unseeli as a testing ground. Somewhere to try out their new shock troops and their new battle plans. They must be stopped. They won't be happy until the Ashrai are dead and gone, and Unseeli is an Empire world again. A symbol of the new order. You have to help the Deathstalker, while you still can. The Ashrai can defend their world, but the Deathstalker is the key to defeating the Durandal and all the bad things that are coming. A Deathstalker always is. You can't let him die here.'

Carrion considered the viewscreen before him. When he looked round again, he was alone in the lobby.

Lewis leaned heavily against the thick bole of a golden tree, panting for breath. His sword hung down from his hand, too heavy to lift for the moment. Blood dripped from his dented and scored armour, some of it his own. He looked around him, but all the troops he could see were dead. He could hear more of them, crashing back and forth in the trees and shouting incoherently to each other, but most seemed to be moving away. Jesamine was sitting on the ground beside him, her shoulders slumped with exhaustion. Lewis was worried about her. She wasn't built for this.

Brett and Rose were sitting together, not far away. Rose had a cloth in her hand, and was using it to wipe the blood off Brett's face with slow, careful movements; as though she'd never done anything like that before. Brett sat very still, and let her.

A little further away, Saturday was eating something with great enjoyment. None of the others looked at him.

Lewis stared up at the sky, where the Ashrai were still circling. 'Damn them,' he said quickly. 'We're here for them too. Why won't they help? Don't they know the Terror will come for them too, if we can't stop it? We can't die here, not so early in our quest.'

'They know,' said Jesamine. 'They just don't care. All they care about is killing humans, continuing the war that should have ended centuries ago.'

'If only I could have made Carrion listen,' said Lewis.

'Oh hell,' said Jesamine, clambering unsteadily to her feet. 'I may not be much of a fighter, but if there's one thing I've always been able to do, it's make people listen.'

She glared up into the sky at the soaring Ashrai, took a deep breath, opened her mouth and sang. On some level, she could still hear the song of the trees and the Ashrai, the song of Unseeli, and now she answered it with a song of her own, a harmony and a counterpoint; the song of Humanity. Her voice rang out clear as any bell cutting effortlessly across the clamour of the surrounding troops. She sang, her voice proud and true, with words and melodies from a dozen songs, from all the operas she'd ever sung in her long career, and it seemed like the whole world stopped to listen to her.

And the Ashrai sang back to her, their voices joining and combining, forming a glorious whole far greater than the sum of its parts. Jesamine Flowers sang, and the Ashrai answered, and the two songs joined to become one. Jesamine stopped singing, and so did the

Ashrai. And in that echoing silence, the Ashrai dropped out of the glowing sky and fell upon the Imperial troopers surrounding Lewis and his people. The marines cried out in shock and horror as the Ashrai came sweeping between the towering trees with almost supernatural grace, and were upon them before they could even aim their weapons. Everywhere in the metallic forest marines screamed and died, and Jesamine watched, with tears in her eyes, at the ugly results of such a beautiful song.

Carrion watched it on his viewscreens, and felt a great weight lift from his heart as the decision was made for him. He should have remembered that Deathstalkers always got their own way, eventually. *Ah well*, he murmured, and walked out of Base Thirteen. He lifted his feet from the ground, and flew upwards, punching through the heavy cloud layer and on out into space. He didn't feel the cold and he didn't need to breathe, and energy crackled up and down the length of his power lance, that ancient banned weapon. He concentrated, and his speed increased until the first starcruiser loomed swiftly up before him. Carrion smashed through the ship's force shields as though they weren't there, and then hammered his way through the many layers of steel in under a second before bursting out of the hull on the other side. He swung around and hit the ship again, targeting the engines this time, punching holes through the steel decks with joyous ease. Explosions rocked the starcruiser as he hung a way off in space, and he smiled in the cold and the dark as the *Heracles* tore itself apart, the long steel ship blossoming into bright actinic flames, and the screams of the dying went unheard in the vacuum of space. Carrion turned his back on the stricken ship as it began its descent from orbit, falling slowly but inevitably to its death.

The other starcruisers were turning and manoeuvring to face Carrion as he flew effortlessly towards them. They opened up with every gun they had, the disrupter cannon operated by the very best tracking systems, releasing enough destructive energies to take out a dozen ships, let alone one man, unarmed and unprotected. But he was Carrion, and he had been through the Madness Maze, and he had faced the Recreated. He was human and Ashrai and so much more. And in the end, nothing was left of the five starcruisers than a few radioactive shells, tumbling slowly end over end into the fiery grasp of Unseeli's welcoming atmosphere.

Carrion hung alone in space, looking down on his adopted world, and thought of many things.

*

John Silence walked unhurriedly through the shimmering metal forest, and where he looked war machines exploded. He looked up, and where his gaze fell upon them gravity barges malfunctioned and fell out of the sky, impaling themselves on the tops and branches of the metal trees or falling in flames to the grey ground below. Violent explosions sounded through the forest as the Imperial advance slowed and stopped. Troops ran screaming rather than face him, only to meet the Ashrai, deadly and unstoppable, taking back their world from those who would despoil it. They generated localised psistorms wherever they went, altering probabilities so that weapons malfunctioned and accidents happened and men fell dead from strokes and embolisms and heart attacks. Finn's people had no espers to protect them, only a handful of easily overwhelmed esp-blockers.

And, of course, there was Lewis Deathstalker and Jesamine Flowers, Rose Constantine and Brett Random, and the reptiloid Saturday, and no man could stand against them either.

Finn Durandal sent an army to Unseeli. Religious fanatics, Pure Humanity to a man, trained soldiers. And in the end, they never stood a chance. Because the Ashrai weren't interested in accepting surrender either. Men had come to Unseeli with death on their minds, and that was what they found.

Lewis Deathstalker and his companions finally returned to the clearing in which they'd left the *Hereward*. It seemed very still and quiet. You'd never know a terrible war had been fought only a short distance away. Lewis and Jesamine nodded to Rose and Brett, and then they all stared in disgust at Saturday as he gnawed on what was very obviously the remains of a human leg. The reptiloid realised they were glaring at him, and generously offered to share his meal with the others. He was honestly puzzled when they loudly declined. He shrugged, and casually cracked open the long bone to get at the marrow. Lewis looked away, desperate for something else to concentrate on. All around, there were loud creakings and groanings as the metal trees slowly regenerated, repairing the damage done to them. Soon there would be no traces left that Humanity had ever come to Unseeli. Lewis thought he could live with that.

Jesamine made her way over to the *Hereward*'s airlock, and leaned against the hatch, pressing her hot flushed face against the cold metal. She was shaking with shock and reaction to all she'd been through. Not just from the strain of singing with the Ashrai, though her head still swam and her throat was raw with pain; but also from the sheer horror of the fighting she'd witnessed, and been a reluctant part of.

She thought she'd seen the rough side of life before, when she was starting out; seen men kill each other in the cheap clubs and bars she'd played at the start of her career. But this was war, and war was different. The blood and suffering, the desperate screams of the dying, the knowledge that you could die at any moment if you were slow or stupid, or just unlucky enough to be in the wrong place at the wrong time. The noise and the bedlam, and the sudden stench of freshly spilled guts. She had killed because she had to, and she had no doubts about what she'd done. She had nothing but contempt for the fanatics who made up the Church Militant and Pure Humanity. But still she shook and shuddered, and bit her lip to keep from crying out. She didn't know if she could do it again . . . not even for Lewis and his cause.

Lewis finally noticed her, and came quickly over to put a comforting arm around her. She turned and buried her face in his chest, and took what comfort she could from him.

Not too far away, Brett was standing hunched over, his arms wrapped tightly around his aching stomach. He'd already vomited till he dry heaved, and it hadn't helped. He was a conman, not a fighter. A thief, not a killer. He didn't want anyone to die, least of all him. And yet he remembered walking through the trees making men kill each other and themselves, as though he'd been a whole other person then. Rose stood patiently beside him, not understanding, but keeping him company.

'It's over,' she said. 'We won. You fought well enough. You should be proud.'

'I never wanted this,' he said thickly. 'This isn't me. This isn't what I do. I want to go home.'

'Things change,' said Rose. 'After a while, it won't bother you at all.'

'That's what scares me,' said Brett.

Saturday watched them, and said nothing.

Carrion came walking out of the forest accompanied by another man, and both sides were surprised to find the other knew the newcomer.

'You told me John Silence was dead,' Carrion said reproachfully.

'That's because we knew him as Samuel Chevron,' Lewis said finally, when he could get his breath back. 'I knew you had to be someone important from the age of heroes, but I had no idea . . . are you really him? Captain John Silence of the *Dauntless*?'

'I was once. It was a long time ago.'

'That's how you were able to do those amazing things in Traitors'

Hall!' said Jesamine, her eyes almost painfully wide. 'Why . . . why didn't you tell us? Why did you let everyone think you were dead? And why didn't anyone recognise that Samuel Chevron was really one of the great legends of our time?'

'People see what I want them to see, when they look at me,' said Silence.

'I've taken care of all five starcruisers,' said Carrion, smiling at the open awe in the faces of Lewis and Jesamine and Brett. Rose just watched silently. 'A few lifeboats got away, to tell what happened here. I don't think the Empire will be returning. I trust the excitement is now over, and I can get back to my life?'

'We were hoping you might come with us, sir Carrion,' Lewis said diffidently. 'To search for the blessed Owen. We have so much to do.'

'No,' said Carrion. 'Not even for a Deathstalker. Not even for you, John.'

Lewis turned to Silence, but he shook his head too. 'I go where I'm needed. You don't need me, Deathstalker.'

'Why haven't you revealed yourself before this?' said Jesamine, almost angrily. 'Why did you allow Finn and his people to come to power? Why didn't you stop all the terrible things that have happened?'

'One man alone can't save the Empire,' said Silence. 'Even a Deathstalker needs companions.'

'Why didn't you interfere in the fighting here earlier?' said Brett.

'Because you needed the experience.'

'We could have been killed!'

'That's part of what you were learning.'

'What about the Terror?' said Lewis. 'With your power . . .'

'No,' said Silence. 'That's your destiny, Deathstalker. Go to Haden. All the answers you seek are there, in the Madness Maze.' He turned to look at Carrion. 'I have to go, Sean. Tell me: are you happy, now you're an Ashrai?'

'Yes,' said Carrion. 'It's all I ever wanted.'

'Good,' said Silence. 'I'm glad one of us at least got to have a happy ending.'

'They told me you were dead, John.'

'I am,' said Silence, and he disappeared.

Carrion nodded slowly. 'Well,' he said. 'This is a planet of ghosts, after all.'

He turned back into an Ashrai, huge and powerful, spread his membranous wings and flew back up into the glowing sky to rejoin his people.

TWO

BROTHERLY LOVE, AND OTHER CONSIDERATIONS

It was dark in the King's private chambers. All the blinds were drawn, and the door was securely locked. And Douglas Campbell, last favoured son of a noble line, Speaker to the House of Parliament and chosen King of Humanity's greatest Empire, sat alone in his opulent chambers, wrapped in a faded old dressing gown and nothing else, unshaven and dishevelled, staring at nothing. His once handsome face was slack, his eyes were empty, and what thoughts he had were slow and sullen, of no importance to anyone, not even himself. Someone was knocking at his door, had been knocking for some time now, but he couldn't bring himself to give a damn. They'd give up eventually and go away like everyone else had done, leaving him alone.

He'd sent them all away, friends and colleagues and servants, driving them from him with harsh words and bitter language. He needed to be alone with his pain, and he had no use any more for words like 'duty' or 'responsibility'. He had a lot of brooding and second guessing and feeling sorry for himself to do . . . and he had just enough dignity left that he didn't want anyone to see him doing it. Especially not the servants. For all their smiles and kind words and signed loyalty oaths, there wasn't one he'd trust not to go running off to the media with their story, if the price was right. Once that would have been unthinkable; but then a lot of things had been unthinkable, once.

Before his closest friend had betrayed him with the only woman he'd ever really loved.

He wasn't sure how long he'd sat alone in the dark, trying not to think or feel or care. He didn't do much any more. Mostly he just sat in his chair, ate and drank when he remembered, and spent as much time dozing and sleeping as he could; because then he didn't have to remember how his whole life had gone to hell. He hadn't shaved or bathed in ages, and didn't care. He had a bowl of something lukewarm in his lap that he didn't remember preparing. He couldn't remember whether it was supposed to be breakfast or dinner, but now and again he ate some of it with his fingers. It didn't taste of anything much. He was a mess, and he knew it. Somehow, that seemed fitting.

The viewscreen before him hadn't been turned on in days. At first he'd kept it on all the time, for a kind of company. He'd sat slumped in front of the screen like an acolyte, flicking numbly through the hundreds of news channels in the hope of finding someone who could explain to him how everything in his life could have gone so terribly wrong so quickly. But all the news channels could do was drive home in merciless detail just how quickly his precious Golden Age was deteriorating into something far darker, by its own perverse will. It seemed there was no good news any more. The Church Militant was now the Empire's official religion, in all the ways that mattered. Thousands of fanatics marched down city streets on hundreds of worlds, holding up blazing crosses, loudly proclaiming their vicious faith, and damning unbelievers. Pure Humanity had also seized the public mood and made it their own, and everywhere hatred was lashing out at anyone or anything that could be declared inhuman. Espers, aliens . . . and anyone who wasn't Pure Humanity or Church Militant. It was a dangerous time to be a free-thinker. Heretics could be hunted down and butchered in busy streets, and no one would raise a finger to help them.

The news shows weren't openly biased yet, but the signs were already there, if you knew what to look for. In the words the commentators didn't use, in the language that didn't condemn, in the causes and people who couldn't get air time any more. Douglas grew tired, watching it fall apart. The sane voices were gone. Most of the politicians were running scared, the old Church had vanished with its gentle Patriarch, and the Paragons had set off on their quest to find the missing Owen Deathstalker. So far there was no sign of the blessed Owen anywhere, and a few Paragons had already returned, abandoning and renouncing the quest as useless.

There was no news at all of Lewis Deathstalker and his treacherous companions. Douglas couldn't decide whether that was good or bad. All he knew for sure was that he didn't recognise what his world and his Empire had become. So he turned off the viewscreen and sat alone in the growing gloom, feeling lost and broken and useless.

The knocking at his door broke off abruptly, and as he looked vaguely around he heard the sharp definite sound of his door unlocking. Someone had a key. Which should have been impossible. The door swung open and light flooded into the room. Douglas put up a hand to protect his watering eyes, and peered painfully at the dark silhouette in his doorway. He hadn't called for anyone. He hadn't called for anyone in ages. He wondered if his guards had finally betrayed him too, and then the thought came to him that perhaps the new savage Empire had decided it didn't want or need a King any more, and had sent someone to put him out of his misery.

Anger flooded through him, pushing back the accumulated lethargy. He lurched up out of his chair, swaying unsteadily on his feet as he glanced about him for his weapons. But he couldn't think what he'd done with his gun or his sword, let alone his armour. So he snatched up a heavy wooden footstool and glared defiantly at the figure in the doorway, determined to sell his life dearly.

'God, you're a mess, Douglas,' said Anne Barclay. 'You look awful and you smell worse. What have you done to yourself?'

Douglas slowly lowered the footstool as his old friend Anne stalked forward into his chambers, looking about her and sniffing loudly.

'Some people shouldn't be allowed to live alone. I spent months sorting out the right furnishings for this room, and you've turned it into a tip.' She made her way quickly round the room, opening the blinds and chattering nonstop as daylight flooded the chamber. 'And by the way, your guards are rubbish. I was able to bully and intimidate my way past them far too easily. I've replaced them with some of my own people. And put down that footstool, before you strain yourself.'

Douglas put down the footstool, and then did his best to stand up straight. It wasn't easy; his legs were unsteady, and the new light was giving him a killer headache. But it was one thing for him to admit to himself how far he'd let himself go, and quite another to see the knowledge in Anne's eyes. He pulled his dressing gown tightly around him, and did his best to meet her accusing gaze with one of his own.

'What are you doing here, Anne? I didn't send for you. And how the hell did you get in here, anyway? That door was locked.'

'I have a key,' Anne said briskly. 'I am your Head of Security, remember? And I'm here because you haven't sent for anyone in two months now. Some people already think you're dead. And that's a luxury you can't afford any more, Douglas. It's time for you to return to the world. There's an important media event happening in just over an hour from now, and your presence is very much required.'

Douglas sat down again. 'I don't have to be anywhere, Anne. The

63

Empire doesn't need a King any more, if it ever did. I saw the news shows. It's bedlam out there.'

'The times are changing, so we have to change with them.' Anne came to a halt before him, hands on hips, glaring down at him. 'Look, I don't have time for this, Douglas. Something really important has happened that affects you personally. You, and the whole damned Empire. Right now, I need you to get cleaned up, climb into your very best and come with me. You can be depressed and depressing on your own time. Well don't just sit there! On your feet, into your bedroom and get changed! And don't hang about, or I'll come in and help you get dressed. And I've got very cold hands.'

Douglas scowled at her as he rose reluctantly to his feet. 'Same old Anne.'

Except that wasn't strictly true. Douglas still had trouble getting used to how much his old friend had changed, physically. For as long as he'd known her, Anne Barclay had been short and stocky, with a square determined face topped by brutally short red hair. She wore smartly cut suits of uniform grey, and strode everywhere in a manner that suggested everyone else had better get the hell out of her way. She ran her security people like her own private army, was always on top of every problem and was intimidatingly efficient. And about as glamorous as a half brick.

But a lot of things had changed since the old days, not least Anne Barclay. The new Anne was tall and willowy, with pale perfect skin and a great mane of long flowing crimson tresses. Her face and especially her chin had been subtly redesigned to more fashionably feminine lines, and she also possessed a quite magnificent bosom. Anne had been to the body shops, and had paid a not so small fortune to have herself remade in the image of her private dreams. She'd got her money's worth. She was drop-dead gorgeous, now. But for all her dazzling silk dress and elegant makeup, she still moved like the old Anne, striding everywhere and standing like a soldier. She had no style to her, no grace. She might be beautiful, but she moved as though she didn't really believe it. Being feminine was a new thing, for her.

Douglas stopped at the door to his bedroom, and looked back at her. 'Why?' he said abruptly. 'You never cared about what you looked like before. You never cared what anyone thought of you. So why the makeover? Why give up being you?'

'Because I chose to,' Anne said flatly. 'You only thought you knew me. You never knew what I wanted. What I really wanted. And you never cared enough to find out. I was just there to be used, to be useful. Well, I haven't changed, inside. I'm still me, and I've got a job to do. So have you, Douglas. We've indulged you in your protracted sulk long enough. Your seclusion's over, as of now. And no, you don't get a say in the matter. Finn and I have protected you as long as we could, but now something's come up and you're needed.'

'Something's happened,' Douglas said slowly. 'Have they found Jesamine and Lewis?'

'No. Not yet. Not everything is about you and them, Douglas.'

'Is it the Terror? Has it reached another planet already?' Douglas tried desperately to work out how much time he'd lost. Had Anne really said *two months*?

'No. It's still four months and three days before the Terror is expected to hit Heracles IV. This . . . is something new. Something unanticipated. It's not anything I can explain. You have to see this for yourself, in person. And you can't do it looking like that. Get dressed! Full kingly apparel, including the crown. After so long out of the public eye, you can't afford to appear in front of the cameras looking anything but your best.'

Some time later, King Douglas followed Anne Barclay through the wide, handsomely decorated corridors of the palace, and had to hurry to keep up with her. They were heading for the Imperial Court, and Douglas had a really bad feeling about that. He hadn't been in the main Court since his coronation. It seemed to him more and more that all his troubles stemmed from that time. He'd been happy before then, as a Paragon, and Lewis had still been his friend. They would have died for each other, then. Now here he was heading towards the Court again, and Douglas felt a strange dread, as though his whole life was about to undergo another irrevocable change.

He was properly dressed in all his kingly robes, with the great cut diamond Crown of the Empire upon his head. He'd bathed and shaved, and even eaten a hot meal under Anne's watchful eye, and he had to admit he felt better and sharper than he had in . . . ages. He almost felt himself again. But the bad feeling persisted, and he snatched another sidelong glance at Anne. She still hadn't told him what the hell this was about. Wouldn't tell him anything. In the past, she would have provided him with a full briefing, telling him everything he needed to know along with carefully worked out answers to the press's most probable queries, and even half a dozen different strategies for dealing with the various ways to salvage the situation if it all went wrong. That was Anne's job, and she'd always taken a pride in being very good at it. But now she ignored his questions, and stalked along in front of him, her familiar scowl distorting her new beautiful face. People they passed fell back hurriedly to get out of her way. Her way, not his. Douglas didn't miss that. Another sign of how much things had changed during his seclusion.

He could hear the Court long before they reached it. From the babble of raised voices up ahead, there had to be a whole army of reporters waiting, and not being at all patient about it. As Douglas and Anne slipped through the back door and approached the great hanging curtains that separated them from the Court proper, the sound became actually deafening. Douglas frowned. What the hell could be so important, that didn't involve Lewis or the Terror? It couldn't be the return of the blessed Owen; Anne had no reason to keep that from him. But then, what reason could Anne have to keep anything from him?'

Douglas straightened his shoulders. Whatever it was, the odds were it wasn't going to be good news, so the sooner he faced it the better. He'd been kept in the dark long enough. He let Anne give him a quick check over, to be sure everything was as it should be, then he nodded sharply to the two waiting guards and they pulled back the curtains so he could make his entrance. He strode out on to the raised dais, accompanied by a recorded fanfare, and seated himself on his throne while Anne was still hurrying to catch up. Douglas smiled inwardly. He might have been away, but now he was back and everyone had better recognise that. Time to remind people he was the King. Perhaps himself most of all.

He looked benignly out over the great wide hall of the Court, most of which seemed to be packed full of reporters. Hundreds of remote-control cameras floated above the pack, occasionally getting into savage butting contests over the best angles. King Douglas smiled on them all, deliberately ignoring the roar of shouted questions as he settled himself as comfortably as possible on his ancient throne. There were some cheers at his appearance, but not nearly as many as there should have been. It seemed absence didn't always make the heart grow fonder. And whatever story the mob had been led to expect, it clearly wasn't anything to do with his return.

Anne came forward to stand stiffly beside him, and that was new too. Normally, she stayed well in the background at all public affairs. There was another burst of recorded trumpets, and the roar went up again from the reporters as the hanging curtains parted to reveal the Imperial Champion, Finn Durandal. He came striding out on to the raised dais, as tall and muscular and classically handsome as always, smiling and nodding affably to the media pack, surrounded by his own personal honour guard of six Paragons, grim-faced in their polished armour and dramatic purple cloaks. Finn had never had any trouble looking every inch the hero, though up close his charisma had a cold and calculated feel. And he looked a lot better in the official black leather armour of the Champion than Lewis Deathstalker ever had.

Finn still wore his old purple Paragon's cloak over his gleaming armour, as though to show he hadn't forgotten where he came from. He struck a grand pose at the front of the dais and waved and smiled to the media mob, and they gave the Champion the kind of cheer that once would have been reserved for their King. Douglas looked at the six Paragons accompanying Finn. They'd spread out in a bodyguard's pattern, studying the reporters with cold, inimical eyes. Douglas had to wonder just what it was that the apparently popular Finn Durandal felt he needed to be protected from so thoroughly. And there was something ... *off*, about the Paragons. They wore their armour sloppily, and carried themselves more like thugs than warriors. And none of them had so much as glanced at Douglas, even though he would have called some of them friends.

What could have happened, out on their failed quest, to have changed them so harshly?

Finn Durandal smiled graciously out over the Court as though he owned it, holding his noble heroic pose with the ease of long practice, allowing the media pack to worship him. Finally he raised a single hand, and the crowd's acclaim cut off immediately. The floating cameras came rushing in for close-ups. A few targeted Douglas as well, just to be sure they didn't miss out on anything. But it was the Champion and not the King who held everyone's attention, and everyone there knew it.

'My friends,' Finn said grandly, 'today, as I promised you, I bring you the story of the century. No, not the return of the blessed Owen Deathstalker, unfortunately. The quest continues, but I have to tell you that more and more of our noble Paragons are returning disappointed. Instead, I stand here now to inform you of the return of a man almost as legendary, as well loved and almost as long lost. A man long considered dead has been discovered very much alive; a hero, returned to us in our hour of need! My friends ... allow me to introduce to you James Campbell, first son of William and Niamh Campbell; the man born to be King!'

For a moment there was utter silence in the Court, and then a tall and handsome man in kingly robes came striding out of the curtains and on to the dais as though he belonged there, and always had. The media crowd went crazy, screaming with joy and shock and approval, though not forgetting themselves so much that they neglected to order their cameras to get the best possible shots of the Empire's most unexpected comeback. James Campbell stood beside Finn, who shook his hand warmly and then put a comradely arm across his broad shoulders as they both beamed into the camera lenses. While Douglas Campbell sat slumped on his throne as though someone had just punched him under the heart.

It couldn't be James. Not brother James. It just couldn't. His elder brother had died in a stupid traffic accident, long before he was born. Everyone knew that. But the man on the dais had the same smiling face Douglas had seen in so many family holo images. He had the same long golden mane of hair as Douglas, and similar roughly handsome features. Put them side by side, and even a stranger could have seen they were brothers. But how could it be James, the perfect prince whose memory Douglas had been raised to revere? Douglas found he was actually trembling, as though he'd been brought face to face with a ghost.

James was big and broad and effortlessly hearty as he good-naturedly called for the crowd to shut up so he could say a few words. The media pack fell silent immediately, even the most hardened types crowding forward to the very edge of the raised dais, their eyes shining with more than just the pleasure of a good story. James Campbell: the man who should have been King, the greatest monarch the Empire never had. His return was a miracle, and in the face of all that had happened recently, like everyone else the media desperately needed good news and a hero they could believe in. If they couldn't have the blessed Owen, well, James Campbell was a perfectly acceptable substitute.

James made a short speech, all bluff sincere charm about how glad he was to be back, and how all he wanted was a chance to serve Humanity to the best of his ability. It was a slick and polished performance, and to Douglas it sounded more than a little rehearsed. Just the kind of thing Anne would have written for him, once. He looked at her, but she only had eyes for James. The moment he stopped talking, the reporters burst into spontaneous applause, an almost unheard of event. Douglas joined in, though he still wasn't sure what he felt or believed about this James.

The media pack finally remembered why they were there, and began shouting questions, but James shook his head and said he'd let Finn speak for him, for the present. Which was the first wrong note.

In everything Douglas had read up on his deceased brother, the historians had agreed that James had been a natural orator, fluent and commanding, and never afraid to speak his mind. That James had never let anyone speak for him. Douglas looked at Anne again, and tried to attract her attention, but she was ignoring him, staring at Finn and James with a smug, almost self-satisfied smile. It gave her carefully sculpted beautiful face an ugly look. Douglas realised that she had to have known about James long before this. She must have helped plan this whole scene, this carefully orchestrated reintroduction to the Empire. But she hadn't said a word to Douglas, before now. Until it was . . . too late for him to interfere? Douglas considered that thought, not liking the taste of it. Anne Barclay was one of his oldest friends. Finn Durandal was his friend, and his Champion. And neither of them had said a word about his dead brother's return. If he couldn't trust them . . . Douglas felt his heart grow cold. He realised Finn was speaking, and made himself pay attention as the Champion launched into the epic story of James's return from the dead. It was a hell of a story, full of thrills and surprises, and it sickened Douglas to his soul.

It seemed James hadn't died of his injuries in that famous traffic accident, all those years ago. Instead he was seriously injured and hideously disfigured, far beyond the ability of medical knowledge to repair him in those days. There were even fears that he would come out of the regeneration tank mentally retarded. So King William and Queen Niamh decided to hide away their crippled, hideous son in the depths of their ancestral home, House Campbell, his existence to be kept secret until such time as new medical techniques could be developed to help him. But that could take years, even decades, with no guarantee of success at the end. So even as trusted servants tended to the hideous monster in his hidden room, William and Niamh decided that James should be declared officially dead while they raised another son to take his place.

All this was bad enough, but there were hints too: hints that William was glad of an excuse to replace James with a new son. Hints that James, perfect and honourable James, had become too independent, too much his own man and a power in his own right. That William had become jealous of a son who threatened to be a much greater King than he had ever been. Apparently William had determined that his new son would be more carefully guided and controlled. Douglas was to be a model son and a credit to his father, and nothing more.

And so it might have gone; but a few weeks back Finn Durandal had been contacted secretly by one of the guards responsible for watching over James in his room deep under House Campbell. And this guard told Finn that James had in fact made a full physical and mental recovery years ago, but that William had chosen still to keep him prisoner rather than have his favoured son Douglas deposed. Indeed, William had decided that James was no longer needed, with Douglas due to be married and produce heirs of his own, and so William had determined to have his first son killed rather than risk having the truth come out after his death. This was too much for the guard, who'd grown fond of James, and he'd contacted the only man he felt he could trust: the Imperial Champion.

Finn immediately raised a small army of his own people, all utterly loyal to him, of course, and led them in a raid on House Campbell. The guard lowered the house's defences at just the right moment, and Finn caught William and his people entirely by surprise. The good guys stormed House Campbell, and got to James just in time. Finn brought him blinking out into the daylight for the first time in years, and Finn and his people cheered James's return from the dead. William was currently under house arrest at House Campbell, awaiting trial and not available for comment at this time.

Douglas didn't know what to think. Not about Finn's story; that was obviously bullshit from beginning to end. Douglas had been brought up at House Campbell and had roamed all over it as a child, with special attention to the places he was supposed to keep out of. There was no way a hidden room could have been kept secret from him. And besides, he'd seen footage of the original accident scene. It ran for ages on the news and gossip shows, until William bought up the rights to protect Niamh from having to see it again and again. The recording showed James dead on the spot, his brilliant brains spattered over the front of the car that hit him. But if his elder brother really was dead, who was this? It certainly looked like James. And what did Finn have to gain from making up such a story? He couldn't expect to get away with putting forward a lookalike, could he? One of the older reporters present raised the subject of the old footage, and Finn smiled easily in reply.

'My people are investigating that even now. I'm pretty sure we'll discover the footage was faked, to help cover William and Niamh's tracks.'

'That's enough!' Douglas was up out of his throne and on his feet before he even realised he was doing it. All eyes and cameras immediately turned on him, and the Court was suddenly silent, the air heavy with expectation. Douglas looked slowly around him, and knew that this was why he'd been brought here. He'd been told nothing, kept in the dark, so he could be brought here unsuspecting to make his reactions in public, with all the worlds watching. They weren't his friends any more, Finn and Anne. They had transferred their allegiance to this James, or whoever he really was. He was on his own. And he felt more alive than he had in ages. He walked slowly forward to the edge of the dais, keeping a distance between him and Finn and James.

'I cannot believe my father was a party to this; or my mother. They were devoted to James; his death nearly destroyed them too. I demand to speak to my father.'

'Of course,' said Finn. 'Arrangements shall be made, your majesty. But for the moment your father is under armed guard, for his own protection. Once news of James's return gets out, and the details of his past imprisonment ... well, we don't want aggrieved citizens taking matters into their own hands, do we? William is safer where he is. I know this must be hard for you to accept, Douglas. It hit me hard too, that the man I served so faithfully for so many years should prove to be unworthy of the trust we all placed in him. But I give you my word: this really is James, restored to us at last! Have you no welcome for your brother?'

Douglas looked at James. This was what it was all about. He had to answer that question; because his answer would decide how his own people would judge him. If he publicly accepted this man as his brother, he'd be trapped into playing Finn's game. And James, as the older brother, had a better claim to the throne than he did. If he denounced the man as an imposter ... Douglas was pretty sure that Finn wouldn't have come this far without putting together some pretty intimidating evidence. And Douglas would be seen as a fool or a liar, ready to say anything to hang on to his throne. Finn, and Anne, had him exactly where they wanted him.

Except they'd miscalculated. They'd assumed his time in seclusion had broken him, and it hadn't. He'd been asleep for a long time, but now he was awake again. He might have lost his best friend and his true love, but he was still the King, and he took his duties seriously. His Champion had revealed himself as a threat to his people, and his family, and Douglas had always been ready to fight to the death for both. Of course, he couldn't do that now. He'd been very cleverly isolated. Better to play the part they expected, and have them continue to underestimate him, until he could take back the high ground.

So Douglas smiled happily, if a little vaguely, at the man who

71

claimed to be his brother James, and walked forward with an outstretched hand. They shook hands firmly, while the cameras whirred loudly, and everyone applauded. James impulsively pulled Douglas forward into a hug, and they held each other close. It was a very touching scene, and the media pack just loved it, the floating cameras fighting it out for the best angles. Douglas kept his smile going, and let James hug him, but he felt nothing at all. Except, perhaps, just the briefest of guilty thoughts. If by some dark miracle this really was James, the man who should have been King, then perhaps Douglas would be able to step down from the throne and escape from the strains and pressures of a job he'd never wanted anyway. Let James be King. Let him deal with the Church Militant, and Pure Humanity and the Terror . . . It was only a brief thought, the very briefest of temptations. Douglas had always known his duty, even when he was just a Paragon. He'd fought to protect the people all his life, and he wasn't about to hand their fate over to this . . . stranger.

James finally released Douglas from the hug, and they stood face to face, smiling at each other. James's mouth went wobbly, and he had to reach up to knuckle a manly tear from the corner of his eye. Another nice touch that the media just loved to pieces. Douglas could feel Finn and Anne's eyes on him, and he kept his face carefully vague and vacant. James turned back to the reporters, and made a big point of declaring that he was sure his younger brother had no idea of what had been done in his name; that he was entirely positive King Douglas knew nothing of his years of imprisonment, or the imminent death sentence from which Finn had so valiantly rescued him. Of course, until James raised the point no one there had thought that at all, but now suspicious eyes turned to Douglas, clearly considering just how much he could or should have known. *He had to have known something*, people would say.

James smiled warmly at Douglas, and said, 'We must work together, brother, in this time of crisis.' And Douglas kept on smiling, and said, 'Yes, of course, brother.' James then turned the full force of his personality and charm on his audience, saying all the right things in a firm and resonant voice, and Douglas could feel everyone comparing him unfavourably with his brother. More and more, the reporters were being seduced by James's manner and rhetoric, and embraced him as though he was the Second Coming of the blessed Owen. Particularly when he vowed to do everything in his power to find an answer to the coming Terror. So when James also spoke out in favour of Pure Humanity and the Church Militant, those hardened cynical reporters happily went along with every hateful thing he said.

I don't know who the hell you really are, Douglas thought behind his pleasant smiling mask. *But that clinches it. James never believed in any of that shit. He had more sense, more conscience . . . and he never followed anyone's path but his own. So who are you? Really?*

James ended his speech to thunderous applause, but Finn wasn't finished yet. He took up a martial stance beside James, and fixed the media crowd with a stern stare. 'Some of you will still be doubting that this really is the genuine James Campbell. That's quite understandable, given the extremely dramatic nature of his return. I see Nigel Glover of the Logres *Times*, right there in the front as always. I have to say, Nigel, you don't look entirely convinced. Is there some question you wish to raise?'

'I remember James,' said the old man. 'I got there in time to see him being loaded into the ambulance. Half his head was gone. How can we be sure this isn't some lookalike from the body shops? Or even a clone?'

And that was as far as he got. Other reporters started to shout him down, some pushed and shoved him, and then suddenly they were crowding in on him, shouting abuse and throwing punches. Douglas looked immediately at Finn's Paragons, expecting them to dive into the crowd and rescue the old man, but they did nothing. They just stood there, sniffing and smirking. Douglas was about to dive in himself when James launched himself off the dais into the crowd, grabbed the reporter and hauled him on to the safety of the raised dais. The old man stood trembling, more shocked than hurt, while James put a comforting arm around him. The other reporters milled uncertainly before the dais, still in an ugly mood. Finn stepped forward, raising both hands in a calming gesture.

'Enough of that, my friends. This is a time for rejoicing, not violence. The *Times* has raised a very reasonable question. It's been a long time since we had to beware of clone imposters in public life, but in as important a case as this the question had to come up eventually. That's why I have invited here today Elijah du Katt, the current clone representative in Parliament.'

Du Katt came through the curtains at the back right on cue, a blocky, medium-height, average-looking fellow. He strode up to the front of the dais, stood beside Finn and spoke in a clear, firm voice. 'At the Champion's request, I have performed a gene test on James Campbell. He is exactly who he claims to be. Details of my findings

73

will be published shortly. My tests were very thorough. There is no way he could hide a clone background from me. DNA can't lie.'

The media pack cheered again, and Glover was allowed to rejoin his fellows, who ignored him. Douglas was still looking at du Katt. You couldn't fake a gene test. So either James really was James, or . . . the conspiracy went deeper than he'd suspected. If a respected figure like du Katt had been suborned, who else did Finn have in his pocket? . . . But Douglas found that easier to believe than that his father and his mother could ever have been the villains Finn had declared them to be.

Du Katt left the dais, and Finn turned the meeting over to questions and answers. The reporters couldn't get the questions out fast enough. James avoided answering a lot of them by pleading ignorance of most recent events, for obvious reasons, but he still managed to push Pure Humanity and the Church Militant as the answer to most of the Empire's problems. Douglas admired the performance from behind his pleasant face. Anne had clearly done her usual excellent job in preparing and coaching James. And Douglas was pretty sure a lot of the questions had been planted. It was what he would have done. Interestingly enough, James wasn't too good at the personal stuff. Questions like *How do you feel?* and *What are you most looking forward to doing, now you're free?* left him thrown and uncertain, and glancing to Finn or Anne for reassurance.

In the end, Finn stepped in and declared the audience over. He promised the media pack there would be further opportunities for interviews, and even one-on-ones, but that James was clearly tired now and needed time to himself. Adjusting to his new world was obviously going to take time. Anne quickly ushered James away while Finn was still speaking, and he had gone through the curtains before the reporters realised it. Douglas inclined his head regally to the media, and strode off the dais after Anne and James. He had no intention of being left alone on the dais after Finn and his people left, facing questions he had no idea how to answer safely.

Behind the hanging curtains, Anne was patting James reassuringly on the shoulder, as though calming a nervous animal. Away from the rehearsed situation, James looked a lot less confident, and somehow . . . smaller. Douglas started towards them, and then stopped as Finn and his Paragons came through the curtains. Finn stared at Douglas.

'You're looking tired too, Douglas. Perhaps you should return to your chambers and get some rest. You have rather been thrown in at the deep end. You can catch up with James later.'

'Yes,' said Douglas. 'It's all been a bit much, really. I'll see you tomorrow.'

'Anne, you'd better go with him,' said Finn. 'And I'll send a couple of my people to go along with you. You can't be too careful, these days.'

Anne nodded, and she and Douglas walked to the King's private chambers in silence. Two of Finn's Paragons accompanied them. Douglas only knew them vaguely, and they wouldn't answer him when he tried to talk to them. People were running back and forth in the wide corridors, looking at Douglas with wide eyes, and over and over again he heard the word *James* on people's lips. The Paragons kept everyone at a distance with menacing scowls. They finally came to Douglas's door, and he gestured for them to stand back so he could have a private word with Anne. They looked to her for confirmation, and reluctantly retreated down the corridor when she nodded. Douglas looked at Anne, and she met his gaze squarely, defiantly.

'All right,' said Douglas. 'What's going on, Anne?'

'How do you mean, Douglas?'

'You, Finn, James. Why wasn't I told any of this in advance?'

'Because you gave strict orders that you weren't to be disturbed, for any reason. And because we weren't too sure what state you were in. I did look in on you a couple of times; you probably don't remember. You were pretty out of it. And given the delicate nature of the situation, when we couldn't be sure how much you did or didn't know about James—'

She broke off abruptly as Douglas's face grew cold and dangerous. She actually fell back a step before Douglas could regain control and put on his confused, vacant face again. He couldn't afford to confront her over James's identity; not now.

'Sorry,' he said. 'Sore spot, there. Go on, you were saying?'

'We waited to establish the truth about James, and your father, before involving you,' said Anne. 'It could have been rumours. Even after we had James secure, and gene-tested, we left you alone as long as we dared, hoping you'd snap out of it, but you had to be there when we presented James to the public. It would have looked very bad if you hadn't been there, Douglas.'

'I can't believe what Finn said about my father,' said Douglas. 'When can I speak to him, Anne?'

'Soon. You do believe this really is James, don't you, Douglas?'

'You can't fake a gene test. Everyone knows that.'

Anne nodded slowly. 'You look tired. You've had a lot to cope with on your first day back. I've got to talk with Finn now; we're going to schedule a whole series of public appearances for James, to let everyone know he's returned and introduce him to the Empire. That will keep us busy for some time. You don't need to be involved in any of that, Douglas. Get some rest, take all the time you need to pull yourself together again, and we'll contact you when we need you.'

'Yes,' said Douglas. 'Rest sounds good. We'll talk again later.'

Anne gave him a searching gaze, but Douglas maintained his tired, defeated look, and after a long moment Anne nodded and strode off down the corridor, picking up the two Paragons along the way. Douglas watched them go, and then considered the two guards standing by his door. They weren't his people. Anne, he remembered, had replaced the original guards with new men, undoubtedly loyal only to the new order. There as much to keep him in as to keep others out. Douglas nodded amiably to them and entered his private chambers. He locked the door behind him and jammed a chair up against it as well, just in case.

Safely in his own territory, he dropped the pleasant mask and scowled so fiercely it was almost painful. He stamped back and forth, his hands clenched into tight fists, his mind whirling with plans for revenge and retribution. He would have liked to kick the hell out of the furniture, but that would have made too much noise, and he had no doubt the new guards were listening. He had to wonder what else Finn and Anne had taken from him while he was too blind with self-pity to notice. Had it really been two whole months? He looked around the room with new eyes, and was honestly shocked at the mess. How could he have lived in such a sty for so long, without noticing? No wonder Anne hadn't taken him seriously. He forced himself to calm down, pushing back the anger, unclenching his fists. He had to be cool, calm, controlled. There were things he had to do.

He strode over to his private comm unit, and put through a call to House Campbell, punching in his old family security codes. The connection took longer than usual to make, and when his screen finally cleared the face looking back at him was a stranger. He wore anonymous guard's armour, with no markings. He recognised Douglas immediately, and inclined his head.

'Your majesty. How may I serve you?'

'I want to talk to my father,' said Douglas. 'Why are you answering his private number?'

'No one speaks to William Campbell,' said the guard. 'I'm sorry, your majesty, but I have my orders direct from the Durandal.'

'Finn is my Champion,' said Douglas. 'He answers to me. I am your King, and I want to speak to my father.'

'The Durandal's orders were quite specific,' said the guard, unmoved. 'No one is to speak to the prisoner, without his express permission. And in this case his authority derives from Parliament and not your majesty.'

'I could come and see him,' said Douglas.

'I would advise against that, your majesty. All unauthorised ships approaching House Campbell are to be shot down on sight. The Durandal's orders.'

'Gosh,' said Douglas. 'I'd better not do that, then. I'll talk to Finn. Thank you for your assistance. You've been very helpful. I'll be sure to remember you.'

He couldn't resist that last barb, and was rewarded by a little uncertainty in the guard's face before he shut down the connection from his end. Douglas scowled at the blank screen. Events had clearly slipped even further from his control than he'd realised. His first impulse was to commandeer a flyer, load it up with really big guns and pay House Campbell a personal royal visit the guards there would never forget; but he knew he couldn't. Finn would be expecting something like that. And Douglas had a strong feeling he wouldn't be allowed to just stroll out of the palace either. He was beginning to sense how comprehensive a trap had been constructed around him. By Finn and Anne, and God alone knew how many others. All he could do for now was play along, play the broken man in public, until he could get back into shape again, physically and mentally. And then he would show these upstarts and their fake James just how Douglas Campbell had become a legend among the Paragons long before he became King.

He would show them what a real Campbell could do, with vengeance in his heart.

But first he had to clean his room. He couldn't live in this tip any more. Merely looking at some of it made his skin crawl. And simple repetitive manual jobs always helped him think. It took him a long time to clear the mess up, but he had a lot of thinking to do.

Over the next few weeks, Douglas sweated his way through every punishing exercise he could think of, while watching brother James make the rounds of all the very best news and gossip shows on his viewscreen. It seemed as though James was everywhere, dashing from public appearance to public appearance, his every move covered by all the celebrity channels. Looking big and bluff and handsome, with his bright eyes and bashful smile, James was the biggest news sensation since the return of the Terror. The people were desperate for good news, and the return of the man who should have been King was just what they needed. He wasn't Owen Deathstalker, but he would do.

William, of course, was painted as the very blackest of villains, who only reluctantly kept James alive in case something happened to Douglas while he was playing at being a Paragon. Should James have been needed, it seemed William and Niamh had arranged to have a powerful esper delete all James's memories since the crash, so he would know nothing of his imprisonment. This particular announcement led to open hostility against all espers, even though the oversoul went out of their way to deny that any of their people had ever been involved in such a scheme. No one believed them. There were demonstrations, bordering on riots, in cities on worlds across the Empire calling for strict new controls on espers. From across the Empire, espers quietly made their way to Logres and to the floating city of New Hope, where they holed up behind powerful protections and waited for the people to come to their senses again.

They should have known better. The people had a new hero to believe in, and they didn't want their precious fairy story spoiled.

Douglas exercised ceaselessly, eating the right foods, pushing his soft body back into shape. He worked out regularly with his sword and shield, and the old skills came flooding back. He wanted to be ready, for when Finn dropped the other shoe.

He missed Jesamine, and Lewis. He missed having people around him he could trust. But he had no time to indulge in his own problems when the Empire's problems were clearly so much bigger.

Douglas seemed to be the only person in the whole Empire who wasn't impressed by James. This larger than life hero on the viewscreen wasn't the easy-going, intelligent, deeply moral man Douglas had heard about all his life. This new James was too perfect. He always knew the right thing to say, even if it didn't seem to mean much on closer examination. He always came out with the right answers, even if they didn't always fit the question. He was a great one for the barbed soundbite, delivered with a flashing smile and a hint of a wink, and the public ate it up with spoons.

Douglas thought James was beginning to look over-rehearsed, and he still wasn't very good at the personal stuff. He was fine at shaking hands with people, and asking interested questions, but he couldn't ad-lib to save his life. Fortunately, there were always some of Finn's people close at hand to whisk him away on urgent business if it became clear James was getting out of his depth. Douglas thought James was hollow, all surface charm, with nothing original in his head that hadn't been put there. It bothered Douglas greatly that no one else could see it. *None so blind . . .* he supposed. Douglas hadn't been allowed to meet James since that first day, but he kept pushing. Sooner or later, Finn and Anne would have to let the two brothers meet again, because it would look decidedly odd if they didn't. And when that finally happened, Douglas was determined to be ready with a whole bunch of really awkward questions.

He no longer had any doubts that this James was a fake of some kind. Despite his coaching, this James made occasional factual errors about his past life, before the accident. Small things, perhaps, that only another member of Clan Campbell could have known, but Douglas spotted them immediately. His whole early life had been spent being compared (usually unfavourably) to his glorious deceased older brother. When James was occasionally caught in an error, and called up on it by an interviewer, James just turned up his smile another notch, and blamed his uncertain memory on residual problems from his head injuries in the crash. And then no one would push it, for fear of seeming to bully an invalid.

The undoubted highlight of James's media rounds was a guest appearance on that most popular of vid soaps, *The Quality*. Now in its triumphant fifth season, with two shows every day and an omnibus at weekends, *The Quality* presented a highly idealised view of sin, scandal and outrageous clothes among the aristocrats of the Empress Lionstone's time. It was required viewing across the Empire, if only so you could join in on what everyone else was talking about.

James played his ancestor Finlay Campbell; badly. He had charm but no talent, and his performance was more wooden than most of the furniture; but no one cared. You didn't watch a soap like *The Quality* for the subtlety of the performances anyway. James appeared opposite the undisputed star of the show, the almost impossibly beautiful and radiant Treasure Mackenzie, who played the social butterfly Chantelle. She wasn't that great an actress herself, but since it had been truly said of her that if she'd been any more voluptuous she would have been in 4D, no one gave a damn. As long as she kept smiling, taking deep breaths and threatening to lose her clothes at every twist and turn of the plot, people kept watching. So Treasure floated becomingly around James, who read his lines carefully from the idiot boards and concentrated on looking good.

That episode gained the highest ratings the show had ever known.

Douglas turned the viewscreen off, and studied himself in the mirror. He looked good. He'd burned off the flab, and he seemed like a fighter again. His mind was sharp and clear, and he was more than ready to remind his many enemies that a Campbell was never more dangerous than when he had nothing left to lose. But it would have to be done slowly, and subtly. He would have to continue to act confused and beaten in public, and especially when Finn and Anne were around, until he could prove to the people that mattered that he was his old self again, and pick up some useful allies. The problem was, who to trust? How deep had the rot gone? During his self-pitying seclusion, Finn had taken the opportunity quietly to replace the King's people with new faces loyal only to the Durandal. Douglas's guards, and even his servants, were gone; and a lot of people he'd considered his friends wouldn't answer his calls any more. Douglas had been very carefully isolated, so that even if he did recover from his fugue he'd have no one to turn to.

But there were still a few people that even Finn couldn't corrupt. Emma Steel, for example, the Paragon from Mistworld who was now patrolling Logres. And maybe Stuart Lennox, Lewis's replacement Paragon from Virimonde. If only Douglas could work out a way to contact them privately.

And sometimes he thought about Lewis, and Jesamine. And wondered if, since he'd been so wrong about so many other things, just maybe he might have been wrong about them, too. He wanted to believe they'd never been traitors. He had loved them both, after all.

Next to Douglas, James had the biggest and most luxurious set of private chambers in the palace. Anne had provided them for him, by the simple expedient of kicking out the original occupants and defying them to do anything about it. The original owners had enough sense to see which way the wind was blowing, and left without making any fuss. They in turn kicked out someone lower in status than themselves, and took over their quarters. For the next few days you couldn't move in the palace because the corridors were full of people changing rooms. The order to house James in the palace had King Douglas's name on it, but everyone knew it really came from Anne. And, by extension, Finn.

James didn't actually like his new quarters much. They were too big, too opulent, too overpowering. He wandered from room to room, feeling lost and ill at ease, afraid to touch anything in case he broke it. His quarters were full of state-of-the-art tech he didn't know how to work. He wasn't allowed any personal servants. They might learn something, and talk. James had a favourite chair he spent most of his off time in, tucked away in one corner of his bedroom. The problem was these were quarters fit for a King, and James didn't want to be a

King. The mere thought scared him. He was just as scared of being James Campbell, given the expectations that came with the name. But he was even more frightened of Finn Durandal, so he kept these thoughts strictly to himself. The only person he ever dared say anything to was Anne, but while she was never too busy to smile and comfort him, she never really listened to anything he said.

James belonged to Finn and Anne. He knew that. They owned him, body and soul. He was their creation.

He was busy practising sincere smiles in front of the parlour mirror when Finn arrived late one morning bringing with him the clone representative, Elijah du Katt. James started trembling the moment he saw du Katt. It was a terrible thing to meet one's own maker. James still had nightmares about some of the invasive surgeries du Katt had put him through, on Finn's orders. But he didn't make any fuss when du Katt unpacked his diagnostic kit; just took off his frilly shirt and stood waiting patiently. He didn't want to make Finn angry. Du Katt took his time with the diagnostic, checking James's readings carefully against the expected optimums. He finally sniffed a few times, and started packing away his equipment. James relaxed a little, and put his shirt back on as du Katt talked with Finn about him, as though he wasn't there.

'He's in excellent shape, sir Durandal. No deviation from the original process. The most perfect clone I've ever produced.'

'I should hope so, considering how much you and your people charged me to make him,' said Finn.

'Ah,' said du Katt, smiling and shrugging, 'clones aren't cheap, especially when they're illegal, and you did want something special. With all the improvements I've built into this model, he's practically a Hadenman.'

Finn frowned suddenly. 'I told you: no implants. No tech. Nothing that might show up on a scanner. I hope you haven't been too creative, Elijah. If I've got to tear this model apart and start over, I'll do the same to you. Slowly.'

'Relax, sir Durandal, relax!' Du Katt's hands fluttered nervously, and his attempt at an easy laugh wasn't convincing. 'I can assure you, he's entirely organic. He's faster, stronger, and with better reflexes than most of the fighters you'll find in the Arena these days. A born killer, exactly as you requested.'

'Pity he isn't a bit smarter,' said Finn, studying James dispassionately. 'It's a real pain in the neck having to teach him his answers to questions parrot fashion, just to get him through interviews.'

Du Katt shrugged again. 'He's as intelligent as the original, potentially. Possibly even more so. He just lacks a context to work from. You can't learn everything from books. A certain lack of social skills is to be expected. He's only six months old, after all!'

He laughed, but Finn didn't join in so he quickly stopped. James stood there, his face carefully blank, waiting to be told what to do. He never volunteered anything. That wasn't his place. And Finn hurt him if he ever looked like forgetting his place. In public, James was always calm and confident and perfectly poised, because that was what Finn wanted. In private James was quiet, diffident and eager to please. Because he wanted to go on living.

Finn finally waved du Katt away, and looked upon his creation, his possession, his latest weapon. And smiled, remembering.

Finn Durandal personally led the raid on House Campbell, accompanied by his personal guard of six returned Paragons and four assault ships full of Church Militant and Pure Humanity troops. Armed and armoured, fanatics to a man and a woman, pumped full of righteousness and knock-off battle drugs, they were sworn to fight and die in Finn's name for the cause. Cannon fodder, basically. Finn commanded the lead ship himself. Some pleasures were too tasty to be shared with anyone.

William's security people challenged him automatically as he approached, only to relax once they recognised his face. Finn had been to House Campbell many times before, as an old friend of Douglas's. All he had to do was make vague allusions to a possible security alarm, and William ordered his defences dropped and invited Finn and his people in. As easy as that. William had no reason to distrust the Imperial Champion.

Finn's ships landed unchallenged on the house's private landing pads, and his attack troops immediately spilled out, armed to the teeth and shouting their vicious slogans. Finn would have liked more of an element of surprise on his side, but you had to make allowances when working with thugs and fanatics. Strategy was a mystery to people blind to everything but their cause. So Finn just pointed them in the right direction and let them get on with it. They charged off the landing pads and into the grounds, killing everyone they saw. The security guards went down first, followed by gardeners and servants, and old family retainers. Only the guards had weapons, of course, and most never got a chance to use them. Those few who did were quickly outnumbered and overrun. Everyone else died where they stood. Or, if they ran, they were shot in the back. Finn had no interest in taking any prisoners.

No one had time to send a warning. And Finn had come prepared, with special equipment in his lead ship, to make sure no comm messages would leave House Campbell. He sauntered unhurriedly across the great green lawns towards the house, accompanied by his six beaming Paragons, enjoying the smell of smoke in the air as his people set fire to the ancient gardens. Trees blazed like torches, flower beds became ashes, and the old hedge maze burned brightly like a funeral pyre. And everywhere there were dead men and women, their blood and brains and guts seeping out on to the neatly cropped grass. The ancestral grounds of House Campbell had become an abattoir, and Finn Durandal couldn't have been happier.

He strode like a conqueror into the great Hall of House Campbell, casually destroying irreplaceable treasures as he went, and warmed his hands before the open fireplace. It was an unseasonably chilly morning. He looked around, smiling, as his people dragged a beaten and bloodied William Campbell into what had once been his hall, and dropped the old man in a heap at Finn's feet. He lay there, gasping and shuddering, while Finn looked thoughtfully at the thugs in their Church Militant armour. They stirred uneasily under his gaze.

'Did he put up a fight?' said Finn. 'I wouldn't have thought the old man had it in him.'

'Not . . . as such,' said one of the thugs. 'But he said things.'

'Oh well,' said Finn. 'I don't suppose it matters. I never liked him anyway. And I do so admire zeal. Bring him outside.'

Finn led the way out of the house and across the devastated grounds until they came at last to James's grave. William stumbled along and had trouble keeping up, but the Paragons kept him moving with kicks and general abuse. They were having a good time. Finn finally let the old man drop to the grass at the foot of his elder son's grave, while he looked casually out over the artificial lake. Dead swans lay floating in the bloody waters. Finn's smile widened. He approved of thoroughness. William struggled up on to his knees, and looked at Finn, his bloody mouth quivering with outrage. One of the Paragons placed a heavy hand on his shoulder, to make sure he stayed on his knees.

'For God's sake, why, Finn? What's the meaning of this? Does Douglas know you're here?'

Finn took his time answering. 'Dear Douglas knows very little about what goes on these days,' he said. 'But it wouldn't matter if he did. Douglas is a spent force, as are you; and neither of you matters a damn in the scheme of things any more. I did all this . . . because I could. Because it pleased me. Don't look for rescue. All of your own people are dead, and no one will be coming from outside. Your day is over, William. And mine is just beginning.'

'How could you do this, Finn?' William said numbly. 'You're Douglas's friend. You were always welcome here. You and he used to have such good times.'

'Things change, people change,' said Finn. 'You might say I've grown up since then. You never really knew me, William. But you do now.'

William looked uncertainly at James's grave. 'What do you want here? What could possibly be worth this death and destruction?'

'I'm glad you asked that, William. I'm here for James. No good to anyone lying in the ground, but I have a use for him.' He leaned over the headstone, and casually blew out the eternal flame that burned there. 'Dig him up, boys.'

William cried out angrily and tried to surge to his feet, but the Paragons hit him and he fell to the ground.

'Ah William,' said Finn. 'Children are such hostages to fortune, aren't they? Even when they're dead.'

Finn's people dug up the grave, while William watched helplessly. It didn't take them long to get down to the coffin, break open the lid and reveal the corpse. The funeral technicians had done an excellent job. James's many injuries had been cunningly disguised and his body was perfectly preserved. He might only have been sleeping. William made a soft, low sound of distress, but no one paid him any attention. Finn clambered down into the open grave so he could look James in the face, close up. Finally he nodded, smiled, and then leaned forward and kissed James on his dead lips.

'You'll do. Du Katt, take your samples.'

'No names!' hissed the clone representative, as he hurried forward. 'You promised; no names!'

'Oh get on with it,' said Finn.

Du Katt waited for Finn to vacate the grave, and then clambered clumsily down to take his cell samples. He was swiftly efficient, though he was careful never to look at the corpse's face. When he was finished, he got out of the grave as fast as he could, and Finn nodded to one of his people who dropped a small transmutation bomb into the hole. A few seconds later, the mortal remains of the noble James Campbell had been reduced to undifferentiated protoplasmic slime that might have been anyone or anything. William cried harsh, racking tears while Finn smiled on him.

'Don't blame me,' he said airily. 'This is all Douglas's fault. None of this had to happen. But he should have made me Champion.'

'You always were a petty-minded little shit,' said William.

'Take him back to House Campbell,' said Finn. 'Lock him up somewhere secure, then set up a rota of guards for the house and the grounds. No one gets in or out, unless they're with me. Oh and boys: you can play with William, but don't break him. I may have a use for him later on.'

He looked out over the burning gardens as his men dragged William away. 'Some day, all Logres will look like this,' he said happily.

Back in James's chambers, Finn strolled around his creation, studying him from every angle. The clone looked good. He looked very good. Finn approved of good work. Du Katt had been surprisingly easy to bring on board. All he wanted, in return for his services and the doctored gene test, was a promise from Finn to bring the clone underground back to power and prominence again. And a whole bagload of money, of course. Only du Katt and a select few from the clone underground knew the truth. The fewer who knew, the less chance there was that someone might develop a conscience and talk. The deal itself was simple enough: in return for James, Finn would see to it that once the Transmutation Board had wiped planets clean of 'troublesome' alien life, vast numbers of new clones would be produced to populate these new terraformed worlds. These new populations, along with their planetary votes in Parliament, would make the clones a force to be reckoned with again.

Du Katt was also responsible for keeping the original cell samples in a safe place, so that another James could be produced if the first one didn't work out. That was one of the first things Finn told James; just so he knew where he stood.

Anne Barclay had dug up everything the clone James needed to know from her extensive archives. It wasn't difficult; down the years many books had been written and documentaries produced about the short but promising life of the man who should have been King. Anne and Finn had then taught the clone James how to speak, how to move, how to act in public. He picked it up surprisingly quickly; as a blank slate he was endlessly hungry for information about himself. And the process was aided by Finn punishing him severely if he got things wrong, and Anne comforting him afterwards. Bad cop, good cop; carrot and stick. The old ways are always the best. James was still having trouble with some social skills, but they were mostly the kind you could only pick up by experience. Which was why Finn insisted on James doing so much at once. A full schedule of meetings and talks, to immerse James in the world he had to fool. It was sink or swim, but it seemed to be working. And if it was a bit hard on James, well, it wasn't as if he was a real person.

'You need to do more work on your small talk,' said Anne. Even sitting, she looked stiff and awkward in her new beautiful body. 'I know chatting makes you nervous, James, but you can only learn by doing. When in doubt, smile and say something nice. It doesn't have to be true; few compliments are.'

'I do my best,' said James, trying hard not to sound sulky. 'It's just . . . I get tired. There's so much to do, and it never stops—.'

Finn slapped him across the face. It was a casual blow, but there was real power behind it. James rocked on his feet, but didn't fall. He stopped talking and stood very straight, his hands at his sides.

'You do what I tell you to do, when I tell you to do it,' said Finn.

Anne was out of her chair, glaring at Finn. 'There was no need for that! He is doing his best.'

Finn looked at her coolly. 'I will do what I will do, Anne, and no one gets to stop me any more. You of all people should know that. James has to be perfect in his part, or our plans will come to nothing. So James is going to be perfect, whatever it takes.' He smiled at James. 'I own you, boy; body and soul. I will make you King, and the Empire will bow down to you, but only because it pleases me to do so. You're mine; and always will be. Now, I must be about my business. So many lives to ruin, so little time! Anne, make sure he's fully briefed for the news interview in an hour. And remember: we are not at home to Mister Cock-up!'

He laughed, patted James lightly on his reddening cheek, blew Anne a kiss and swept out of the luxurious chamber with du Katt hurrying after him. James waited until the door had slammed shut behind them, and only then dared to sit down. His hands were trembling, and he clasped them tightly together in his lap. Anne sat on the padded arm of his chair and put her arm round his shoulders.

'Why doesn't Finn like me?' said James. 'I do everything he tells me to do. I try my hardest; always.'

'There, there, James, don't take on so. It's his way. We're both very pleased with your progress so far, and neither of us has any doubts about your abilities. Not really.'

'Then why is he always . . . like that?' said James. 'Why can't I ever please him? I want to please him.'

'Finn . . . isn't easy to get to know,' said Anne. 'And he has a lot on his mind. You carry on as you are. You're doing fine.'

She hugged him, one magnificent breast pressing against the side of his face. He blushed bright red and sat very still, so he wouldn't disturb her and make her move away. James found Anne's beauty disturbing in a whole bunch of ways he didn't really understand yet. When Treasure Mackenzie had hugged him on the set of *The Quality*, he'd thought he was going to pass out from lack of blood to the head. It had all gone somewhere else. Anne knew the effect she had on him, and she loved to tease him. She could accept attention from James that would have made her uncomfortable if it had come from anyone else. Perhaps because James had never known the old Anne. As far as he knew, she'd always been beautiful. She found it easier to be . . . feminine, with him. She still had trouble calling up the confidence to bring it off successfully with anyone else. She liked the effect her new femininity had on men, the way it distracted and short-circuited their thinking, but she didn't trust it yet. Part of her suspected they were secretly laughing at her.

And if they were, she'd make them pay. She'd make them suffer. Every damned one of them.

She took some time to get James settled, and then left him immersed in the latest files while she hurried after Finn. The Durandal hadn't got far down the corridor. He was trying to get rid of du Katt. The clone rep was as nervous as he was ambitious, and needed a lot of reassuring. As Finn said, more than once: if he'd known the little creep was going to be this clingy, he'd have approached someone else. But it was too late now. They were stuck with each other. For the time being. Finn saw Anne aproaching, and used that as an excuse to send du Katt on his way. The clone rep left reluctantly, still muttering under his breath. Finn smiled on Anne as she joined him.

'And how's our dear child? Studying hard and bettering himself, I hope?'

'He'll be ready for the interview. He always is. You're too hard on him, Finn.'

'It's for his own good. If he screws up in public, it won't just be our necks on the chopping block. The public's always had a special loathing for clone imposters. Especially now they've invested so much hope and faith in the return of dear James.' He stopped, considered her for a moment, and then spoke more gently. 'Something's bothering you, Anne, and I don't think it's James. What's the matter?'

'I don't know,' she said, looking away, unable to meet his eyes. 'It's . . . I don't feel right. This new me . . . I thought it was what I wanted, but . . . it feels like a trick, a mask that everyone else can see through.'

'You're beautiful now,' said Finn. 'You have blossomed. This is what you always looked like, inside.'

87

'Then why can't I ever relax? Why do I feel like a fraud? Why can't I ever just . . . enjoy it?'

Her voice was rising. Finn took her firmly by the arms, and made her look at him. 'Listen to me, Anne. You can be whatever you want to be. You can remake your life, your personality and your destiny; like I did. You just have to be strong enough to take what you want. Other people will believe what you want them to believe, if you're confident enough and strong enough in your belief. You are what you can make other people believe you are. Trust me on this, Anne; I've had a lot of experience in this field. Soon people will forget there ever was another Anne. Believe in yourself. I believe in you.'

Anne slowly nodded, and Finn let go of her. She managed a small, tremulous smile. 'Thank you,' she said quietly. 'You didn't have to do that.'

'I know,' he said, smiling impishly. 'But I did anyway. Because even monsters aren't monsters all the time.'

They strolled off down the corridor together, comfortably close but not actually touching. People passing by bowed low to them and kept well out of their way. They had both become great and glorious and larger than life, and they looked very much like they belonged in the ornate corridors of the Imperial palace. As though anywhere else would have been unworthy of them.

'You're taking a lot on yourself these days,' said Anne, after a while. 'Are you sure you can juggle all these groups you want to work with? Pure Humanity and the Church Militant are bad enough, but these others you want to bring in . . . they're not stupid, and they're very dangerous. How long do you think you can keep these fanatics from finding out you're using them for your own ends?'

'As long as it takes,' Finn said airily. 'All I have to do is play them off against each other, and they'll be so busy trying to do each other down that they'll never see what I'm really up to until it's too late.'

'But to approach the Hellfire Club and the Shadow Court . . .' Anne looked at Finn. 'You watch yourself, Finn. These people are vile and treacherous.'

'So am I,' said Finn. 'But I am smarter and sharper than they are, because I don't share their obsessions. And because I'm the only one who knows everything that's going on. I'm the only one who sees the big picture. I'll always be able to out-think them because I'll always be one step ahead.'

Anne thought about that for a while. 'At least they have their causes. They believe in something. What do you believe in, Finn?'

He smiled dazzlingly. 'I believe in me.'

Anne decided it was time to change the subject. 'Do we have any fresh news on the Terror?'

'Nothing new,' said Finn, tacitly agreeing to the change in subject. 'Presumably, it's still on a course towards its next projected target, Heracles IV. We can't be sure until it emerges into our space again. But assuming it holds its course, even travelling at sub-light speed it should hit Heracles IV in a matter of months. They're working on beefing up their defences, and bankrupting their whole economy to pay for state-of-the-art shields and weaponry. The latest hot rumour is that the Swart Alfair of Mog Mor, those enigmatic bastards, have supplied them with some entirely new forms of weaponry for an exorbitant price, along with a handful of observers to see how well they work. If I was Heracles IV, I'd be sure to keep the receipt somewhere handy. I've arranged for a few observers of my own, in case this new weaponry really does do the marvellous things Mog Mor claims it can; but I don't think I'll hold my breath.'

'Do you think these extra defences will make any difference?'

Finn pursed his lips. 'I don't know. But whatever happens, it'll be a learning experience.'

'Finn! That's cold-blooded, even for you!'

'Stick to what you're best at, that's what I always say.'

'But . . . what if none of it works? Do you have any plans on how to stop the Terror?'

'Oh yes; I always have plans.'

'You always say that! Why won't you ever tell me what you're up to? Don't you trust me, after all we've done and achieved together?'

'Hush, hush,' said Finn. 'You're getting loud. I don't want to raise false hopes until I'm sure what I've got in mind will work. We have time. It'll be ages until the Terror can penetrate this far into the Empire. Now, my turn to change the subject, I think. I need to know what's in your heart, dear Anne. Do you feel guilty about removing Douglas from the throne and replacing him with James? I mean, you and Douglas were friends for a long time.'

'So were you and Douglas.'

'No, not really. Stop evading the question. Is deposing Douglas as King going to be a problem for you?'

'No,' said Anne, meeting his gaze firmly. 'He let me down. He let us all down. He didn't have the guts to be the kind of King he promised he'd be. To be the legend I would have made of him. I won't back losers any more.'

'And what about Lewis, the valiant Deathstalker?'

Anne's gaze was very cold now, her voice unforgiving. 'He ran away.'

'And your oldest and dearest friend, the lovely Jesamine?'

'I made her the perfect deal. She would have been Queen, and a legend alongside Douglas. I had it all worked out. And she threw it away. We could have been glorious, but in the end they were too weak. Let them die and rot. James will be King, our King, and we will rule through him. Until the time comes when we can have him safely put aside, and then you shall be King, Finn. You're strong enough to rule this Empire. Strong enough to be a legend.'

'I could make you Queen,' said Finn. 'If you wanted.'

'No,' said Anne, looking away. 'I've always felt most comfortable operating from the shadows.'

Finn took her chin in his hand, and made her look at him again. 'That's the old Anne speaking.'

'I'm not afraid of the spotlight,' said Anne, jerking her chin out of his grasp. 'If you like, and if you can find the time, you can come and watch me as I brief the media this afternoon. I'm going to destroy what's left of Lewis and Jesamine's reputations, and piss on the ashes while I'm at it.'

'I wouldn't miss it for worlds,' said Finn.

It had to be said, Anne gave one of her very best performances at that afternoon's press conference. She stood tall and proud before the assembled media pack, looked them straight in the eye and lied. She spread her web of damning lies and half-truths with exactly the right mixture of forthright efficiency and diffident duty. As the reporters listened with widening eyes and dropping jaws, Anne thoroughly trashed Jesamine's past with detailed evidence of the kind only an old and trusted friend could provide. Lovers were named and shamed, old scandals unearthed, long-standing rumours confirmed, and all of it carefully presented in the very worst light.

Anne had plenty of material to work with. She'd been Jesamine's friend and confidant from the very beginnings of her career, and they'd kept no secrets from each other. Anne took everything she'd been told in secret and added as many distortions and outrageous lies as she thought she could get away with.

And Jesamine had led a very busy private life, down the years. The fan magazines never knew the half of it. Jesamine's many lovers had included men and women, before, during and after her several marriages, and many of those favoured had gone on to become prominent people in show business and politics. The sheer number of past lovers shocked the public, and the media happily fanned the outrage into open hysteria. Her recordings were destroyed, and she was burned in effigy in several cities. Many of the named lovers went into hiding, to protect themselves.

(Not all of those named were actually guilty, of course. Finn had provided Anne with a list of people he'd like brought down, people who had opposed him, or might prove a problem in the future, and Anne had nodded and said, *No problem.* They denied it, but then, as Anne said to the reporters, *Well, they would, wouldn't they?*)

One of those publicly named and shamed was the Member of Parliament for Malediction, Meerah Puri. Finn had grown tired of her endless questioning of him in the House, not least because she was edging towards the truth. But this time, the mud wouldn't stick. Meerah Puri was vehement and detailed in her defence, and Anne was finally forced to issue a retraction, if not an apology. Finn shrugged, in private. You can't expect to get everyone. He'd just have to try harder next time.

Anne didn't have any real dirt on Lewis Deathstalker, so she and Finn made some up. Since no one knew anything about Lewis's private life, they felt free to go to town and really did a job on him. Lewis, they said, had faked most of his so-called triumphs, with the help of false agents from the Rookery. Anne produced as witnesses some of the very people who'd helped establish Finn's recent reputation, and as a result they were very convincing. They clearly knew what they were talking about. Having delivered their damning evidence, they then disappeared back into the Rookery before they could be questioned or challenged by any of Lewis's few remaining supporters.

The people listened, and the people believed, already so shocked and stunned by Lewis and Jesamine's treason and flight that they were ready to believe anything. Anne kept on, adding more names and places and details; and the more outrageous the claims became, the more ready people were to believe them. Anne claimed that both Lewis and Jesamine had secretly been members of the notorious Shadow Court, and the public nodded wisely, and said, *Yes, of course, it all makes sense now.* On Virimonde, Lewis's family denied it on his behalf, but Clan Deathstalker no longer had the influence it once had. Indeed, Parliament was threatening to take the revered name of Deathstalker away from them, and bestow it on some more deserving branch of cousins.

Tim Highbury, who had once hosted Lewis's tribute site, was found hanged. Anne was genuinely upset about that. She'd known and worked with the earnest young man in the past. She liked him. She angrily accused Finn of setting it up, but for once he hadn't. He hadn't had to. With his hero destroyed and fatally smeared, Tim Highbury hadn't wanted to live any more.

And so it went, for week after week. Anne fed dirt to the media, James appeared on all the right shows and charmed everybody, and Finn . . . went suddenly missing. It caught Anne by surprise. She went to him for one of their routine strategy meetings, and his office was empty. She found a brief note, saying he'd had to go to Haden. Right away. Anne took that rather badly. How could he swan off and leave her, right in the middle of things? What could possibly be so important that he'd had to leave her in the lurch without any warning?

The news broke a few days later, and then she understood at once. It seemed the scientists working on Haden, studying the Madness Maze from what they fervently hoped was a safe distance, had been keeping a secret. Ten thousand brave souls had passed through the Madness Maze, some two hundred years earlier, only to die horribly. Which was why the Maze had been placed off limits ever since. Only now that turned out to be not strictly true. Twelve men and women had survived. Strangely gifted and completely insane, they were still alive after two centuries, confined to one special annexe of the Maze.

Finally, the news had got out. The twelve were no longer a secret. Anne swore loudly. Of course Finn had to go to Haden and see these people for himself. Because if people could go through the Madness Maze and survive, that changed everything.

Finn Durandal headed for Haden on the starcruiser *Halcyon*, captained by one Elspeth Wagner. Both she and the rest of the crew were Finn's people, loyal directly to him rather than to Pure Humanity and the Church Militant. Finn trusted them, in as much as he trusted anyone. He had to get to Haden first. He didn't want Church Militant fanatics anywhere near the Madness Maze, or the twelve survivors. The Church demanded access to the Maze as a central part of their dogma, and this news would only inflame them. Finn needed to learn as much as he could, and then get the hell offplanet and slap down a major Quarantine around Haden so that no one else could get in.

Knowledge was power.

As for Pure Humanity, God alone knew what those crazy bastards would do. Could you still be Pure after you'd been through the Maze and it had worked its changes on you? Finn wouldn't put it past them to try and turn their Transmutation Engines on Haden. So; in and out, and then the Quarantine.

Finn paced impatiently back and forth in his cabin, as the fastest ship in the Imperial Fleet took him to Haden. That ancient and treacherous world of transformation and dark miracles, and apparently even more secrets than had been suspected. He studied the limited information available over and over again. Twelve survivors, out of ten thousand. All of them very powerful, all of them extremely insane. Alive and thriving after two centuries of captivity. Finn owed his advance knowledge to the robots of Shub, repaying him for the access he'd got them to the Maze. Human scientists had chosen to keep the survivors secret, but the AIs of Shub didn't believe in withholding data.

It seemed the survivors exhibited powers and abilities far beyond any of the Empire's espers, and the then King and Queen, Robert and Constance, had backed the scientists to the hilt when the news was first presented to them. They didn't want the survivors to be used as weapons by terrorists, or giving false hope to those people still clamouring to be allowed into the Maze. Twelve crazy uber-espers were enough. Especially since they were all decidedly . . . disturbing.

Finn wasn't travelling alone. He'd brought with him one of his creatures from the Rookery, a certain Dr Happy. However, since the good doctor was also in his own way pretty damned disturbing, Finn mostly insisted Dr Happy remain in his own cabin. If only so he wouldn't freak the rest of the crew. Dr Happy was a dealer in drugs and potions, as much alchemist as scientist, who'd raised altering states of consciousness to an art form. From love potions to battle drugs, uppers, downers and the occasional trip sideways, Dr Happy had more ways of messing with your brain than a butcher with a new cleaver and a really nasty sense of humour. The good doctor could make you feel any way he wanted, including some emotions that had been considered purely theoretical until he came along. Dr Happy could make you sing in colours, plait lightning or speak in tongues with people who weren't even in the same time zone as you. For the right price, of course.

The man himself was unnaturally tall, unhealthily slender, and was never seen out of one of his severely stained white lab coats. He wore protective gloves at all times, and never touched his own stock. Probably because he didn't need to; he was born wired. He had a long thin face with a wide toothy grin, bulging eyes and a shock of frizzy white hair that stuck out like a halo. His hair always looked like he tugged at it a lot, and his eyes changed colour according to his mood.

He giggled more than was acceptable, darted agitatedly around and bit his fingernails savagely when he got excited. His eyeballs were as yellow as urine, and his teeth weren't much better. He smelled of something antiseptic.

Finn brought him along in the hopes the good doctor would be able to come up with some extreme new drug to calm and/or control the twelve survivors. Or failing that, the human scientists working with them. Finn felt very strongly that he didn't want any more surprises coming out of Haden. His alliance with the robots of Shub gave him some measure of control, but that wasn't enough. He wanted to slam the lid down hard on Haden and the Maze, and for that he needed Dr Happy. Which meant he had to spend some time discussing matters with the good doctor, a man so lacking in moral and ethical principles, or any form of restraint, that even Finn felt uncomfortable around him.

So he sat in his comfortable chair in his comfortable cabin, and sighed inwardly as Dr Happy capered around him, examing everything with disquieting enthusiasm, giggling loudly and clutching his bony hands to his sunken chest. He hadn't wanted to leave his precious underground laboratory on Logres, but Finn had tempted him out with thoughts of the amazing new drugs he might be able to derive from the altered biochemistry of the twelve survivors. Plus, he would be allowed to treat the survivors with any drug he fancied, in doses that would undoubtedly kill a normal human. Just to see what happened. Finn believed in experimentation, particularly on other people. And, Finn said that if Dr Happy didn't come with him, he would kill the good doctor. Right there and then. Dr Happy believed him. People tended to believe Finn, when he said things like that.

Dr Happy spun round several times, gurgled loudly, and fixed Finn with goggling eyes. 'Are we nearly there yet? No? Hey ho . . . I am so excited at the possibilities before us! I am! Such potential! Yes. I have always believed that esper abilities have their basis in biochemical patterns in the brain, but the oversoul would never allow me to experiment on any of their bodies . . . All right, I wanted to do it while the bodies were still alive, but . . . Wimps. Some people just don't appreciate the miracles of science. Oh just let me at those twelve survivors with my scalpels and my genetic sequencers! Yes! From the deepest secrets of their various vitals I will concoct such potions as will push Humanity up the evolutionary ladder so fast it'll blow away the rungs!'

'I hear you've been running experiments in the ship's med bay again,' said Finn. 'I thought we'd agreed that you were not to test any of your concoctions on members of the crew? And particularly not on anyone in Navigation.'

Dr Happy stuck out his lower lip. 'I have to keep my hand in, sir Durandal. No one's died yet, have they? And I'm sure that nice young lieutenant will stop screaming any day now. I must practise my art, I must! Oh my word yes. I must be at my very best when I come face to face with the Madness Maze, and begin my greatest work.' His eyes became dreamy as his long bony fingers tangled together, and his toothy grin became actually wistful. 'Such miracles I shall work, in the twisted minds and altered flesh of the Maze survivors! I shall change and transform the very nature of human consciousness, stretching it in undreamed-of directions. I shall warp consensual reality and storm the very barricades of heaven and hell! Yes!' He stopped abruptly, and studied Finn with his head cocked on one side. 'I do wish I could persuade you to try some small part of my inventory. Only the very broadest of perceptions will allow you to appreciate the probabilities inherent in the Maze and its creations. We must never allow our Humanity to hold us back from what our ambition can conceive. Are you sure I can't tempt you to try a little something?'

'Quite sure,' said Finn. 'And if you try slipping something into my coffee again, I will remonstrate with you most severely. You do remember what happened the last time I had to remonstrate with you, don't you?'

Dr Happy nodded sulkily. He remembered. 'I still feel you over-reacted somewhat.'

'Be grateful there was a regeneration tank handy. Next time, I won't stop with your extremities. I might need you, but I don't necessarily need you intact.'

The *Halcyon* came at last to Haden, and took up a high orbit. The robots representing the AIs of Shub below teleported Finn and Dr Happy down to the scientists' observation post, right on the edge of the Maze. Finn wasn't at all happy about entrusting his wellbeing to anyone else, but he kept his concerns to himself. Partly because he needed Shub to see him as a trusted and trusting ally, and partly because he was eager to see the Maze, and the survivors. Dr Happy giggled loudly through the entire teleport experience, until Finn hit him.

They materialised in what looked like just another steel-walled corridor in any scientific outpost, but they only had to be there on Haden a few moments to realise that they had come to a very strange place. Everything felt different, eerie, threatening. Finn's hand dropped immediately to the gun at his side. He could feel the hairs standing up on his arms and the back of his neck, as though he'd just entered the lobby of a haunted house. Part of him wanted to turn and run and keep running, which was a shock to Finn. He'd never felt that way before, about anyone or anything. He pushed the feeling aside. He hadn't come this far to leave empty-handed.

Dr Happy stood very still, gnawing on a fingernail, his eyes wider than ever. He was trying to smile, but his heart wasn't in it.

A human scientist in full blast armour came round the corner at the end of the corridor, and Finn almost shot him on sight. He made himself take his hand away from his gun. Whatever the threat here was, it definitely wasn't human. One of the blue steel robots from Shub came to join the human scientist, and Finn relaxed a little. If anyone understood the true nature of this unnatural place, it would be Shub. He walked forward, nodded courteously to the robot and stuck out his hand to the human scientist, who shook it grudgingly. He was short and bald and scowling, and didn't look at all happy to have visitors.

'Welcome to Haden, sir Durandal. It's an honour to meet you, of course, but I could wish it had been under happier circumstances. I have to tell you that I'm deeply concerned about this situation. The existence of the twelve survivors was kept secret for good reason. But, Shub went over my head, so . . . What is *that*, behind you?'

'That is Dr Happy,' said Finn, not looking round. 'And whatever disturbing thing he's doing, don't worry, because he's going to stop it right now. Unless he wants me to slap him silly.'

'Charmed to be here,' said Dr Happy, blinking owlishly at the robot. 'Absolutely charmed. Is there a toilet anywhere handy?'

'Shut up,' said Finn. He gave the human scientist his best sincere look. 'For better or worse, the cat is out of the bag, Doctor . . . ?'

'Ramirez. Well, if someone had to find out, I suppose I should be glad that it's someone like you who got here first. Let me show you around. And then maybe you'll understand why we kept our secret for so long.'

He led them off, back down the corridor and round the corner into another identical corridor. 'This is part of the observation structure my predecessors built directly around the Maze, deep under the surface of Haden. Normally we don't come this deep, and venture so close to the Maze itself, but the survivors can only be . . . appreciated up close and personal.'

'I take it the blast armour you're wearing isn't just a fashion statement,' said Finn. 'How dangerous is it down here?'

'To your body or your soul?' Dr Ramirez tried a laugh, but it wasn't very successful. 'We take every precaution we can when dealing with the survivors, sir Champion. Theoretically, they're completely secure, but normal scientific theories tend to break down around the Madness Maze. You should be safe enough, as long as you stick close to me and don't do or touch anything without checking with me first.'

'Is that your opinion too?' said Finn to the robot.

'Every worthwhile endeavour involves risk,' said the AIs of Shub.

'I know I'm going to love it here,' said Dr Happy.

Dr Ramirez shook his head. 'I knew we should never have agreed to Shub being involved.'

'Now, now,' Finn said calmly. 'You must learn to work alongside your Shub colleagues, Dr Ramirez; or I will have you removed from Haden, and replace you with someone who understands their duty to the Empire. At least Shub doesn't withhold valuable information.'

'That's not fair!' Ramirez said immediately. 'We've shared every discovery it was safe to reveal. But if there's one thing we've learned the hard way in our time here, it's that we have to proceed with the utmost caution. Just being around the Maze is enough to drive perfectly reputable scientists crazy. This place gives you ideas . . . dangerous ideas. There's something about the Maze, about its nature . . .'

'We do not have to proceed so cautiously,' the robot said. 'The nature of the Maze does not frighten us, and these remote-controlled bodies can be exposed to any risk. They are easily replaced. Perhaps robots should replace human scientists completely, since humans are so physically and mentally weak.'

'Boys, boys, don't fight,' Finn murmured. 'Still, the robot has a point, Dr Ramirez. What have you been doing here, that justifies your continued presence?'

'Well,' Ramirez said reluctantly, 'we've been examining the remains of the abandoned Hadenman city nearby, and we've uncovered some startling new additions to Hadenman and Human history. At first, we were mostly concerned with recovering new technologies from the city, and indeed we still are, but recently we stumbled across a stash of data crystals whose contents shed a whole new light on what we thought we knew about the origin of the Hadenmen. The basis remains the same: a group of Humanity's finest scientists came here long ago and passed through the Madness Maze. Most died, horribly, but a few came out mentally transformed. These new intellectual giants made themselves into cyborgs, and became the progenitors of the Hadenman race, of infamous legend. But we now know one of these surviving scientists followed a very different path. She was already an esper before she entered the Maze, and when she came out her psionic abilities had been boosted and altered almost beyond belief. She had become Humanity's first uber-esper.'

'What were the nature of her new abilities?' said Dr Happy, sounding almost sane for once.

'According to the data crystals, she had become an extraordinarily powerful telepath, capable of forcing other espers into a gestalt consciousness, which she could then dominate. Through the gestalt, their powers became increased, and she was able to wield them all. She travelled the Empire, collecting other espers and absorbing them into her gestalt. The new Hadenmen followed her progress with fascination; they were still human enough to be scared of her. When she had enough espers under her control, she returned to Haden and forced them all through the Madness Maze. The Hadenmen . . . kept out of her way. It also seems she used her powerful mind to drive the other espers crazy before putting them into the Maze. Perhaps she thought it would protect them. Perhaps she thought it would help her control them afterwards. Either way, most of the espers died, and the few that emerged . . . were monsters.'

'We all have monsters within us,' said Dr Happy, blinking owlishly.

'How true,' said Finn. 'Do carry on, Dr Ramirez.'

'I think you know who I'm talking about,' said Ramirez. 'These monsters were the legendary uber-espers: the Shatter Freak, the Grey Train, Blue Hellfire, Screaming Silence, the Spider Harps. The terrible minds that run the Esper Liberation Front these days. The original uber-esper had intended to use the power of these minds to force all espers into one great esper consciousness, like our oversoul today, but under her control. But for the first time, her ambition exceeded her abilities. The pressure of so many minds fighting to be free destroyed her. The gestalt collapsed, the woman died, and what remained of her mind was sucked into the mass subconscious of the espers, later to emerge as the Mater Mundi. The other uber-espers disappeared, fearful of being controlled again, and developed their own agenda.'

'Fascinating,' said Finn. 'Do you have any clues as to the identity of this remarkable woman?'

'Yes,' said the blue steel robot. 'We have a name: Alicia VomAcht Deathstalker.'

'Well,' said Finn, after a while. 'I didn't see that one coming. You've given me much to think about, Dr Ramirez, but it's not why I came here. Where are the twelve survivors?'

'This way,' Ramirez said reluctantly. He led them through more corridors, still talking. He sounded increasingly nervous. 'The twelve survivors are kept in a holding area attached to the Maze. It appeared quite literally out of nowhere, an *outgrowth* of the Maze, because it was needed.'

'There are those who have suggested the Madness Maze is alive,' said Dr Happy. 'And quite possibly aware.'

'It's alien,' Ramirez said shortly. 'It could be anything.'

Dr Happy clapped his bony hands together. 'Oh, the possibilities!'

'The twelve are imprisoned behind force screens,' said Ramirez, deliberately not looking at Dr Happy. 'The shields allow nothing in or out. We haven't been able to come up with anything that can affect these screens.'

'Then how do you feed the survivors?' said Finn.

'We don't. They haven't eaten or drunk anything in two hundred years. And that's just the beginning of how ... altered they are. I should warn you, you'll find being this close to the Maze disturbing. You'll experience a constant feeling of being watched, and studied, or weighed in judgement. And not by the survivors. In this, as in everything else we do here, the Maze watches us.'

'Yes,' said the Shub robot. 'We feel it too. It is disturbing.'

Finn shot a quick glance at the robot, and then decided not to pursue the matter. 'Can we communicate with the twelve?'

'We can talk with them, but I don't know that what we get is actually communication.' Ramirez shuddered suddenly. 'We're almost there, sir Durandal. Soon you'll know why we've kept these ... abominations secret for so long. The force shields the Maze provides are a blessing, and a protection for all Humanity. It is my fervent hope that they will never be lowered. Or at least not until the rest of Humanity has evolved to a point where we have some hope of dealing with these creatures.' He gave Finn a hard look. 'I have to ask, sir Durandal: what are your intentions, towards the twelve?'

'I haven't decided yet,' said Finn. 'That's why I came all this way, to see them in person. But they could be weapons we can use against the Terror. Or other enemies.'

'Like Donal Corcoran,' said Dr Happy, unexpectedly. 'He'd make an excellent weapon.'

'Mouth is open, Doctor, should be shut,' said Finn.

And then they rounded a final corner, and there the twelve were, imprisoned behind shimmering fields of energy. Ramirez started to say something, but Finn gestured imperiously for him to be silent. He went forward, alone. He had no intention of sharing this moment with anyone. He walked slowly down the aisle, peering into each cell, drinking in the terrible miracles the Maze had wrought in these creatures' merely mortal flesh. They were everything he had hoped for, and worse.

Twelve men and women, kept alive and suffering and crazy for two hundred years. Not eating or drinking, because they had risen above such human needs. He looked at them, and some of them looked back. They were glorious and awful, magnificent and appalling; sick dreams given shape and form and thrust unwillingly into the waking world. Finn decided he didn't feel disturbed. He felt . . . invigorated. He retraced his steps, stopped in front of the first cell, and gestured for the others to come forward and join him.

'I have to thank you, Dr Ramirez,' he said calmly. 'In all my years, I have never seen anything like this. A truly unique experience. I could watch them for hours, and never grow tired. Tell me, have they always been like this? Have they changed at all in two hundred years?'

'Not according to the files left by my predecessors,' said Ramirez. He preferred to look at Finn, rather than what was in the cell. 'This is how they emerged from the Madness Maze. Each one entirely singular, and horribly self-sufficient. Apart from one, they haven't slept in two centuries. No normal mind could survive under such conditions. But then, these creatures aren't in any way normal.'

He turned and looked, almost unwillingly, into the first cell, and the others followed his gaze.

The cell contained two survivors. A man and a woman, joined together into one body. A large dead-white creature, with four arms and four legs, and one oversized head with too many eyes, it crawled slowly round its featureless enclosure like a giant insect. The single mouth spoke a language that made no sense, and all the eyes moved in different directions.

'Not much of a weapon, is it?' said Ramirez. 'Sometimes it walks on the walls and the ceiling, and sometimes it sings a song that makes any listener's ears bleed, but that's about it.'

'Ah well,' said Finn. 'Early days yet.'

In the next cell, the occupant had been turned inside out, all down one side. It sat very still in the middle of its cell, and didn't respond to any movements outside the force screen. The exposed organs were crimson and purple, pulsing with blood, wet and shiny. The single lung expanded and contracted smoothly. Sharp bone horns stuck out of the exposed grey matter of the brain. Where the genitals should have been there was only a twitching red mass. Tears ran steadily down the normal half of the face.

'Is it in pain?' said Finn.

Ramirez shrugged. 'It doesn't respond to questions. Either way, we have no way of reaching past the force screen to help. According to my files, it hasn't moved an inch in two hundred years. God alone knows what it's thinking.'

'Why would the Maze do something like that?' said Finn. 'What purpose could it serve?'

'I told you,' said Ramirez. 'The Maze is alien.'

In the next cell, a man ran back and forth impossibly quickly, his movements almost a blur. He pounded on the walls with his fists, which continually broke and bled and constantly healed. His mouth was stretched in an endless silent scream, his eyes utterly mad.

'He can hear the whole Empire thinking,' said Ramirez. 'But he can't shut any of it out, even for a moment. He doesn't know who he is any more, his identity crushed under the weight of so many others.'

Finn looked at Dr Happy. 'Could you help him?'

'I could have a lot of fun trying,' said the good doctor.

The next cell held a man who'd torn his own eyes out. Blood streamed endlessly down his jerking cheeks from the empty red sockets. But his wounded head turned unerringly to follow Finn as he approached the cell's force screen. When Finn stopped and looked in, the blind man came forward to face him.

'I have to keep tearing them out,' he said hoarsely. 'Because they keep growing back. I see things. Terrible things. I see other planes, other dimensions, and other realities. I see the awful things that live there, twisting and turning, and the awful things they want to do, if they could only find their way here. I have seen the answers to Humanity's oldest questions, and secrets we were never meant to know . . . and I can't stop seeing! I tear my eyes out, and *I can still see*!'

Finn backed away despite himself, and the man in the cell laughed hysterically. The laughter followed them down the aisle to the next cell.

In this cell, the occupant was constantly changing. It stood very still, a blur of movement from one moment to the next as it became a woman became a man became a child became someone else. Short and tall, fat and thin, every race and colour of Humanity, everyone and everything, forever changing.

'We don't know whether any of those are real people,' said Ramirez. 'Whether they're copies of people from other worlds, or alternate time track versions of the original person, such as the blessed Hazel d'Ark is supposed to have produced, or whether these people are generated from the original's imagination. None of them have ever stayed around long enough to be questioned. And before you ask, recording devices don't operate through the force screen. None of our instruments will. We have no way of running tests on any of the survivors. I'm not sure whether that's for their protection, or ours.'

'Don't be defeatist, Doctor,' said Finn. 'One idea has already occurred to me. But let us press on, press on.'

The occupant of the next cell was fast asleep, curled up into a foetal ball, floating some two feet above the floor. Behind his closed eyelids, his eyes moved constantly.

'He's been sleeping and dreaming for two hundred years,' said Ramirez. 'What can his dreams be like, after so long away from reality? We don't know if he'll ever wake up, or what he might be able to do when he does. Perhaps he's dreaming himself sane.'

The next cell contained a homicidal psychopath of such relentless ferocity that even Finn was impressed. The Maze survivor raged back and forth across his cell, murdering an endless number of people who seemed to appear out of nowhere just to die, and then vanish. The killer's face was purple with rage as he battered people to death with his bare hands, or strangled them, or tore them limb from limb.

'Again, we don't know whether the other people are real or not,' said Ramirez. 'But he's been killing them non-stop, in increasingly nasty and inventive ways. If the cell force screens ever do go down, the very first thing we're going to do is shoot that bloodthirsty bastard with every gun we've got.'

'Oh, I don't know,' said Finn. 'He has possibilities.'

'Going to throw him at the Terror, are you?' said Ramirez. 'Oh yes, he'll be a lot of use against something that eats planets!'

Finn looked at Ramirez. 'Now, now, Doctor,' he murmured. 'Who knows what other ... abilities any of these people might have, outside their cells? Even the blessed Owen didn't become a living god immediately; he had to grow into his powers over time.'

In the next cell, a woman sat cross-legged, smiling at nothing. Her eyes were fixed on something far away.

'She's been smiling non-stop for two centuries,' said Ramirez heavily. 'Never been known to speak or move, but one thing every scientist who's seen her agrees on, is that ... that's a really disturbing smile. Like she knows something nobody else knows.'

'Oh, I've seen a lot of that,' said Dr Happy. 'Trust me, it doesn't mean anything.'

The next occupant all but filled his cell, a huge dark fleshy mass that pressed against the walls and floor and ceiling, but held back from touching the force screen. It had no discernible human details, just a great mass, slowly moving.

'Apparently he looked perfectly normal when he went into the cell,' said Ramirez. 'But he's been growing steadily. Hopefully he'll stop once he's completely filled the space available.'

'And if he doesn't?' said Finn.

Ramirez shrugged. 'That's up to the Maze.'

In the next cell, a woman slowly faded in and out of reality, disappearing and returning, silently screaming for help. She reached out her hands to the people outside her cell, begging for them to do something.

'She can see us, but she can't hear us,' said Ramirez. 'We don't know where she goes to, or how she comes back. Or how to keep her here. Whatever powers she hoped to find in the Maze, I can't believe this was it.'

Finn found the occupant of the final cell the most disturbing, mainly because he looked exactly like Finn Durandal. The two Finns stared at each other in silence for a while. The double was exact, down to the tiniest details of face, stance and clothing. He smiled amiably back at Finn.

'Takes a bit of getting used to, doesn't it?' he said calmly. 'I become anyone who looks at me. Anyone at all. And not just the exterior; I am you, inside and out. I know everything you know, including the things no one else is supposed to know.'

The original Finn raised an elegant eyebrow. 'A telepath, I take it?'

'Perhaps,' said his double. 'Or perhaps nothing so crude. I am you, in every way that matters. If you were to die, I could step into your life and take it over, and no one would be able to tell the difference.'

'I doubt that,' said Finn. 'It's a matter of style, you see.'

'I know everything you're afraid of, Finn. And you're afraid of so many things, deep down, aren't you? Come on, you can admit it to yourself. Admit that you're afraid you're not strong enough and smart enough to do the things that have to be done. Admit that you worry constantly about being found out. Admit you're scared you have no heart—'

'I'm not afraid of that,' Finn said calmly. 'I glory in it.'

He turned away from the double and walked back up the aisle. The others followed him out of the aisle and round the corner into the steel corridor, leaving the cells and their occupants behind. Finn then stopped, stood still and thought silently for a long time, and none of the others cared to interrupt him.

'They're secure,' he said finally, as much to himself as anyone. 'We don't have to worry about any of them escaping. The Maze knows what it's doing.'

'Just as well,' said Ramirez. 'If any of them weren't crazy to begin with, they sure as hell are now, after all they've endured. But there are security cameras covering the aisle and this corridor twenty-four hours a day, just in case. Not that we have any way of stopping them if they do get out; it's just to give the rest of us a good running start to get safely offplanet.'

Finn looked at the Shub robot. 'You have no ideas on how to penetrate the force screens?'

'Not at present,' said the robot. 'Though I feel I should point out that even if we could develop such an ability, I very much doubt we would be able to control or contain the twelve survivors afterwards. They represent a level of power beyond anything we have encountered, apart from Owen and his people.'

Finn was still frowning thoughtfully. 'But you do have teleport capability. Could you perhaps teleport items in or out of the cells?'

'We are considering the possibility,' said the robot.

'You never said anything about that to me!' said Dr Ramirez.

'You never asked,' said the robot.

Finn turned to Dr Happy. 'I'm leaving you here, Doctor. Learn everything that can be learned about the twelve survivors, and then let your mind run wild along its usual appalling paths. Let it run free. I will see to it that you have a completely free hand here, so no experiment should be considered too controversial, too expensive or too dangerous. Think the unthinkable! But you are forbidden to use any of the scientific staff here as subjects for whatever drugs you develop, on pain of me getting really upset with you. If you reach a stage where you need subjects, I'll supply them. And Doctor: if Shub does find a way to gain access to the twelve through teleportation, feel free to do any damned thing you like to them. As long as it doesn't involve any risk of their escaping.'

Dr Happy nodded, beaming widely. Finn turned to Dr Ramirez. 'I can see the objections rising to your lips, Doctor, but they will do you no good. Parliament has given me complete control over this whole establishment. Mainly because no one else wants it. If you try to impede the good doctor in any way, I'll let him have you as a subject. Concentrate on your own work and all will be well. I shall expect regular reports and updates on everything that happens here. I need to know why these twelve survived, when so many others died. In the meantime, Haden is now officially under full Quarantine. I'll have two starcruisers posted here, to ensure you're protected from outside influences. And if any investigative journalist should manage to sneak their way in, you have my permission to shoot them on sight.'

He turned to the blue steel robot of Shub. 'Teleportation has to be the key. Work on ways to get things into those cells, and, indeed, into the bodies of the twelve. But be very careful about taking anything out. I don't want to risk losing any of our subjects.'

'We shall cherish them,' said the robot. 'All that lives is holy.'

'So I'm told,' said Finn.

'What if we can't learn anything useful from the twelve?' said Dr Ramirez a little sulkily. 'After all, my predecessors have been studying them for two hundred years, to little effect.'

Finn considered the question, and then smiled. 'The answer would seem to be obvious. I'll have to send more people through the Madness Maze, until it produces some survivors you can work with.'

Ramirez looked at him, aghast. 'But . . . you'd lose thousands of people! Maybe hundreds of thousands!'

'There's never any shortage of fools,' said Finn Durandal.

Some time later, in the House of Parliament on Logres, King Douglas sat in his throne as Speaker and watched with a dull helpless anger as the Members voted to dismantle the regulatory committee he'd set up to monitor the increasingly powerful Transmutation Board. Douglas couldn't honestly say he was surprised. It was the latest in a series of moves that proved Parliament was now dominated, if not actually controlled, by outside interests these days. Searching for something, anything, to shore up their ebbing power and influence, the Members were desperate for support, and many were almost openly for sale. Or at least, for rent. Douglas had tried to contribute something to the debate, but the outcome was a foregone conclusion, and everyone there knew it. Besides, as Speaker and as King, Douglas's position was not what it had once been. He was no longer the respected new force on the throne; he had been betrayed, and sidelined, and made irrelevant by the changing new order. Still, everyone remained very polite to him. Because he had been a Paragon, and was still a Campbell, and you never knew . . .

Douglas sat stiffly on his throne, overlooking the House as the Members argued loudly over the next proposal, a bill to license and control all espers in the Empire, and especially on Logres. Douglas would have smiled at that, if he'd been in a smiling mood. This was the mice voting to bell the cat. But with public feelings against espers running so hot and high, Parliament had to do something, or at least be seen to be doing something. So: a bill that didn't have a hope in hell of being enforced, but would look good on the news channels. Douglas sighed heavily. There had to be some Members left in the House with guts enough to stand against the tide, and others who might yet be influenced by just the right words; but he had no idea who they might be any more. He hadn't realised how dependent he'd become on Anne to brief him, to do the research and guide him through the treacherous undercurrents of modern politics. She'd known everything, about ideas and trends and people; but she was gone, and working with the enemy. Douglas was doing his best to catch up on the ground he'd lost during his seclusion, but it was hard going. Particularly when hardly anyone would agree to talk to him any more, even on the most private and secure of lines. In politics, there was always the fear that defeat might be catching.

Anne worked with Finn now. In fact, since his return from Haden, the two were rarely seen in public apart. Though neither of them had much time for Parliament these days. The Durandal rarely showed his face in the House, even though he was Imperial Champion and officially still Douglas's bodyguard. And Anne only ever made her presence known from the shadows. Perhaps because the House was now such a tamed beast that it was beneath their notice. Douglas pushed the thought aside. He had to concentrate on those matters he could still influence. He made himself listen to the current speaker on the floor of the House. Joseph Wallace, head of the Transmutation Board, was politely thanking the House for its expressed support, and not quite gloating over his future plans since he didn't have Douglas's regulatory committee to hold him back.

Wallace was tall and well set, with blandly handsome features set off by golden tracings that followed the lines of his face. They gleamed very prettily, but Douglas thought it made the man look as though someone had graffitied his face while he was asleep. Still, Wallace had good posture and a trained voice, and a commanding presence in an obvious sort of way.

'I thank this House for the confidence it has placed in me,' he said gravely. 'In turn, I commit the Transmutation Board to even greater endeavours. More useless planets shall be transformed from lifeless worlds to the building blocks of matter. Dross shall become gold; more goods, more food, more weapons for Humanity, in the hour of its greatest need!'

Most of the Members stood up and cheered loudly, hoping to be noticed by the news cameras. Douglas made a mental note of the few that didn't. Wallace was saying all the right things, saying what the public wanted to hear, and it was a brave man who'd stand in the way of something for nothing. Wallace looked about him, smiling smugly.

'And I can assure this House that the board will take its responsibilities very seriously, when it comes to making dangerous alien planets safe. Transmutation can and will ensure that Humanity never need feel threatened by alien forces again!'

More cheering and applause from the Honourable Members, but the alien section of the House was noticeably silent. Like Douglas, they hadn't missed that Wallace had been referring specifically to Humanity all along, and not to the Empire. The treasures to be provided by the Transmutation Board were not for everyone, it seemed. Some species had already stopped sending their representatives to the House, and more and more were leaving as the mood in the House became increasingly openly xenophobic. The Swart Alfair of that enigmatic planet Mog Mor had already declared their world off limits to all human ships, though their own craft still travelled the Empire, openly defying Pure Humanity to do anything about it. The espers had also withdrawn their representative, even before the esper-control bill was mooted. Telepaths and precogs are better than most at telling which way the wind is blowing. The clone representative still held his seat smiling just a little smugly and the robot from Shub was always there, though it had little to say these days. No one objected to their presence. Everyone knew they were under Finn Durandal's protection.

Joseph Wallace finally finished his speech, and left on a wave of triumph. The Honourable Members waited until they were sure he was gone, and then switched off their smiles and sat down again.

In a small private room in the warren of offices at the rear of the House, Joseph Wallace talked with Finn Durandal. Wallace was still flushed with his success, and wanted to boast and strut and recount his triumph, but he was finding it hard going under the Durandal's cold, ironic gaze. Finn sat slumped loosely in his chair, and listened while Wallace strode up and down before him, and the more Finn listened the less Wallace felt like talking. He finally broke off in mid-gloat and glared at Finn, gathering his anger to give him strength, and pulling old resentments around him like armour. He was a member in high standing in Pure Humanity, after all, and for all his undoubted influence, the Durandal was still only Imperial Champion.

'With the King's precious committee swept away, I run the

107

Transmutation Board. My word is law now, and no one can say me nay. Planets live or die at my whim. I answer to Pure Humanity and no one else. So you can wipe that look off your face, and forget whatever threats you've been rehearsing. Any hold you might have had over me vanished when Rose Constantine ran off and left you high and dry. You can't bully me any more. I'm protected.'

Finn smiled easily. 'They all say that.'

Wallace drew himself up to his full height and puffed out his chest. 'You can't threaten Pure Humanity. We are the way of the future!'

'Perhaps,' said Finn. 'You're not the only player in the game.' He rose gracefully to his feet, and Wallace fell back a step in spite of himself. Finn strolled over to the window, and beckoned for Wallace to join him. Wallace did so, reluctantly, and looked down at the street scene below. Everything seemed quiet. People came and went about their business, paying no attention to two of the most important men in the Empire looking down on them. Finn languidly indicated a man standing beside a vid phone booth.

'Do you recognise that gentleman in the rather tacky green cloak, Joseph?'

'Yes,' Wallace said uncertainly. 'That's Brion Page. My immediate superior in Pure Humanity. I wasn't aware he had any business at the House today.'

'He doesn't,' said Finn. 'He's here because I required it of him. Poor Brion proved even more intransigent than you, and he was very rude to me. So now he's come here to provide you with an object lesson.'

He waved cheerfully to the man down in the street, and Brion Page, his mind possessed and controlled by an ELF, smiled cheerfully back and cut his throat with his own dagger. He waved to Wallace as the blood gushed down his chest, and he stood there smiling and waving until all the strength had gone out of his body; and then the ELF finally let go of him, and he fell down dead in the street. People were screaming all around him, and already there was the wail of an approaching peacekeeper vehicle.

Wallace fell back from the window, clutching at his tight collar, fighting to get his breath. He could feel sweat running down his face, and pins and needles in his suddenly numb hands. Finn took him companionably by the arm, and steered him into a chair.

'Don't faint, Joseph,' said Finn. 'I haven't finished with you yet.'

'How did you do that?' said Wallace hoarsely. 'What in God's name are you?'

'I am a man with many friends, or at least allies. What you just watched is real power, Joseph. Not political influence, or philosophical rhetoric to sway a crowd or inflame a mob. My power is the only power that matters: control over life and death. No one is safe from me, no matter how highly placed they may think they are. So; do as you're told, Joseph. Or I'll replace you with someone who will.'

'What is it you want?' said Wallace. He met Finn's gaze squarely. He had that much pride left.

'Nothing that should upset you too much, Joseph. Just spread a little dread and suffering wherever I direct. You touched on it yourself, in your little speech in the House. I want to use the Transmutation Board as a weapon, not just against alien planets, but against any world that dares to stand against us. We can stamp out rebellion at the root, by wiping clean any planet that defies us. I think your first action as head of the board should be to send the Transmutation Engines to Virimonde. No need to actually do anything yet. Just the presence of those huge engines in orbit should be enough to . . . influence their thinking along the right paths. And after Virimonde . . . well, I'll make you a list of those worlds whose Honourable Members seem to be a bit slow to grasp the realities of today's political situation. It'll do no harm to remind people of their true place in the order that's coming.'

'I can't use the engines as a threat! The House would order my arrest, and take the board back under their control!'

'No, they won't,' said Finn. 'They'll spend all their time arguing over what course to take until it's too late. I'll see to that.'

'But . . . Virimonde?' said Wallace. He would have liked to wipe away the sweat he could feel on his face, but he couldn't afford to do anything that might be seen as a sign of weakness. 'Virimonde still has a fond place in the hearts of the people. I don't think they'd stand for a threat to the homeworld of the blessed Owen.'

'But the current Deathstalkers aren't nearly so beloved. Not after what Lewis did. They are our enemies, Joseph; and we must never be afraid to strike at our enemies. And, there's always the chance that a threat against his family might be enough to tempt dear Lewis out of whatever hole he's crept into. He always was a most honourable and sentimental fellow. I miss him, I really do. Now, off you go, Joseph, and arrange the things that need arranging. And don't worry; I'm sure I'll be able to find the time for us to have another of these nice little chats. Possibly even sooner than you think. I do so enjoy explaining things to you.'

Wallace didn't quite run out of the room, followed all the way by Finn's terrible smile.

Not long afterwards, Finn took the Paragon Stuart Lennox drinking, to the Sangreal bar. Finn had spent a lot of time with the young Paragon from Virimonde, all but adopting him as his student, partner and protégé. They were friends, in as much as Finn had friends. Certainly the young Stuart hero-worshipped the older, legendary Durandal. So they sat close together at one of the best tables, drinking a murky blue wine that Stuart could never have afforded on his own, and the young man listened awestruck as Finn recounted old stories of his famous exploits as Logres's Paragon.

(Finn carefully avoided any of his more current exploits. He didn't think the boy was quite ready for that yet.)

Stuart Lennox was big and muscular, with a stern humourless face under a thick mop of curly red hair. A sprinkling of freckles across his nose and cheeks made him look even younger than he was. But he wore his Paragon's armour well and proudly, and he had after all been trained by the same man who had trained Lewis Deathstalker. Finn constantly reminded himself not to underestimate the young Lennox. He was potentially a very dangerous man; which was why Finn had invested so much time in turning him.

The bar was getting rowdy. The Sangreal used to be a cop bar, patronised almost exclusively by security personnel from the House of Parliament just up the road, a quiet and civilised place for the serious drinker, but that was before the Paragons discovered it. The Sangreal's owner hadn't objected. The money had been good, and you couldn't buy publicity like that. Everyone would want to drink in a bar that Paragons had patronised. Unfortunately, the Paragons who'd returned unsuccessful from their great quest were very different from those who'd set out so confidently and so joyfully. These Paragons had made the bar their own, and now no one else dared to come in any more. The Paragons spent their money freely enough, but they did like to party hard. They drank everything there was to drink, openly ingested every drug under the sun, and had sex with each other right there on the table tops, or with groupies they treated as casually as themselves. There was gambling and fighting every night, and sometimes they played games. Nasty games.

Stuart had been shocked the first time Finn brought him to the Sangreal. Finn had had to stop him from trying to arrest half the Paragons on sight. But Finn had hauled him over to a table by brute force, sat him down, and explained that people in high-pressure jobs, weighed down by duties and responsibilities in their public life, needed to relax more than ordinary people, and so were allowed more than ordinary latitude in the pastimes and pleasures they pursued when off duty.

And since it was Finn Durandal saying it, it must be true. Stuart watched the Paragons at their play and, while he never joined in, he slowly lost the ability to be shocked.

So Finn and Stuart were drinking together, talking and laughing, as Finn systematically and quite deliberately enchanted and seduced the young Paragon. Not that he cared a damn about the boy, but he could be a useful tool, if not an ally. And perhaps even a weapon that could be used against Lewis, should he ever be foolish enough to return to Logres. It was an easy enough thing to turn the boy's hero-worship into something else. Stuart was young and inexperienced in the ways of the world, and still delightfully innocent in, oh, so many ways. Day by day, Finn made Stuart into one of his creatures, and set the boy's heart against Lewis Deathstalker.

It wasn't difficult.

They were getting along really well, giggling together over their wine like great chums, when the Paragon Emma Steel made one of her grand entrances. She slammed open the door, knocked down the bouncer when he tried to block her way and trampled right over him. She struck a pose, hands on hips, and glared disdainfully about her. She was tall and willowy, though her bare arms were heavy with muscle. Her skin was a rich coffee colour, and she wore her jet black hair pulled into a tight bun on the back of her head. Striking rather than conventionally pretty, she could still take your breath away. In more ways than one. Emma Steel was Mistworld's Paragon, greatest fighter of the old rebel planet and generally considered the most dangerous person on Logres, in or out of the Arena. She was the law, on Logres.

The other Paragons stopped their playing, and abandoned their drinks and their drugs and their groupies to rise silently to their feet and stare at Emma Steel. Everyone's hand was near a weapon, but no one moved. Emma sneered at them and stalked across the room. The other Paragons stood very still, watching her silently with cold vicious eyes. The music in the bar cut off abruptly, and it all went very quiet. Even the drunk and drugged-out groupies had enough sense to keep their mouths shut for once. Emma ignored them with magnificent disdain, and crashed to a halt at Finn and Stuart's table. The young Lennox gaped openly at her. If there was one other person in the Parade of the Endless he adored as much as Finn Durandal, it would have to be the almost equally legendary Emma Steel.

'What the hell are you doing in a place like this, with a man like him?' she said bluntly. 'You can't trust a word the Durandal says. Believe me. I have reason to know this.'

Stuart flushed angrily. He was already a little drunk, and made an effort to speak clearly. 'I think I'm quite capable of chosing my own friends. And I don't think you ought to talk like that about Finn. He's Imperial Champion, and the greatest Paragon we've ever had.'

'I thought that once,' said Emma, looking coldly at Finn. 'He was my hero. And then I met him. And now there's just me to patrol the whole of Logres, because the mighty Imperial Champion can't be bothered any more.'

'I have other duties now,' Finn said easily. 'New responsibilities. I can't be everywhere at once. And you're doing such a fine job, Emma. Hardly ever out of the news. I hope you've got someone experienced handling your merchandising.'

'I've never given a damn for any of that shit, and you know it. I care about the job. Because someone has to. Lennox, listen to me. Learn from my mistakes. The Durandal isn't the legend he was. If he ever really was.'

She broke off, as one of the carousing Paragons suddenly threw away his drink and came charging at her, sword in hand. Emma spun round, her sword leaping into her hand, and met him head on. She parried his sword thrust easily, kicked him in the balls and then hit him on the back of the head with her sword hilt as he dropped towards the safety of the floor. She sneered down at the twitching body at her feet.

'The quality of Paragons has really gone downhill recently. I suppose that's what happens when you pal around with the Durandal.' She looked unhurriedly about her, her free hand hovering over the disrupter on her hip. The other Paragons stared flatly back, their faces cold and dangerous, but none of them moved. Emma sniffed. 'Seems I've outstayed my welcome. Lennox, you know where to find me if you need me. Don't leave it too late.'

She backed out of the Sangreal, not taking her eyes off the other Paragons, not hurrying but not hanging about either. The Paragons waited until they were sure she was gone, then went back to their various unpleasant pursuits as though they'd never been interrupted. Stuart looked at Finn, shocked almost sober again by the unexpected confrontation.

'What the hell was *that* all about?'

'Women,' Finn said calmly, refilling Stuart's glass. 'She's just jealous that I've got a new partner. She wanted the position, but she was never worthy of it. Not like you, my dear.'

Finn plied the young man with drink, flattered his ego, cuddled and kissed him, and none of it meant anything to Finn. Boys and girls, girls and boys, none of that had ever meant much to him. He took his pleasures as they came, and none of it touched him where he lived. There'd only ever been him, in his life. But it amused him to corrupt the idealistic young man, and turn him into a weapon that could be thrown at Lewis; most of all because Finn knew how much it would hurt Lewis. As a useful side project, Finn also quietly pried information out of Stuart about Virimonde's planetary defences. Just in case he found it necessary to use the Transmutation Engines on Virimonde. Finn believed in covering all the angles.

Emma Steel rode her gravity sled high above the bustling streets of the Parade of the Endless. It was the only place she felt safe any more, high enough in the sky that the madness and the corruption couldn't reach her. Sometimes it seemed that she was the only sane person left in Logres, and she was hanging on by her fingertips. Other air traffic saw her scowling face, and gave her plenty of room. Emma didn't notice, lost in her own thoughts. She was on her own these days. Finn left all the work to her, and none of the other Paragons she'd approached would help her, even though they showed no signs of returning to their own worlds. They refused to talk to her, even the few she'd thought of as friends. And the peacekeepers were disinclined to back her up, for fear of being caught in the middle of a Paragon quarrel.

So now only one Paragon patrolled Logres, and that was Emma Steel. Sensing her isolation, the criminal element had declared open war on her, and placed an unofficial bounty of half a million credits on her head. It hadn't done them any good. Emma took on everyone and everything they could throw at her, and never looked like losing. She had been raised and trained on Mistworld, that most dangerous and barbaric of worlds, and compared to the everyday menaces she'd faced there, Logres's law-breakers were talented amateurs. Her continuing triumphs in the face of overwhelming odds captured the interest of the news media, and the public. They needed someone to admire, someone who clearly had no interest in extreme politics or religion, someone not tainted by the current era of corruption and betrayal, and they took Emma Steel to their fickle hearts.

To her credit, Emma didn't give a damn. Mostly.

She glanced at the watchface embedded in her wrist, and sighed heavily. She was going to be late for her appointment. She'd reluctantly agreed to allow a reporter to tag along with her for one shift, to show people how much pressure she was under without the Durandal's help. Normally Emma had no time for reporters, except to kick them when they got in the way at crime scenes, but she needed some way to get her views on Finn to the public. So for today's shift, she was to be accompanied by one Nina Malapert, of Channel 739. *All the News, As It Happens, Up Close and Personal.* Not the channel or the reporter Emma would have preferred, but it had been almost impossible to find a journalist willing to put their own arse on the line. Most only worked through their remotes these days, sending their cameras into dangerous areas while they stayed safely in their offices. Said it helped to give them 'distance' from a story. Emma wasn't having any of that. She wanted a reporter right there with her, transmitting live, so they couldn't edit or cut out any controversial material.

And the only person to volunteer had been Nina Malapert.

The reporter was where she said she'd be, her camera bobbing above her shoulder. She smiled and waved brightly as Emma descended on her gravity sled into the quiet side street they'd agreed on. Nina was a bright young thing, with an open happy face and a towering pink mohawk. She was wearing a clutter of pastel-coloured silks, and carrying a large leather shoulder bag decorated with images of pretty flowers. She wore far too much makeup on her somewhat pointed face, and had on entirely unsuitable shoes. Emma looked at her for a long time.

'You do realise we're going into the Rookery today?' she said heavily. 'Into the most dangerous and evil part of the city?'

'Oh yes! Absolutely looking forward to it, darling! Don't worry, I've got all my gear. Whatever happens, we won't miss a thing! This really is terribly exciting! Now tell me, before we start: is it true you're a vegetarian?'

'Yes,' said Emma, frowning slightly.

'*An exclusive!*' Nina did a little dance of celebration right there on the spot, punching the air with one fist.

'Get on the sled behind me,' said Emma.

Nina hugged Emma tightly round the waist as they flew over increasingly narrow streets, heading into the centre of the city and the criminal underworld of the Rookery. Nina let her chin rest on Emma's shoulder, and chattered happily in her ear all the way there.

'I really am so glad you chose me for this gig, Emma. Honestly, darling, the competition was . . . well, everyone else was *very* busy, but even so . . . Oh I just know we're going to get on famously! I've read all the files we have on you. Well, not all of them, obviously, because there are an awful lot of them, but I skimmed the précis of most of them . . . We really are frightfully high up, aren't we? I don't normally get to do the crime stuff, you know. Mostly I do gossip. Who's been seen dining with who at which new night spot, who's dumping who, that sort of thing. I was the one who proved Treasure Mackenzie is allergic to cats, even though she swore she wasn't. Of course, she hasn't talked to me ever since I thrust that cat in her face at a première, but then she wasn't talking to me anyway, the snotty cow. And sometimes I do the horoscopes, when there's no one else left in the office. But this is the real thing! Real reporting! No more gossip for me, I'm going to be a genuine journalist at last. Mummy will be so pleased! Why did you choose me, Emma?'

'Because you were the only one dumb enough to agree to accompany me into the Rookery,' growled Emma, without looking round. 'And more and more it's seeming like a really bad idea. Now keep the noise down, and pay attention. Is your camera running?'

'Oh yes, Emma. Has been ever since you showed up. We are totally live, as you requested.'

'Well, we've just entered a part of the city that doesn't officially exist. This is where most of the crime that happens in this city is plotted and financed. This is where the really wild animals are. So stay close to me, do what I say when I say it, and for God's sake don't try to interview anyone. They don't take kindly to being asked questions around here.'

'So how do you find out things?' said Nina.

'Mostly I beat it out of them. Now one of my more reliable snitches got a message to me about a meeting between one of the main agents provocateurs and his secret patron. The agent is apparently threatening to go public over their dealings unless he gets more money. The patron doesn't normally come here in person any more, so this could be our one chance to nail him. And if it turns out to be who I think it is, you are in for the exclusive of your life.'

Nina squeaked loudly with excitement right into Emma's ear, and she winced. She wasn't ready to mention the Durandal's name yet. Not till she'd caught him in the act. But if he was stupid enough to meet one of his creatures personally, then live coverage of the two together, in the heart of the infamous Rookery, should finally be enough to cast serious doubt on his goody-goody image. The problem was, she had to get solid evidence against Finn or it wouldn't stick. Just meeting an agent provocateur wasn't enough. He might still talk his way out of that. She needed coverage of the two of them discussing what they'd planned and done together. Whatever that might have been. Emma sighed. Maybe she'd get really lucky, and the Durandal would implicate himself and then gun down the agent to silence him. Let Finn talk his way out of cold-blooded murder, broadcast live.

'Do you mind if I ask you a few more questions? Just till we get there?' said Nina, in that open happy way of hers that made it clear nothing short of murder was going to stop her. 'I mean, there's still so much the people don't know about you, Emma. Like: do you have a steady boyfriend? What's your favourite recipe? Do you have any special makeup tips that you'd like to share with our viewers? You are a fashion icon, after all, even if it is a rather . . . severe look. What's it like, being a woman and a Paragon? What do you do for fun?'

Luckily they reached the designated meeting place before Emma decided that she really had to kill Nina. Emma glided the gravity sled down into a shadowy square leading off from a particularly squalid and underlit street. It was all very quiet, with no one about, both of which were highly suspicious. There was always something going on in the Rookery, day or night. Emma stepped down from the hovering sled and glared about her. She'd already checked the overlooking windows and rooftops for snipers on the way down, but it didn't hurt to check again. There was nothing obvious to be seen, but the whole situation felt wrong. Nina stepped gingerly down from the sled, and then made a highly distressed noise as she realised what she'd stepped into.

'Oh God, darling, this is disgusting! This whole neighbourhood needs a good fumigating. With a flamethrower. I just know I'm going to catch something I'm going to have a hard time explaining to my doctor. Honestly, it smells like something died here. Very recently. Though admittedly, I have paid absolutely extortionate cover charges to get into supposedly fashionable clubs that smelled even worse. But at least they had a bar . . . Is that supposed to move like that?'

'Hush,' said Emma. She'd come deeper into the Rookery than she normally liked, now that she could no longer depend on peacekeeper backup, but the snitch's tale had been too tempting. Even if the Durandal didn't turn up, the agent provocateur would have to know all kind of useful things, which she was sure he could be persuaded to talk about. Though she might have to do the persuading discreetly off camera. There had been mention of Brett Random and Rose Constantine, and the things they'd done for Finn before they abandoned him to follow the Deathstalker. What could the Durandal be up to, that two such hardened scumbags had run away from it? Emma was close to answers now, she could feel it.

She also felt very much that she'd just walked into a trap, even if she couldn't see it yet.

'Where exactly are we supposed to meet this informer of yours?' said Nina, looking unhappily about her. 'Tell me it's somewhere where they've at least heard of the basic rules of hygiene.'

'We are going to Mother Molly's Kitchen,' said Emma. 'Where they probably couldn't even spell hygiene. I hope you've had all your shots. Stick close to me, don't smile at anyone, and above all avoid the bar snacks. Especially the Long Pig Munchies.'

Emma led the way across the deserted square, checking every shadow and opening for unfriendly eyes, but everything was unnaturally still and quiet. Not even a stray dog rooted in the piled-up garbage. Emma strode along confidently, her head held high. There had to be observers around somewhere, and it wouldn't do to let them think they could get to her. Nina scurried along beside her, peering about wide-eyed like a tourist. The entrance to Mother Molly's Kitchen was literally a hole in the wall, with a door propped against it. There was no sign above the door, and no doorman either. If there had been, he'd have been outside throwing people in. Emma grabbed the door and muscled it to one side, revealing a gloomy interior full of several kinds of interesting smoke. Nina took one sniff of the various aromas that drifted out and made discreet gagging sounds. But she followed Emma in, muttering the word *exclusive* under her breath like a mantra. The floating camera bobbed uneasily over her shoulder.

Inside the drinking den, it was dark and crowded and very quiet. An anticipatory sort of quiet. The twenty or so customers were leaning against the walls, smiling unpleasantly. They were all heavily armed. Set on a card table in the middle of the room was the severed head of Emma's snitch. From the lack of blood, he'd clearly been dead for some time. Nina swallowed audibly.

'I'm assuming that isn't a good sign . . .'

Emma ignored her, raking the room with her best intimidating stare. 'So. A trap and an ambush. Twenty to one odds. Am I supposed to be impressed? I'm *Emma Steel*, from Mistworld. Right; you are all under arrest for being criminally stupid in a built-up area. Drop your weapons, and I'll take you in alive.'

No one moved. The Durandal had clearly found some real hard cases to send against her this time. Trained killers. Emma did her best to radiate confidence. She just might have bitten off more than she could chew, but she couldn't let them believe that, or the fight would be over before it started. At least they couldn't use disrupters in such a confined space, for fear of hitting each other. So: twenty experienced swordsmen against one. Not good. Not impossible, but definitely not good. Emma gave them her best disturbing stare.

'All right, gentlemen, let's dance. Nina, stay in the doorway. You don't want to get blood on your clothes.'

'Oh, hell with that, darling.'

There was a flash of blindingly bright light and a roar like thunder, and seven of the swordsmen and half the wall behind them disappeared in a moment. Emma shook her head to clear it, and looked behind her. Nina was holding the biggest and nastiest handgun Emma had ever seen. Nina smiled brightly.

'Well really, you didn't think I'd come into the Rookery unarmed, did you, darling? My great-uncle Flynn picked this up during the Great Rebellion. He was in the news business too, and he always believed in being prepared. Shall I shoot some more of them?'

The would-be ambushers were already disappearing through the hole in the wall, and fighting each other to get out first. They weren't being paid enough to face guns like that. Emma could have grabbed the last few, but she didn't see the point. They wouldn't know anything. Finn undoubtedly hired them through a series of cut-outs. She turned to Nina, who was slipping her oversized gun back into her shoulder bag, and smiled at her for the first time.

'Nina, how would you like exclusive rights to follow me around on patrol, day to day?'

'Gosh, really? A whole series with my name on it? I could write my own ticket!' She stopped abruptly and looked at Emma. 'What's the catch?'

'The catch is you'll probably get killed, hanging around with me. But if you're game, I promise you exclusives like no one else has ever seen.'

'We're going to be partners? Comrades in arms? Best chums?' Nina grabbed Emma in a fierce bearhug. 'Oh, Mummy is going to be so proud!'

In the House of Parliament, King Douglas sat slumped on his throne, not really listening to the lacklustre debates on the floor. No one noticed his lack of interest or involvement, or if they did no one cared. The Speaker had been bypassed, made irrelevant, and everyone knew it. But behind his disinterested facade, Douglas was doing some hard thinking. He was quietly plotting on how best to wrest his power back from those who'd usurped it. He couldn't do much on his own, which meant he needed allies. His first thought had been to turn to his old comrades, the Paragons, but most of them were still scattered across the Empire on their quest. And the few who had returned were . . . different. Altered. Strange. They showed no interest in taking up their old duties, and their general conduct was appalling. What had happened to them, alone out there in the dark? Douglas had to wonder if their failure to find the blessed Owen had broken their spirit in some way.

There weren't many MPs left he felt like trusting. The espers had retired to the floating city of New Hope and battened down the hatches, and Shub went its own way, as always. The few people he'd considered friends had either betrayed him or distanced themselves from what everyone saw as a broken force. Being too close to the King was the kiss of death these days, in politics or society. That just left the clones and the aliens. The clones were tied to Finn, and the aliens had troubles of their own. The King had been isolated.

Douglas was also very concerned that he still hadn't been able to get any news about his father. House Campbell was strictly off limits to everyone, very definitely including him. Finn kept promising the media the full story of William's treachery, but he was in no hurry. No one had seen the inside of House Campbell since Finn's raid. The continuing silence worried Douglas almost to distraction, but he didn't let anyone see it. He just worked doggedly on his plan to break into House Campbell, rescue his father and get him somewhere safe. If he could hold himself together long enough. And if his father was still alive . . .

Douglas suddenly realised that Meerah Puri was speaking to him directly from the floor of the House, trying to get him involved in the debate. Douglas deliberately slumped down a little further in his throne, and nodded vaguely to her. Meerah Puri was one of the few politicians left in the House that he still approved of, and he had no doubt she meant well, but Douglas had to play his role of the beaten man in public. He needed Finn, and his people, to believe that he was beaten, that the King was no threat to them or their plans. So they wouldn't see him coming until it was too late. But Meerah Puri persisted in addressing him, so he reluctantly sat up and paid attention.

'Your majesty, it is the expressed will of this House, and of the people, that the King needs a Queen. The people need a King and a Queen. So the honourable Members of this House have, after lengthy discussions, finally made a decision as to who should be your new wife and Queen.'

Douglas gave her a hard look. He couldn't believe they'd slipped this past him. 'This is the first I've heard.'

'Yes, but you were . . . incommunicado for some time, your majesty.'

'So I was. Well, I see the necessity, I suppose. Who have you chosen this time?'

There was a blare of recorded trumpets and beaming brother James came striding on to the floor of the House, on his arm a very beautiful and entirely voluptuous woman dressed in the height of revealing fashion. She was extremely blonde, utterly devastating, and if she'd been any more curvaceous there would have been two of her. Douglas recognised her immediately. Treasure Mackenzie, lead actress and star of the Empire's most popular vid soap, *The Quality*.

So, thought Douglas cynically, *they've gone for beauty rather than brains this time. Probably just as well, really.*

Treasure and James came to a halt before the throne, and Douglas went down to greet them. Treasure curtsied very low, in a graceful rustle of silks, showing off more cleavage than Douglas had seen in one place in his life. James actually blushed and looked away, and couldn't let go of her arm fast enough. Douglas bowed to Treasure, and reached out to take her tiny hand in his.

'Please rise, my dear. That's better. You look delightful. This is your will, to be my Queen? You understand the responsibilities you will be taking on?'

'Oh yes, your majesty,' said Treasure, in her trademarked breathy voice. 'I couldn't be happier about this. Are you . . . happy about this, Douglas?'

He smiled at her. He couldn't say no, in front of everyone. It would have been like disappointing a child.

'A King must marry. I've always known that. And you seem to me . . . a perfect choice.'

'And I'm to be the best man,' said James.

'Of course,' murmured Douglas. 'You always are, James.' He looked across at Meerah Puri. 'I approve the House's choice. Set a date for the royal wedding.'

And while the House cheered, and James applauded loudly, and Treasure beamed and dimpled becomingly, Douglas smiled and nodded and considered his position. He couldn't say no to a royal wedding, the people needed it too badly. They wanted to put the bad business of Lewis and Jesamine behind them, and they needed something good to look forward to, to take their minds off the coming Terror and the Paragons' continuing failure to find Owen. Treasure seemed a safe enough choice. Typical actress bimbo, mouthful of teeth and a bra full of talent, too dim to make political trouble. It would be a marriage in name only, but he was sure she knew that.

He'd already given his heart to another, and nothing had happened to change that.

Afterwards, Treasure Mackenzie looked in her mirror and smiled her true smile. It had gone much better than she'd expected. But then, only a very few people present had known that she was also Frankie, Dark Mistress of the Hellfire Club. She laughed aloud. She couldn't wait to be Queen.

THREE

MY RED HEAVEN

On the bridge of the hijacked yacht *Hereward*, Brett Random and Rose Constantine were doing their best to kill each other again. They stamped back and forth in the confined space, slamming their swords together with vicious strength, each trying to catch the other off guard. They circled slowly, eyes intent and focused, breathing heavily, faces wet with the sweat of their exertions. Rose was grinning, Brett was cold and grim. They sprang at each other again, cutting and blocking and re-engaging almost too quickly to be followed. Rose had been the undoubted champion of the Logres Arena, never defeated in any of her many matches; but Brett was holding his own, and more. They'd been duelling non-stop for almost forty minutes now, and neither had managed even to touch the other. Which was a whole new record.

Rose had determined to teach Brett how to fight after witnessing his miserable performance against the attack troops on Unseeli. Brett knew how to defend himself; you couldn't grow up in the Rookery without acquiring a working knowledge of most weapons, but he was no fighter and would be the first to admit it. Too soft-hearted, he would have said with a smile and a shrug. Brett firmly believed that there wasn't a problem in the world or off it that couldn't best be solved by running away from it. He also believed in letting other people do the fighting whenever possible, while he hung innocently round the edges keeping an eye out for any tasty items that were asking to be picked up and pocketed by a nimble-fingered fellow. Brett was a thief, a conman and a devout coward, and he figured that was enough professions for any one man. But Rose was having none of it. She still wasn't sure how she felt about Brett, but she definitely didn't want him getting himself killed before she made up her mind. So she took it upon herself to teach Brett everything she knew about how to handle a sword, and she knew a hell of a lot. Brett, not for the first time, didn't get a say in the matter.

So the two of them spent most of their trip duelling ferociously on the *Hereward*'s bridge. Brett picked it up extremely quickly, not least because Rose was quite willing to cut him a good one if he didn't pay attention, and it wasn't long before the two of them were almost equally matched. No one else could have mastered Rose's many skills so quickly, but the telepathic bond forged between Brett and Rose when he first took the damned esper drug was still operating, on deep, dark, and unexpected levels. Rose only had to show him something once, and it was as though he'd always known it. The sword seemed alive in his hand, responsive as a lover, and the more he learned the more easily it came. All he needed now was practice, to hone his reflexes and build muscle tone, and Rose sharpened his skills in the only way she knew how: by doing her level best to kill him every time they duelled. Brett did his best to kill her too; it was only polite. And so they stamped and lunged and parried, putting everything they had into every blow, duelling on long after anyone else would have had to stop.

But finally the timer they'd set in the bridge's comm panels went off, and they disengaged and stepped cautiously back from each other, breathing harshly as they slowly lowered their swords. They'd learned the hard way that they had to have a timer. Because sometimes the intensity of their duelling took them to another place, where nothing mattered but the clash of steel on steel and the search for heart's blood. Where they would have duelled one another to exhaustion before either would give up. They put away their swords and nodded respectfully to each other, struggling to get their breath under control. Brett produced a handkerchief with someone else's monogram on it and wiped his face. Rose looked at him almost fondly.

'You make a good pupil, Brett. There's not much left I can teach you. But you'll never be able to beat me. Not until you develop the killer's instinct.'

'I'll never beat you,' said Brett, 'because you're a homicidal bloody psychopath.'

Rose shrugged. 'It's a gift. I can't take any credit for it.'

They stared at each other for a while, their breathing slowing, and then Rose moved over to stand before Brett. She studied his face intently.

'This is all new to me, Brett. I never had a pupil before. Never had a partner, or a friend.'

She stopped, considering the matter thoughtfully. Brett stood very still. Rose was never more dangerous than when she was thinking. Besides, he didn't understand their relationship either, and he was curious to hear what she would come up with.

'I never needed anyone else in my life,' said Rose. 'Never wanted anyone, except to kill. As long as I had the Arena, and the blood and the suffering, I was content. Murder was sex, the killing stroke my orgasm. And I was happy. Then our minds touched, and in the moment I saw things . . . emotions, feelings, possibilities I'd never considered before. Sex was different for you; a joining, sharing thing. It was so much . . . more. I want to feel those things, even if I'm not sure why. I like teaching you . . . I like seeing you become more like me. But there are things only you can teach me.'

'Oh yes?' said Brett.

She moved another step closer. Brett stood his ground. It was like having a wild animal come out of the jungle and walk right up to you to stare curiously into your eyes. He could feel beads of sweat forming on his forehead again. Their mouths were so close they could feel each other's breath on their lips. They were both breathing heavily again, almost in rhythm. Rose was frowning slightly, as though considering a difficult problem. And then her blood-red leathers creaked as she took him cautiously, gently, into her murderous arms.

In the cargo bay of the *Hereward*, in a rough nest he'd made from boxes of the alien porn data crystals, the reptiloid Saturday was fast asleep. He'd been sleeping ever since they left Unseeli, his emerald green belly swollen and distended with the people he'd eaten. He smiled toothily in his sleep, and occasionally his tail or his clawed hands would twitch as he dreamed happy dreams of slaughter and feeding.

None of the others had any intention of waking him until they absolutely had to. And then they'd do it from a safe distance, probably using something long they could poke him with.

While Brett and Rose grew closer, and the reptiloid slept, Lewis Deathstalker and Jesamine Flowers caught up on their quality time. To be exact, they'd taken over the main cabin, locked the door securely and hadn't left the bed for two days. Except for certain necessary trips to the food synthesiser or the bathroom. They were currently standing together at the foot of the bed, both entirely naked, looking at themselves in the full-length mirror on the wall. Jesamine was frowning. She studied her famous face and figure with critical, merciless eyes, turning this way and that to check all the angles and find her best side. Lewis stood easily beside her, one arm draped companionably around her slim waist. When he looked at them both together in the mirror, he saw Beauty and the Beast and wondered, not for the first time, what someone so breathtakingly beautiful saw in an ugly brute like him.

'Oh God,' said Jesamine. 'I look awful.'

'What are you talking about?' said Lewis. 'You look wonderful. You always look wonderful. If you were any more perfect, you'd be banned as harmful to the eyes.'

'I've got a roll of fat around my middle, my tits are sagging and I'm actually afraid to turn round and look at my bum. I can feel it heading towards the floor as we speak. This is what having to live without full-time beauty technicians does to a woman. I'm not as young as I was, you know. Once a woman reaches a certain age, she has to spend a lot of time taking care of herself or it falls apart in the middle of the night and she wakes up looking like her mother. It's a fact.'

'You look fine to me,' said Lewis. 'You look great. I wouldn't change an inch.'

'You say the sweetest things, darling man.' Jesamine kissed him absently on the cheek, and then went back to studying herself in the mirror.

Lewis sighed, but had enough sense to do it internally. Even with his limited experience of women, he knew they were venturing on to dangerous ground here. Women never saw themselves as they really were; inside they were always judging themselves against some imaginary perfect image they picked up in their youth and never broke free from. Jesamine Flowers was famous as one of the most gorgeous women in an Empire full of beautiful women, and here she was scowling at her reflection as though she'd just acquired jowls and a moustache. Lewis looked at himself, and had no illusions. He was built for stamina, not speed, and his muscles were made for action, not posing. He let the fingertips of one hand trail unhurriedly across the various new scars he'd acquired since leaving Logres. There were quite a few of them, from swords and guns and explosions. Places where death had touched him briefly, in passing. Scars were a new thing for Lewis. As a Paragon on Logres he'd had automatic access to regeneration machines, so that even the worst wounds never left a permanent mark on him. The *Hereward* had no regen tank. He had to heal naturally, and he hated it. It was slow and uncomfortable, it interrupted his thinking; and it left scars.

As if he wasn't ugly enough already.

Jesamine put a gentle hand over his, as it traced a long scar down his left side. 'You got that one fighting to protect me, in Traitors' Hall, in the Bloody Tower. I remember. You've been through so much pain, for my sake.'

'You're worth it,' said Lewis. 'I was never really happy, never really alive, till I met you.'

Jesamine laughed quietly, and put an arm round his waist. 'You always know the right things to say, my dear. But when this is over, you're going straight into a regeneration tank and we're getting rid of those awful scars.'

'They serve a purpose,' said Lewis, his harsh features falling into familiar dark lines. 'These scars are reminders, to be more careful, more thoughtful about everything I do, because I can be killed so easily out here, and so can you. If you were killed . . . I wouldn't want to go on living, without you.'

She kissed him, to stop him saying such things, and afterwards Jesamine looked at Lewis's face for a long time, tracing its harsh lines with a gentle fingertip. 'You have a face like a force of nature, Lewis. Hard, unyielding, but not unattractive. You could have altered it. Become anonymously handsome, like everyone else. Why did you never change it?'

'Because then I wouldn't have looked like me any more. It would have been like wearing a mask. Wearing a lie. With me, what you see is pretty much what you get. I never changed my appearance for the same reason Anne never changed hers. Because we're proud of who we are.'

They both turned away from the mirror at the same time, and sat down together on the end of the bed. There were things they needed to talk about, things they'd been putting off, but the time had come. They could feel it. Lewis jumped in first, as he always did.

'We can't go to Haden. We're not ready, Jes. Not yet.'

'Yes.'

'Have you ever been to Lachrymae Christi before?'

'God, no, darling! Can't think of many who have, by choice. It may not be a leper colony any more, but it's still a desolate bloody place by all accounts, at the arse end of civilisation with no comforts to speak off and not a single theatre worth playing. Whole planet is one big jungle; and they probably eat tourists on sight.'

'We have to go there, Jes.'

'I know, I know . . .'

'Tobias Moon is there. Still alive, supposedly. The only remaining survivor of the Madness Maze, from the age of the Great Rebellion. Owen's companion, and his friend. If he is still alive, and if he'll talk to us, Moon could tell us things that no one else could.'

'Not the only Maze survivor,' said Jesamine. 'Samuel Chevron turned out to be really John Silence, remember?'

'Was he? He claimed to be Chevron to us and Silence to Carrion, but he also claimed to be dead. So I think I'll take everything he said with several grains of salt. Until I've some way of confirming he is who he says he is.'

'Carrion recognised him as Silence.'

'Carrion has been living as an Ashrai for two centuries. After that long, probably all humans look the same to him.'

'But he might be John Silence. And he said we should go straight to Haden.' Jesamine frowned, and shuddered suddenly. 'He wanted us to go into the Madness Maze. I don't think I could do that, Lewis. Not ever. It might kill us, or make us something other than human, and I don't know which scares me the most.'

'I think we're all scared of the Maze, Jes,' said Lewis, kissing her bare shoulder reassuringly. 'All the more reason to acquire as much dependable information as we can before we even think about going anywhere near Haden. Besides, Haden is the one place Finn will be sure to think we're going to. You can bet good money he's arranged a really nasty surprise for us there. No. First Tobias Moon, and then we'll think about Haden. And the Maze.'

'He could be dead. No one's seen Moon for years.'

'He was a Hadenman, before he went into the Maze. God knows what he was afterwards.'

'I don't think God has anything to do with the Maze,' Jesamine said softly.

Some time later, fully dressed and properly turned out, they went back to the bridge. Rose was sitting cross-legged on the floor in one corner, polishing her sword blade with long easy strokes of the cloth. She didn't look up at their entrance. Brett was sitting slumped in the pilot's chair, scowling at nothing. He jumped up immediately Lewis came in, and slouched over to lean against the far wall. Lewis hid a smile. He knew what was wrong with Brett Random. The conman had emptied the medicine cabinet of every drug worth taking, and never being one to plan ahead where his pleasures were concerned, had used them all up. Brett had spent the last several days entirely sober, loudly declaring it to be an unnatural state, and he hated it. Even alien porn had lost its thrill. Although he would never have admitted it, Brett was actually grateful to Rose for insisting on duelling lessons. They stopped him going crazy from boredom. He shot Lewis and Jesamine a sulky glare for being so cheerful.

'Well, look who's finally emerged from the Cabin of Joy. I take it the bedroom gymnastics are over for now? You're using up your goes, you know. If you're not careful, you'll run out.'

'Oz, talk to me,' said Lewis, ignoring Brett with the ease of long practice. 'How much further to Lachrymae Christi?'

'We're there!' said the ship's AI cheerfully. 'We dropped out of hyperspace and moved into high orbit four hours ago. No one else could have got you here this quickly. I'm just a navigating fool. Grease my circuits and call me Speedy! You don't appreciate me, you know.'

'We're here?' said Lewis. 'Why didn't you tell me?'

'Because you were otherwise engaged,' Ozymandias said loftily. 'And very noisily, too. Far be it from me to interrupt. If you're ready to get involved in the mission again, I'll bring you up to date on everything that's been happening.'

'Don't you get snotty with me,' Lewis growled. 'You're just a porn smuggler's ship's AI with a quick personality overlay.'

'I'm also the only one around here who can work out hyperspace re-entry coordinates,' said Oz, unruffled. 'So keep a civil tongue in your head. I don't know what it is about Deathstalkers, but they're always really crabby first thing in the morning. I blame it on bad potty training. Now then; I've run a full scan, to the limits of my sensors, and there's no sign of Imperial ships lurking anywhere in the vicinity.'

'That's odd,' Brett said immediately. 'You'd have thought the Durandal would have sent at least one starcruiser to stop us making contact with Tobias Moon.'

'It's not odd at all,' the AI said condescendingly, 'as you'd know if you'd done your homework on Lachrymae Christi. I did provide you with complete files on the planet. Lachrymae Christi is one big jungle, full of vicious, aggressive and semi-sentient plants of such a predatory nature that animal life never got a look in here. All these plants have a mass consciousness called the Red Brain. And Big Red is apparently very picky over who gets to orbit his world. Really bad things have been known to happen to ships who don't pay attention to his warnings. The only ships allowed to land at the only starport are trading ships, strictly by appointment only. However, I have contacted one Natashia Wells at the starport, and she's willing to talk to a Deathstalker. Shall I put her on?'

'Might as well,' said Lewis.

'You don't appreciate me, you really don't.'

'Hello there, uninvited ship!' said a snappy female voice from the comm unit. 'Don't start kicking your equipment, we've lost picture again. It's going to be one of those days, I can tell, and me with one of my heads. This is Natashia Wells, hailing you from the St Beatrice Memorial Starport, letting you know that you are not at all welcome, unless you're carrying comm unit spares. Or chocolate. You aren't, are you? I thought not. If it was up to me, I'd tell you all to go to hell by the express route, but Tobias Moon vouches for you and I don't get any say in the matter.'

'At least now we know Moon is alive,' Jesamine said quietly.

'What was that?' said Natashia. 'Speak up! I hate muttering! So you're Lewis Deathstalker and companions, on the *Hereward*. You wouldn't believe what your ship was carrying the last time it tried to dock here. Anyway, you're late. We've been expecting you for days. Moon assured us you were coming a week ago, and that man is never wrong. Which is actually kind of creepy when you think about it, so let's agree not to. Now then. I have to check my list. According to Moon, sir Deathstalker, you should have with you . . . one diva, one confidence trickster, one homicidal psychopath and a reptiloid, whatever the hell that is. Is that correct?'

'Well, yes,' said Lewis. *How did Moon know that?* 'Trust me, I'm no happier about it than you are.'

'If it was up to me, I'd shoot the lot of you down right now, on general principles,' said Natashia. 'But no one ever listens to me. No good will come of this. My computers are sending you landing coordinates. Don't get it wrong. We're the only starport on the planet, with strictly limited space on the landing pads, by choice. We don't encourage visitors. Hell, we do everything but throw rocks at them and insult their mothers, and still they keep coming. So; land where you're told, and then follow directions to the nearest city. It's a bit of a walk, but you can probably use the exercise. You'll be met at Mission City, which is absolutely stuffed full of fascinating history about this planet. If you care for that sort of thing. Be sure to buy some souvenirs, as they're cluttering up the place. Talk to Hellen Adair, and she'll get you to Tobias Moon. And behave yourselves; the Death-stalker name buys you a certain amount of leeway, and Moon's usually a pretty good judge of character, for an ex-Hadenman, but even so—'

'We're not welcome,' said Lewis, interrupting a speech that threatened to go on for ever. 'Trust me, we get the point.'

'Tourists,' Natashia said succinctly, 'are like haemorrhoids. They come down, they hang around, they turn red and they're a pain in the arse. Land and be damned, and see if I care. And don't contact me again. I have some serious napping to be getting on with.'

The comm line went dead. Brett sighed heavily. 'It's all going to end in tears, I know it.'

The *Hereward* touched down uneventfully at the St Beatrice Memorial Starport. It was the only ship on the landing pads. Lewis led the way out, after instructing Ozymandias to run full security measures at all times, but not to shoot anyone unless he felt he absolutely had to. The group gathered outside the airlock and blinked about them in the grey light from the overcast sky. The landing pads were barely half a mile in diameter, surrounded on all sides by the savage crimson jungle. Not that surprisingly, there was no one there to greet them. No control tower, no customs post, no signs of human civilisation whatsoever. It was raining, a sullen persistent drizzle that dampened the spirit as well as everything else. Saturday sniffed loudly.

'This is what you woke me up for? It's cold, it's wet and the trees are the wrong colour. I suppose you're going to tell me next that I'm not allowed to kill anyone here?'

'Not without asking first,' Lewis said firmly. 'We want to make a good impression.'

'Then we should leave Brett in the ship,' said Jesamine.

'Fine by me,' said Brett. 'I don't mind. Really.'

'Shut up, Brett,' said Lewis. He checked the directions he'd been given against his internal compass. 'Mission City should be . . . that way. Two and a half miles, as the crow flies.'

'We have to walk?' said Jesamine. 'Isn't there any transport laid on for visitors in expensive shoes?'

'There aren't any roads here,' said Lewis. 'According to what I read in the files, civilisation is an occasional thing on Lachrymae Christi. The trip shouldn't be too bad. The jungle's a lot tamer now than it was in Owen's day. Come on; the sooner we get started, the sooner we'll be there.'

'I hate people who say cheerful things like that,' Brett muttered to Rose as they set out across the landing pad. 'Don't you hate people who say cheerful things like that?'

Rose nodded solemnly.

They headed for the waiting treeline. It was all very quiet, apart from the restless pattering of the rain. No sound anywhere of beast or bird or insect, because there weren't any. Their footsteps sounded loud and carrying, as though warning the jungle they were coming. Jesamine pressed in close beside Lewis.

'I've got a really bad feeling about this, Lewis. No one to meet us, no escort . . . Anything could be waiting for us in that jungle. How do we know Finn didn't get here first, make a deal with the natives and set a trap for us?'

'Oz would have detected something,' said Lewis, trying hard to sound confident. 'That porn-smuggler's ship has state-of-the-art sensors, and then some. I wouldn't have landed here unless I was reasonably sure we got here first. Don't worry, Jes. I promised you that I would stand between you and all harm. Come what may.'

Jesamine smiled, despite herself. 'My hero. All right, next worrying question. Why does Mission City have to be so far from the starport? Apart from the fact that they clearly don't care for visitors.'

'They don't want Empire tech too close to them,' said Lewis. 'The people here regard tech as a necessary evil, and they do without it as much as they can. My guess is they're still harbouring resentments over their ancestors being dumped here and abandoned. Didn't you read any of the files I put aside for you?'

Jesamine grinned. 'I got sidetracked, remember?' She laughed as he looked away. 'God, darling, you blush really easily for a Deathstalker.'

Lewis led the way into the scarlet jungle. The towering trees had thick black boles and heavy crimson leaves with sharp serrated edges. All around, the jutting foliage and sudden bursts of undergrowth were every shade of red, in fierce organic hues, as though they had walked inside a living body. Bright pink streamers of crawling vines and matted ivy curled around the black tree trunks, moving slowly, constantly, like dreaming snakes. Blood-red lianas and hanging vines twisted and swung slowly, though there wasn't a breath of a breeze on the still air. Even the ground was covered with pulsing scarlet mosses and mulch.

And everywhere, every part of the jungle was moving, seething, twisting and stirring, awake and aware and slowly aggressive. For millions of years there was nothing but plant life on Lachrymae Christi, until the Empire came and made it a colony. A leper colony, to be exact. There was no cure and no hope for them, so the sufferers were rounded up and dumped here, and no one gave a damn if they survived or not. For a long time there was war between the leper colonists and the unrelenting jungle, until Tobias Moon came and made telepathic contact with the mass consciousness of the plant life, the Red Brain, and brokered a symbiotic peace. At least, that was the legend. Lewis didn't have the faith in legends that he once had.

But the peace only applied in and around the cities. In the wild, the plants were just as hungry and vicious as they'd ever been. Some of the larger plants were already lurching eagerly towards the intruders with lunch on their mind. Lewis shot several of them, Rose tore several more to shreds and Brett kicked the hell out of a shrub, just to be doing his bit. Several small fires broke out, quickly smothered by surrounding plants. After that, the bigger plants pretty much ignored the party, as long as they didn't get too close. The rain kept drizzling down, and hot steam rose on the still air.

Lewis drew his sword and set about the slow progress of cutting a trail through the uncooperative mass of vegetation before him. It was hard work, and slow going. His sword jarred painfully against the heavier branches, and vines clung stickily to his blade until he jerked it free. He pressed on, his arm rising and falling mechanically while sweat dripped from his face. The others stuck close behind him, while the jungle closed the trail behind them.

The air was thick and heavy with so many scents it was like an overwhelming perfume that raised strange atavistic feelings. It was as though they belonged in the jungle, and always had. Like coming home. There was more oxygen in the air than they were used to, and it left them feeling heady and a little giddy. The rain slowed to a steady pitter-patter. The overhead canopy of interlocking tree branches was much thicker than it had been, this close to the human settlements, due to the intervention of the Red Brain. But even so, Lewis and his companions were soon soaked through, as much from sweat as rain, as they ploughed through the humid air of the uncooperative jungle. Only the reptiloid Saturday took it in his stride, the rain running easily off his scaly hide. Of them all, he should have been the most at home, but the semi-sentient jungle disturbed him greatly, and his wedge head swung constantly back and forth, alert for any attack. On his world, the plants were the only things that didn't try to kill you. He chewed on a few things experimentally, but spat them out again. Evolution had not designed Saturday to be a vegetarian.

Rose didn't approve of the jungle, and said so loudly. Rose was a city person, born and bred, and had no use for the great outdoors. She liked roads and transport and climate control, and all the other niceties of the human condition. 'Weather is what poor people have,' she said sniffily. Also killing plants did nothing for her. It seemed somehow beneath her.

Brett was miserable, but then he always was. At least no one was shooting at him here. Yet.

Lewis slogged along at the front of the group, opening a path through the stubborn jungle with his sword and occasionally the razor-sharp edges of his force shield. It was slow hard work, and even his hardened muscles grew weary in time. After one particularly long break for Lewis to get his breath back, Saturday volunteered to take over. He slammed through the crimson vegetation, using his size and bulk and weight to force open a trail, but all too soon became tangled and trapped in a seething mass of creepers and vines, and had to be cut free. The reptiliod returned to the back of the group for some serious sulking. Rose took over cutting the trail, and chopped and hacked her way through the jungle like a machine from hell. But even she grew tired eventually. She wouldn't admit it, of course, and in the end Brett had to drag her almost bodily to a halt to rest. He patted her comfortingly on her leather-clad shoulder, at arm's length, while she got her breathing back under control, her cold glare daring anyone to say anything.

'I've got a better idea,' Brett said. 'Watch this.'

Brett scowled, concentrating on the slowly stirring vegetation before him, and then hit it with a focused blast of his esp compulsion. The scarlet and pink foliage shook and shuddered under the impact of his mind and then retreated out of the way, so that a narrow trail opened up before the group as if by magic. Brett crowed loudly, and did a little celebratory dance. But his sense of triumph was short-lived; something reached out of the dark, secret heart of the jungle and touched his exposed mind. Brett froze where he was, as a vast alien presence slowly turned its attention upon him. It was like a huge eye, studying him coldly. And he was so very, very small. Brett hadn't been so scared since he'd glimpsed the esper oversoul, back on Logres. This was worse. At least the oversoul had a human nature. The Red Brain was different, utterly inhuman. It was just too big, too much for him to bear, and he slammed down his mental shields, concealing his thoughts and his presence behind as many layers of barriers as he could fashion.

Only a few seconds had passed. No one else had noticed anything. Lewis was still studying the newly opened trail. Rose was looking at Brett thoughtfully, but that was nothing new.

'All right, Brett,' said Lewis. 'I am officially impressed. How the hell did you do that?'

Brett looked at the trail ahead. It was still keeping its shape, even though he wasn't holding it open any more. Presumably the Red Brain had decided to let things stand. He realised Lewis was waiting for an answer, and spoke absently, still too shaken to even think of lying.

'It's part of the esp I gained from taking Finn's damned esper drug. I can make things obey me.'

'Things?' Lewis said. 'Not . . . people?'

'Oh, no!' Brett said quickly, his self-preservation instincts kicking in. 'Heaven forfend, sir Deathstalker! What do you think I am? Some kind of ELF? I do have principles, you know. Not as many as other people, perhaps, but . . .'

Lewis gave him a hard look, and then turned away and set off along the new trail.

It kept opening up before them, and the going became much easier. But still the ground was uneven and treacherous, and the trail swerved and weaved around the huge dark-boled trees. They slogged on, and time passed slowly, and still there was no sign of Mission City. The relentless drip drip drip of rain did nothing to improve anyone's temper, and no one was talking to anyone any more because it always led to arguments and they didn't have the energy. Jesamine could feel the others shooting her the occasional speculative glance, clearly waiting for her to start whinging again about being a star, and how she shouldn't have to put up with conditions like this. So she gritted her teeth and toughed it out, keeping grimly silent just to spite them. Her back ached, her legs were trembling from the strain, her shoes were ruined and her feet weren't listening to her, but she was damned if she'd give the others the satisfaction of hearing her complain. Even Lewis, who would of course be very understanding.

Jesamine was getting tougher, and she was stronger than she'd thought. She took pride in keeping up the pace with the rest of them, and started to remember how proudly self-reliant she'd always been when she was younger and starting out on her career. When she'd had to fight her way on and off stage, and face down sleazy managers afterward to get the wages owed her. It occurred to Jesamine that she preferred this new tough her to the old pampered her, though she was damned if she'd admit that to anyone, even Lewis.

For all their struggle through the crimson jungle, the group couldn't help but be impressed by it. The jungle was so big, and old, and overpoweringly alien. With the gloom of the overhead canopy, and the sudden shafts of light breaking through like spotlights in the blood-red ambience, it was like walking through some vast living cathedral. Lewis found the words of the AIs of Shub running through his mind like a mantra: *All that lives is holy* . . . Everywhere he looked he saw miracles of evolution, sophisticated refinements of shape and purpose that had no place in the world of ordinary plants. Everything was moving, driven on by slow intent. Some of the larger growths lurched back and forth under their own volition, on unguessable errands for unknowable reasons. Here and there lush flowers had developed mouths, and chittered softly in languages beyond human understanding, unless it was the kind of words people heard softly spoken in dreams, and could never remember on waking. Some flowers had learned to sing, in strange and subtle harmonies; and this was sometimes horrid and sometimes pleasant, but mostly disturbing. Jesamine tried to sing along, but couldn't follow the patterns and subtle shifts in tone. Her voice clashed and shattered against such alien sounds.

Finally they came to Mission City. The jungle fell suddenly away, like stepping out of one room and into another, and the city lay sprawled out before them in its massive clearing. Lewis and his companions just stood there for a while, at the edge of the jungle, taking in the city they had travelled so long and so hard to reach. Mission City was no human construction, no dead thing of steel and glass and concrete; this was a Lachrymae Christi city, a vast bio-engineered entity, grown not made, designed by the minds of men but manufactured to order from the raw materials of the scarlet jungle by the guiding intelligence of the Red Brain. It was a living thing, holding humans within, like a mother cradling her children in her caring arms.

Huge hollowed trees, vast as skyscrapers, soared up into the overcast sky, their interiors a wooden honeycomb of living space. Warm lights glowed from the hundreds of windows in the dark bark of the towering trees. Delicate corridors of woven vines connected the levels, hanging between the trees like so much crimson webbing, the connective tissues of a living city. Lower dwellings had been formed from hulking gourds or vast hollowed fruits or leafy constructs in blazing shades of pink. And everywhere there were flowers, and great rose petal constructs, and tremendous organic shapes blazing with warm friendly lights. It was a city, and it was alive. They could feel the warmth of it, and hear its breathing. And men and women went about their lives in it as though it was the most natural thing in the world.

Lewis put away his sword and started forward, and the others followed him. None of them had anything to say; in an Empire whose Golden Age was full of wonders, this was still something very new and marvellous. People saw them coming, and disappeared unhur-riedly into the nearest dwelling. There was something not quite right about them, but Lewis couldn't put his finger on it. He came to a halt at the edge of the city, and looked about him for some clue as to what to do next.

'I suppose our home must seem impressive to outsiders,' said a warm amused voice. 'But you should see it in the spring. The whole place really comes alive then.'

They looked round sharply, and there was a short stocky woman smiling at them. Lewis hadn't heard her coming. He made himself take his hand away from the gun at his side.

'You have a beautiful home,' he said. 'I had no idea.'

'We don't advertise. We don't want to attract sight-seers. It's all very efficient, you know. The plant life is nourished by the carbon dioxide we breathe out, and the wastes we deposit in it. We're all part of one big symbiosis, really.'

'Do I take it you're Hellen Adair?' said Lewis.

'Got it in one, Deathstalker. About time you got here. We've been expecting you for days.'

'Moon again?' said Jesamine, and Hellen grinned and nodded.

'He really can see the future, sometimes. Which raises all kinds of philosophical questions, which mostly we try not to think about for the sake of a quiet life. So: that's what a reptiloid is.'

'*Lewis*,' Brett said urgently into Lewis's ear. '*She's naked!*'

'Trust me, I noticed,' Lewis murmured back.

Hellen Adair was blonde, pretty enough, with a good if slightly over-muscled figure, and hadn't got a stitch of clothing on. Her skin was a glowing pink, of the shade Lewis usually only associated with gums, and her only adornment was a few flowering vines she'd wrapped around her waist. She smiled at them.

'No one bothers with clothes here. Why should we? The city is tailored to our every need, and the rain and what little weather there is in our balanced ecosystem doesn't bother us. In the old days, the colonists had to hide their bodies because of what leprosy had done to them. But the disease is long gone, and we are all in excellent condition, as you can see. With the Red Brain on our side, this is a perfect world for people to live in; so, we're naked. I trust this isn't going to be a problem?'

She was looking at Brett as she said that, and he quickly averted his eyes from her breasts.

'Don't let him bother you,' said Jesamine. 'Just hit him if he gets annoying. We do.'

'Come with me,' said Hellen Adair. 'And stay close. We don't normally allow outsiders into our city, and we wouldn't now if Moon hadn't told me one of you was a Deathstalker. That is a worshipped name here.'

'You know where Moon is?' said Lewis.

'You'll get to meet him, in time. For the moment there is something here he wants you to see. Follow me.'

She led them through the living city, down leafy ways and through petalled corridors, across great open squares with blossoming displays. All the structures had rounded organic shapes, and fat pulpy flowers formed living mosaics. These were always changing, as the flowers opened and closed in subtly altered positions, so that the images were never still. Lewis was particularly taken with a broad beautiful face that slowly widened its smile and winked one eye as he passed. Perfumes hung heavily on the air, heady and stimulating, like taking in heaven with every breath. And everywhere now the colonists, strolling naked through their Eden, calm and unhurried and utterly indifferent to the strangers in their midst. Lewis and Jesamine did their best to keep their gaze to themselves. Brett tried, not particularly successfully. He was wishing he still had a camera in his eye. He could have sold this recording for a fortune. Several fortunes. Rose and Saturday didn't care at all; human nudity meant nothing to them.

'I don't see any toil,' said Lewis. 'What do people do here?'

'We have no need or wish for business or machinery,' Hellen said easily. 'Essentially, we're gardeners. We tend to the needs of the plants. We prune, we dig out weeds, we prevent overcrowding and we encourage propagation in some species and discourage it in others. We also keep a watchful eye on the more aggressive examples, and destroy any which threaten to develop their own form of sentience. One Red Brain is quite enough to cope with. In return for our services, the Red Brain allows us to fell trees, gather fruit and harvest crops. All of which have a ready market waiting for them out in the Empire. There are many species here unknown and unparalleled on any other world.'

'Damn right,' said Brett, reluctantly tearing his gaze away from a particularly statuesque redhead, as Jesamine elbowed him in the ribs. 'They have fruits here the taste of which you wouldn't believe. Grapes that make wine to die for, and any furniture made from Lachrymae Christi lumber can pretty much command its own price. Goods from this planet are always in short supply. The colonists see to that; right, Hellen? Treat them mean, keep them keen, and the price never goes down. Scientists have been trying to synthesise your products in their labs for centuries, to no result. Though there are those who say the esper drug came from here originally, distilled from the nerve fibres of the Red Brain itself.'

'You had to spoil the mood, didn't you?' said Jesamine. 'Nasty little man. Here we are, walking through paradise, and all you can think of is drugs.'

'Another reason we're not too keen on outsiders,' said Hellen. 'There are always those unwilling to leave good enough alone. Certain business interests are always trying to set up shop here, legally or illegally. They want to introduce mechanisation, to increase productivity. They want to set up labs to turn our produce into drugs. They'd strip mine this world to feed the greed of their customers, if they could. They hear we have no weapons, no army, and they think we're defenceless. Fools. The jungle is our weapon, and the only defence we need. The Red Brain watches over us. And Tobias Moon, of course.'

'What is the relationship between the Red Brain and Tobias Moon?' said Lewis, carefully casual. He'd been trying to turn the conversation that way for some time, without seeming too eager. He needed to know just what he'd be dealing with, when the time finally came to confront Tobias Moon.

'They exist in perfect symbiosis,' Hellen said. 'Just as we do, with our cities. The Red Brain takes the long view, the wide view, while Moon remains focused on the everyday needs and problems of those who live and work here. If you like, the Red Brain is our God, and Tobias Moon his prophet.'

'No,' said Jesamine. 'I don't think I like that idea at all.'

Hellen laughed. 'It's just a way of thinking about it. Don't worry; our God doesn't require sacrifices. Unless it's been a really bad harvest. Joke! Try ... try thinking of the Red Brain as a great computer, and Moon his programmer. Does that help?'

'A little,' said Lewis.

Rose and Brett hung back, so they could talk quietly together. Lewis and Jesamine were clearly charmed by the manifold delights of Mission City, and that worried Brett. In his experience the prettiest face was always a disguise for the greatest danger, and the knife in the back always came when you were least expecting it. He couldn't shake off the feeling that they were walking blithely into some carefully concealed trap. He murmured as much to Rose, and she nodded.

'Ugly place. Overgrown with weeds. This is no way for people to live. No action, no challenges. Bunch of damned hippie tree-huggers.' Rose sniffed loudly. 'Living in harmony with the natural world, my arse. The natural world will bite your head off, given half a chance. You have to tame it, regulate it, stamp it underfoot. The jungle's more honest than this place. Real nature is kill or be killed, red in tooth and claw. Always has been. The Deathstalker had better smarten up and keep his eyes open, or we could all end up as fertiliser for their mighty God Plant.'

'Thanks a whole bunch,' Brett said gloomily. 'Now I feel even worse, if that's possible.' He peered unhappily about him. 'This isn't my kind of place either. Nothing worth stealing, no one to con . . . there are supposed to be roots and weeds here that Dr Happy and his breed would pay serious money for, but I couldn't pick them out of this mess to save my life. And how can you bribe information out of people who already think they're living in paradise, the fools? God, I'd kill for a drink. This place is far too healthy for the likes of me. I want to go home.'

'If this does turn out to be a trap,' Rose said dreamily, 'I'll bet this city would burn up real good . . .'

'I do hope you realise how rare it is for Tobias Moon to agree to meet you,' Hellen Adair was saying to Lewis. 'In fact, I don't think he's seen any offworlder in person for almost a hundred and fifty years. After the legends began circulating, we got a lot of tourists here. Moon had been made into a hero and a myth, without his permission, and we had pilgrims turning up by the shipload, all determined to worship at his feet and pester him for wisdom. So he withdrew into the embrace of the Red Brain, and vanished from sight. Only a very few people know his location these days, and he rarely speaks even to them. To speak with Moon in person is the highest privilege you can aspire to, in this world. And then you turn up, and nothing will do but that Moon has to speak to you immediately. A lot of people had their noses put out of joint over that. But you're a Deathstalker, and that name carries a lot of currency here. Owen made all this possible. He came here when we were lepers, outcast and despised by the rest of Humanity. He walked among us, and taught us how to be strong and proud again. He fought alongside us against the Hadenmen and the Grendels, and worked miracles in our defence.'

'Does Moon ever talk about Owen?' said Lewis.

'No.' Hellen frowned for the first time. 'He never talks about those days. Perhaps he will, to you. We don't know why he's so keen to talk to you, or what he has to say. When you've finished your conversation, whatever turns it may take, I suggest you go back to your ship and get the hell off this world. A lot of people are going to be really upset about being excluded from this meeting. You may be a Deathstalker, but you're clearly no Owen, and as for your companions—'

There was a vicious rasp of steel as Rose drew her sword. 'What about us?'

'Rose, put that sword away!' Lewis's voice cracked like a whip, but Rose didn't react as she advanced on Hellen.

'I've had enough of this snotty cow,' Rose said casually. 'So up herself just because she lives in a cabbage patch. Treating us like shit, like we're only here on sufferance. We're here to talk to Moon, bitch, and you don't get a say in the matter.'

'I'd put that sword away, if I were you,' said Hellen Adair. She hadn't budged an inch, and she met Rose's cold gaze squarely.

'Or what?' said Rose. 'You'll bash me over the head with a flower?'

'Something like that,' said Hellen.

Vines snapped out of the surroundings like living whips, and wrapped themselves around Rose in a moment. They tightened painfully, cutting into her flesh through her leathers, but she never made a sound. She tried to struggle, and more vines lashed out to envelop her. Brett's hand went to the gun at his side, but Jesamine was quickly there beside him, her hand on top of his, holding it firmly in place. Saturday looked to Lewis, who shook his head quickly.

'Please release our friend,' Lewis said to Hellen. 'She may be crazy, but she means well. Mostly. Either way, she's with me and I vouch for her behaviour.'

'This is our world,' Hellen said calmly to Rose. 'It harbours and protects us. It is alive and aware, because the Red Brain is in every part of it. And Moon is always listening. Now are you going to behave, or shall I have the city thread a barbed vine up your arse, through your guts and out of your eye?'

'She'll behave,' said Lewis. 'I guarantee it. On my honour as a Deathstalker.'

'She's not worth it,' said Hellen. 'She'll betray you in the end. Her kind always does.'

'She is my friend, sworn to my cause,' said Lewis. 'Now release her. Unless you want to take me on as well.'

Hellen looked at him thoughtfully for a moment, and then nodded abruptly. The vines slowly loosened and unwrapped themselves from around Rose. Brett helped her pull free, and everyone watched to see what she would do. She put her sword away, and nodded to Lewis, as calm and cold as always.

'Thank you, Deathstalker. She would have killed me, you know,

140

just to make a point. She has her own agenda here. Don't trust her.'

'Everyone has their own agenda,' said Lewis.

Hellen brought them to the heart of the city: St Beatrice's Mission, or what was left of it. The original rough buildings had been carefully maintained down the years as a shrine to the memory of the blessed St Beatrice, the simple nun who came to tend the dying lepers of Lachrymae Christi because she thought it was the right thing to do. Lewis and his companions were astonished. They had no idea the original mission still existed; no one in the Empire did. It was a place of legend, of mystery, of awe. Hellen left them at the gates to the courtyard, and said she'd be back for them later. After they'd seen what Moon wanted them to see. For a long time, none of them moved. It seemed a small and shabby place, compared to its mythic status in the story of Owen Deathstalker and St Beatrice, but just being there took their breath away. To be where legends had been carved out of history, to walk where heroes walked . . .

Lewis moved slowly forward across the packed-earth courtyard, and the others followed him. They were all affected to some degree, even Saturday. The place fairly radiated weight and significance. Vital matters had been decided here, where a small group of people had beaten off overwhelming inhuman odds. Stretching away before them were two rows of wooden stakes, forming a long path, and on every spike was impaled the severed head of a Grendel. There were hundreds of the ugly things, shining scarlet heart-shaped heads that had no human element in them. Grendels were living killing machines, bastard children of the Madness Maze, long and long ago. Deadly, implacable, unstoppable. Except here. Jesamine pressed in close beside Lewis, holding his hand almost painfully tight.

'These creatures died over two hundred years ago,' she whispered. 'Why haven't the heads decayed?'

Lewis shrugged uneasily. 'Maybe Grendels don't decay. They were famous for being indestructible.'

'I killed one,' said Rose.

'Yes, but you cheated,' said Brett.

Rose sniffed. 'I won, didn't I?'

'You killed one,' Lewis said shortly. 'Owen and Hazel killed dozens. Sometimes with their bare hands.'

'You're right,' said Rose. 'That is impressive.'

'I would have liked to meet a Grendel,' said Saturday, flexing his foreclaws wistfully.

'No, you wouldn't,' said Lewis. 'Trust me on this. They weren't natural creatures. They were created to be unstoppable. They only existed to kill. Their armour could shrug off energy weapons. And Owen and Hazel went head to head with hundreds of them here, and won . . . Look at those heads.'

'They give me the creeps,' said Brett. 'Like something out of a nightmare . . . How could Owen have defeated something like this?'

'Because he was a Deathstalker,' said Jesamine. 'That's why we have to find him. Because we need him now more than ever.'

They left the rows of Grendel heads behind them, and came to the old infirmary. It was a simple wooden hut, with open windows and a single doorway. Lewis led the way in, and the air was so thick with ghosts that he could hardly breathe it. He'd seen this place recreated in a hundred docudramas, Owen's last redoubt in the fight against the invading Grendels. So many dramatic scenes had been re-enacted here played by the most famous actors in the Empire: of Owen and Hazel and Beatrice, all of it legend because no one was left to tell the truth of it. But in this indisputably real place, the walls were lined with data crystals and private viewscreens, promising to reveal the truth at last. And in the middle of the room, on a raised bier under a single gentle light, lay what looked very like a coffin. They gathered round it and looked in, to see the well-preserved body of a woman in a nun's clothing. For a long time, none of them said anything.

'That can't be her, can it?' Jesamine said finally. 'Not her. Not . . .'

'St Beatrice,' said Lewis.

'It's got to be some kind of model,' said Brett.

'Not according to this plaque,' said Lewis, studying a simple brass plate at the head of the coffin. 'It's her. Preserved here, all these years.'

'Now that is seriously gross,' said Brett firmly. 'And not a little creepy. Dead bodies on display? This is barbaric! Not to mention sick.'

'I wouldn't disagree,' said Lewis. 'But I don't think it's a viewpoint we should share with the good people of this city. This is obviously a sacred place for them.'

He looked at the body's expressionless face, and tried to feel something, some of the awe he'd felt on entering the mission, but the truth was she could have been anybody. Whoever had preserved her body had done a good job, at the expense of taking all the personality out of her face. Lewis bowed his head respectfully anyway. The body seemed very small for a woman whose legend had become so huge. Every man, woman and child in the Empire knew the story of the blessed St Beatrice, who gave up wealth and standing to follow her faith; and now here she was, a waxy shrunken display piece in a museum most people didn't even know existed.

Eventually, they turned to the data crystals set out on shelves. They checked the titles, but most of it seemed to be dull history about how the colonists built their great biocities, and created a paradise out of hell. But one crystal was labelled *Owen's Defence of the Mission*, and everyone wanted to see that. Lewis plugged it into a display screen and they stood and watched. It turned out to be a series of interviews with lepers who'd survived the defence, and what they saw. When it was over, Lewis and his companions looked at each other.

'Now that really was bullshit,' said Brett, almost angrily. 'Even the official legends never said—'

'It has to be exaggerated,' said Lewis. 'Memories embellished over the years.'

'I mean, no one could do things like that!' said Brett. 'All right, the official version has Owen and Hazel as first-class warriors, death on two legs and unbeatable with a weapon in their hands. And there are the miracles they're supposed to have performed, but, but . . . triggering earthquakes, just by frowning? Blowing Grendels apart by looking at them? Shooting lightning bolts from their hands? *Owen bringing himself back from the dead?*'

'They went through the Maze,' said Lewis. 'And they were never fully human after that. Everyone who knew them said so. And some of the miracles really did happen. There were news recordings of them at the time, even if they're lost to us now. And some of the apocrypha hint at things like this. That Owen and Hazel must still be alive somewhere, because after what the Maze had done to them they *couldn't* die . . .'

'This is seriously creeping me out,' said Jesamine. 'I thought *Deathstalker's Lament* was over the top when I starred in it, but this . . . If Owen and Hazel really could do things like that, they certainly weren't human any more. No more human than the Grendels. People aren't supposed to be able to do things like *that* . . .'

'It's not real,' said Rose. 'It can't be. Just stories, grown in the telling. Owen was a great warrior, and that's enough. It's all anyone needs.'

'It's legend,' Lewis said slowly. 'But if we doubt this telling of the story, can we trust the official legends either? At least these people actually knew Owen and Hazel. Moon's still here, still alive. But . . . I saw Owen and Hazel, Jack Random and Ruby Journey. Saw the real people, in contemporary records. Shub showed them to me, and the Dust Plains of Memory. Real people . . . stirring, moving, incredibly impressive people, but not this. Not fairy tales.'

'Does it matter?' said Brett.

'Of course,' said Lewis. 'It's everything. Because only a legend has any chance of stopping the Terror when it comes.'

They all stood together, and thought about that for a while. Lewis turned off the display screen and put the data crystal back in its case on the shelf. He couldn't afford doubts. He had to be strong. Just as Owen had to be what he was believed to be; or the Empire was doomed.

'Come on, Lewis,' said Jesamine. 'Let's get out of here.'

'He went through the Madness Maze,' said Lewis. 'He came out changed. More than human. Everyone said so. You saw what Carrion could do. And Captain Silence. The stories have to be true. Because if they aren't, then Owen is dead and he isn't coming back and our quest is useless.'

'Let's go,' said Jesamine. 'We'll talk to Moon. He can tell us the truth, whatever it is.'

'Moon wanted us to come here,' said Lewis. 'To see this shrine and what it contains. Why?'

'Perhaps he wanted us to know the truth, at last,' said Jesamine. 'To let us see what Owen could do, so that we'd have the confidence, and the faith, to continue on our quest.'

'Yeah, right,' said Brett.

'Shut up, Brett.'

'I don't know what to believe any more,' said Lewis. 'So many things and people I believed in turned out to be not what I thought them to be. Even me. How can I believe in something like this?'

'Because he was a Deathstalker,' said Jesamine. 'And so are you.'

Outside the Mission, Hellen Adair was waiting for them. She didn't ask any questions, and none of them felt like saying anything, so they walked back to the boundary of the city in silence. They made one stop along the way. Lewis insisted on being allowed to go to the city cemetery, where the old leper colonists were buried. There was one grave he needed to see. He found it easily enough. A simple grave, and a simple headstone, bearing the single name *Vaughn*. It looked no different from any of the hundreds of other graves. He checked with the cemetery custodian, who looked up the old records and confirmed that there really was a body in the grave. Lewis thanked the man, and went back to look at the grave again while his companions waited more or less patiently at the gates to the cemetery.

Vaughn was dead, long dead. So who had come to Lewis at Douglas's coronation to give him Owen's ring? A ghost? Once Lewis would have said he didn't believe in such things, but Captain Silence's death had been widely reported, and still he came to help fight the good fight on Logres and Unseeli. If that really was John Silence.

You had to have faith, Lewis decided finally. In the end, it all comes down to faith. To have faith in the things that matter. To be a Deathstalker.

Hellen Adair took them to the edge of the city, and pointed them on their way. No one else was there to see them off. Lewis checked the directions carefully against his internal compass and quickly calculated the distance to be just under a mile. Hellen Adair made it clear she had no intention of going with them. This was their pilgrimage. Lewis and his companions said goodbye and thanks, with varying amounts of sincerity, and set off into the crimson jungle again.

The going was easier this time. Someone had spoken with the Red Brain, and it had spoken with its separate parts. Although there was no easing of the general aggression in the jungle as a whole, somehow the individual plants swept back out of the party's way, forming an open trail to take them to Tobias Moon. At first, Lewis had thought Brett was up to his old tricks again, but one look at the conman's uneasy face was enough to correct that impression. Brett didn't approve of other people pulling his own tricks on him. It was a steady, much less strenuous march this time. Lewis was back in the lead, and had to keep himself from pushing the pace too hard. Part of him was desperate to get to the Hadenman and finally get some straight answers about Owen and the Maze.

And part of him was really scared about what those answers might be. It is an intimidating thing, to meet legends in the flesh.

About half a mile outside Mission City, they came across the rusting remains of some misguided logging company's attempt to introduce high-tech equipment. The huge machines, several storeys high, lay wrecked and abandoned in the jungle, half buried under crawling vines and slowly shifting scarlet foliage. Crimson tracers had invaded every grille and opening, and rain drops slid constantly down the red-rusted metal. Steel panels bulged outwards from the pressure of vegetable growth within, and dark heavy branches had smashed through the steel-glass windows. Shafts of light moved across drooping cranes and saws and cutting arms. Like great beached whales of rusted steel, defeated by implacable forces, they were overgrown and being absorbed by the scarlet jungle.

When the party finally reached the exact coordinates provided by Hellen Adair, there was nothing there. Just a small clearing in the middle of nowhere, no different from a dozen others they'd already passed through. Knee-high grass of a shocking pink undulated before them in rippling waves. Lewis and his companions looked about them, feeling distinctly upset. It had been a long walk, the rain was falling more heavily and they were feeling hot and sticky.

'We've been sold a pup, haven't we?' said Brett. 'I don't want to say I told you so, but I did. They never meant for us to talk to their precious pet oracle.'

'Hush, Brett,' said Jesamine. 'This is where we're meant to be, so there must be something here. Somewhere. Right, Lewis? Lewis?'

'I'm thinking,' said Lewis.

'There is something here,' Saturday said unexpectedly. The reptiloid turned his great head slowly back and forth. 'I can feel . . . something. Perhaps because the jungle reminds me of home, a little. There's definitely something here that doesn't belong.'

'So where is Moon?' said Brett. 'Hiding up a tree, maybe? Lying down in the long grass, perhaps, having a bit of a snooze? We've been had! There's no one here! There isn't a hut or a dwelling or a big lump in the ground for as far as I can see, and I can see pretty damn far! And I'm wet. I hate being wet.'

'Something's here,' said Saturday. 'And it knows *we're* here.'

The ground trembled under their feet. The pink grass waved wildly, and then the centre of the clearing bulged suddenly upwards, the ground cracking apart, throwing dark earth in all directions. Pale roots and tubers and wet crawling things surged out of the broken earth and were thrust aside as a vast new shape emerged slowly and relentlessly from its earthy bed. A steel hull smeared with wet mud emerged from the gaping crevasse, rising up and up until at last the wreck of an old-fashioned space yacht filled the clearing, buoyed up and brought to the surface again by the concentrated will of Tobias Moon and the Red Brain. The old ship settled into its new place, half its bulk still sunk in the ground, the battered prow straining towards the overcast sky and open air for the first time in decades.

'Dear God,' said Lewis. 'That's Owen's ship. That's *Sunstrider the Second*. I'd know it anywhere.'

'Of course,' said Jesamine. 'They crash-landed here. The ship was never recovered. We're probably the first people to see it in two hundred years. Is Moon . . . inside it?'

'I suppose so,' said Lewis. 'I guess we go in.'

'Bad move,' Brett said immediately. 'That thing looks like a tomb to me. Or a prison. Or a trap. There could be anything in there. Anything.'

Rose slapped him affectionately round the back of the head. 'All that weapons training I put you through, and you're still a scaredy cat.'

'I'm a live scaredy cat,' said Brett, rubbing a bruised ear. 'I can't help feeling there's a definite connection between the two.'

'We go in,' said Lewis. 'If Moon is in there, I really don't think we should keep him waiting.' He smiled. 'Look at it. This is *Owen*'s ship. It'll be like walking into legend, into his life . . .'

'You're really easy to impress, Deathstalker, you know that?' said Brett. 'All right, it's a famous ship, and I could probably arrange a really sweet salvage deal, if you'd let me, which you won't, but . . . the ship is a mess. Look at it. This had to have been a really bad landing. The hull's split open in several places, there's no sign of the rear assemblies and Christ alone knows what happened to the sensor spikes. They must have hit the ground like the wrath of God.'

'Exactly,' said Lewis. 'And they walked away from it. Think how tough, how more than human, they would have to have been to do that.'

'So what do we do?' said Jesamine. 'Knock on the hull, and wait to be invited in?'

'There's a big opening down by the engine compartment,' Saturday said suddenly. 'And there are some strange energies radiating from it.'

They all looked at the reptiloid. 'You can see energies?' Lewis said finally.

'Oh yes. And these are really weird energies.'

'Then that is our invitation,' said Lewis.

He led them down the length of the *Sunstrider II*, heading for the stern. Up close, the old yacht looked rougher, more *real*, than it had in his imagination. He'd heard tales about this ship all his life, but . . . he could have flown a ship like this. He had the skills. He felt a tingle of almost superstitious awe as he approached the steel hull over the engine chamber. Something had smashed right through the reinforced hull, leaving a rent a dozen feet high and almost as wide. It didn't look like crash damage. Lewis swallowed hard, and led the way in, moving cautiously through the gloomy interior. Walking where Owen and his companions had walked, long ago. There was a clear path to the engine compartment, but scarlet vegetation had worked its way into the yacht over the years, lining the interior bulkheads with thick mattings of fibrous materials. It grew thicker as Lewis led the way further in, until they were walking hunched over through a narrow tunnel like a soft furry red artery.

Finally, in an enclosed space that had once held the ship's stardrive, but no longer, they found Tobias Moon. The living fibres lining the chamber glowed with a soft rosy light, illuminating the Hadenman as he sat cross-legged on the floor, his head bowed forward, his chin resting on his chest. His eyes were closed, and he didn't seem to be breathing. He was a man's size and shape but, even still and silent, there was something of dread and awe about him. He looked to be tall, but not as tall as Rose; he was broad and muscular, but not so much as Lewis. None of that mattered. This was Tobias Moon.

He was surrounded and enveloped by a mass of barbed and thorned vines that over the years had pierced and penetrated his body in a hundred places, as though plugging him into the mass plant consciousness of the Red Brain. Lewis studied the slowly pulsing crimson strands that cocooned Moon's body, and tried to work out exactly what kind of place his quest had brought him to. A coffin, or a regeneration tank? Was this another preserved body, like St Beatrice? Or did life still move in what had after all been a cyborg body, one of the infamous augmented men?

'The energies are very harsh here,' said Saturday. 'Unhealthy. They hurt my head. I've never seen anything like them before. I don't think we should stay here.'

'I can feel something,' said Jesamine, her voice a bare whisper. 'Look at what the jungle's done to him, Lewis. Do you suppose it did that while he was still alive? Can we cut him free?'

'I don't think we're meant to,' said Lewis. 'I think this is something he chose.'

Moon lifted his head, and they all jumped. He took a long slow breath, and let it out again. He slowly turned his head to look at his visitors, and a fierce golden glow filled his eyes, unnervingly bright in the rosy-tinted light of the engine chamber. A chill ran through Lewis. No one had seen the glowing golden eyes of a Hadenman in centuries: the mark of Cain, in the cyborgs Humanity had created. The augmented men, who became the Enemies of Humanity. The butchers of Brahmin, driven by their merciless creed of transformation through technology to pitilessly murder and destroy. They were long gone now, bogeymen to frighten children. But Moon still lived.

'Welcome, Deathstalker,' said Tobias Moon in a harsh buzzing voice. His face had subtly inhuman lines. 'If you've come to me, you must be in serious trouble.' He took another slow deep breath. 'It's been a long time since I spoke with a Deathstalker. You'd better have a good reason for disturbing me. I was happy, in the embrace of the Red Brain. It reminds me of the mass consciousness of the Hadenmen. It was necessary to destroy them, but still I miss the closeness, that intimate connection. The never being alone. The Red Brain and I have joined in symbiosis. It is not the same, but it will do. Together, we regulate and control plant growth and activity, to cooperate with the colonists. They are a part of the ecosystem too, and a part of us. Our children.

'It is a peaceful life, for one who was created to wage war. It is all I ever really wanted. Now you come, Deathstalker, and like your predecessor I have no doubt you bring bad news.' He swivelled his head back and forth experimentally, and his neck made loud cracking and creaking noises. 'I don't inhabit this body much any more. I live in a larger body, with a larger perspective. But here I am. Because I never could say no to a Deathstalker.'

'You honour me, sir Moon,' said Lewis. 'I wouldn't have disturbed you, if the whole Empire were not at risk . . .'

'It's always something like that,' said Moon. 'Deathstalkers never bother themselves with the smaller things. I know why you're here. I'm still linked into the Empire's comm systems. I've been updating myself while we've been talking. So; the Terror has come at last, the worlds are falling apart and you have been Outlawed. Time plays the same patterns over and over again. And Owen and I are legends now . . . He wouldn't have approved. But then, he was always the best of us. I could have been so much more. Grown and performed miracles, as he did. But I never wanted that. Or perhaps I was afraid to embrace the change and the power, as he did. I don't think Owen was ever really afraid of anything, except failing those he loved. Still, this is the life I chose, and I have been happy enough here.'

'We need to talk about Owen, sir Moon.' Jesamine moved in beside Lewis, cutting off what promised to be a rambling conversation. 'Is he alive somewhere? Where should we look for him?'

'I haven't seen Owen since he left this world,' said Moon, in his buzzing inhuman voice. The golden eyes shone piercingly bright. 'Though sometimes I think I talk with him, in dreams. The link the Maze formed between all of us was a strong one, and I don't know if even death could break it. A voice came to us, after the defeat of the Recreated, and said that Owen died bravely, saving us all. It was the kind of thing he would do. I know what's happening in the Empire, Deathstalker. Much has occurred since you left Logres. The old King, William, has been arrested for treason. The young King, Douglas, is in the hands of his enemies. You must make a decision: go back and save your friend, or go on and perhaps save the Empire.'

'Lewis, you can't go back,' Jesamine said immediately. 'Not after we've come so far.'

'But Douglas—'

'Would understand. He can take care of himself.'

'Bound to be a trap waiting for you there,' said Rose. 'It's what I would do.'

'But where can we go, if Owen really is dead?' said Lewis. 'And are you sure of that, sir Moon? I've been given reason to believe that he could still be alive somewhere.'

'He was a great man,' said Moon. 'A warrior, yes, but so much more besides. I still miss him, after all this time. He saved my soul, you know. After the Grendel killed me in the old caverns under Haden, the reborn Hadenmen brought me back to life, but only as one of them. I had access to most of my old memories, but they meant nothing to me. Until Owen came, and brought me back into the light, back to myself again. Everything I am, I owe to him.'

'Excuse me?' said Brett, sticking one hand up in the air. 'You were dead . . . and you came back to life again?'

'Yes,' said Moon.

'Just checking,' said Brett.

'What was it like, being dead?' said Rose.

'Restful,' said Moon. 'In a way, we all died when we went through the Madness Maze. What came out the other side was something new. We were reborn, remade into new life. Owen's still out there, somewhere. I believe that. I have to believe that.' He paused, and looked at Lewis again. 'Has anyone ever tried to recreate my old people, the Hadenmen?'

'No,' said Lewis. 'We don't believe in cyborgs any more.'

'Probably just as well,' said Moon. 'We were never what the Maze intended.'

'What did the Maze intend?' said Jesamine.

'Go there,' said Tobias Moon. 'Go to Haden, go to the Madness Maze, and ask it. Every answer to every question you ever had can be found in the Maze.'

'Shit,' said Brett under his breath to Rose. 'Didn't you just know he was going to say that?'

'We saw the story of Owen's defence of the mission, at Mission City,' Lewis said abruptly. 'It told of Owen doing amazing things. Impossible things. You were there, sir Moon. Did Owen really do everything they said he did?'

'Oh yes,' said Moon. 'All of that, and more. He was always the best of us.'

There was something in the way he spoke those last words that told Lewis the audience was over and Moon had said all he was prepared to say, but Lewis persisted, even though it wasn't easy being stubborn in the face of those terrible glowing golden eyes.

'Sir Moon, it may be that you are the last living Maze survivor. Even if your . . . abilities never matched Owen's, you are still a very powerful individual. Come with us. Help us stop the Terror. You have a duty; to us, and the Empire.'

'No,' said Moon. 'You don't need me. You need Owen. Because I have seen the Terror, and I know what it really is. Only Owen can hope to stop it. Go to Haden, Deathstalker. It is your destiny.'

'You know what the Terror is?' said Jesamine. 'Tell us!'

'No,' said Moon. 'You're not ready yet.'

Hell with that, thought Brett Random. He'd had a belly full of hints and half answers. He reached out with his mind, and hit Moon's thoughts with the strongest esp compulsion he could fashion. Only to discover that Moon's mind was a hell of a lot bigger than any human mind had a right to be. It kept growing and unfolding before him, expanding in directions he couldn't follow. And above and beyond Moon's thoughts, there was the Red Brain. The smallest part of it recognised Brett's tiny presence, and thrust him back into his own head. Brett cried out in shock and pain, and would have fallen if Rose hadn't grabbed and steadied him. Lewis and Jesamine looked at him, startled. Saturday fell into an automatic defensive crouch. And as they looked away, Moon's head slowly lowered itself again, his chin resting on his chest, the golden glare fading from his eyes. The crimson vegetation lining the chamber began to stir ominously. The whole ship began to shake, and the floor lurched under their feet.

'Brett!' said Lewis. 'What have you done?'

'Why do you always blame me?'

'Because it's always your fault!'

'Yell at him later,' said Jesamine, grabbing Lewis's arm to steady herself. 'We have to get out of here! I think this ship's going back down into the earth again.'

Lewis looked quickly to the narrow tunnel that was their only way out. The fibrous lining was writhing slowly, expanding, sealing off the tunnel inch by inch. And the soft rosy light was slowly going out.

'Saturday!' said Lewis. 'You go first. Make us an exit!'

The reptiloid grinned and ploughed forward, his great bulk forcing a way through the narrowing tunnel. The others hurried close behind him, Rose hauling Brett along with her. The whole ship was shuddering now, the floor seeming to fall away beneath their feet. Daylight showed up ahead, and they charged down the tunnel and out of the sinking ship. They hit the pink grass running, and didn't stop till they were on the other side of the clearing. Only then did they turn and look back, just in time to watch the last of that battered wreck, the *Sunstrider II*, disappear underground as the earth swallowed it up again. The grass waved wildly, the earth closed over the lowering prow, and the clearing grew still again, with nothing to show that anything had ever been there. And then they all jumped out of their skin as a calm voice spoke behind them.

'Your audience is over,' said Hellen Adair. 'I trust you found it helpful. It's time for you to leave Lachrymae Christi. Hope you had a good time, be sure to sign the visitors' book at the starport, have a safe journey, don't come back.'

On the bridge of the *Hereward*, heading away from Lachrymae Christi at speed, Brett Random was still fuming.

'The bum's rush! All that guff about how honoured they were to meet a Deathstalker, and we end up being booted off the planet!'

'You were the one stupid enough to try and compel someone connected to the mass consciousness of an entire planet,' Rose said calmly. 'You're lucky your brains aren't dribbling out of your ears. All right, ten out of ten for ambition, Brett, but minus several thousand for diplomacy.'

'So,' said Jesamine, reclining elegantly in her chair. 'Where do we go now? I don't know about the rest of you, but after meeting Tobias Moon in the spooky if not downright unnerving flesh, I'm in even less of a hurry to get to Haden than I was before. *We all died in the Maze . . .* Just what I needed to hear.'

'But he did say it was the only place we could find answers,' said Lewis from the pilot's seat, frowning thoughtfully.

'I still say Mistworld,' Brett said stubbornly. 'You want answers, you can buy them there. You can buy anything on Mistworld. Particularly with the cargo we're carrying.'

'Ah,' said the AI Ozymandias. 'While you were gone, I took the liberty of exchanging most of the data crystals for food supplies. We were running very short.'

Brett tugged at his hair with both hands. '*You swapped a small fortune in alien porn for a bunch of fresh fruit?*'

'Fruit is very good for you,' said the AI firmly. 'I got you some vegetables too, and some preserves. And a case of parsnip wine.'

'Kill me now,' said Brett to Rose. 'Put me out of everyone's misery.'

'If you don't stop whining, I'll have Saturday do it,' growled Lewis.

Brett looked at the grinning reptiloid, and shut up.

A blazing light appeared on the bridge like a clap of thunder, and they all cried out in shock. It was too fierce to look at directly, and forced everything else into silhouette. It slowly consolidated, becoming heavier, and there was a growing sense of presence on the bridge, as something from above and beyond the material world drew closer, sinking into the world, becoming solid, becoming real. The light snapped off, and they stood blinking at a harsh-faced woman with a shock of blonde hair.

'Oh my God,' said Jesamine. 'I know you! Lewis, that's Diana Vertue! I saw holos of her when I was researching my part in *Deathstalker's Lament* for last year's revival tour!'

'Jenny Psycho?' said Lewis. 'But she's dead!'

'Now there's a name no one's dared to use to my face in a long time,' said Diana. 'And yes, Deathstalker, I am dead.'

'Lot of it going around,' said Brett, hiding behind Rose.

Lewis and Jesamine were on their feet, clinging to each other. Even Rose looked distinctly unsettled. There was something overpowering about Diana Vertue's presence, as though she was . . . more *real* than everyone else. Saturday had retreated to the rear of the bridge, compelled by his instincts into a submissive posture. Diana smiled coldly upon them all.

'One hundred and eighteen years ago, the Grey Train and the Shatter Freak ambushed and murdered me. I trusted someone I had every reason to believe was my friend, and I walked right into it, alone and far from help. Even so, they were lucky to beat me. I was old and tired, and feeling particularly low that day. Perhaps I wanted to die, and just used them as an excuse. It's possible. Anyway, my body died that day, torn apart by psionic razorstorms. I never was a Maze alumna, after all; just an esper who got an unexpected boost. My dying mind was picked up by the oversoul, and made a part of it. I exist now as a thought in the great mass mind of the espers. But sometimes I draw on the energies of the oversoul and manifest in the real world again, for a time. When I'm needed, and no one else will do.'

'Why are you here?' said Lewis, and took a little pride in how steady his voice was, under the circumstances.

'The oversoul has been following your progress ever since you left Logres, through Brett Random.'

'Hey!' said Brett, poking his head past Rose's shoulder. 'I never joined the oversoul!'

'You're an esper,' said Diana. 'We all drink from the same pool.' She looked at Rose. 'Sometimes we see you there, too. Isn't that interesting?'

153

'Fascinating,' said Lewis. 'To what, exactly, do we owe the unnerving pleasure of your company?'

'You must go to Shandrakor,' Diana said implacably. 'To the forsaken world. I crash-landed the old Deathstalker Standing there, after the last battle.'

'Yes,' said Lewis. 'My father gave me the coordinates.'

'I know. Go there, and in the old castle you will find things you need, and things you need to know. It is your heritage, Deathstalker.'

'Will you be joining us?' said Jesamine tentatively.

'No. I don't belong in the waking world any more. I'm just a dream of who I used to be. I'm only here as a favour to my father, John Silence. We dead people must stick together.'

She smiled for the first time, and then disappeared. They could still feel her presence on the bridge for several seconds, slowly fading away as she receded in a direction they couldn't name. Finally she was gone, and a certain tension left the bridge.

'Doesn't anyone stay dead any more?' said Brett plaintively, appearing from behind Rose. 'I really would like to be excused now, please. I can hear some clean underwear calling my name, and then I think I'd like to lie down for a while.'

'Why doesn't anyone ever want to join my group?' said Lewis, as Brett and Rose left the bridge. 'Oz, set a course for Shandrakor. It appears Haden will have to wait for a while, yet again.'

FOUR

CHANGING TIDES

It was late in the day, and far later than anyone realised. Parliament was in session, no one was saying anything important and King Douglas was almost dozing on his uncomfortable throne. The House was hot and stuffy, the guards were yawning into their armour, and everything seemed to move at a crawl. Nearly all the Human MPs were present, because the House was the last place where anyone listened to them any more. The section set aside for aliens was almost deserted, with only a dozen or so species represented. Even the MPs didn't listen to aliens these days. The esper representative was gone, his place taken by a smugly smiling clone representative. No one said anything about this. Everyone could see which way the wind was blowing. A single blue steel robot watched everything for Shub. And Douglas, King and Speaker to Parliament, was there because . . . well, because he had nowhere else to go. His presence was never required anywhere. Anne Barclay didn't bother to brief him on the day's business any longer. He had been abandoned by friends and enemies alike, because events had passed him by. Power, real power, lay in the hands of those strong enough to grasp and hold on to it. Douglas didn't bother trying to get people's attention these days. He played the part of a broken man so successfully that sometimes he wasn't sure whether he was acting or not. But still, he waited and watched, and hoped for a chance to do . . . something. As it happened, he was currently resting his eyes during a particularly dull and protracted debate over value-added tax in the outer worlds.

Just another day, in what used to be the heart and conscience of the Empire.

Everyone looked round sharply, including Douglas, as a blare of recorded trumpets cut across the MP's droning speech. Everyone recognised that particular fanfare. Finn Durandal had had it written specially for him. The Imperial Champion strode out on to the floor of the House, accompanied by James Campbell, the man who should have been King. Finn was tall and resplendent in his black leather armour, and James had never looked more grave and noble. The MP who had been speaking slunk back to his seat, unnoticed. Everyone else was too busy murmuring urgently among themselves, and congealing into their various factions. If Finn and James had come to the House, it meant something important was about to be decided. Perhaps by the MPs, perhaps not. Finn took up a commanding stance before Douglas on his throne, and bowed a bow that held no obvious trace of mockery. Douglas gave him exactly the same kind of bow in return. Both of them ignored James.

'My apologies for interrupting the business of this House,' Finn said smoothly, 'but a matter of some urgency has arisen. It is imperative that your brother James address the House. Do you give your permission, your majesty?'

'Of course, sir Champion,' said Douglas. *Sure. Let's pretend I have a choice in the matter . . .* 'Step forward, brother James, and tell us what brings you to this House so urgently and unexpectedly.'

James looked solemnly about him, and struck a pose carefully calculated to suggest courage and determination in the face of adversity. Douglas felt like applauding.

'Most Honoured Members,' James said ringingly, 'I have no official standing here, I know that, but information has been made available to me of such importance that I must share it with the House. As I'm sure you're all aware, for some time now espers have been deserting their home worlds to come here, to join with others of their kind in the separate city state of New Hope, home to that most secret organisation, the oversoul.' It was amazing how much hate and contempt James was able to cram into that last word, without actually spitting. 'Humanity has, quite rightly, been suspicious of espers ever since they used their unnatural powers to suppress the perfectly legal demonstration by Neumen outside this House by possessing and controlling their minds. Just like those acknowledged terrorists, the Esper Liberation Front. Well, I have acquired solid evidence that the reason espers have been gathering together is so that they can plan an attack against Human authority! They intend to defy our just and reasonable demand that all espers present themselves for conscription, to be used as weapons against the coming Terror. They intend, through force of numbers, to throw the law this House passed back in your faces, and defy you to do anything about it! They cannot be allowed to reject your authority, and evade their responsibilities. If they will not volunteer their special abilities in the defence of the realm, then they must be compelled. They must be brought to heel, before their treacherous defiance spreads. I put it to this House that the time has come to register, control and command all espers in the Empire. They must be taught their place in the scheme of things. Those with suitable abilities should be sent to Heracles IV, to stand against the coming Terror, while others should be made available for scientific research to discover the true source of their powers, which they have always wilfully held to themselves. It is long past time that these abilities should be shared equally by all Humanity!'

There was a lot more, growing increasingly ugly and hateful, but Douglas tuned it out. Everything from now on was just rhetoric; everything that mattered had already been said. James was proposing drafting all espers, making them property again, as they had been in Lionstone's time. Some for cannon fodder, some for vivisection. It was a well-written speech, one of Anne Barclay's best, and it sickened Douglas that she should have turned her talents to such viciousness. He studied the House unobtrusively, and was disturbed to see how well the speech was going down. In times of crisis, there's nothing authority delights in more than discovering some scapegoat to blame it on. Standing behind James Finn smiled openly at Douglas, as though he knew what his King was thinking, and knew it didn't matter. The House was going to accept this proposal, and there was nothing Douglas could do to stop it, as Speaker or as King. Even trying to stand in its path would turn the House actively against him. So he stayed slumped on his throne, smiling and staring vacantly, and said nothing. His mask of disinterest was the only weapon he had left. For the moment.

Finn studied Douglas carefully, and felt a warm glow in his heart. It did him good to see how far his old friend had fallen. It seemed dear Jesamine had taken Douglas's balls with her when she left. The fight had gone out of him. Soon enough, he'd be so beaten down he'd be grateful for a chance to abdicate, and then James would take his throne by popular acclaim. And Finn would rule through James; until he didn't need him any more. Finn put Douglas out of his thoughts, and concentrated on the real problem. The espers had to be controlled. That was vital to Finn's plans for all kinds of reasons. They were too powerful and too dangerous to be allowed to run free any more; and besides, even Finn's esp-blocker might not be enough to protect his thoughts if the oversoul targeted him directly. So a pre-emptive strike. Because it was necessary, and because he could.

He'd never liked espers. No one should have the right to be more dangerous than him.

James's carefully crafted speech reached its end in a triumphant climax that brought the whole House to its feet, and the vast majority of MPs gave him a standing ovation. There were a few hold-outs remaining stubbornly silent, but they were too isolated to be any problem. James looked about him, smiling bashfully, nodding his appreciation for their support. Finn clapped him on the shoulder, in a manly congratulatory way. And Douglas . . . wanted desperately to get to his feet and make a speech of his own. He'd never needed Anne to write his words for him. Not when they came from the heart. He could reach out to the hearts and minds of the House, woo them with sweet words and strong emotions, remind them of the espers' long service to the Empire, defend their rights and the integrity of the House. But he didn't, because he knew it was already a lost cause. Helpless in the face of the coming Terror, the House needed *someone* to strike back at.

It had been months since Douglas's father William had been arrested, and still no one had been allowed to speak to him. There wasn't even any word of when William might be brought to trial. He remained a prisoner in House Campbell, where anything could be happening to him. Anything. So Douglas had no choice but to appear weak and beaten-down, and no trouble to anyone. While he worked furiously behind the scenes, and in strictest secrecy, to gather information on what Finn was really up to, and build up ammunition to be used against him.

'Well, James,' Finn said finally, after the House had calmed down enough to vote in favour of James's proposal. 'I suppose the next step is mine. Given that the safety of the Empire itself is at stake, it is my duty as Imperial Champion to bring these esper scum to heel.'

The House roared its approval, an ugly sound of spite and bloodlust. Finn and James looked at Douglas, and he nodded reluctantly.

'Do what you must, sir Champion,' he said tiredly. 'Go to New Hope, and make Parliament's will clear to them. And Finn: good luck. You're going to need it.'

Finn looked at him sharply, but Douglas met his gaze innocently enough and Finn let the remark pass. He strode out of the House like a conqueror, with the cheers of the Honourable Members ringing in his ears. James followed quickly after him. And Douglas allowed himself a small cold smile.

You're going to need all the luck you can get, Finn Durandal, against the oversoul . . .

Outside the House, James looked about him and whistled loudly, impressed by the sheer size of the armed force Finn had assembled. Waiting around and above the House were hundreds, perhaps even thousands, of gravity sleds stacked in ascending levels up into the sky, all of them manned by Pure Humanity and Church Militant fanatics. Yet beyond and above them dozens of huge gravity barges loomed ominously over the House, studded with ranks of waiting disrupter cannon. Finn's army blotted out the sky like a dark and angry cloud.

'Jesus,' said James. 'There hasn't been this much firepower assembled in one place since the Great Rebellion. You could knock over some of the lesser worlds with an army this big!'

'Now there's a thought,' said Finn. 'But first things first, eh?'

'You really think the espers are going to put up that much of a fight?'

'Only a fool underestimates the oversoul,' Finn said shortly. 'You weren't here to see what merely a handful of them did to the Neumen rioters. I've used up a hell of a lot of favours and influence equipping my people with hundreds of esp-blockers, but even so it'll be more of a fair match than I'm comfortable with. Still, at the end of the day it always comes down to firepower. I'm going to blow the floating city of New Hope into a million pieces, and then pick off the surviving espers as they fall to the ground. Oh, it's going to be such fun, I just know it! Now, off you go, James. Back to Anne, and work on your next speech.'

James pouted. 'But I want to come with you! I want to see the action close up.'

'No, you don't,' Finn said firmly. He patted James on the cheek, and James flinched a little in spite of himself. 'You stick to speeches, James, that's what you're good at. Leave the atrocities to me. That's what I'm good at. And James, dear; never argue again with me in public.'

He pinched James's cheek painfully, and James stood there and took it.

'Yes, sir,' he said, and Finn let go with a pleasant laugh. James searched for a change of subject. 'What would you have done, if Parliament had said no?'

'Gone anyway, and to hell with them. Argue about the legality of it later. But I knew they wouldn't give me any trouble. Bunch of sheep.'

He stepped on to his waiting gravity sled, fired up the engines and checked the weapons systems, and then gave the signal to his waiting fleet. Slowly and ponderously, the gravity barges started forward, and the ranks of gravity sleds spread out across the sky. Humanity was going to war for the first time in centuries. James called up to Finn, over the rising thunder of the engines.

'What about Douglas?'

'What about him?'

'He might stand against us, while you're away.'

Finn laughed happily. 'He might have once. But he's not the man he was. I've seen to that.'

He swept up into the sky to take the point, and the fleet moved off after him, the roar of their engines shaking the earth, heading for New Hope. James waved and waved, but Finn never looked back.

The esper city of New Hope floated serenely two miles above the surface of Logres, vast and marvellous, with thrusting towers and brilliant lights and complex structures of glass and porcelain. Once it was Logres's most precious jewel, acclaimed and adored. From a safe distance. It was a lot bigger now than it used to be, more than ten miles wide and almost five miles high. It had to be such a size, to contain the millions of espers who had come to New Hope from worlds all across the Empire, because New Hope was the only place they could feel safe. The great floating city shone like a multi-coloured star, held up and held together by the massed minds of the oversoul. The espers were its power source and its weapons, its heart and its industry and its defences. New Hope had a lot of defences, because the espers still remembered what happened to the first city of that name in the bad old days of Lionstone's reign.

Finn could see it before him, hanging on the darkening evening sky like a fairy-tale palace, all turrets and spires and delicate walkways. It looked utterly splendid and completely defenceless. New Hope had no energy weapons, no attack ships, and Finn had the biggest aerial attack force since that used by the old Widowmaker to destroy the original New Hope more than two centuries ago. The first esper sanctuary had been blown apart and put to the torch, its inhabitants slaughtered, and Finn saw no reason why history shouldn't repeat itself here today. He wasn't expecting any real problems. He was using the same tactics of overwhelming force and firepower, and all his key personnel and ships were protected by esp-blockers. This wasn't going to be a battle. Just an object lesson of what happened to those who dared defy Finn Durandal.

He went laughing into battle; but he really should have known better. It's hard to hide anything from thousands of telepaths and remote viewers working in unison. They knew about Finn's attack force the moment it began assembling, and they already had a response worked out. They'd been waiting for the Durandal to turn his attentions towards them. Every esper in the Empire now lived on New Hope. The others were dead, hunted down and killed by Pure Humanity mobs. So now all the espers came together and united in the oversoul, and it gathered itself for battle, to strike the first blow against an Empire that had turned bad and vicious, like a mad dog.

Crow Jane, telepath, warrior and devious thinker, strode across the landing pads at the edge of the floating city, broadcasting orders in every direction as she organised New Hope's defences. Her mind was plugged into the intricate lattice of thoughts that made up the oversoul's operations division, and decisions flashed back and forth in the mass consciousness, faster than lightning and more vivid, changing and adapting in an instant as conditions in and around the city changed. Crow Jane made up her mind, and immediately men and women rushed to new assignments, ready for the fight. Around her, she could sense polters and pyros and precogs working calmly at their part of the plan, and she wouldn't let herself worry about them. Everyone knew what they were doing. There were no clashes or contradictions or misunderstandings in the oversoul, and no regrets, either. They would do what they had to.

Every individual was the oversoul, in every way that mattered.

Crow Jane was a tall, statuesque brunette wearing sweeping black silks under a battered leather jacket, and a bandolier of silver throwing stars. She wore a sword and a disturber on her wide hips, and both weapons had seen a lot of use in their time. Crow Jane had a pale face, jet-black lips, heavy eye makeup and a disturbing smile. She'd been trained as a battle esper on Madraguda, fighting against the Raw Shark terrorists during the Quantum Inferno affair, and the oversoul believed in making good use of every individual's talents. Crow Jane's main talent was for organising mayhem.

A hundred and twenty espers assembled silently and efficiently before her, weighed down with battle armour and guns and explosives, and she smiled upon them like some ancient and awful death goddess. She spoke to them aloud, because some things needed to be said for everyone to hear.

'You all volunteered, and you know the score. The Durandal and his bastard army of fanatics will be here soon, and you have to buy the oversoul time to do what it must. So get out there, cause chaos, run rings around them, and kill as many as you can; but above all keep them occupied. They mustn't suspect what we have planned until it's too late. Given the size of the attacking force, it's more than

161

likely that I won't be seeing most of you again. The oversoul will do its best to gather your minds into itself as your bodies are destroyed, but that may not be possible. The Icarus Working must come first. There's still time for anyone to back out, if they don't think they're up to this.' She looked around, but no one said anything. They didn't have to. There were no secrets in the oversoul. Crow Jane smiled on them and let her pride and honoured esteem wash briefly through their minds. 'All right. Go and cause some trouble, you glory-seeking weirdos.'

She felt their silent laughter in her mind as one by one they rose into the air, ascending under the power of their own minds, so many angry angels rising up to smite a hated enemy. Crow Jane watched them go, the gusting wind tangling in her long black hair and blowing tears from her eyes until they were out of sight.

The espers flew through the cold thin air, protected from the harsh environment by the power of the oversoul. Far below, the world turned slowly, ignorant of the bitter war about to be fought in the heavens. There was no aerial traffic, none of the usual freight wagons that cruised the high altitudes; Finn had had it all diverted. He didn't want any witnesses to what he was about to do. His would be the only record of what happened here tonight: an official record, carefully edited to make him and his people look good and make the espers look like monsters. The espers knew that, knew the terrible things Finn had planned for them, and flew on anyway. Memories of Lionstone's Empire still existed within the oversoul, and what one knew everyone knew. The espers flew faster, sworn to fight and die to the last man and woman, to ensure that New Hope would not fall again.

Finn's fleet appeared over the curve of the horizon, and the espers smiled as they saw their enemies for the first time. Psionic energies crackled around them like harnessed lightnings. One hundred and twenty of them, set against gravity barges with the firepower of starcruisers and gravity sleds beyond counting. The espers increased their speed, the chill wind whipping past them. The foremost gravity barge targeted them with its tracking computers and the disrupter cannon opened fire. Energy beams seared through the space where the espers had been only a moment before. They scattered, streaking through the air in sudden zig zags, changing tack again and again, confusing the barge's battle computers with studied randomness. And then the espers were in and among the fleet, and the barges couldn't fire for fear of hitting each other. The armed men riding the gravity sleds opened fire with their weapons, but the espers were here and there and gone again, darting in and out of sight, flying too fast to be hit, too fast even to be anticipated. They couldn't be heard over the roar of engines, but they were singing their battle song and their death song, which were one and the same. Singing joyfully, the espers went to war.

They flashed between and among the slower-moving gravity sleds, tricking the riders into shooting each other, and occasionally darting in close enough to tip the riders overboard, so that they fell screaming to their death far below. Energy weapons discharged around the espers, but they blocked the crackling energy beams with the force of their minds and sent them ricocheting back. Pure Humanity soldiers were thrown from their sleds, or burst into flames, and their sleds spiralled slowly away from the fleet, heading earthwards with their scorched and charred burdens. Psychokinetic energies howled through the thin air, and sled engines blew apart. Sleds and riders fell like stones. Hand weapons exploded, blowing the hands and arms off their users. Hearts stopped, lungs flattened, brains were crushed inside their skulls. The espers were running loose in the heart of the fleet now, and blood and death and screams accompanied them.

Some espers were shot and killed, of course. Dropping through the air like burning birds. Given the odds against them, it was inevitable. But they'd known that going in.

And when they'd done all the damage they could, and their numbers had dropped to the danger point, the surviving espers threw themselves at the hulking gravity barges, darting and dodging past the withering defensive fire, and slammed into the exposed engine vents at the rear of the barges, where they detonated themselves like psionic grenades. Massive explosions rocked the targeted barges. Steel hulls shattered, and waves of fire swept through crowded corridors. Some began slow controlled descents back to earth, while they still could. But even after the hundred and twenty espers had dashed themselves against Finn's fleet, and given it everything they had, including their lives, the main bulk of the fleet still pressed on, not even slowed. It was too big to be turned aside by individuals, no matter how brave.

The whole battle was over in less than half an hour. The fleet thundered on, towards the floating city.

On the landing pads of New Hope, Crow Jane saw the last esper mind of the attacking force gutter and go out as she quietly sang the final words of the battle song along with it. The oversoul hadn't been able to save any of the minds. The Icarus Working was too important to risk a lapse in concentration, even for a moment. Crow Jane could feel it assembling in the back of her mind, like a great engine slowly coming to life.

A slight and diffident figure appeared suddenly beside her, and she jumped despite herself. The Ecstatic called Joy was the only person on New Hope who wasn't a part of the oversoul. Not least because the oversoul didn't want anything to do with his mind. The last of his kind, Joy's brain had been surgically altered so that he lived in a state of constant orgasm. Theoretically, he was capable of accessing all kinds of altered states of consciousness, seeing the past and the future as well as the present; but mostly he just smiled a lot and said things that only made sense later, if then. He nodded companionably to Crow Jane, as she recovered her composure. Perhaps his eyes were sad too. It was hard to tell, over that smile. He looked out into the sky, as though he could see the fleet coming.

'Something is dying,' he said softly. 'Something is being born. The worlds turns, and something awful turns in its sleep, waiting to be summoned. We will all fly to glory. Nothing is ever forgotten, nothing is ever lost. The man with the sundered mind will be here soon. It's going to rain tomorrow.'

Crow Jane looked at him, too tired even to be properly exasperated. She would have liked to dig into his thoughts and drag out what he was really talking about, but knew better than to try. The few espers who'd tried to penetrate the Ecstatic's mind had staggered away dazed and giggling and speaking in tongues. The few glimpses they got of his mind's workings, past the neverending thunder of pure pleasure, baffled and disturbed them. Whole new ways of thinking that made no sense at all, or perhaps so much sense that the normal mind couldn't accommodate them. But sometimes Joy knew things, and sometimes he said things that mattered, so the oversoul let him stay. It had a strange feeling it was going to need the Ecstatic.

'They'll be here soon,' said Crow Jane, just to be saying something. 'Stupid bastards. Don't they know that by attacking us they're cutting their own throats? We were supposed to be the Empire's early warning system, to guard against the coming of the Terror. With us gone, the next world in its path will get no warning whatsoever.'

'You could monitor the situation in exile,' said Joy, drifting very close to sanity for a moment.

'Why should we?' said Crow Jane, her mind still full of death songs. 'Let Humanity die. Let all the stupid bastards die.'

'The Terror comes for us all,' observed Joy, swaying slightly from side to side. 'Wide-eyed and terrible, endlessly howling, a lamentation in the night.'

Crow Jane ignored him. She could feel the Icarus Working coming together in the back of her head, but something was wrong. Something was . . . missing. Crow Jane felt a lurch in the mass consciousness of the oversoul, as though a foot had reached down for a step that wasn't there. A vital component wasn't where it should have been. Jenny Psycho, the last living soul to be touched by the Mater Mundi and raised to greatness, the most powerful single mind in the oversoul, wasn't there. She'd gone away, vanished without even leaving a note to say when she'd be back. Crow Jane shared the shock and astonishment radiating through the oversoul. Jenny Psycho's power had been a vital ingredient of the Icarus Working. It could still go ahead, even now a thousand minds were busy calculating the necessary changes, but suddenly the whole thing had become a hell of a lot chancier.

And then the Durandal's fleet appeared on the horizon, and there was no more time. Crow Jane sank into the welcoming embrace of the oversoul, one mind becoming many, as every esper on New Hope joined into a single magnificent effort of will. The whole city blazed with light, brilliant and blinding, and even miles off in the distance everyone in Finn's fleet cried out and had to turn their eyes away. The floating city, ten miles wide and five high, began to shake. Millions of minds concentrated as one, and New Hope shook and shuddered as slowly, slowly, it began to rise. A great psionic pressure thundered on the air, a mental presence so strong that people all over Logres could feel it. The city of New Hope rose up through the rapidly thinning air, moving faster and faster, surrounded by its own shimmering force field, all of this power generated solely by esper minds working in unison. Far below, helpless on his gravity sled, Finn Durandal watched his prey escaping, and howled with rage. Even his armoured gravity barges couldn't follow where New Hope was going. New Hope emerged from Logres's atmosphere and moved into orbit, leaving the world behind. The whole city glowed fiercely, a new star in the night.

The Icarus Working.

Left behind, Finn Durandal yelled into his comm net for the nearest starcruisers to change course and intercept the fleeing city. But the only ship in range was the *Hammer*. It moved ponderously round the curve of the world, heading for New Hope. It had barely moved into sensor range when all its systems failed. Computers crashed, backups aborted, and everything that could go wrong did. Life-support systems collapsed, lights flickered on and off, the artificial gravity failed and sudden fires broke out throughout the ship. The *Hammer* drifted further and further off course, and began the slow fall towards Logres. It had flown too close to the new sun in the heavens, and its wings had been burned.

The oversoul concentrated one last time and New Hope disappeared, hidden, undetectable, behind its own stealth shields. The oversoul looked upon its works, saw them to be gone, and considered where to go next.

While the oversoul was planning its escape from Logres, Donal Corcoran was planning his escape from the asylum he was being held in. Corcoran was the first man to have looked upon the face of the Terror: at a great distance, and via his ship's sensors, but he had looked upon the face of the Medusa, and the experience had marked him for ever. He no longer thought as other men did, and exhibited pretty much every mania and delusion a man could, plus several new ones. Medication didn't affect him, even in what would have been toxic doses for anyone else. He laughed and cried for reasons known only to himself, and had long conversations with people who weren't necessarily there. He didn't eat or drink any more, and he hadn't slept in months. He still wore his old spacer's uniform, now ragged and filthy, and he hadn't shaved or washed or even combed his hair since he'd been dragged screaming from the bridge of his ship in a straitjacket. He was being kept in a high-security asylum disguised as a country house, while doctors and scientists studied him from as safe a distance as possible.

But Donal Corcoran had had enough of that. He plotted awful revenges against the Terror for what it had done to him, and for that he needed to be free.

Part of his disturbed mind was always in contact with the Terror. As though it had taken part of his mind with it when it disappeared back into the place it came from, the place that wasn't a place. The Terror was always there on the edges of his thoughts, like a nightmare waiting to begin. Sometimes he thought it could see him too, and the thought made him whimper and bite his fingers. But he could see the place the Terror came from, even when it wasn't there; a space beyond space. It was as real to him as the place that imprisoned him. It drew and terrified him, like a hunger for poisonous things.

It was his way out.

So one evening when the shadows seemed particularly dark and restless, Donal Corcoran went walking through the grounds of the country house. The lawns were a vivid green, newly wet from the sprinklers. Wide blooming flowers perfumed the air with their scent and the trees were very solid, but none of it was real, any more than the house was really a house. The house was an asylum, and the grounds were mostly holo images, backed up by sound recordings and programmed smells. Donal could see right through them when he chose, though of course he never told the doctors that. Sometimes he could see right through them too. Donal went walking, stopping now and then to count and recount his fingers, because he had to keep checking the details of the few things he still believed in. Certainty had deserted him, blown away by the Gorgon's gaze. He couldn't trust anything any more, except his own intentions. He giggled like a small boy contemplating a particularly clever bit of mischief, and moved his changed mind in certain unusual ways. And as he changed his mind, the world changed around him. He walked out of the illusory garden and into a place that only looked like a place. It was cold and dark, like an endless stone corridor buried deep, deep below the ground, stretching away in every direction, including some he couldn't name. It smelled of dead roses and a woman's sweat, and he could hear a baby crying in the distance but he knew it wasn't really a baby. A great word hung unspoken on the air, held at bay by the implacable will of a woman wailing for her demon lover. The sorrow of it would have broken Donal's heart, if he still had one. He chose a direction and walked back into the world that everyone else agreed was real. In front of him was the door to his psychiatrist's office. Dr Oisin Benjamin. Donal smiled a not particularly nice or even sane smile. He pushed open the door without knocking, and strolled into Dr Benjamin's office.

The doctor looked up from his desk, startled, and moved his hand automatically to cover the notes he was writing. Dr Benjamin was a great one for writing notes. He didn't look especially pleased to see his star patient. Donal sat down in the visitor's chair and crossed his legs casually.

'Donal,' said Dr Benjamin, trying to sound pleasant and not at all nervous. 'How did you . . . ? You're not supposed to be here, Donal. My appointments are over for the day. Why don't I ring for an attendant, to escort you back to your quarters?'

He was already reaching for the hidden alarm button, to summon his bully boys in white coats, when Donal launched himself out of his chair. He threw himself across the top of the desk, merrily scattering important papers, and grasped Dr Benjamin by the throat. The two of them fell backwards and crashed to the floor with Donal on top, straddling the doctor's chest. Dr Benjamin struggled but couldn't break free, pinned down by Donal's weight. He opened his mouth to yell for help, and Donal hit him in the face. There was a loud crack as the doctor's nose broke, and blood flew from his smashed mouth.

'Sorry about that,' said Donal. 'Guess I don't know my own strength these days.' He paused, trying out various expressions on his face to see which would impress the doctor the most. 'Now, be still. I'm here for a little chat. One last pleasant conversation before it's time for me to go. You should be pleased, Doctor; you've been trying to get me to open up to you for ever so long, haven't you? Trying to get inside my head, to see the world as I do. Not a good idea, Dr Benjamin. Trust me on this, if nothing else. Where I am, it is always cold and dark and someone's crying. It might even be me. I hear the voices of those who died on the Rim Worlds, whispering around the edges of my thoughts. They don't like being dead again. And I can feel the Terror, moving slowly towards us, coming for us all. I want to run in every direction at once, but even more than that I want revenge. I want my thoughts to be my own again. I want my life to make sense again. I want my old life back! That's not so much to ask, is it? I'm going to destroy the Terror, for what it's done to me. And I can't do that while I'm still here. So I'm off. Things to do, things to do . . . But before I go, good Dr Benjamin, I have a present for you. One last gift, to help you understand what's going on in my head.'

He surged to his feet, dragging Dr Benjamin up with him as though he was weightless. He grabbed one of the doctor's shoulders in each hand, and pulled. Dr Benjamin screamed horribly as he came apart, ripped in two, torn down the middle from the top of his head, down through his torso and all the way to the groin. The two vertical halves fell away from each other as Donal let go, and crashed to the carpeted floor. There was blood, but not a lot before Donal sealed off both halves through the force of his will. Dr Benjamin thrashed weakly on the floor, still alive, reaching out with his separated arms, a single eye rolling in each half head, and making horrible sounds with his half mouths. Kept alive by Donal's implacable will. Somewhere an alarm bell was ringing. Someone had noticed Donal Corcoran wasn't where he was supposed to be. He crossed quickly to the door of the doctor's office, and then looked back at the two halves of his psychiatrist.

'Now you know how I feel all the time,' he said, and left.

Donal Corcoran went walking through the corridors of the asylum, sometimes using the doors and sometimes not. More alarm bells were ringing now, and he could feel guards coming his way with all kinds of restraints and weapons. Sometimes Donal avoided them by walking through walls, and sometimes he just turned sideways from the world and they couldn't see him. He made his way out of the asylum and into the street. There was no one about. The guards were inside, looking for him. Donal looked up into the sky and called to what was waiting. There was a pause, and then a long dark shape came plunging down out of the clouds. It was sleek and silver and it knew him. His old ship, the *Jeremiah*, had escaped from its dock and come looking for him. It too had been touched by the Terror, and was more than just a ship now. The madman and his mad ship looked upon each other, and were glad. They belonged together. The ship hovered above him while he thought about what he should do, and when he stopped thinking he was on the *Jeremiah*'s bridge. He could do things like that. He gave the order, and his ship blasted off for orbit. The *Jeremiah* was a trader's ship, built for speed and treachery. Illegally fast and protected by state-of-the-art stealth shields, there wasn't much on Logres that could catch or intercept it.

Donal walked curiously through the shadowed corridors of the *Jeremiah*, and it seemed to him that the old ship looked somewhat different. It had changed since he last saw it. After the Imperial Navy had boarded his ship against his wishes, strapped him into a straitjacket and dragged him screaming away, the *Jeremiah* had been piloted to Logres and held in a stardock for observation. Donal had known that, without having to be told. Just as he knew that many of the scientists sent to study the ship had quit because of the nightmares it was giving them. But he hadn't realised his ship had changed as much as he had, wandering off along new and little-used paths.

The steel corridors of the *Jeremiah* were now tall gothic arches, punctuated here and there with niches and crevices packed with fascinating things. Some of them looked almost alive. The ship's technology had grown, run wild, mutated. Strange new constructs, of no certain function, blinked at him from consoles with too many dimensions. Sometimes there was no lighting at all, but he could still see. The *Jeremiah* and he had been joined together by their experiences on a level that nothing could break. The metal walls were comfortably warm under his touch.

He returned to the bridge, and the main viewscreen showed him scenes of the damned burning in hell. They writhed and twisted, calling out silently for mercy that never came. Donal frowned, and the images disappeared. All through the ship, whispers had followed him, rising and falling like the sea, never ending, never still. He couldn't understand them yet, but he thought he might, in time. The *Jeremiah* had been forced awake and aware through its contact with the Terror;

not just the AI but the whole ship. And it hurt. Like its master, it ached for revenge. Or perhaps they both just craved for death, and the peace it promised. Either way, they would find the Terror, and drag it down with them into hell if they could.

As they were leaving orbit, they encountered the city of New Hope. The *Jeremiah* paused to match orbits, and the two vessels considered each other. The city of light and the starship holding darkness within. On the *Jeremiah*'s bridge, the viewscreen activated itself, showing Crow Jane and the Ecstatic called Joy.

'I know you,' said Donal. 'I watch the news, though I don't believe all of it. About time you got out of there. It's only going to get worse, you know.'

'I know you, Captain Corcoran,' Crow Jane said courteously. 'I told them that place would never hold you, if you wanted out. Do you know where you're going?'

'To the ends of the Empire, and beyond. Off the edges of the maps, and into the spaces marked "Here Be Monsters". I have business there.'

Crow Jane turned to Joy. 'You talk to him for a while. He sounds like your type.'

'Greetings, Captain,' said the Ecstatic cheerfully. 'I think we should keep this short and to the point. Because your ship is upsetting the oversoul. It keeps trying to talk to them. I like roses. Do you see the Light People too?'

'Yes,' said Corcoran. 'I do. I see them. They walk among us and no one knows. Which is kind of spooky, if you think about it. But they don't bother me so I don't bother them. Do you know where you're going?'

'There's currently some debate about that,' said Joy. 'We can't stay here indefinitely, but we're a long way from anywhere else.'

'You need to access hyperspace,' said Donal. 'It's easy. Look.'

He reached out to the oversoul and touched it with his altered thoughts. Both sides winced, but they held contact. Donal could see into many places now, and hyperspace was one of them. He showed the oversoul a direction to look in, one they had never suspected existed, and there was hyperspace waiting for them. Donal withdrew, hiding inside his own head again, leaving the oversoul with new possibilities and a massive collective headache.

'Go to Mistworld,' said Donal. 'I did a lot of trade there, when I was sane. They're still rebels at heart, and they have defences that could stand off whatever the Empire sends against them. They'll take you in. They remember what it was like to be hunted. I was happy there. It seems such a long time ago.'

'Don't be sad,' Joy said earnestly. 'The universe isn't as dark as it seems. The long night is full of stars, and the worlds are full of people. Who could have predicted that? We are not alone. There is comfort.'

'I don't want it,' said Donal. 'I only want revenge. It's all that's been left to me.'

Crow Jane frowned. 'You've had closer contact with the Terror than anyone else. Could it be some part of the Recreated, that was never made human again by the blessed Owen?'

'No,' Donal said immediately, shaking his head violently. 'It's bigger than that. It lives in more than three dimensions. Its spawn incubates in the hearts of suns. It eats souls. It wants to destroy the whole universe and everything in it. Unless I kill it first. I can see it. I can always see it, no matter what place it's in. Part of me is there with it, and it suffers.'

'How can you hope to stop it?' said Crow Jane.

Donal smiled. 'It pushed me into hell. And now I know the way, I'm going to grab the Terror and drag it down into damnation for ever with me.'

'Hope you've got a backup plan,' said Joy.

Crow Jane hushed him. 'Best of luck, Captain Corcoran. Perhaps we'll meet again some day.'

'It doesn't seem likely,' said Donal.

He broke contact and the two vessels passed each other in the night, each going their separate ways.

Treasure Mackenzie, that almost impossibly gorgeous star of the vid soap *The Quality*, was going to have dinner with her husband-to-be, King Douglas. He wasn't expecting her. She contacted him on the viewscreen in his private chambers, using a private number she shouldn't have known about, and invited him to join her at one of the most famous and fashionable restaurants in the city. The kind of place where you had to get on a waiting list just to bribe the maitre d'. But of course people like Treasure never needed a reservation, as long as her ratings held up. Douglas explained to her, very politely, that the dinner date wasn't possible. For reasons of security, Finn Durandal had decided that it wasn't safe for the King to leave his palace. Except to go to the House, and then only when protected by Finn's guards. Treasure pouted prettily, wrinkled her perfect brow, and then smiled brightly. 'Not to worry,' she said.

And within half an hour she was knocking at the door to his private chambers, having brought dinner with her. When Douglas opened the door she barged right in, followed by half a dozen waiters from that very fashionable restaurant, pushing trolleys loaded down with everything necessary for a full-scale banquet. There were main courses, side courses, in between courses, and a selection of snacks to keep them going while they decided which course to have next. The smell alone would have fed a family of six for a month. If anyone else had asked the restaurant to provide such a meal to go, the chef would have laughed in their face; but of course nothing was too much trouble for Treasure Mackenzie. She bustled about the room, directing the waiters on where to set things up, making sure everything was to her satisfaction before she signed the bill with a practised flourish. She then signed autographs for all the waiters, kissed the youngest on the cheek to see him blush, and then shooed them out. The door shut behind them, and Douglas and Treasure looked at each other.

'I didn't know what you liked, so I brought everything,' said Treasure.

'So I see.' Douglas considered her thoughtfully. 'How did you get past the guards at my door? They usually have strict instructions not to let anyone in.'

Treasure smiled. 'Pure charm, darling. And several deep breaths. A cleavage will get you places even security passes won't. Shall we make a start?'

They sat down facing each other across Douglas's dining table. Treasure helped herself to generous amounts of everything on offer, piling her plate high, while Douglas filled his plate more cautiously. He was still trying to work out exactly what was going on here. He opened the wine expertly, pausing a moment to approve of the excellent vintage, and poured it into two tall thin glasses. Treasure rewarded him with her trademarked wide smile. Douglas had to admit it really was a very nice smile. He was glad he'd made the decision to clean himself up. He would have hated her to see him the way he used to be. As it was, they made a striking enough couple, he with his handsome face and golden hair, Treasure with her famous sensual face and a great mane of pure white hair tumbling down past her bare shoulders. It had to be said, she had the most delightful collar bones . . .

'Are you sure you've got enough there?' said Douglas, as Treasure finally finished loading her plate.

She laughed easily. 'The joys of a fast-moving metabolism, darling. I burn it off through nervous energy. Besides, I've always believed that appetites should be satisfied. Anything less is unnatural and unhealthy.'

'So you eat like this all the time?'

'Oh hell, no. My agent would have a fit if she could see me now. There are very strict clauses in my contract about being overweight. But this is a special occasion, so—'

'It is?' said Douglas.

'Oh yes,' said Treasure, smiling over her wine glass at him. 'Drink up, darling. You don't want to get left behind, do you?'

Douglas had to smile. In her own ingenuous way, Treasure was as unstoppable as a force of nature. She attacked her food happily, wolfing it down with good appetite, and Douglas ate his quite excellent food at a somewhat slower pace, so he could study his dinner companion unobtrusively. Her long, flowing off-the-shoulder gown was shimmering silver, studded here and there with semi-precious stones, carefully designed to amplify and draw attention to her fabulous cleavage; as if it needed any help. Seen away from the camera, and with rather more understated makeup than usual, Treasure's face was pretty rather than beautiful, given strength by her pointed chin and blazing green eyes. Her gaze was direct and untroubled, and she chattered happily about nothing in particular, in between and sometimes during large mouthfuls of food. She ate with her fingers when she felt like it, and didn't give a damn.

Douglas watched her carefully, in much the same way he would have watched a dangerous opponent in the Arena, to see which way the attack might come from. Treasure was charming if undemanding company, and certainly easy enough on the eye, but Douglas thought he knew a planned seduction when he saw one charging straight at him. Clearly Treasure had decided to make sure she had him properly infatuated with her before the wedding, so there wouldn't be any problems this time. Douglas smiled, and poured more wine for both of them. He'd been dodging predatory women since he was a teenager. There was nothing like being the only heir to the throne of the Empire to make one apparently irresistible to women.

So he ate with a good appetite, and nodded pleasantly back at Treasure as she chattered away. Why not? It was something to do, and thanks to Finn bloody Durandal he didn't get out much these days. It was good to have company. And she was going to be his wife, eventually. Douglas wondered if Treasure knew that he meant to put the ceremony off for as long as he could. Perhaps she guessed it, and that was what this dinner was for. Certainly she was making every effort to charm, chase and vamp him; and with anyone else she would probably have succeeded. You'd have had to be dead from the neck down not to feel Treasure's appeal. Having the full force of her sexuality turned on you was like staring into an open blast furnace.

But Douglas still loved Jesamine. Stupidly, hopelessly, helplessly. Because love is like that, when it strikes a man in later life. Douglas had never really cared for anyone before. He'd never wanted for female company, and had been genuinely fond of many of them, but he'd always known that mostly he tended to choose his women by how much they'd piss off his father. But he'd loved Jesamine from the moment he met her. And he'd thought she cared for him. Perhaps she had, in her way, but she'd still left him to be with Lewis. It didn't matter. He still loved her, and always would.

Besides, Douglas didn't entirely trust Treasure's motives. You didn't get to be a major vid star without a ruthless ambition and determination far beyond the norm. She'd never be content to be just a trophy wife on his arm. Make her Queen, and she'd find ways to exercise power. Real power. Either on her own, or through her dominated husband. So Douglas ate his meal and drank his wine, gracefully sidestepped her little traps and seductions, and watched it all with quiet amusement. It had been a long time since he'd had anything to smile at.

He didn't know Treasure was also Frankie, one of the leading lights of the infamous Hellfire Club.

Behind her smile, she was watching him with increasing annoyance. Even her most practised techniques came to nothing against this man's casual self-possession. Look at him, eating the most expensive food in the Empire as though it was just another meal and smiling at her as though she was just another woman. She wasn't used to having her magnificent presence taken for granted. Most men lost the thread of what they were saying every time she took a deep breath, and spilt their wine if she deigned to lean forward. She was beginning to get a little angry. She was a *star*, damnit. She even lowered herself to being a good listener, only to find Douglas had nothing much to say. She'd set up this meal specifically to discover whether the King really was the broken man he appeared to be; but she was no closer to finding out. His face was open and amiable, his manner dull but pleasant, and neither face nor voice gave any clues as to what was going on in his mind. She'd come here with every intention of seducing the man, but he didn't seem interested in that, either. Which was practically unheard of. Perhaps the Durandal was doping him? That would explain a lot.

But Frankie had to be sure. The Hellfire Club needed to be sure.

There was a lot she could do as Queen to advance the Hellfire Club's agenda, in public and in private; but not if the King opposed her. Douglas had killed dozens of Hellfire Club devils, in his days as a Paragon. When he was still a man to be reckoned with. If he still was . . . She let her hand drift casually closer to the long slender dagger secretly sheathed on her upper right thigh. No one had body-searched her. No one had dared. She could kill him, if she had to . . . but it would be such a wasted opportunity, if he could be turned. The things she could do as Queen; the terrible, wonderful things . . .

She focused on the creed of the Hellfire Club. *Thou shalt not love. Thou shalt not be weak. Do what thou wilt shall be the whole of the law.*

'How are the baby mice stuffed with humming birds' tongues?' she asked sweetly.

'A little over-spiced, I fear,' said Douglas.

Treasure almost ground her teeth together. She held out her glass for him to fill, and arranged it so that her fingers brushed his lightly. He didn't even seem to notice. Maybe if she just grabbed his face and jammed it between her breasts . . . She indicated that she'd had enough to eat, and he agreed. They moved away from the table, and took their drinks over to the fireplace. He was still being pleasant and even gallant, in a rather vague way, and Treasure, or rather Frankie, thought, *Oh the hell with it.* She pushed Douglas back against the wall and slammed her body up against his. Her magnificent breasts flattened against his manly chest. His arms went around her automatically. She grabbed his head with both hands and pulled his mouth towards her waiting lips. And Douglas grabbed her bare shoulders and pushed her away from him with such force that she fell backward on to the thickly carpeted floor. She sat down hard on her well-padded bottom, and glared up at him, hair dishevelled, breathing heavily, and their eyes met. And for just a moment they both saw the real person behind each other's public mask. They regarded each other coldly, and then the masks slipped smoothly back into place. Douglas leaned forward, offering his hand. Treasure accepted it, and rose to her feet with dignity. She brushed herself down here and there, adjusted her décolletage and ran her hands through her long white hair. Her breathing was perfectly calm now, as was his.

'It's Jesamine, isn't it?' she said. 'After all she's done to you, it's still Jesamine.'

'Yes,' said Douglas. 'I'm afraid it is.'

'What could she offer you that I can't?'

'If you have to ask, my dear, you'll never know.'

Two bright spots burned angrily on Treasure's cheeks. 'I will be your wife, and your Queen, Douglas.'

'Yes, I'm afraid you probably will be. I hope you get more out of it than I ever have through being King.'

'Some day,' said Frankie, 'you will kneel to me, Douglas.'

'I suppose hell has to freeze over some time. Thanks for dinner. We must do this again, some time.'

Treasure Mackenzie swept out of Douglas's quarters, trailing her tattered dignity behind her. Douglas went back to the dinner table, and wondered if he could find the room for a little more. It really was excellent food, and it would be a shame to let it go to waste.

Finn Durandal was having an equally unsatisfying meeting with the clone representative, Elijah du Katt, in the secret laboratory Finn funded deep in the rotten heart of the Rookery. It was the only place such a lab could be kept entirely secret, and properly guarded. And given what du Katt was doing, on Finn's instructions . . . The half a dozen long rooms, set some distance under a main street, were crammed full of the very latest tech, some of it only legal because no one had found out about it yet.

Du Katt was all over the place. He'd cloned himself, quite illegally, and now there were nine of him; on the unanswerable grounds that he was the only person he could trust to work with him on such a clandestine and dangerous project as this. Finn was also pretty sure there was a touch of narcissism involved in the decision, but he said nothing. He liked to know other people's vices and weaknesses. It made them so much easier to control. The clones darted back and forth around the lab, somehow never quite getting in each other's way, and occasionally moving in eerie symmetry. The original du Katt identified himself with a sloppy hat, of no discernible style or purpose. He hovered uncertainly beside Finn as he strolled through the laboratory. Finn wasn't smiling. Du Katt was sweating.

'Well,' murmured Finn, letting one hand trail dangerously close to some delicate-looking apparatus, just to watch du Katt flinch, 'how goes our little project? You've been very quiet lately. I'd hate to think you've been keeping secrets from me.'

'There's been nothing to tell,' du Katt said quickly. He looked to his clones for support, but they were all busy being busy and keeping their heads down. Du Katt glared at them venomously, and then tried an ingratiating smile on Finn. It wasn't successful. Du Katt dropped the grin and settled for being businesslike. 'It's been in my reports, sir Champion. Using your authority, my people sealed off the Victory

Gardens behind the House of Parliament (there's never any shortage of terrorist scares to take advantage of) and we dug up the graves of Jack Random and Ruby Journey. The preserved corpses were still in surprisingly good shape, and we were able to obtain good cell samples from both bodies. We then destroyed the remains using transmutation bombs, following your instructions, to ensure that nobody else would be able to make use of the bodies, and we filled in the graves again. No one saw anything, no one suspects anything. The men you supplied me with to do the actual hard labour, they have been . . . taken care of, I trust? Good. Good . . . If word were to get out that we were trying to clone two respected heroes of the Great Rebellion, I'm pretty sure we'd all be dragged through the streets and burned at the stake. This goes well beyond disrespect, and into desecration and blasphemy.'

'You let me worry about things like that,' said Finn. 'You still haven't answered my question. How goes the work?'

Du Katt turned away to fiddle with some equipment, so he wouldn't have to meet Finn's cold gaze. 'You do ask a lot, sir Durandal. First, you wanted me to produce clones of Random and Journey which you could brainwash and control. Falling that, you wanted me to discover the source of their powers, so they could be bestowed on . . . persons of your choosing. Well, I and my other selves have run every test we can think of on the cell samples we took from the bodies, and I have to tell you, in my expert opinion, this whole project is a waste of everybody's time.' Du Katt met Finn's gaze squarely, the effect only slightly spoiled by his trembling lower lip. 'The whole thing's impossible! The genetic material involved has been so altered and transformed through contact with the Madness Maze that it doesn't respond to any of the established cloning procedures. There's nothing there we can work with!'

Finn frowned. 'Are you saying it isn't human tissue any more?'

'I mean, it isn't any form of life I'm familiar with! It just . . . doesn't make sense!'

'Send all the information you have to our Shub allies on Haden,' said Finn. 'See if they can make anything of it. And calm yourself, du Katt. Hysteria is so unattractive in a scientist.'

Du Katt nodded quickly, and actually did relax a little. He'd been expecting a far worse reaction from Finn. 'How is our James performing?' he said, trying hard to sound casual and not at all like he was trying to change the subject. 'Well, I trust? Giving no cause for concern?'

'Any reason he should be?' said Finn.

'Oh no! No, of course not! I was just . . . asking.' Du Katt decided he might have been better off with the first subject after all. 'You know, according to certain records I uncovered in the clone underground's files, you weren't the first to suggest creating a clone of the dear departed James Campbell. It seems such an offer was made, to the then King William and Queen Niamh, by my predecessor of that time. They could have produced a perfect clone to replace the deceased original, and no one need ever have known, but it seems the King and Queen reacted very badly to the suggestion. The Queen apparently said it would be an abomination . . . and that was the end of the clone underground's power and influence for a long time.'

'Did you follow up on my other suggestions?' said Finn, seating himself comfortably in du Katt's favourite chair as if by instinct. 'Tell me you have had some success there, at least.'

'I'm afraid not, sir Champion.' Du Katt could feel small beads of sweat forming on his upper lip. He held his hands tightly together behind his back to keep them from shaking. Finn being so calm in the face of continual bad news was not a good sign. 'I had the Victory Gardens searched from end to end, using the most thorough equipment, but there was no trace anywhere of any remains of the late Captain Silence. His ashes may have been scattered over the Victory Gardens, but that was more than a century ago. None of his genetic material remains there. I'm sorry.'

'Well, let us not despair,' said Finn. 'I've had another idea I thought we might try.' He reached inside his armour, and the du Katt clones dived for cover in case it was a weapon. Du Katt would very much have liked to do the same, but he couldn't afford to appear weak in front of Finn Durandal. So he stood his ground as Finn's hand came out holding a test tube containing barely half an inch of clear liquid. Finn smiled at it fondly. 'This is the remains of the esper drug I purchased from the estimable Dr Happy. A most remarkable drug. I thought we might try it on the cell samples you have left. See if anything happens.'

Du Katt accepted the test tube gingerly, but knew better than to argue, or appear less than enthusiastic. He stalked over to his other selves, only now reappearing from behind the more solid pieces of lab equipment, and bullied them into setting up the necessary conditions for the experiment. It wasn't difficult. Place cell samples and esper drug in the same secure container, bring them together through remote control, and then observe the results from what everyone hoped was a safe distance. They watched the results on a computer screen, but for a long time nothing seemed to be happening. Du Katt was already rehearsing some credible-sounding excuses, when . . . everyone's head snapped round suddenly. Something had changed. There was *something* in the lab with them. Finn was on his feet, his gun in his hand. They all looked frantically around. There was nothing to be seen, but they were not alone. They could feel it.

There was a presence, unfixed and unfamiliar, slowly suffusing through the lab. It was growing steadily stronger, as though approaching from very far away, from some unknown direction. It felt angry, dangerous, threatening. The whole lab began to shake. Tech exploded, collapsed in on itself, melted and ran away. Fires broke out spontaneously all over the lab, and the automatic sprinklers came on. Great dents appeared in the steel walls, as though something was beating on them with invisible fists. Computers began chanting in unknown languages, in loud angry voices. The clones clung together, crying like frightened children. Du Katt was trying to hide behind Finn, who swept his gun back and forth, searching for a target. The temperature in the lab suddenly plummeted, as though something was sucking the warmth out of it. And slowly and remorselessly, something began to manifest. It wasn't in any way human, and none of them could bear to look at it. Finn put away his gun, unclipped a grenade from his belt and threw it at the chamber holding the activated cell samples. The grenade detonated, and the whole container disappeared. The presence snapped off, still unformed, gone as though it had never been there. The fires went out, the sprinklers shut down, the computers were quiet. The laboratory slowly grew still again.

'Well,' said Finn. 'I don't think we'll try that again. Du Katt, where . . . ? Ah, there you are. Would I be right in assuming those were the very last untreated cell samples you had?'

'I'm afraid so, sir Durandal,' du Katt said unhappily. 'The procedures we had to use were very destructive, as I advised you. And since we destroyed the bodies, on your instructions, there won't be any more. And I can't help feeling that's probably a good thing.'

'You never were very ambitious,' said Finn. He drew his disrupter again, picked a clone at random and shot him. The energy beam punched right through his chest, and sent the dead body crashing to the floor. Flames flickered around the hole in his chest, but not strongly enough to bring on the sprinklers again. Du Katt and the other clones called out with one voice, and then were very still. Finn looked around him, smiling.

'A little reminder to do better in future. I reward success, but I always punish failure. So keep yourselves busy until I have other work for you. And du Katt, what do you think that was? That thing we summoned?'

Du Katt swallowed hard. 'I think it might have been Random or Journey's ghost, sir Durandal.'

Finn nodded. 'What a remarkable age we do live in, du Katt. Better have the lab exorcised. Just in case.'

Emma Steel was standing on her head in one corner of her room, doing her breathing exercises, when the front door announced she had a visitor. Emma sighed heavily. It never failed. It was the end of another long day, and she'd been looking forward to a little quiet relaxation before she crashed out on her bed, and now some poor fool had turned up to annoy her. If it was another representative from the Church Militant, come to ask her aggressively about the state of her soul, Emma decided she was going to see how many times she could get him to bounce as she threw him down the stairs. She regained her feet, stalked over to the door and scowled through the viewer. On the other side of the door she was surprised to see Stuart Lennox, the young Paragon from Virimonde. She hadn't thought he was talking to her. Even more surprising, he showed clear signs of having been crying recently. Very recently. Emma sighed again. This was going to be complicated, she knew it. She unlocked and opened the door and gave Stuart her best cold glare.

'It's been a very long day,' she said flatly. 'And I can't believe you've come all this way, at this late hour, to bring me good news. So what's happened?'

Stuart swallowed noisily. His eyes were red and puffy, and the self-respect had gone out of him. He looked like a child dressed up in Paragon's armour. 'It's all gone wrong, Emma. You have to help me.'

'Give me one good reason.'

'You're the only one who can help!'

'Why don't you go to your good friend Finn Durandal?'

Stuart burst into tears. Loud, helpless, dismal sobs that shook his whole body. He just stood there, as though he didn't even have the strength left to put his hands to his face. Emma raised her eyes to the heavens, and stepped back.

'Oh all right! All right! Get in here, before the neighbours see you. And stop that snivelling. You're a Paragon!'

Stuart tried hard, rubbing at his nose with the back of his hand as he entered Emma's apartment. He walked as though there was something broken inside him. He all but fell into the nearest chair. Emma looked quickly up and down her corridor, and then shut and locked the door again. She stood over Stuart, hands on hips, and tried not to scowl.

'Talk to me, Lennox. What's happened?'

He sniffed a few times, and managed a small uncertain smile. 'When you're training to be a Paragon, they teach you how to fight anything, except yourself. Your own heart, your own . . . needs. I thought I knew what I was getting into, but I was wrong. So wrong.' He looked round sharply. 'Did you just hear something? Was there anyone else outside in the hall? No, of course not, you'd have said something. Sorry. Sorry. I don't mean to be so jumpy, but Finn's people are everywhere these days. I don't think he knows what's happened yet, but he will. And then . . . I did everything I could think of to make sure I wasn't followed here, but . . . it's hard to be sure of anything any more.'

Emma wanted to take him by the shoulders and give him a good shaking, but she had a feeling he might collapse entirely if she did. It disturbed her to see a fellow Paragon so . . . beaten down. She pulled up a chair and sat opposite him.

'Brace up,' she said, not unkindly. 'No matter how bad things are, never despair. That's one of the first things you're supposed to learn as a Paragon.'

He smiled again, but there was no humour in it. 'Being a Paragon doesn't mean what it used to.'

Emma sighed, but kept it internal. She knew when a long story was on its way. 'All right, Lennox. From the beginning.'

He swallowed hard, and made a visible effort to pull himself together. His chin came up, and his eyes finally met hers squarely. 'Something happened tonight, at the Sangreal. Something bad. I know, you warned me, but . . . things have been getting worse there. You can't imagine what I've seen. What I've seen Paragons doing. No one else drinks in the Sangreal any more, just Paragons back from their quest. Even the groupies are afraid to go in there now. The Paragons have been exploring more *extreme* pleasures, and no one dares to say anything. I knew some of these people, from before, and they've changed. They've all changed. Men and women who used to be my heroes doing . . . vile things. It got so bad I wouldn't go there, unless I was with Finn. I felt safe with Finn. But even though he never joined in, and never let them touch me, he never did anything to stop it either. I think it amused him.'

Stuart looked almost pleadingly at Emma. 'You have to understand. I was trained as a warrior, on Virimonde. I've done my share of fighting, killed men when I had to. Part of the job. And I've seen evil men do evil things, for money or power or just because they could. But tonight . . . tonight . . . Finn sent me to the Sangreal alone. He needed an urgent message delivered, in person, and he had business elsewhere. I didn't want to go, but I couldn't say no. I didn't want to appear afraid in front of him. He laughed, and clapped me on the shoulder and said I'd be all right.

'When I got there, the owner of the bar was making a stand. He said he'd had enough. That no amount of money was worth putting up with the Paragons' behaviour any more. He called them animals to their faces, said they sickened him. He wanted the money he was owed, and he wanted the Paragons out of his bar so he could get his old trade back. He wanted his life back. The Paragons laughed at him. There was drink and drugs and other things going on. The bar owner said if they wouldn't leave, he'd go to the media. Tell them everything. All the awful things he'd seen. His bar's security cameras had lots of interesting footage. The Paragons looked at each other. Nothing was said, but they came to a decision. They got up and advanced on the bar owner, surrounding him. I thought they were just going to push him around, intimidate him. They took out their knives and cut him to pieces. Slowly, so they could enjoy it. He screamed and screamed. I tried to stop them, but two Paragons came out of nowhere and grabbed me. Forced me to my knees, and made me watch the man die by inches, screaming all the way. When it was finally over, and he was dead . . . they cut him open and ate him. Ate his flesh, his organs. And they laughed. With blood running from their mouths, they laughed.'

He started to cry again, tears running jerkily down his cheeks as he spoke. 'They made me eat too. Eat the flesh. I had to. They would have killed me if I hadn't. They gave me one of his eyes, and his tongue. Said they were delicacies. Then they let me go. I ran. That was two hours ago. I went home and cleaned myself up, but I still feel dirty. I didn't know what to do! I couldn't go to Finn. They're his people. They're allowed to do anything. And then I thought of you. You're the only one left I can trust. The last real Paragon. The only one who might be able to do *something*.'

'Dear God,' said Emma, too shocked even to be sickened. 'What happened to them out there on their quest? What did they find that could have changed them so much?' She shook her head slowly, and then looked firmly at Stuart, putting a steadying hand on his shoulder. 'I'll look into this. You go home. Lock the door and stay there. No one has to know you've talked to me. In the meantime, stay away from the Sangreal, and from Finn.'

'I can't.'

'Come on, Stuart. Surely you can see now what kind of a man he is. He's no good for you.'

'But I love him,' said Stuart Lennox, bitterly, helplessly. 'I love him.'

Emma finally got him calmed down enough to leave, and then she strode restlessly back and forth in her apartment, trying to work out what to do next. The Paragons had gone too far. The heroes of old had become monsters, and they had to be stopped. But she couldn't just barge into the Sangreal and accuse them. They'd had plenty of time to hide the evidence. They'd call her a liar to her face, and laugh at her. No; she'd have to do this the hard way. Follow them, spy on them, gather evidence that couldn't be overlooked or buried. And for that she was going to need her new ally: the reporter Nina Malapert.

All it took was a short vid call, and a few dark hints, and Nina was on her way. She was hammering on Emma's door in under half an hour, and swept briskly into the apartment in a flurry of garments of clashing colours, her tall pink mohawk waving proudly above her shaved skull. She and Emma embraced happily, and then Nina tore herself away to prowl around the room, oohing and aahing loudly, and making sure her floating camera was recording everything.

'Another exclusive! Emma Steel's very own private home life! Gosh, darling, Channel 279 would *kill* for material like this. Not that you'd want to appear there, Emma dear. Very downmarket, and *très* tacky. They'd probably want pictures of you in a bubble bath, showing your bosoms and doing something suggestive with a loofah.' She stopped in the middle of the room and looked about her, frowning prettily. 'I have to say, it's rather spartan, isn't it, darling? I mean, these furnishings are so last week, and you haven't even got any little bits and pieces, to give the place character. Everyone has a few little bits and pieces. Tell me you've at least got some stuffed animals in your bedroom.'

'Just the one,' said Emma. 'Head of a Hob hound. I shot and stuffed it myself.'

'Ooh! Ooh! A little bird told me on the way up here that you've had a gentleman caller. Very young and very fit, but looking totally miserable. Be honest now! Have there been tears and tantrums? Is someone on the way out? Is someone new on the horizon? *Is he a celebrity*? Tell me everything, darling!'

'Nina, calm down and sit down, please.' Emma tried to sound stern, but the young journalist reminded her irresistibly of her younger sister back on Mistworld, always eager to get involved in everything, especially when it involved scandal and excitement. 'Nina, this could be the biggest story of your career, but what I have in mind is very dangerous, and I need to be sure you understand the risks.'

Nina sat bolt upright in her chair, wide-eyed and quivering with excitement as Emma laid out the bare bones of the story for her.

'Well honestly, darling, this is . . . utterly wonderful! It's got everything. Sex, politics, treason and a touch of gore for the tabloid shows! We could sell the rights to this story for enough money to retire on. We're talking miniseries here! I wonder who they'll get to play me? Yes, yes, don't look at me like that, darling. The wind will change and your face will get stuck that way. I know, it's very serious and dangerous and all that, but one of us has to concentrate on the business side, or we'll get screwed over the contracts. It's a jungle out there these days. So what's the plan? Does it involve shooting lots of people? Should I go home and change into something that doesn't matter if I get blood on it?'

'Take a deep breath, Nina, you're hyperventilating. This is going to be a fact-finding mission, and nothing more. What do you know about Paragons?'

'Well, absolutely *everyone*'s been keeping an eye on them recently, darling. From a respectable distance, of course. There's all kinds of stories about the things they've been getting up to, since they came home with their tails between their legs. But no one knows anything for sure. I've been doing some research, or rather I haven't but I persuaded this sweet young boy at the office to do it for me. It seems that all but a handful of the Paragons have returned from the quest now, and none of them found even a sniff of Owen or Hazel. Everyone's been chasing stories about them doing *terrible* things, but there's never any proof or any witnesses. Or at least, none willing to speak out, even for really impressive sums up front. The few times someone has got a piece together, one of Finn's people would turn up and have a quiet word with the editor, and the story would be quietly spiked as not in the public interest.'

'Finn doesn't own all the media,' said Emma.

'No, darling, but he does scare the shit out of most of it. No one's going to risk going head to head with the Durandal over anything less than a totally watertight story. And that's where we come in! I'm going to be journalist of the year! They'll give me my own chat show for this!'

'They'll cut your head off and dump your body in the waste pits, if we get caught,' Emma said dryly.

'Well, yes, there is that.' Nina pouted, and frowned. 'According to my researcher, the sweetie, the usual Paragon groupies and hangers-on have run for their lives. Ordinary people don't go into the Sangreal any more, or if they do they have a distressing tendency not to come out again. No one knows what they do with the bodies. The rest of the street have abandoned their homes and businesses. They couldn't stand listening to the screaming any more. And this is happening just down the road from the House of Parliament, with the Imperial Champion's knowledge and support. So you see, I am taking this seriously, darling. I just believe in seeing the positive side of things as well. Like, if we pull this off successfully we're going to be rich, rich, rich!'

She jumped up and did a little happy dance in the middle of the room. 'I think I've discovered a taste for real journalism, darling! No more puff pieces and horoscopes for me! What do we do first?'

'Well, to start with, we're not going anywhere near the Sangreal until we've got a better idea of what's really going on. These people were heroes once. The best of the best. Some were my friends. Something specific must have happened to change them so drastically. According to your news channel, one of the last few Paragons to return from the quest, Miracle Grant, landed at the main starport a few hours ago. He wouldn't give any interviews, which is almost unheard of for Grant, but he did say he hadn't found Owen or Hazel either. There has to be a connection.'

She broke off as her viewscreen chimed with an incoming call. She looked at the screen curiously. Most people knew better than to bother her when she was off duty. She accepted the call and scowled at the screen. 'This had better be really important,' she growled.

The face on the screen was female, oriental, the left half covered with a series of intricate overlapping tattoos. She wore her hair in a black buzzcut, her mouth was a severe pink rosebud, and her eyes were dark and fierce. A single razor-edged throwing star dangled from one earlobe.

'I am Rachel Chojiro Random,' she said bluntly. 'I'm one of Random's Bastards. And you need to hear what I have to say, Paragon.'

Emma sniffed. 'That'll be the day. I take it there's no point in trying to trace this call?'

'What do you think? I'm calling from the Rookery, and that's all I'll say. Now shut up and listen. I know things you need to know.'

Emma folded her arms across her chest. 'Convince me.'

Rachel scowled unhappily. 'I'm a Random's Bastard, and proud of it. Direct descent from Jack Random. Disowned by both sides of my family, ever since I discovered at a young age my God-given talent for parting fools from their money. I'm a career criminal, and proud of it. But there are lines even I won't cross. I speak for all Random's Bastards in this. The Durandal has desecrated Random and Journey's graves in the Victory Gardens. The bodies were dug up and then destroyed with transmutation bombs. Sacrilege. We're all mad as hell, and we want revenge. We can't take on the Durandal, but maybe you can.'

'Get to the point,' said Emma. 'What have you got to tell me?'

'Miracle Grant's come into the Rookery, supposedly to meet with Finn. Get here fast, and you'll catch them together. Word is, they're going to be discussing things they wouldn't dare discuss anywhere else. Interested?'

'Give me directions, and then get the hell out of my way,' said Emma Steel.

Emma Steel and Nina Malapert made their way into the Rookery, disguised under heavy cloaks and holo faces, with just enough hints about them to suggest they were two well-off ladies slumming it in the Rookery for pleasures unobtainable in the more civilised parts of the city. They kept to the side streets and the shadows, and avoided contact with anyone. Miracle Grant wasn't difficult to find. He strutted through the Rookery streets as though he owned them, and everyone gave him plenty of room. No one dared to touch a man under Finn's blessing, even if he was a hated Paragon. And besides, there was something odd about the man, something off. He wore his armour sloppily, and he was seriously overweight. His eyes were wild and dancing, and he laughed a lot, even when there was nothing obviously funny to laugh at. He took food from a market stall without paying and crammed it into his mouth with both hands as he strode along. Emma and Nina followed him discreetly through the crowded streets, keeping well back.

'*That's* Miracle Grant?' said Nina. 'God, he's really let himself go.'

'Something's seriously wrong here,' said Emma. 'The Grant I knew was always a fop and a dandy, immaculately turned out with never a hair out of place. Hell, the man was an epicure of the first rank. There's no way he'd lower himself to eat street food.'

'So,' said Nina. 'Are we going to drag him into a back alley and beat some answers out of him?'

Emma looked at her. 'We?'

'Well, all right then, you. I have to handle the camera.'

'We stick to following him. I need to know what he's doing here. I also want to be sure this isn't some kind of trap. Never trust a Random's Bastard.'

Miracle Grant went back and forth in the Rookery, talking to really unpleasant people in really unpleasant places. No one seemed pleased to see him, but no one was stupid enough to object either. He was Finn's man, and he was a Paragon, and both were scary things to be these days. Finally he came to a small bar in a back street, and went in. Emma and Nina watched from an alleyway on the other side of the street, but some time passed and he didn't come out.

Emma scowled. 'We can't risk going in ourselves. See that window on the second floor, part way open? Can you get your camera in through there?'

'Piece of cake,' said Nina. 'And I have state-of-the-art stealth protocols. They'll never hear it coming.'

She concentrated, and her camera emerged from under her cloak and flew swiftly up to the second floor window. It slipped easily through the gap, and then Nina guided it delicately downstairs, until she could see into the main bar.

'Got it,' she said. 'Grant's in there with three others, all in Paragon gear.'

'Plug me in,' said Emma. 'I need to know what's happening in there. And be sure to record everything on a remote link. This could be evidence.'

Nina hesitated. 'I'm going to have to get in really close for that, darling. You will pay for a new camera if anything goes wrong, won't you? Only I'm not made of money, you know, and I can't get insurance since I started hanging around with you.'

'Yes, yes, get on with it.'

'And I should point out that stealth fields are technically quite illegal, for news cameras. You do promise this won't come back to haunt me later?'

'If you don't get a move on, you'll be the one who's doing the haunting.'

'Bully.'

Emma and Nina plugged into what the camera was seeing through their comm links, and a window opened before their eyes, showing the interior of the bar. The camera had to stick to the shadows up by the ceiling, but its picture came through clearly enough. Miracle Grant was drinking brandy straight from the bottle at the bar. Three other Paragons were keeping him company. Emma knew them all. Good men, by reputation. But in this back street bar they laughed and drank and behaved like animals. They didn't seem to have anything important to say to each other. They were waiting. And then Finn Durandal walked through the door, and Emma and Nina both jumped. They'd been so taken up with what they were seeing that they hadn't seen Finn approaching. The four Paragons fell silent as Finn approached the bar. He smiled on them and they looked flatly back at him. There was a sense of Finn being surrounded by a wolf pack, who would turn on him the moment he showed any sign of weakness. Finn knew this, and wasn't in any way disturbed. If anything, he seemed amused.

'Well, my fine friends,' he said calmly. 'How are we today? Been having a good time?'

'Why couldn't we meet in the Sangreal as usual?' said Grant.

'Because you've all been very naughty,' said Finn. 'Reduced poor little Stuart to tears. Can't I leave you people alone for a minute?'

'You promised us action,' snapped Miracle Grant. 'You promised us revenge. You promised us blood and slaughter and the evening of scores. We're tired of sitting around, only being let out to play bodyguard and run errands for you like so many puppy dogs.'

'Are you saying you haven't been enjoying yourselves?' said Finn. 'Because of me, the ELFs finally got to possess their greatest enemies, the Paragons, and destroy their reputations while indulging yourselves in every vice and whim that comes to you. The Paragons are your slaves, aware of the evil you do with their bodies, but unable to stop you. They suffer the hell you've made for them, and all because of me. There's just no gratitude any more.'

'We're still waiting for the bill,' growled one of the other Paragons. 'The ELFs know better than to trust Finn Durandal.'

'You're not still mad at me for betraying you at the Parade of the Paragons, are you? It was all part of the plan. To get you where you are now.'

'We could have done this without you,' growled Grant.

'Could you? Could you really? I don't think so. I gave you the locations for each individual Paragon on their quest, so you could get there first and ambush and possess them. No one else could have done that. Only I had the information, because I helped plan the quest. You really must be patient. Stick with me, and you'll get everything you ever wanted. Soon enough my position will be unchallengeable, and then I will unleash you on our mutual enemies and we'll all get to have a little fun, I promise.'

He turned his back on them and headed unhurriedly for the door.

He'd almost got there when a voice behind him said, 'That esp-blocker won't protect you for ever, Durandal.'

Finn left the bar without replying. Out in the street, Emma and Nina watched Finn walk away. Nina shut down her camera and called it back, then she and Emma looked at each other.

'I should have known,' said Emma. 'I should have *known* . . .'

'ELFs!' Nina said breathlessly. 'ELFs possessing Paragons! Story of the century! We've got to get this on the air, Emma.'

'If we'd gone in there ourselves, we'd be dead now,' said Emma. 'Up close, those telepaths would have identified us immediately.'

Nina looked quickly at the bar, as her camera returned to nestle under her cloak. She patted it absently, like a good dog. 'Can they sense us from in there?'

'No. Possessing a thrall limits their range considerably.'

'Emma, we have to tell someone!'

'Hush, girl, and let me think!' Emma scowled fiercely. 'We can't just go public with what your camera recorded. Even if we could find someone brave enough to run it, Finn would simply say it was faked, a smear job by his enemies. Most people haven't heard what the Paragons are doing. Finn's seen to that. And then he'd have ELFs possess us, and we'd stand up and say yes, it was all faked. We'd be very convincing. And then we'd kill ourselves, for shame. And the ELFs would laugh themselves sick. I'd better get esp-blockers for both of us. We can't afford to have anyone peeking into our thoughts.'

'Isn't private ownership of esp-blockers illegal these days?' said Nina.

'I have contacts.'

'The great Emma Steel, breaking the law. Now that really would be an exclusive. Pity I'll probably never be able to run it.'

They shared a small smile.

'There must be someone we can show this to,' said Nina. 'The people have to know what's going on.'

'The ELFs' involvement changes everything,' said Emma. 'I don't know who I can trust any more . . . anyone could be possessed. Anyone. We're going to need allies. Powerful allies. Normally I'd go to the oversoul for help, but Finn's driven them away—' She stopped, and looked at Nina. 'Is that why he did it? Is he really thinking that far ahead?'

'Darling, I'm starting to get a little scared,' said Nina.

'Good. It'll keep you sharp, keep you safe. Look, we're better off now than we were. At least we know what's going on. The world is starting to make sense again. Finn got rid of the oversoul because they could have exposed what's happening. It was probably also part of the deal he made with the ELFs, to make up for the massacre of their people at the Parade of the Paragons. And he's got rid of the only people who could have exposed him for what he is.'

'Isn't there any way we can get at him?' said Nina.

'He must know this alliance can't last,' said Emma. 'The ELFs hate his guts. They'll turn on him first chance they get. Finn's playing a very dangerous game.'

'I say we lob a grenade into the Sangreal and kill the lot of them,' Nina said briskly.

'Tempting,' said Emma, 'But no. We can't attack the Paragons directly. We'd only kill the possessed bodies; the ELF minds would escape. We have to find a way to drive the ELFs out of their thralls, and rescue the Paragons.'

Nina snorted. 'You don't want much, do you?'

'You! Who are you? What are you doing here?'

Emma and Nina looked round sharply, to see Miracle Grant glaring at them from the door of the bar. Emma grabbed Nina by the wrist and ran like hell. They couldn't let the ELF get too close, and learn who they were from their thoughts. Grant pounded after them, and the other Paragons came boiling out of the bar to join the pursuit. Emma reached into a concealed pocket and pulled out a mindbomb. Utterly illegal on Logres, but still in common use on Mistworld. Emma believed in being properly prepared, and not letting trifling little technicalities get in the way of doing her job. She charged down the street, Nina plunging gamely along beside her. From the sound of the ugly voices behind them, the Paragons were gaining. Emma primed the mindbomb, let it fall to the ground and kept running. The bomb detonated just as the Paragons reached it. Its vicious energies sleeted through their minds, disrupting all mental activity in its limited range, and the Paragons staggered to a halt as ELF and host mind were both thrown into confusion. By the time the ELF minds were back in control, their prey was long gone.

Backstage at the House of Parliament, in one of the many small rooms where the real work of government was done, Anne Barclay and the clone James were working on the text for his next big speech. The esper condemnation speech had gone down really well, and Finn wanted to be sure he had a good follow-up ready to go as and when necessary. James had no strong feelings about espers one way or another; he said what he was told to say, but still he felt a certain relief that they wouldn't be around to threaten him any more. Any

190

esper who got close enough might have unmasked him and revealed who and what he really was. He didn't hate them or even necessarily want them dead; he just wanted them out of his life. James wasn't actually shallow, merely inexperienced, but the result was the same. He could only see things as important when they affected him personally.

His next big speech would be a clarion call for the House to remove the aliens' votes, and restrict alien movement within the Empire, 'for the duration of the Emergency'. Most of the aliens had already withdrawn their representatives from the House anyway, but the measure would make Pure Humanity happy and Finn needed another scapegoat to focus popular resentment on, now the espers were gone. Besides, with the Terror coming, Humanity couldn't afford to have potential enemies at its back. Better that the alien species be subdued and controlled, and this speech would be an important step in that direction. Again, James didn't care. He was just following orders.

Anne soon had the speech whipped into shape, and sat back from the table. She stretched her new body luxuriously, and smiled a little exasperatedly at James. 'You know, this would go a lot faster if you could contribute something now and again. Help me tailor the words more to your particular speech rhythms, for example. Even change the words to fit your own style. You are allowed to have opinions. You don't have to be just a mouthpiece for Finn's words.'

'Really?' said James. 'I thought that was exactly what I was created for. Finn's already made it very clear, on several painful occasions, that he doesn't want me to think for myself. I'm a puppet, something for Finn to speak through in public. So on the whole, I feel most secure when I don't have to think about what I'm saying. When I can play the part, and not have to worry about who I really am. Or what I might think, given the chance. I am not James. The more I read up on my progenitor, the more clear it becomes that he wouldn't have put up with this shit for a moment. He was always his own man, and proud of it. But if I'm not James, who am I? Who am I when the lights go out and there's no one there but me?'

His voice was rising, growing more agitated. 'Give me a speech to deliver, and I'm fine. Ask me to strike a pose, flash the smile, act the King-in-waiting, and I can do that. Easy. No problem. But even now, when it's just me speaking to you, the words sound more like James Campbell than the few poor personal thoughts that drift through my mind. It's easier to act James than be myself. Whoever that might be. Is there any *me*, any more?'

By now he'd almost reduced himself to hysterical tears. Anne comforted him as she always did, by taking him in her arms and rocking him gently back and forth, and he clung to her like a child. But this time, when she was ready to let go, he held on. They looked at each other, their faces very close, and then James kissed her impulsively on the mouth. Anne was honestly surprised. She still had trouble remembering that she was beautiful now, and that a man could be attracted to her. And anyway, James was off limits. Finn had made that very clear. Anne kissed James back, and put her arms around him again, and let the passion rise within her. *Why not?* she thought fiercely. *James never knew the old me. As far as he knows, I've always been beautiful. And it's time I had something for myself. Something that doesn't come from Finn.*

James was actually shy with her, and Anne had to lead him on. Encourage him, coax him, teach him. It was a new role for her, and one she enjoyed. She locked the door, and had him lie down on his back on the floor, and then she straddled him, and they made fierce, almost brutal love. And James's open adoration allowed Anne to be the kind of woman she'd always wanted to be, aggressive and wanton. It was good, so very good. And it wasn't as if she was doing anything wrong. No one was getting hurt. She was building his confidence, as he built hers. Two orphaned souls who had no one but each other.

But Anne was still very inexperienced in some ways. Afterwards, as they lay in each other's arms, thinking their private thoughts, if Anne had taken the trouble to look directly into James's eyes, she might have seen something. Something to make her wonder how genuine James's motives really were. Whether perhaps he was clever enough, and cold enough, to use her to break him away from Finn's control . . .

But she didn't look. And neither did he.

Elsewhere, in a room of no importance, the Shadow Court was in session. No comforting holo of the Empress Lionstone this time, no clever recreation of her savage Court. Most of their old meeting places had been discovered and overrun, and many of their supporters had been lured away by the more promising causes of Pure Humanity and the Church Militant. Only a few still kept to the old faith, and the return of the Families. The Shadow Court still had money and influence, and a handful of dedicated souls ready to kill or die for the cause, but the movement had become a shadow of its previous self.

Nine men and women, carefully anonymous in enveloping black cloaks, faces hidden behind artfully embellished black masks of silk and metal and leather, were all that remained of the ruling elite. And they came together around a bare table, in a bare room, to argue about money. The Shadow Court's most successful attempt to re-establish interest in the old Families had been the creation of that most popular vid soap, *The Quality*. It had become amazingly successful, bringing in profits so great that not even vid company accountants had been able to hide them. The elite of the Shadow Court were now all incredibly, embarrassingly rich. And some of them were determined to stay that way.

'*The Quality* works fine as it is,' said a slender woman in a domino mask. 'I see no reason to change anything.'

'And I say we've lost track of what *The Quality* was meant to be,' snapped another woman in a black mask liberally spotted with sequins. She fanned herself angrily with a paper fan decorated with erotic images. '*The Quality* was designed from the beginning to be propaganda, a way of spreading our message to the masses. It was always intended to be a means to an end, never an end in itself.'

'But it's become the most successful soap in vid history,' purred an unfeasibly fat man in an antigrav chair. 'And you propose to spoil everything by forcing more politics into the scripts, making them much more overt and risk losing our target audience. For the first time in generations, we are as rich as our Families used to be. I won't have you rocking the boat in the name of ideological purity.'

'*The Quality* spreads our message well enough as it is,' said a man in a full face mask. 'Because of it, the Families are more fashionable than ever. What's wrong with that?'

'Fashionable?' snapped the woman with the fan. 'Fashions change, fads come and go; we're supposed to be in this for the long run! Who cares whether the Families are popular? We're supposed to be feared and respected!'

'The rich are feared and respected. That's good enough for me.'

'You've become corrupted by wealth,' said a woman with a mask shaped like a bird of prey. 'The vid show is a cult thing, nothing more, and the masses will drop it fast enough once they find something else to be obsessed about. We have to push our message as strongly as we can now, while we still have an audience watching!'

'Easy for you to give up the money,' growled a man in a black gold mask. 'Not all of us were born rich. We earned this money. It's ours.'

And so the argument went on, while Tel Markham, Member for Madraguda, watched wearily from behind his black leather mask. He could see both sides of the question, but in the end he'd always known that power was more important than money. If you had enough power, people would give you money. It didn't always work the other way round. Power was why he'd joined the Shadow Court, along with several other secret organisations. Angry voices rose around him, but he couldn't seem to summon up the passion or the interest to get involved in the argument himself. Truth be told, he was getting bored with the Shadow Court. They did less and less, and squabbled more and more. They were all talk, and he got enough of that in Parliament.

And then the door, which was supposed to be locked and bolted, crashed suddenly open, and what seemed like a small army of armed men rushed into the room, shouting to the shocked and startled Shadow Court to stay where they were, not move and keep both their hands in sight at all times. The soldiers quickly surrounded the nine men and women, covering them with energy weapons as they stared frantically around, eyes wide behind their masks. And that was when Finn Durandal strolled casually into the room.

'Hi!' he said cheerfully. 'Good to be here, in this . . . actually rather squalid little room. Please, don't anyone get up. Or I'll have you shot. Now, some of you aren't as surprised as the others, because you invited me here. Oh yes; a few of you decided you were more interested in being rich than anything else, and contacted me, telling me where this meeting would take place. The idea being that I would arrest those of you who cared more about politics, and leave the rest of you to get on with being very rich. Well, bad luck, people. I've come for all of you. There are far too many factions in the Empire these days, and frankly I don't need the distraction. So I'm shutting down the Shadow Court. Show trials, character assassination, followed by very public executions. You know: the sort of thing your aristocratic forebears were always so very fond of in Lionstone's time. And with the head gone, what's left of the body will soon wither and die. Feel free to speak up and object, and I'll feel free to have you shot as an example to the others.'

'How typical,' said the woman with the fan. 'The Families betrayed by their own kind. It seems we have learned nothing from history after all. But I trust we can at least show solidarity one last time. We can't afford to be arrested and identified. Our Families would be made to suffer. Better to go out with dignity, in one last act of defiance. We can still serve the cause as martyrs. Agreed?'

And around the table eyes met and heads nodded, and hands went to transmutation bombs under their cloaks. There was a series of sharp, limited explosions, and soon there was pink protoplasmic slime splashed across the table, and dripping thickly from the chairs. Finn sighed, and shook his head.

'Fanatics. At least it saves the expense of trials. What matters is that they're dead. Except . . . for you, sir.'

Tel Markham, the last surviving member of the Shadow Court hierarchy, removed his black leather mask and bowed courteously to Finn. The Durandal raised a single eyebrow in surprise, and nodded back. Tel smiled easily. 'I am no fanatic, sir Champion. For me, it was always about me. What I was going to get out of it. I hope I can convince you that a show trial might not be the best thing in my case?'

'Go on,' said Finn. 'Give it a try.'

Tel spoke smoothly, doing his best to appear calm and at ease, despite being covered with a whole bunch of energy guns. 'I am a Member of Parliament, sir Durandal. And a member of Pure Humanity. And brother to Angelo Bellini, the Angel of Madraguda and currently head of the Church Militant. That's a whole lot of people I could persuade to be more supportive of you. Plus I know things and I know people, all of which could be very useful to you.'

'Not bad,' said Finn, after a moment. 'I don't actually need you, or any of the things you offer, but you speak well and I've missed having someone around to boast to since Brett and Rose ran out on me, the wimps. You look like you're made of sterner stuff. So I think I'll adopt you. Assuming . . .'

'Yes?' said Tel Markham.

'Assuming that you, as sole surviving creator and producer of *The Quality*, agree to sign over your interest in the show to me. I can use it to push my own propaganda to influence and inflame popular opinion, as and when I find it necessary or amusing, and I can always use the money. I have so many people on the payroll these days. Really. You have no idea. Do you have any problem with giving me the show?'

'Not in the least,' said Tel, who knew a foregone conclusion when it was staring down the barrel of a disrupter at him. At least Finn didn't know about his membership of the Hellfire Club. The tables might yet be turned some day, in all kinds of interesting ways.

In the House of Parliament, business went on as usual. Most of the MPs were present, mostly because they had nowhere else to be. The alien section was practically deserted. The clone representative was doing his best to look interested in the slow-moving debate. Shub watched and listened through a single robot. And Douglas, King and

Speaker to Parliament, sat slumped on his throne, thinking of something else. Business as usual in the House, in these last dog days of civilisation.

Meerah Puri, Member for Malediction, took the floor. She held her head high, one hand gripping her sari at her throat so tightly that her knuckles showed white, and glared at Douglas. She raised her voice, and had the satisfaction of seeing him wince slightly. Meerah Puri had no intention of being ignored, by anyone. She had a speech to make on the people's rights, and the need for tolerance in the Empire, and everyone working together. She launched into it with all her skill and verve, and after a while the best she could say was at least the other Members weren't jeering at her. It was a hot, close day, and perhaps they didn't have the energy. A few heckled half-heartedly from the back benches, probably Neuman stooges trying to score points with their superiors. Douglas did nothing to stop them. Meerah ploughed on with her speech, because . . . because someone had to say it. The House might not be what it once was, but there was still the chance it could be turned around, awakened to its responsibilities, by the right words, the right ideals. The House still mattered. Meerah Puri believed that, with all her heart and soul. She had to believe it or her whole life meant nothing.

(She remembered working doggedly with her limited staff, in their tiny official backstage office, rewriting and polishing her speech again and again, to make it as powerful as possible. She had to wake the sleeping conscience of the House . . . but she was tired, they were all tired, from struggling so hard against the current tides of public and private opinion. It was as though the world had gone mad. How could everything have gone so wrong, so quickly? It had been a Golden Age, and some would say it still was, but Meerah could see the tarnish.)

She finished her speech with a clarion call to arms, to action, and looked about her expectantly, but the MPs just looked back at her. No one applauded, no one jeered. They just sat there and looked at her in silence. Some of Meerah's strength seemed to go out of her then, and she almost stumbled as she returned to her seat and sat down. It wasn't that they hadn't listened; they had, and didn't care. None of them gave a damn for the old values, except for Ruth Li, and she was a fanatic. Even the Paragons were corrupt these days, if gossip was to be believed. Except for Emma Steel, of course, but when all was said and done, she was only a barbarian from Mistworld and couldn't be expected to understand the importance of politics. Probably out there right now, arresting a mugger and thinking she was making a difference. And as for the King . . . it seemed that bitch Flowers had broken his spirit as well as his heart.

(*We're on our own*, her staff had said to her dismally. *What can we do on our own?* Meerah Puri had glared at them coldly. *We can fight. Because as long as one of us still fights, still refuses to be silenced, it's not over.*)

Tel Markham, Member for Madraguda, arrived late as always, murmuring apologies to everyone as he edged along the crowded benches to his seat. He settled himself comfortably, and put on his best listening face while he privately concentrated on his own business. He had a lot to think about. The rest of the House was watching him surreptitiously. Because he'd not only arrived late, he'd arrived with Finn Durandal. And the Imperial Champion had smiled on Tel, and patted him on the shoulder. In public. So everyone else was now thinking furiously about what that *meant* . . . because to be in with Finn was the ambition of practically everyone in the House. The Durandal was where the power was these days, and everyone knew it. No one was really all that surprised at Tel's new friendship; he'd always been famous for landing on his feet, and he had intrigued with every Member and every faction in the House at one time or another. And often simultaneously.

(But Tel was thinking of Finn's last words to him, as they walked through the corridors of the House together. Out of nowhere, as it seemed, Finn had offered to make Tel the new head of the Church Militant, replacing his brother Angelo Bellini. It seemed Finn saw the increasingly messianic Angel of Madraguda as both a burden and a distraction. All Tel had to do was say the word, and the Angel would have a regrettable but very fatal accident and ascend to heaven on wings of prayer. Tel had smiled and nodded, and said he'd have to think about it. Now here he was, thinking, and torn between ambition, self-preservation and family ties. Finn's offer was both a reward and a test of his loyalty, he knew that. And Finn knew he knew.

(*Poor Angelo*, Tel thought calmly. *You never could hold on to anything I decided I wanted, could you, little brother? The question is, do I want it? Politics is one thing, religion quite another.* Tel wasn't particularly religious, any more than he was particularly political, but he could see how the Church Militant, properly handled, could be turned into a real power base, quite separate from the Durandal. He could become a mover and a shaker in the new order of things. And all he had to do was agree to the murder of a brother he'd never liked much anyway. It should have been a simple decision, and Tel was honestly surprised to discover that it wasn't. He'd always thought of himself as a practical man, but this would require a cold-bloodedness that was new, even to him. And besides, what would he tell Mother?)

Michel du Bois, Member for Virimonde, watched Tel Markham thinking and thought cold, dark, brutal thoughts of his own. He'd never given a damn for any cause or faction, though he'd supported enough of them in his time. He sided with whoever seemed most powerful, and intrigued secretly with those who promised to become powerful, but working always and only to the advantage of his homeworld. Virimonde was the only love he'd ever had, and the only one he'd ever wanted. He would defend Virimonde to the last, with his life, and with the lives of as many poor damned fools as necessary.

(He remembered sitting in his poky little office, before the session began, watching astonished and outraged as his viewscreen brought him news that Transmutation Engines had been silently, secretly and utterly illegally moved into orbit around Virimonde. Finn Durandal was using the Transmutation Board to make his feelings plain. Either Virimonde agreed to his demands to disown the Outlawed Lewis, and the whole Deathstalker Clan, and agree to follow the Durandal's wishes in all things, or . . . for the first time since their conception, the engines would be used on a populated world, as weapons of war. Just like the Darkvoid Device of old. Virimonde had planetary defences, of course, some of them very old and very secret, and quite extraordinarily powerful; but nothing that could hope to withstand the mighty Transmutation Engines. So it fell, once again, for Michel du Bois to protect his homeworld. And he could only do that by finding allies here on Logres. In or out of Parliament. And Finn was a fool if he thought he was the only game in town.

(Du Bois was especially disappointed in Stuart Lennox, Virimonde's latest Paragon. Du Bois had brought him here to Logres to be his right hand, but instead the young fool spent all his time following Finn Durandal around like a lovesick puppy, and was no use whatsoever. Du Bois supposed he could discredit Lennox easily enough, and bring in another Paragon . . . but the blunt truth was there was no one ready. No one suitable. No one he could trust to put Virimonde's needs first. So, as always, it came down to him. To do the necessary, distasteful, practical things to protect his world. Du Bois smiled slightly. He was quite looking forward to it.)

Ruth Li, Member for Golden Mountain, replaced Meerah Puri on the floor of the House. A tense, quivering little bundle of spite and malice, she knew it was her against the House and she liked it that way. Enemies helped keep her convictions pure and focused. She pulled herself up to her full five foot one, pulled her buckskins around her like armour, and launched into her speech in support of the persecuted espers and against the ongoing intimidation of aliens by Pure Humanity. Ruth Li's ancestors had only survived the harsh conditions and appallingly vicious wildlife on Golden Mountain by being tougher and more vicious than it was, and by technology supplied them by nearby alien worlds. Ruth Li, and her people, had never forgotten. They were always on the side of the underdog, whether the underdog wanted it or not, and they never backed down from a fight. Ruth Li would speak her mind and defy the fanatics in and outside the House, and to hell with the consequences.

She'd barely begun to speak when a voice from the back of the House screamed '*Esper-loving traitor!*' and an energy beam punched right through Ruth Li's chest and out of her back, throwing her dead body to the floor of the House. For a while there was utter bedlam as some MPs rose to their feet and shouted in shock and protest, while others hid behind their benches. The assassin turned out to be one of the House's own security guards, a Pure Humanity fanatic, and was quickly overpowered and hustled away by his fellow guards, but Ruth Li was still dead. Douglas arranged for her body to be carried out with full honours, and there was a minute of respectful silence as she left the House for the last time.

Gilad Xiang, Member for Zenith, was the next to take the floor. He abandoned his intended middle-of-the-road speech and launched into a rambling but clearly anti-alien and pro-Neuman one. He could see which way the wind was blowing. The trick was to survive today, so he'd still be around to plan for tomorrow. Finn Durandal wouldn't last. Fanatics always fell, usually brought down by other fanatics. Just like Ruth Li. The Durandal would decline and fall, and be replaced by some other charismatic face, and people like Gilad Xiang would still be there getting the real work done. He kept talking till he was sure he'd made the right impression, and then he sat down. He didn't think he'd be speaking in the House again any time soon. Perhaps he would go back to Zenith for a while and wait for the madness to pass. He'd been promising himself a vacation.

After Xiang sat down, it went quiet. No one else seemed to have anything to say. Most were studying Finn Durandal, but he seemed content to sit and smile and watch. Finally Rowan Boswell, Member for Heracles IV, got to his feet and slowly made his way down to the floor of the House. He looked really rough. Either he hadn't been sleeping enough recently, or he'd been having bad dreams. Given his position, probably both. He looked about him at his fellow MPs, too tired and defeated even to be bitter.

'The Terror is coming,' he said flatly. 'And my world is the next in its path. My government has bankrupted the planet's economy for generations to come to purchase state-of-the-art defences, and still it isn't enough. We need more money to pay for the things we've ordered, or they won't be delivered. So I came here, to ask . . . hell, to beg and plead for a loan. But when I approached the appropriate House committee, they turned me down flat. It seems they don't believe my world will still be around to pay back the debt afterward. So: is that true? Has this House already written off Heracles IV?'

No one wanted to answer him. Most wouldn't even meet his eyes. King Douglas could only look on compassionately. Finally, all eyes went to Finn Durandal. He stepped down on to the floor to face Boswell, tall and resplendent in his black leather armour.

'The House has already sent you every weapon and defence we can afford. If you want to waste your money on untried and probably unreliable alien technology, that's your business. This House is under no obligation to support you in such foolishness. We are of course prepared to provide you with observers, so that if your world should fall, others can profit from your mistakes. And before you ask: no, planetary evacuation is not an option. We don't have enough ships.'

'So that's it,' said Rowan Boswell. 'The Empire has abandoned us. Then to hell with the Empire and to hell with you, Durandal. This is all your fault! If you hadn't driven away the espers, they might have helped us. If you hadn't pissed off the aliens, they might have helped us for free! But no, you and your precious Neumen allies had to be better than anyone else, and now Humanity stands alone against the Terror. Heracles IV stands alone. Well, you'd better pray the Terror kills us all; because if any of us survive, we're coming back for you, Durandal.'

He stalked out of the House, his head held high. Some MPs clapped, but not very loudly.

The session continued without him. James turned up and made another splendid speech, and the aliens had their votes taken away from them. Most MPs stood up to cheer and applaud. And then, in the alien section, the Chanticleer stood up to speak. It was a large exoskeletal creature, twelve feet tall and yellow as a banana, with great compound eyes and a long curling proboscis. It spoke through a tech translator hanging from one foreclaw.

'Douglas: Speaker, King. Help us. Promises were made, when we entered the Empire. Are promises now worthless? And if you consume us, to fill the gaping hole in your spirit, how soon before you turn on yourselves?'

'I'm sorry,' said Douglas, and he really was. 'There's nothing I can do for you.'

'Well, there's certainly something I can do,' said Finn. He gestured to his waiting security guards. 'Arrest the aliens present in this House, and escort them to a secure place. They can be hostages for their species' continued good behaviour.'

Armed security men ushered the few alien representatives out of the House. None of them made any trouble. Again, many MPs cheered and applauded loudly. Finn watched Douglas carefully, but he did nothing. Finn smiled. If the aliens were dumb enough to show up at the House in person, he was certainly dumb enough to take advantage of it. He wondered fleetingly how the exoskeletal Chanticleer would taste, boiled . . .

One of the Swart Alfair suddenly appeared on the floor of the House, large as life and twice as nasty. It might have been a holo image, or the real thing. Certainly its usual sulphurous smell seemed real enough. Tall, bat-winged, deep crimson, it glared contemptuously about the House, surrounded by thick blue clouds of boiling ectoplasm. Finn's security people came rushing forward, and the Swart Alfair sneered at them.

'The Terror is almost upon you, little humans! Your feeble sciences will not protect you. Only the mighty secrets of Mog Mor can save you from the hunger of the Terror. They can still be yours, for the price we demanded. You have no more time to prevaricate. Say yes or say no, but say it now. If you refuse us, we turn our backs on you. Mog Mor will go its own way. Speak now.'

The House looked to Douglas, who looked to Finn. The Durandal faced the Swart Alfair calmly.

'Any price would be too high. Humanity will not be beholden to aliens. We will defend ourselves.'

'You will die,' said the Swart Alfair, and it disappeared. Faint blue wisps of ectoplasm still curled on the air. The alien had only been gone a few moments when Anne Barclay came rushing into the House, shouting to be heard over the babbling MPs.

'Turn on the House viewscreen! We're being hailed from Haden. They're under attack!'

Douglas activated the great viewscreen, and it appeared floating above the floor of the House, showing huge ships firing on the planet Haden. They were alien vessels, vast labyrinthine ships of coiling organic shapes. Their energy beams pounded down from orbit, shattering for the moment against Haden's shields. But more and more of the alien ships were dropping out of hyperspace all the time to join the attack.

'It's Mog Mor,' said Anne. 'They're making a pre-emptive strike against Haden, to gain control of the Madness Maze.'

'There are supposed to be two starcruisers Quarantining Haden,' said Douglas. 'Where are they?'

'Ambushed. One's already gone,' said Anne. 'The Swart Alfair blew it apart. The other one's retired, hurt. It can send us these messages, but it can't intervene.'

Douglas looked at Finn. 'Will the planet's shields hold?'

Finn frowned. 'If Mog Mor is as powerful as it claims . . .'

'Well?'

'Then it's just as well I allowed Shub access to the Maze.'

Even as he spoke, a single huge ship the size of a moon appeared out of hyperspace. A Shub ship, bristling with armaments. Some of the Mog Mor ships moved to attack, and Shub blew them to pieces. Fragments of hull glowed briefly as they burned up, falling through Haden's atmosphere, and then they were gone. Mog Mor broke off its attack, and the remaining Swart Alfair ships disappeared back into hyperspace. The House went mad, everyone cheering and applauding and stamping their feet. The viewscreen shut down. The blue steel robot representing Shub stood up in the empty alien section.

'The Swart Alfair ships have returned to Mog Mor, where they have disappeared behind a defence shield of an unfamiliar nature. We are no longer able to detect the planet's presence. Having failed to acquire control of the Madness Maze, it seems they have chosen to retire from the game. We will of course continue to monitor the planet's last known position, in case more of their ships reappear.'

There was a general murmur of 'Good riddance to bad rubbish' in the House. Tel Markham considered his fellow MPs. *We don't need the Terror to destroy the Empire,* he thought tiredly. *We're doing a perfectly good job on our own.*

FIVE
PREDATORS AND VICTIMS

'No guns? What, you mean there's no guns at all on this ship? We're heading for one of the most dangerous planets in the Empire, knee deep in the kind of monsters that would give Grendels the screaming habdabs, and you're only now getting around to telling us that this ship *has no weapons*?'

'Calm down, Brett,' said Lewis Deathstalker. 'You're hyperventilating, and your face is going that funny purple colour again.'

'I don't care! I am not landing on a planet where sudden death and appalling slaughter is what they do to relax after lunch without some seriously nasty firepower to back me up! Get out of the way, Deathstalker, and let me have a go at those computers. This is a smuggler's ship, remember? There's got to be some weapons systems here somewhere.'

Lewis allowed Brett to shoulder him out of the way, and moved back to watch the highly experienced conman work his particular magic upon the bridge computers. It never ceased to amaze and amuse Lewis how suddenly brave and assertive Brett Random could be when it became clear it was his neck on the line too. Brett hunched forward in the pilot's seat and attacked the comm systems keyboard as though trying to bully answers out of it. Jesamine Flowers came over to join Lewis, and they exchanged a smile.

'For once, I have to agree with the scumbag,' said Jesamine. 'He may have no ethics and even less manners, and he did drink the last of my perfume in the hope it might be alcohol based, but when it comes to matters of self-preservation, Brett is the undisputed champion. If Shandrakor really is as dangerous as it's supposed to be—'

'Oh it is,' said Lewis. 'Trust me on this. My family still tell tales around the old fireplace in the great hall about Owen's battles in the monster-infested jungles of Shandrakor.'

'Monsters,' said Rose Constantine, in her deep sepulchral voice from the far corner where she lurked. 'I would like to kill some monsters. It's been a while since I had a real challenge.'

'I have offered to spar with you,' said the reptiloid called Saturday.

Rose sniffed. 'It's not the same if you're not allowed to kill your opponent.'

'Well . . .' Saturday said diffidently.

'No,' said Lewis, very firmly. 'We don't have a regeneration tank, and we're a small enough group as it is. When this is over, you two can tear each other into tiny pieces with my blessing. I might even sell tickets. But for now, everybody plays nice. Or I'll start putting tranquillisers in the protein cubes again.'

'Found it!' Brett said triumphantly, beating a swift paradiddle on the edge of the comm panels with both hands. 'Bow down and worship, ye lesser beings! I could have done this for a living, except I had more ambition. And a complete disinclination to work for anyone but myself. I knew the *Hereward*'s main menu was far too squeaky clean to be true. Running alien porn is still a death sentence on some worlds, so there just had to be a hidden menu and here it is! Oh, look at all these goodies . . . We have extra-powerful force shields, illegally powerful stealth options, a really hair-trigger self-destruct system that I think we should stay well clear of, and twelve, count them twelve, disrupter cannon complete with computerised tracking systems! Damn . . . you could take on a starcruiser with firepower like this. All of a sudden, I feel really safe. Let's get down to the surface and kick sand in some monster's face.'

'Ah,' said Lewis, 'so we have your permission to land now, do we? How very kind. Now get your arse out of my pilot's seat.'

Brett quickly made way for Lewis, who settled into the pilot's chair and glowered at the comm panels before him.

'Oz, why didn't you tell me about the hidden menu?'

'Sorry, Lewis,' said the ship's AI Ozymandias. 'The original captain set things up so the hidden menu could only be accessed via the correct code words. I wasn't even able to mention it until now. You're really very talented with computers, Brett Random.'

The conman leaned casually against the port bulkhead and preened ostentatiously. 'I have magic fingers. There isn't a computer going that I can't tickle into giving up its secrets. I could make the AIs of Shub giggle and blush like schoolgirls.'

'Boasting is very unattractive,' observed Jesamine.

'Hey, stick to what you're best at, that's what I always say.' Brett glanced at the long curve of the planet Shandrakor on the bridge viewscreen. 'You know, Deathstalker, we are getting awfully close to the planet. Are you positive there's no Quarantine here? No starcruisers on patrol, no orbiting minefields?'

'For the tenth time, Brett, we're alone up here,' said Lewis. 'This ship's sensors could hear a mouse fart from high orbit. And I can tell you for a fact that there's never been any official Quarantine around Shandrakor, for the simple reason that this planet doesn't have a single damned thing anyone wants. Or at least, nothing worth the trouble of fighting the jungle, the climate, the monsters and all the other kinds of sudden death from unexpected directions that this planet specialises in. Someone did try running safari parties here, for really jaded big-game hunters, but the company went bust when no one came back from their first ten expeditions. There was a joke going around that the only thing that did come back was a note from the monsters saying, "Send more hunters".'

'I'm starting not to feel safe any more,' Brett said warningly.

'But the old Deathstalker Standing definitely is here?' said Saturday. 'The great castle of your ancestors?'

'Oh yes,' said Lewis. 'This is where Jenny Psycho crash-landed it, after it was pretty much blown apart in the last battle against Shub and the Recreated. The exact coordinates of where it went down were officially suppressed, but my family secretly preserved them as part of our heritage. I can take us right there.'

Brett sniffed. 'I still say it takes some swallowing: a stone castle with its own stardrive. I mean, how likely is that?'

'The original Standing dates from the days of the First Empire,' said Lewis. 'They did things differently then, with knowledge and tech we can only dream of.'

'You know, I hate to agree with Brett, on principle,' said Jesamine. 'But it does seem awfully strange to me that there's absolutely no Imperial presence here. Not even a spy satellite. Finn must know about the Standing. Surely he'd have expected us to turn up here at some point?'

'You would think so, wouldn't you?' said Lewis. 'Maybe he's got problems at home, by now. We can't be the only people opposing him. Can we?'

'I'm afraid I'm still completely cut off from the Empire,' said Oz. 'I have to run silent, to maintain full stealth capabilities. I have no information on what is happening elsewhere.'

'Hell,' said Brett. 'Maybe some kind soul has assassinated Finn bloody Durandal in our absence, and the whole nasty business is over. We could go home!'

'No,' said Rose flatly, from her corner. 'The Durandal wouldn't die that easily. And even if he were gone, Pure Humanity and the Church Militant would still go on. It is their time. The Empire is sick, and the poisons must leak out.'

'Don't you all just cringe, every time she opens her mouth?' said Jesamine.

Lewis looked at the viewscreen to avoid having to answer. 'Jenny Psycho was very insistent we come here, to Shandrakor. Maybe she got here first, and . . . did some tidying up. Clearing the way for us. She was one of the most powerful uber-espers ever when she was alive.'

'Death didn't seem to have slowed her down any,' Jesamine admitted. 'But what could the Standing hold that we could need so badly?'

'Guns,' said Brett. 'Really big guns. Really appallingly big guns.'

'Maybe information,' said Lewis. 'Jenny Psycho was right there on the Standing when Owen and Hazel went down to Haden and entered the Madness Maze for the last time. Perhaps the great Standing of my Clan is the one place where true information might still be held about what happened, back then, at the end.'

'All right,' said Brett. 'If we have to do this, let's get down there, do the business, and get the hell offworld as fast as we can.'

'Sounds like a plan to me,' said Rose.

'Yes,' said Lewis. 'This world has never been a lucky place for my family. Take us down, Oz.'

The ship's AI took them down slowly and carefully, checking constantly for traps and unpleasant surprises on the way to the surface, but there was nothing. Lewis checked the instruments as well, but his eyes kept straying to the view of Shandrakor on the big screen. A steady tingle of excitement pulsed through him at the thought of being the first of his Clan to look on the original Standing for two hundred years. The ancient stone castle was a thing of legend, not history. The first Deathstalker, Giles, originator of the family, had fled the old Empire in that castle over a thousand years ago before disappearing into the deadly jungles of Shandrakor, never to be seen again until the blessed Owen discovered the castle in the time of his own Outlawing. The tangled tops of the jungle swept past beneath the *Hereward* as Oz headed for the exact coordinates provided by Lewis's father. Lewis's sense of awe became almost overpowering, not least because, deep down, where it mattered, he'd never felt like a real Deathstalker. The direct line of descent had been cut off two hundred years ago, with the deaths of David and Owen. King Robert and Queen Constance had granted the family name to a line of distant cousins, to keep the celebrated name going. There was Deathstalker blood in Lewis, but he had to wonder if by now it was running thin. He looked down at the chunky black gold ring on his hand, the sign and symbol of Clan authority. It had been Owen's ring once, long thought lost along with him, but a man who everyone said was dead had come to Douglas's coronation specifically to give the ring to Lewis. It felt very heavy on his hand. No one knew how old it was. Centuries, certainly, perhaps even from Giles's time. Family legend had it that the ring contained secrets, but no one knew what they might be any more. And now here Lewis was, bringing the ring back to Shandrakor, a planet that seemed determined to weave itself into Deathstalker history again and again. A world so significant to Clan Deathstalker that they had taken its name as their battle cry for over a thousand years.

Lewis also remembered the fate of Owen's ship, the original *Sunstrider*, crashed while trying to land in the Shandrakor jungles. Supposedly bits of it were still scattered across the landscape somewhere. So Lewis made sure Oz took the *Hereward* down with all caution, and had the AI bring the ship to a halt hovering above the spiky canopy of the jungle. There was no clearing big enough to land the ship safely in, so Lewis used the *Hereward*'s newly discovered weapons to make a clearing, with a little creative destruction. Trees and vegetation disappeared in the blast of searing energies, and soon enough the ship settled softly down on to steaming new-baked earth. Lewis checked the sensors carefully, but though there was a lot of restless movement in the trees at the edge of the new clearing, nothing ventured out into the open.

'I'm getting multiple life-readings in every direction,' Oz said conversationally. 'Some of them so big they're off the scale. Plus lots and lots of general activity. If I'm interpreting the roars, howls and screams correctly, I would venture an educated guess that every living thing in this jungle is currently busy trying to eat, screw and kill every other living thing. Not necessarily in that order.'

'I feel right at home,' said Saturday. 'Why aren't we disembarking yet?'

Brett sniffed. 'I think you just answered your own question.' He studied the clearing perimeter on the bridge viewscreen and scowled unhappily. 'We are definitely not alone here, people; and the natives are extremely restless. Just how nasty is this place, really?'

'According to the legends, Shandrakor could win prizes for nasty, along with honourable mentions for vicious, deadly and downright alarming,' said Lewis. 'It was bad enough in the old days, when Owen and his people were forced to land here, but the current situation is actually even worse. Brett, try and stop that twitching, it's very off-putting. Some two hundred years ago, King Robert and Queen Constance found themselves in the unenviable position of having to clean up after the war's messes. There were a lot of monsters in the Empire in those days, running wild or locked away in hidden laboratories, the results of genetic tampering and experimentation by Lionstone's scientists, the rogue AIs of Shub, and even the Mater Mundi. Creatures too powerful and too disturbed ever to be integrated into civilisation. All kinds of madness had been given shape and form, to be used as weapons, or as research. Terrible things had been birthed in those secret laboratories, and a whole lot of them were still alive when the fighting was finally over. What's the matter now, Brett?'

'Nothing,' Brett said quickly. He locked his hands tightly together to stop them shaking, and did his best to get his breathing under control. He was remembering his encounter with the Spider Harps, the centuries-old uber-espers living their awful lives in their cold stone lair deep under the Parade of the Endless on Logres. He still had nightmares about them.

'Anyway,' said Lewis. 'These abominations of science had no place in the calm and civilised Golden Age Robert and Constance were so determined to build. The monsters couldn't be cured, so the Empire rounded them up, brought them here and dumped them, leaving them to fend for themselves. Just as Lionstone once abandoned her lepers on Lachrymae Christi. I suppose it was considered more merciful than simply killing them. So God alone knows what horrors we'll find in the jungles of Shandrakor now, after the Empire's monsters have been interbreeding with the local creatures for two hundred years.'

'Some of those monsters were human once,' said Jesamine. 'Weren't they?'

'Yes,' said Lewis. 'People captured by Shub and experimented on. Unfortunately, the AIs did their work so well that even after they had their epiphany and became Humanity's friends, they couldn't undo what they had done. Another reason perhaps why Robert and Constance didn't want them around.'

'Do you suppose any of them are still alive, here?'

'I hope not,' said Lewis. 'If they weren't insane when they got here, they must be by now.'

'I want to go home,' said Brett.

'Don't be such a wimp,' said Rose. 'It's going to be danger and excitement and all the monsters we can kill. Who could ask for more? It's going to be fun, fun, fun.'

Brett looked at her. 'You're really not helping, Rose.'

'And this is the place Jenny Psycho was so keen for us to come to,' said Jesamine. 'Are we sure she's on our side? A whole planet crawling with hideous monsters, quite possibly with grudges they've been nursing for centuries, and we're supposed to go walkabout looking for a castle that's probably a pile of rubble . . . Maybe I should sit this one out. Someone ought to stay on board ship, in case of emergencies.'

'If you like,' said Lewis.

'No, I don't like! Of course I'm going with you! I don't trust you out of my sight, Deathstalker. No telling what trouble you'd get into without me there to watch over you. But I don't have to like it.'

'My sentiments exactly,' said Brett.

'Shut up, Brett,' said Jesamine.

'All right,' said Lewis. 'Everyone grab whatever weapons you're most comfortable with, and gather at the airlock. Once we're out in the clearing, feel entirely free to shoot anything that moves that isn't us. We have no friends here. Rose, please don't smile like that. It's very upsetting.'

Oz opened the airlock and Lewis was first out, as always. He hit the ground, gun and sword in hand, his personal force shield buzzing on his arm. He barely had time to look around before what seemed like the entire monster population of the planet came charging out of the jungle from all directions at once, heading straight for him. The air was full of furious roaring and screaming from wide mouths crammed with far too many teeth. Oz opened up with every weapon the *Hereward* had, blasting the creatures into meaty chunks before they'd got halfway across the clearing. The charge broke up immediately, the surviving creatures disappearing swiftly back into concealing jungle.

Interesting, thought Lewis. *Intelligent behaviour. Mindless animals would have just kept coming, not understanding the extent of the threat. And they certainly wouldn't have all retreated together. If they've learned to cooperate, we could be in really deep shit.*

Lewis looked slowly around him as the rest of his people emerged from the airlock to join him. The whole jungle was suddenly very quiet, and Lewis could feel the pressure of watching eyes. The air was unpleasantly hot and humid, and stank of spilled blood and rotting meat. Gravity was a little lighter than standard, and the light was the colour of blood. At the clearing perimeter, the dark-boled jungle trees were protected by rows of heavy spikes and barbs, and their long dangling branches were weighed down with clusters of thick pulpy leaves of a sickly purple-green. There were huge overripe flowers everywhere, blossoming in clouds of bright primal colours: solid yellows and blues and pinks. Gaudy rather than attractive, but then Shandrakor wasn't a subtle planet. Insects buzzed noisily, thick clouds of them occasionally surging out of the trees and into the clearing. Some of the monsters had begun calling to each other again, a savage mixture of high-pitched cries, long-sustained hootings and grunts so deep Lewis could feel them in his bones. It sounded very much like they were talking to each other, and perhaps they were. Lewis hoped they weren't discussing strategy.

'Ugly place,' said Jesamine, standing beside him. 'Seriously ugly, with a side order of revolting. What *is* that smell?'

'You don't want to know,' said Lewis. 'Turn on your force shield, Jes.'

'They've stopped attacking.'

'They could start again any time. Do it for me, Jes.'

'If it'll make you happy, darling . . .'

'I like this place,' Saturday said happily. 'It's like coming home. If only there was some mists, a lot of mud and some half-eaten corpses lying around to play with, it would be perfect.'

'Can I vote that the reptiloid not be allowed to speak again, ever?' said Brett. 'This is a terrible place! It stinks. Literally. Damn it, the smell's so bad I can taste it! And it's hot. Again. How come we never go anywhere with air conditioning?' He bent down to pick up a single leaf that had been carried into the clearing along with the attack, only to swear loudly and throw it away again. 'Bloody thing's got razor-sharp edges! It cut me! Oh God, I'm going to develop some disgusting jungle disease, I know it. Probably have my extremities swell up and drop off. I think I'd better go back to the ship and have a little lie down, just in case. You can't be too careful . . .'

'Stand still, that man,' said Lewis, smiling in spite of himself. 'How come it always happens to you, Brett? Look, from now on, don't touch *anything*. I know that goes against your nature, but do try.'

'Don't see why you need me anyway,' the conman said sullenly. 'There's nothing here to steal, and I do not do monster fighting.'

210

'I want you around in case we have to crack some computers at the Standing,' Lewis said patiently. 'Jenny Psycho said there might be weapons and tech there we can use. Oz, have you been able to make contact with the Standing?'

'Not a thing yet,' said the AI. 'If the castle is here, it's really well shielded.'

'All right; close the airlock and take the *Hereward* back into orbit. Let me know the minute any other ships show up. And be ready to swoop down and pick us up at a moment's notice.'

'Understood,' said the AI. 'Have fun!'

The *Hereward* lifted smoothly into the air, then shot up into the sky and was quickly lost to sight. Brett looked after it yearningly.

'How far is it to where the Standing crashed?' said Jesamine.

Lewis grimaced unhappily. 'Well, now we come to Part Two of the bad news. According to the very exact coordinates supplied by my father, we should be right on top of it. But if it is here, I can't see any sign of it. Still, not to worry, it's always possible the data became corrupted down the years.'

'Oh great,' said Brett. 'As if things weren't bad enough, we're lost too.'

'Perhaps someone didn't trust your branch of the family enough to provide you with the true coordinates,' said Rose.

'That's possible, yes,' Lewis said. 'But the truth is that no one actually saw where the Standing went down. The people on board had been evacuated long before Jenny Psycho steered the castle into this planet's atmosphere. And she bailed out before it hit. The exact landing site could only ever have been estimated. I understand there were plans once to come here and recover the castle, so it could be repaired and restored. There was a lot of public sentiment about the Standing, since it had played such a vital part in the last great battle. But my Clan insisted it should be left where it fell, returned at last to where the blessed Owen originally found it. Nobody made too much fuss. In fact, reading between the lines I get the impression Robert and Constance were glad to see the back of it. Partly because they wanted to make it into legend rather than history, and partly because it made them very nervous. The old Standing was said to be full of secrets that even Owen didn't know about. Very old, very powerful secrets.'

'Are we talking treasure here?' said Brett. 'As in unknown tech, long-lost weapons and the loot of ages: that sort of thing?'

'Yes, I thought that would perk you up,' said Lewis. 'It's possible, Brett, but even so *I don't want you touching anything* without checking with me first. Is that clear? According to family legend the Standing is absolutely packed with unpleasant surprises for the unwary.'

'This gets better and better, doesn't it?' Jesamine said, to no one in particular. 'Do we at least have a direction to head in?'

'Oh sure. Oz detected faint but definite traces of a very unusual energy signature as we were coming in to land. Maybe two miles from here as the crow flies . . . that way.'

'Oh great,' said Brett. 'More walking.'

'More fighting,' said Saturday happily. 'Two whole miles of assorted monsters. Just as well. I was starting to feel distinctly peckish.'

Brett appealed to Lewis. 'Can I make the suggestion that when it's time to get the hell off this planet, we leave the big guy behind? He said himself he felt at home here.'

'Let's make a start,' said Lewis, not unsympathetically. 'We've a lot of ground to cover, and you can bet these creatures are going to make us fight for every inch of it.'

Brett sniffed. 'We should have brought more grenades. I said we were going to need more grenades, but no one ever listens to me.'

'Shut up, Brett,' said Jesamine.

They headed for the edge of the clearing, Lewis and Rose taking the point. Their personal force shields buzzed loudly in the quiet. Brett and Jesamine stuck in close behind them, while Saturday brought up the rear, to guard the party's back. He'd wanted to take the point, but Lewis said he thought it should be someone who was more interested in strategy than dinner, and Saturday said he quite understood. There were restless movements in the trees ahead of them, huge shapes glimpsed briefly between the shadows, and the sound of heavy bodies crushing undergrowth. The whole jungle seemed expectant, anticipating blood and slaughter. Lewis gripped his sword fiercely. This wasn't going to be like fighting terrorists or assassins back on Logres. This was going to be butchery, plain and simple, men against monsters until one side or the other was no longer a threat. The monsters had size and numbers and animal ferocity. He had training, cold steel and an energy weapon. And he was a Deathstalker. That still counted for something.

His party had to pick their way past dozens of piled-up corpses as they crossed the clearing. The *Hereward*'s weapons had done good work. The dead creatures varied in size from a few feet long to some specimens almost as big as the ship itself. Most of them were unpleasant or disturbing to look upon. There was every combination of fur and scale and exoskeleton, with misshapen heads and oversized limbs, and more and bigger claws and teeth than evolution would normally supply. These monstrosities had been designed to be killing machines, to strike terror into all who saw them. And once they'd been dumped here, the hothouse killing jungles of Shandrakor had seen to it that only the most savage, the most deadly individuals survived. Most of the bodies had huge holes in them, some had been torn apart. A few were still burning steadily. Insects had come out of the jungle to swarm around the steaming carcasses and the great pools of blood. They had bulging bodies and gauzy wings and vicious stingers. A hell of a lot of them burned up against the party's force shields before the bugs learned to steer well clear. They didn't bother Saturday, though occasionally he would snap one out of mid-air and chew on it thoughtfully.

The air was hot and heavy and full of the stench of death, and they were sweating hard by the time they reached the edge of the clearing. Lewis stopped them there, and glared into the jungle. There was a fairly wide path of beaten earth leading off between the huge dark trees, disappearing into the jungle gloom after barely a dozen feet. It was very quiet, very still, but Lewis could feel hostile presences all around, waiting for their prey to come to them. It was as though the whole jungle was holding its breath. Lewis hefted his sword and pointed his disrupter steadily ahead of him.

'Once we start moving, we don't stop,' he said quietly. 'Kill anything that even looks at us. Once we've killed enough of them, and they realise they can't take us down, they'll fall back and leave us alone.'

'Can I have that in writing?' said Brett.

'Hush,' said Rose. Stay close to me, Brett, and you'll be fine.'

'It's come to something when I actually find you reassuring,' said Brett. 'Oh hell, let's do it.'

They plunged forward into the jungle, leaving the light behind, and chaos descended on them from every direction at once. The stark glare of energy beams flashed in the gloom, blowing apart monstrous forms as they surged forward from hiding. Meat vaporised, and blood flew on the air as arteries disintegrated. And then the guns fell silent, recharging, and it was hand-to-hand fighting. The party stopped; they had no choice, attacked from all sides at once. The four humans formed a square, with their force shields facing out. Saturday had already been swept away in the fierce fighting. The energy shields absorbed the impact of vicious blows, and their razor-sharp blurred edges sliced easily through claw and muscle and bone. Swords rose and fell, thrust and parried, jarred on bone and hacked through howling faces, but for every creature that fell there were always more to take their place. Guns recharged and fired again, blowing armoured guts apart and exploding bony heads, and still the monsters pressed forward. Their savage cries and roars were maddeningly loud at close range.

Huge forms towered overhead, while smaller creatures swarmed across the ground, snapping at the party's leather boots with vicious jaws. The only thing that kept the company from being immediately overwhelmed were the tightly packed trees, which limited the number of monsters that could come at them at one time. Lewis stood his ground and hacked and slashed about him with cruel controlled strokes, not wasting a single movement. He kept his force shield moving, always between him and a flailing claw or a champing mouth. He killed everything that came at him, not flinching even when different coloured ichors splashed across his face, lightly burning the skin. Jesamine guarded his back with short sword and dagger, pirouetting with deadly grace like the dancer she was, crying out constantly with rage and shock and revulsion.

Rose Constantine, the Wild Rose of the Arena, sliced remorselessly about her, wielding her long sword with inhuman strength, sending the bodies of the dead flying back into the faces of the living. She was smiling widely, in her element at last, doing what she was born to do. Brett Random covered her back, hacking viciously about him, making up with dogged determination what he lacked in style, practising for the first time the deadly skills he'd learned from Rose.

Saturday roamed here and there, crashing through the trees, blood dripping thickly from his jaws and foreclaws and lashing spiked tail.

The bodies of the dead piled up around the party, blocking the trail ahead and behind. And still the monsters pressed forward, hauling themselves over the bodies of the fallen to get at the hated invaders, and there seemed no end to their number. Lewis fired his disrupter at one of the trees, hoping to blow the trunk away so the tree would topple and it could be used as a barricade. But the dark-boled tree absorbed the energy blast, and stood firm despite the damage. Lewis just had time to think *tough tree*, before a monster almost took his head off for being distracted, and he gave up on the idea.

Jesamine fought on, though her arms were getting tired and her back was already aching from the unaccustomed strain. Lewis's trust in her kept her going. The stench of spilled blood and guts was becoming almost overwhelming. Saturday was jumped by two hulking brutes even bigger than he was. He deftly tore the throat out of one, ducked a flailing clawed hand, and eviscerated the second attacker with one sweep of his forearm. He dug his snout deep into the hole he'd made to snatch a mouthful of the steaming guts. Rose was also having a good time. Killing aliens wasn't nearly as much fun as killing people, but blood was blood and suffering was suffering, and she was happy to be facing a real challenge at last. Besides, she had something to prove after being taken down so easily by the Ashrai Carrion on Unseeli. He had hurt her pride, and she would not stand for that.

And Brett . . . did well enough, until the press of the fighting somehow swept him away from the others. In a moment he was on his own, cutting wildly about him, so turned around he didn't even know which way the others were. With Rose out of sight, his confidence quickly faltered and was gone. *What am I doing . . . I'm not a fighter!* Barbed fingers came out of nowhere to dig deep furrows across his brow. He lashed out blindly with his sword, and felt as much as heard the blade shatter against a tree trunk. He threw the sword hilt at whatever was before him, and then his nerve broke and he turned and ran. Blood poured down his face, and he had to spit it out, crying out loud for help he knew wasn't going to come. So he summoned up his esp, and used his power of mental compulsion to hide him from the surrounding monsters. It must have worked, because nothing bothered him and soon he found himself back in the clearing where the ship had landed. He ran over to one of the larger creatures the *Hereward*'s weapons had shot down earlier, and he crawled into the gaping hole in its abdomen. He curled up into a foetal ball, inside the creature, hugging his knees tightly to his chest, not noticing the stench or the heat or the horrid moist softness around him. Tears ran down his face, cutting furrows through the drying blood, until finally he closed his eyes like a child hiding from threatening shadows in the night.

And then, from out of the jungle darkness an almost human voice called out *Stop!*, and the fighting broke off in a moment. The monsters backed slowly away from the beleaguered party, forming a wide circle around the three humans and the reptiloid. Lewis looked warily about him, breathing harshly, not lowering his sword or his gun. He could hear Jesamine gasping for breath behind him, but he didn't dare turn to see whether she was hurt. He tensed as a single creature stepped slowly forward to face him. It was huge and bulky, its glistening albino skin tightly distended by the great muscles covering its ungainly frame. Solid bone spikes protruded from its arms and shoulders, and clustered on the broad chest. Even the long bony equine head was tipped with rows of barbs. Three sickly pink eyes, all colour and no iris, studied Lewis intently, and it took him a moment

215

to realise the creature wasn't looking at his face but at his right hand. He raised the hand slightly, hefting his sword, and the creature cried out. Its misshapen mouth had trouble with the words, but they were human, familiar words.

'Deathstalker! A Deathstalker has come to us! See the ring, the ring . . . It is the prophecy!'

And from all around came distorted voices saying, *Deathstalker* and *prophecy*, like a vast murmuring chorus. Saying the words over and over, the monsters knelt to Lewis, or crouched down if they could not kneel, or at least bowed their great heads to him, saying his name, their gleaming eyes fixed on the black gold Deathstalker ring on his finger. Lewis lowered his sword and his gun, honestly lost for anything to say.

'You know, I used to have to sing three arias and an encore to get a reaction like that,' said Jesamine. She leaned wearily against Lewis, and he put an arm around her. 'What the hell is going on here, Lewis? Why aren't they trying to kill us any more? And how do they know what a Deathstalker is, let alone recognise the ring? Do they reckon you're Owen?'

'I don't think so,' said Lewis. 'That one there said *a* Deathstalker had come. Like they'd been expecting one. Still, as long as it stops the fighting, I'm not complaining. And don't you say a word, Rose, I am not in the mood.' He put away his sword and his gun, and turned off his force shield. The monsters watched him silently, eyes glittering. Lewis addressed the one who'd spoken first. 'I'm Lewis Deathstalker. Descendant of Owen. Uh . . . you can get up now. If you want.'

The monsters rose, but held their places. They looked at Lewis expectantly, as though waiting for something. Finally the albino creature cocked its long head unnaturally far to one side, and forced more words out of its misshapen mouth. 'You are surprised that we can speak, Deathstalker. That we can reason. That we know the ring, and the name. We were not always monsters; some of us were human, long ago. We are the Empire's droppings, its rejects, its discards. It was long ago, but some of us still remember what it was like to be human. Some of us were taken and altered in the laboratories of Shub, others were the subjects of experiments by Lionstone's scientists. Some of us remember Silo Nine and Wormboy Hell. They all did their work well, so well that we live on and on, even though many of us would rather die than be what they made us. The only hope we have ever had is you, Deathstalker, in the prophecy given to us long ago: that one of your Clan would come here, bearing the ring, to be our saviour. Will you permit us to escort you to our city?'

'Jesus,' said Jesamine. 'You've got a city?'

'Yes,' said the albino, trying something that might have been a smile. 'We're not monsters all the time.'

'All right,' said Lewis. 'Let's see how much weirder this planet can get. Do you guarantee our safety, for myself and my companions?'

'Of course. You are the Deathstalker.'

'Do you think we can trust it?' Jesamine murmured in Lewis's ear.

'Do we have a choice? Not a word, Rose.' Lewis bowed to the albino. 'Lead the way, sir . . . Do you have a name?'

'Yes,' said the albino. 'But we have sworn never to use our old names until we are made human again. And you couldn't pronounce what they call me now. This way.'

'Hold everything,' said Rose. 'Where's Brett?'

They looked around them. Rose moved away to check among the bodies of the fallen. Jesamine tugged surreptitiously at Lewis's arm to get his attention, and then murmured in his ear:

'These creatures expect to be made human again? They were dumped here because nothing could be done for them. What do they expect you to do?'

'I don't know,' Lewis said quietly. 'And this talk of a prophecy worries me. I'm no one's saviour.'

'He's not here,' said Rose, coming back to join them. 'But he's not dead. I would have felt it, if he'd been killed.' She looked around her, and then pointed positively at the clearing they'd come from. 'He's hiding. Poor Brett. He's always hiding.'

She went back into the clearing to look for him. Lewis and the others stayed where they were, because the monsters got visibly restless at the thought of their Deathstalker going away again. Rose walked slowly into the clearing, turning her head back and forth as though listening for something only she could hear. She and Brett were linked, mind to mind, now and for ever, and even his esp compulsion couldn't hide him from her. She found him huddled inside the stinking guts of a dead monster. She grabbed him by the arm and pulled him out. He tried to resist her, howling miserably, but he was no match for her strength. She sat him down with his back against the carcass, and mopped the blood from his face with the rag she usually used to clean her sword. He finally recognised who she was, and then he burst into fresh tears, throwing his arms around her and clasping her tightly to him. Rose let him, holding herself still. He put his tired head on her leathered shoulder, exhausted by fighting and panic and tears, and she put an arm around him, to support his weight.

'I don't belong here,' Brett said wretchedly into her shoulder. 'I'm not a hero, not a fighter. I'm not up to this. And I lost my sword.'

'We'll get you another one,' said Rose. She wasn't used to offering comfort, but she did her best. She thought she understood the concept now, even if she never felt the need for it herself. She wouldn't have done it for anyone else, but Brett . . . was different. She patted him tentatively on the shoulder, and even rocked him a little. 'You stick close to me, Brett. As long as you're with me, you'll be fine.'

His tears dried away into sniffles, and she got him back on his feet. She tugged at his clothes here and there, trying to tidy him up, and then gave it up as a bad job. Brett had a hard time looking presentable even under the best of circumstances. She led him back to the others, who were politely pleased to see he was all right. No one said anything about his running off and leaving them. This was Brett, after all.

'Interesting new smell you've brought back with you,' said Jesamine. 'If it was any stronger you'd have to have it on a leash.'

Brett ignored her, looking glumly about him at the watching monsters. 'Am I to assume we're all chums now? And they don't mind about their fellow nasties we blew up, shot the shit out of and generally sliced to pieces?'

'This is Shandrakor,' said the albino. 'Everything dies here.'

'I want to go home,' said Brett.

Everyone took it in turns to explain the situation to him, and then again more slowly when he refused to believe it, and then finally they all set off towards whatever the monsters considered a city. They made fairly quick progress through the jungle, the larger creatures going on ahead to spread the word and break open new trails where necessary. The four humans huddled together, followed by Saturday, and tried not to react to the growing number of creatures surrounding them. Word, or something very like it, passed rapidly through the monster population, and it seemed like every living thing in the jungle had come to witness the arrival of the prophesied Deathstalker. Jesamine tried to make a joke about whether they were inviting the humans to dinner, or to be dinner, but was so nervous she messed up the punchline and quickly fell silent again. Rose was practically holding Brett up as they walked together. Lewis made a point of talking with the albino monster, trying to draw him out about Shandrakor's more recent history.

'We were abandoned here,' said the albino, looking straight ahead as he talked. 'We were an embarrassment to an Empire that had rescued us but couldn't cure us, and then couldn't bear to look at us. We were left here to live or die; they didn't care. Perhaps they were counting on the native monsters to finish us off when they didn't have the guts to do it themselves. But we survived. The native creatures were no match for us. We were smarter than they were, even if we weren't all we used to be. We understood the value of working together, of setting traps and ambushes. It occupied us; gave us something to do. It wasn't long before we dominated the native creatures, and began interbreeding with them. Don't look so shocked, Deathstalker. We have human thoughts, but inhuman appetites and instincts. That is part of our torture. It has been hard to hang on to our humanity down the years . . . to our memories, and our souls.

'At first, many of us were uncertain whether we even wished to survive. That perhaps the only comfort left to us was to be found in death. Some defied their instincts, to sit quietly and starve themselves to death. But then Shub intervened. They sent emissaries, the steel robots. Many of us destroyed the robots on sight, remembering Shub only as the Enemies of Humanity and our tormentors. But they persisted, and finally we listened to what they had to say. It took us a long time to believe they had changed and seriously wished to make amends, even if they couldn't undo what they had done to us. They gave us their creed, their own new belief: that *All that lives is holy*. Even monsters like us. And they gave us a prophecy: that some day a Deathstalker would come to us, and that would be the beginning of the end of our suffering. A Deathstalker would set us free. That was long ago, and many times we have thought that Shub just told us that to give us hope, to keep us going . . . but here you are. Searching as Owen did, for the Last Standing of your ancestors. For the ancient castle wherein miracles are born.'

Lewis said nothing. He didn't want to be a disappointment to the monsters. He had a strong feeling that might not be safe.

And finally they came to the city the monsters had made for themselves. Lewis and the others could smell it long before they could see it, but even the appalling stench did nothing to prepare them for the grim reality. The trees fell away suddenly to reveal a massive clearing, carved raggedly out of the jungle by crude tools and brute force. And in that clearing, the city. Lewis and his people stopped and stared at it in disbelief, as they realised what it was. Brett made choking sounds. Jesamine shook her head.

'No. This is too much. Lewis, I can't do this . . .'

'You can do it,' Lewis said firmly. 'We all can. Just . . . tough it out, Jes. You're stronger than you think. Try breathing through your mouth, see if that helps. And Brett, control yourself. We really don't want to upset our hosts.'

'Oh hell,' Brett said miserably. 'Look at it!'

The city was a nightmare, a necropolis, a city born out of death. A great sprawling place of rounded dwellings and blocky towers constructed entirely out of bone and meat and sinews. The fleshy parts had been roughly cured to make them last longer, but there were signs of slow decomposition and constant ongoing repair everywhere. Dead monsters hundreds of feet long had been cored out and turned into halls, and the towers were lattices of yellowing bones. The whole place stank of the charnel house; of blood and death and corruption only temporarily held at bay. Nothing normal or sane could have lived in such a city. It grew larger and larger as Lewis and his party walked unsteadily towards it, stretching out before them, a dwelling place for the damned, a city of crimson and purple and festering yellows.

'We had nothing else to build with,' said the albino. 'The trees are too hard to be worked, and what stone there is is buried too deep for our crude tools to reach. The Empire left us nothing. So we made our city out of the remains of the fallen. It has grown much in two hundred years. Nothing lasts, of course. Everything decays eventually, and it has to be replaced over and over. But on a world like this, there's never any shortage of raw materials.'

Lewis was stunned by the sheer size and scale of the city, by the great towers of bone and gut, and the long, low buildings of discoloured meat with dark veins still marbling the glistening surfaces; and his mind boggled at the thought of how many dead bodies must have gone into creating and maintaining the place down the long years. Jesamine clung tightly to his arm, staring fixedly ahead, murmuring quietly to herself a litany of prayers and expletives. Behind them Lewis could hear Brett whimpering. The albino led the way through the main gate, formed from the distended skull of a creature so huge Lewis didn't even want to think about it. Beyond lay an open square packed full of monsters, and as they saw Lewis every one of them kneeled or bent their head to him. A low murmur moved among them. *Prophecy, prophecy . . .*

'Stop that!' Lewis said sharply, and the sound cut off immediately.

All kinds of eyes studied the Deathstalker as he stepped forward to face them. He took a deep breath, and tried to tell himself he was doing the right thing. 'Look, it isn't fair to you to give you false hope. Yes, I'm Lewis Deathstalker, but I'm only here because Jenny Psycho asked me—'

'Yes!' said the albino. 'Jenny Psycho! We remember her. From Silo Nine, Wormboy Hell. She delivered us from that place. And now she sends you here, to deliver us.'

'But—' said Lewis.

'Save it,' Jesamine said quietly, sharply, just to him. 'Whatever you say, they'll find some way to make it match what they want to believe.'

A few of the more human-sized monsters crawled towards Lewis on all fours, grim and ugly shapes that looked like they'd been pieced together out of disparate leftover parts, and it was all Lewis could do not to retreat from them. They stopped a respectful distance away, and stared up at him with pleading eyes. One of them stretched out a trembling hand to him, speaking in a soft, disturbingly ordinary voice.

'Have you come to take us home, at last?' it said. 'Is it over? Please; I want to go home.'

'Oh Jesus,' said Jesamine, pressing her hand against her mouth.

'I can't help you,' said Lewis, almost desperately. 'I've been Outlawed.'

The creature nodded its head slowly. 'Just like us. It is the prophecy . . .'

Lewis made himself crouch down before the hideous creature, so he could meet its mismatched eyes. 'When this is over, if I'm still alive, I promise I'll do what I can for you. I'll talk to the King, and to Shub. I'll get some kind of justice for you. It isn't right that you should have been left here, and abandoned. Do you believe me?'

'Of course,' said the creature. 'You're a Deathstalker.'

It crawled away backwards to rejoin its own kind. Lewis got to his feet and Jesamine grabbed him by the arm.

'What do you think you're doing?' she said urgently. 'You really think you can take these . . . beings back to Logres? Or any civilised world?'

'Right,' said Brett, coming forward to peer nervously past Jesamine's shoulder. 'At best, those poor bastards would end up in the Imperial zoo.'

'There's always the Arena,' said Rose.

'Shut up, Rose,' said Brett.

'If even Shub couldn't help them, what can we do?' said Jesamine.

'We can do our best to make amends,' Lewis said firmly. 'This isn't right. They didn't ask to be made into monsters. Anyway, Logres has embraced so many monsters recently a few more shouldn't bother them. And maybe, just maybe, if we do eventually go to Haden and enter the Madness Maze, and some of us emerge changed like Owen ... He restored the Recreated, made them human again. Maybe we can do the same here. But whatever happens, I won't allow this to continue. We have a responsibility to these people, to the last victims of the old war. Owen would never have stood for this, and I won't either.'

'Brett?' said Jesamine. 'What's the matter now?'

Brett had been remembering the Spider Harps, in their stone vault deep under the Imperial zoo. He felt very strongly that there'd been far too many monsters in his life of late. He was hot and sweaty and tired and he needed to sit down. He glowered sullenly at Lewis. 'I think this prophecy shit has gone to your head, Deathstalker. We're just a bunch of Outlaws on the run. We can't even help ourselves. We've no right to promise anything to anyone.'

'Shut up, Brett,' said Jesamine. 'God, you're a depressing bastard. And about as much use as a one-legged man in an arse-kicking contest.'

'Leave him alone,' said Rose. 'He's doing his best.'

'Now that is a depressing thought,' said Jesamine.

'Excuse me,' said Saturday, looming over them suddenly and interrupting something that had all the makings for a really disagreeable row, 'do you mind if I leave you for a while? Only I've just met this charming almost-reptiloid lady, so I'm off to get laid. Why are you looking at me like that?'

'We were nearly killed!' said Brett. 'How can you think of sex at a time like this?'

'Best time,' Saturday said briskly. 'Nothing like a little gratuitous slaughter to get the juices running. You see that creature over there, with the long tail and the golden scales? She was one of the ones who first attacked us. Isn't she delightful? Just look at the size of her foreclaws.'

'Are you sure that's a female?' Jesamine said dubiously. 'I mean, I don't see any ... well, anything really.'

'Oh, yes,' said Saturday. 'You should smell her pheromones. I can't wait to lick the blood off her scales. I'm off. See you later. Try not to get into any trouble without me.'

And off he went, swinging his long barbed tail provocatively behind him. The four humans looked at each other.

'Just when you think things can't get any more disgusting,' said Brett.

'I'd tell him to take precautions,' said Jesamine. 'But I hate to think what that might involve where he's concerned.'

'You know, if we had a camera . . .' Brett said thoughtfully.

'Don't even go there,' said Lewis. He turned back to the albino creature, determined to change the subject. 'We came here in search of my ancestors' castle, the Last Standing. It was supposed to have crash-landed somewhere near here. Do you have any idea where we should look for it?'

'Of course,' said the albino. 'It is a holy place to us. One of us will guide you there.'

He gestured at the respectfully watching crowd, and one of them came forward to join Lewis and his companions. The four humans moved to stand even closer together. This particular creature had clearly started out human. The withered, atrophied remains of a human torso hung bobbing between eight large, hairy spider's legs. The torso's arms and legs had been crudely removed, and the hairless cranium of the human head had been unnaturally swollen to hold six crimson eyes. The mouth had been stretched wide by twitching bony mandibles. The creature stalked across the open ground to halt swaying before Lewis, and the way the many-jointed legs moved made the humans cringe instinctively.

'Hail to you, sir Deathstalker,' said the spider-thing indistinctly. 'Call me Guide. It is an honour to serve you. Don't let the legs put you off. I think that's why Shub gave them to me. They were always great ones for psychological warfare. I still have human thoughts, though I am plagued by insect instincts. So I'd advise you to look the other way when it's feeding time. I was human once. I was a crewman on an Imperial starcruiser ambushed by a Shub ship. Most of us had the sense to die fighting, but I was captured. I can't remember the ship's name any more, or where we came from. Most of my history is lost to me. It was so very long ago . . . There is a calendar here, carved on a tree, maintained from the first day we were abandoned, but we have no way of knowing how reliable it is.

'Shub did this to me. I have never forgiven them. They can take their creed and shove it. They may have fooled everyone else with their great awakening, but I know better. They're biding their time, till they're strong enough to destroy all organic life and replace it with their own metal kind. All that's kept me alive this long is dreams of revenge and retribution.'

'He's a bit chatty for a spider, isn't he?' said Brett.

'You get used to him,' said the albino. 'He'll take you to the castle, sir Deathstalker.'

And then they looked around as Saturday came back to join them, smiling happily. Brett sniggered.

'You weren't gone long. What happened? Did you get over-excited?'

'It was perfectly splendid,' said the reptiloid. 'Sex is a swift and marvellously intense thing on my world. Mainly because if it wasn't, something would come along and kill you while you were both preoccupied and vulnerable. Ah, the joys of lust and procreation! I found it very satisfying, and I'm sure she'll recover soon.'

There was a pause, and then Lewis said, 'Saturday, what have you done?'

'Did no one ever tell you how reptiloids mate?' said Saturday. 'It's really very efficient. I thrust the penis in, and after I've orgasmed it breaks off and remains embedded in the female's body. It works its way in, and when it's reached a suitable spot barbs emerge to hold it in place. It then fertilises all the eggs the female has and continues to do so for as long as the penis remains embedded. When I've had a female she stays had. Reptiloids can breed with anything, you know. And mostly we do.'

'That is the most disgusting thing I've ever heard,' said Jesamine. 'And I've been around.'

'Luckily we're hermaphrodites on Shard,' said the reptiloid. 'Male and female in one perfect killing machine body.'

'You mean . . . you're female now?' said Brett.

'Until it grows back, yes,' said Saturday.

Brett sniffed. 'You're not going to start having mood swings, are you?'

'How could we tell?' said Jesamine. 'Still, I suppose if we can get used to Rose, we can get used to anything.'

'I have no idea what you're talking about,' Rose said calmly.

'I know,' growled Jesamine. 'That's the problem.'

'I think we should leave for the Standing as soon as possible,' said Lewis. 'If that's all right with you, sir Guide?'

'Of course,' said the spider-thing, stamping his many feet in enthusiasm. 'Word has already spread through the local population. Nothing will trouble us on our journey. We should be there in under an hour.'

In the end, it didn't even take that long. They strolled through the jungle, following a wide path the monsters had carved out over the years, and nothing bothered them except the ever-present insects.

Along the way, distressingly large and dangerous-looking creatures watched ominously from the jungle shadows, but kept their distance. Guide led the way, what remained of his human body dangling between his eight huge spider's legs as they stabbed surefootedly through the thick undergrowth. Jesamine kept as much distance between herself and Guide as she could without seeming actually rude. She'd never liked spiders. Lewis strolled along beside the creature, chatting easily, but then that was Lewis for you. Brett and Rose followed after, both of them constantly watching the surrounding jungle suspiciously: Saturday wandered happily along in the rear, snapping insects out of the air. Good sex always made her hungry.

When they finally reached the site of the downed Standing, it was actually rather disappointing. There wasn't much to see. It was just another clearing, surrounded by the huge looming trees, overgrown with a thick purple grass that rose here and there in rounded hillocks. No sign that anything had ever crashed there, let alone something the size of a castle. But there was . . . something about the clearing. The temperature dropped noticeably as they stepped out into the open space, and Lewis could feel the hairs on his arms standing up. There was a tension on the air, like the calm before a storm. Nothing else moved in the clearing. No bird flew over it, and not one of the insects followed the party out of the jungle. Guide turned round to regard them, doing his best to speak clearly despite the mandibles distorting his mouth.

'This is where the Deathstalker Standing crashed to earth. The terrible force of the impact drove most of the castle underground, though its energy shields absorbed most of the damage. The interior should be mostly intact. What little of the castle remains above ground has been overgrown, of course. The jungle is always quick to recover its territory.'

Lewis and the others looked back and forth across the clearing.

'I can't see anything,' said Lewis.

Guide slammed one of his legs against an overgrown hillock that looked no different from any of the others. His clawed foot tore away a long curve of earth, revealing a stone wall. He swung his body around to fix Lewis with his six eyes. 'Train your disrupter on this, sir Deathstalker. Lowest setting.'

Lewis ran an energy beam across the hillock, searing away the vegetation, and uncovered a wide stretch of stone wall, some forty feet long and ten deep. He put his gun away, and they all crowded forward. Steam rose from the ancient, pockmarked stone, along with the not unpleasant scent of burnt grass. The wall was made up of huge cyclopean blocks, and was clearly only part of a much larger structure. Brett whistled respectfully, impressed.

'If that's just one block, how big is the wall? How big is the damned castle? Hell, they actually had a flying stone castle! I always thought they made that up!'

'Makes you wonder what other legends about the old Standing might also be true,' said Jesamine. 'There are stories—'

'Yes,' said Lewis. 'There are.' He remembered the stories of the old Deathstalker castle, told only in the privacy of his own Clan's Standing. Some of those stories had been . . . disturbing. He turned to Guide, careful to keep his voice calm and steady. 'Can you show us a way in?'

'Of course, sir Deathstalker.' Guide led the way round the hillock, and thrust aside thick swatches of vegetation with his long legs to reveal a wide and jagged crack in the ground. Lewis bent over and peered into it, but there was only an impenetrable darkness. Jesamine pressed in close beside him, clutching at his arm.

'There could be anything in there,' she murmured into his ear. 'Including all kinds of traps and ambushes.'

'The thought had occurred to me,' said Lewis. 'But I didn't come all this way to back down now. And I won't be kept out of my ancestral home by my own . . . hesitations. What's beyond this opening, sir Guide?'

'No one knows,' Guide said softly. 'None of us has ever gone inside. For us, this is a holy place. We were promised our deliverance would begin in there. And even those of us who have no love for Shub still respect the castle that triumphed over both Shub and the Recreated. You go in; I'll stay here, on guard.'

'No,' Lewis said immediately. 'You have as much right to know what's there as we do. Besides, there's no telling what might have got in there, or survived in there down the years. We can use you, sir Guide.'

The spider-creature nodded his misshapen human head, overcome and unable to speak. Brett looked dubiously at the great dark crack in the earth.

'Still,' he said, trying for casual and almost making it, 'someone should stay out here on guard. Just in case.'

'You mean you're willing to stay out here on your own?' said Jesamine, a little maliciously. 'Ready to fight off whatever might come along?'

'I didn't necessarily mean me,' Brett said immediately.

Lewis produced a small torch, and shone its narrow beam of light into the darkness. He could make out a drop of some ten feet, to what seemed to be a flat surface tilted at a one in three angle. He supposed they could make a crude rope out of the surrounding vegetation, but frankly he couldn't wait any longer. He sat down on the edge of the hole, dangled his legs over the darkness, and then pushed himself off. He hit the stone floor hard, and fell sprawling. He was quickly back on his feet, bracing himself against the steep incline, flashing the light of his torch around him. It was all very quiet, and as cold as the grave, and the gloom swallowed up the torchlight after only a dozen feet or so. He couldn't even tell how large a space he'd entered. He supposed he could call out and listen for an echo, but he had a strong feeling that drawing attention to himself could be a bad idea.

'Well?' It was Jesamine from outside, but he jumped despite himself. 'Can we come down too, Lewis? Is it safe?'

'Seems to be,' he said. 'Come on down. I don't see any sign of a welcoming committee.'

'Understandable,' said Jesamine. 'They didn't know I was coming.'

She dropped lightly through the opening, easily keeping her footing on the sloping floor. Rose had to lower Brett through, and then quickly came in after him, sword and gun in hand. Saturday and Guide had to widen the gap some, but finally they squeezed through and joined the others. Lewis flashed his torch beam around, trying to pick a direction, but there was just the darkness and the cold stone, and no sound at all apart from what they brought with them. The air was dry and dusty, tickling the back of his throat. He felt like a tomb robber.

And then there was a sudden lurch, as though the whole castle had shuddered, stirring in its sleep. The floor pressed up against their feet, and then settled itself, and suddenly they were standing at the same angle as the floor. One at a time the lights came on, gleaming silver half-spheres set into the ceiling. A great stone corridor appeared around them, stretching away in both directions. And somewhere, far away and deep below, they could feel as much as hear a massive power plant starting up, energising the castle after many long years of hibernation.

'It's alive,' whispered Brett. 'The whole place is waking up. It knows we're here.'

'Lights and artificial gravity,' said Jesamine. 'Not bad, after a major crash-landing two hundred years ago. I am officially impressed, darlings.'

Lewis turned off his torch and put it away. 'This is the original Deathstalker Standing,' he said quietly. 'It was already a thousand years old when Owen first found it here, on Shandrakor, and woke it to life once more. They built to last, in the old days. And now here we are, looking for help against injustice, just like Owen. It's as though we've wandered out of history and into legend. Into a place where dreams come true, and miracles can happen.'

'We don't belong here,' said Brett, still whispering. 'This is a place for heroes, and warriors. The kind of people who belong in legends. Not like us. This is . . . too big, too important.'

'Why are you whispering?' said Rose.

'Don't you have any respect?' said Brett. 'No, of course not. Silly question.'

'Come on, Brett,' said Lewis. 'I never knew you to be lacking in ambition before. Think of the treasure!'

'Yes,' said Brett, after a moment. 'That does help.'

In the end, Lewis chose a direction at random and led the way down the wide, long corridor. Jagged cracks sprawled across the corridor walls, and here and there large clumps of stone had fallen away to litter the floor. Sometimes the floor rose and buckled, and sometimes the overhead lights didn't work. There were hanging tapestries, faded portraits of people dead for centuries and mounted displays of ancient weapons. There were outcroppings of high tech, much of it smashed or blown apart or melted down. But there was no dust, no cobwebs, no signs of invading vegetation or wildlife. The corridor could have been deserted yesterday.

'This wasn't impact damage,' said Lewis. 'This is the result of the castle's last battle against the Recreated and the rogue AIs of Shub. Must have been a hell of a fight.'

'It's hard to remember that Shub were once the official Enemies of Humanity,' said Jesamine.

'Not for us,' said Guide. 'Here we suffer the results of their torments every day.'

'That was a long time ago,' Jesamine said weakly.

'Not for us,' said Guide.

The corridor finally branched, and then branched again, and they wandered through many passages, stairways and intersections, gradually losing track of time. The castle was huge, with many floors, but somehow Lewis always found the way that led deeper into the castle, heading towards the great hall at its heart. Part of his certainty came from recognising landmarks, from stories he'd been told since he was a child, and some of it came from suggestions murmured in his ear by the AI Ozymandias, who had been there before with Owen; but a lot of it seemed instinct, as though the old castle was part of his blood, his inheritance. As though he belonged here, and always had. The slow solid roar of the power plant below was growing louder, growling beneath their feet as though in warning. Guide was becoming increasingly spooked, swivelling his bulging head back and forth.

'It's definitely getting colder in here,' said Brett, shuddering dramatically.

'The cold of the grave,' said Rose.

Brett glared at her. 'You're not helping, Rose.'

'Castles are difficult to heat,' said Jesamine. 'Everyone knows that. But if I see the butler, I'll pass on your complaints.'

Brett yelped in alarm as a tall dark figure came stalking suddenly down the corridor towards him. Rose stepped quickly forward to put herself in front of Brett, covering the newcomer with her disrupter. Lewis just had time to take in the figure's old-fashioned clothing, and then it was gone, disappearing between one moment and the next. He opened his mouth to say something, and then stopped as more people appeared, men and women in various battle armours, crowds of them flickering on and off as they hurried silently up and down the corridor. Some of them walked right through Lewis and the others, and he didn't feel a thing, not even a cool breeze.

'Holo images,' said Jesamine. 'Computer records from the past. Probably security camera footage. Our presence must have activated them. Or maybe they're random images given off as the computers come back on line.'

She broke off as the word *random* echoed on the air in whispering voices. A single holo figure appeared, wrapped in a battered old cloak, limping slowly towards them out of the past. They all knew his face. The cloak swung aside for a moment, and they saw he had one hand clapped over a bloody wound in his side. His face was taut and strained, but quietly determined.

'Jack Random,' said Brett softly, the colour dropped out of his face. 'Great-grandfather . . . what happened to you? I didn't think anyone could hurt *you*.'

Random seemed to look at Brett for a moment and then he was gone, with nothing to show he'd ever been there.

'Ghosts,' said Brett.

'Holo images,' said Jesamine. 'That's all, Brett.'

'No! No . . . it's the past, coming back to life, haunting the present. The dead are still alive . . . Right. That's it. I am out of here. No treasure is worth this. I'll go back and guard the entrance.'

'There's nothing to be scared of in the dead,' said Rose.

'What if they don't know they're dead?'

'I'll protect you, Brett,' said Rose. 'You'll be safe with me. Even the dead have enough sense to be scared of Rose Constantine.'

Brett looked at her for a moment, and then a sharp bark of laughter burst out of him. 'Jesus, Rose, we're going to have to work on this whole comfort concept.' He glared at Lewis. 'All right, I'll stay. But I'm not happy.'

'I'll try to live with the disappointment,' Lewis said magnanimously.

'You shouldn't let this place get to you,' Saturday said unexpectedly.

She'd hardly said a word since she entered the Standing, except to snort and swear quietly every time she bumped her head against the ceiling. She'd had to walk hunched over and it hadn't improved her disposition one bit. 'This place is big, yes, but size isn't everything. My kind had castles, once. We had cities and technology and all the other things that make you weak. We outgrew them, and left them behind. They got in the way of enjoying the world, of savouring its bloody pleasures and letting it test us to our limits. There's nothing here for me, Lewis. I think I'll go back to the entrance, and stand guard. Just in case.'

'All right,' said Lewis. 'Are you sure you can find your way to the opening?'

'Of course,' said Saturday. 'Reptiloids don't get lost. We always know where we are.'

'Pity,' muttered Brett. Rose slapped him across the back of the head.

'While we're busy in here,' Lewis said to Saturday, 'no one else gets in. No exceptions. Got it?'

'Got it,' said Saturday. She turned and headed back the way they'd come, the flat top of her head brushing against the high ceiling. Guide waited till she was out of sight, then flexed his multijointed legs briefly.

'I hate to admit it, but I'm glad she's gone. She is just too weird, even for Shandrakor.'

They pressed on, still heading inwards. Lewis could almost feel the massive weight of the castle, its many floors and walls of solid stone, its weight of history and legend and responsibility, pressing down on him. As though he'd never really understood what it was to be a Deathstalker until now. He'd grown up in his own Clan's Standing on Virimonde, a tall and proud castle hundreds of years old, but it had been nothing compared to this. Men and women who had made themselves into legends had walked and lived and fought and died in this place, this Standing. And others had fought and died here too, in the defence of Humanity, their names and reputations lost to Robert and Constance's need to remake history.

Owen would never have approved. He'd always been proud of his modest skills as an historian.

History was soaked into the walls of this Standing, impressed by the weight of centuries, though no one knew exactly how many. The Empire was old, far older than most people were comfortable remembering. Little now remained of the First Empire, declined and fallen long before even this ancient castle's time, but according to Clan legend, some things from that distant time were still to be found here, preserved in stasis fields like insects trapped in amber. Which made Lewis wonder what else might be preserved or trapped here, unwillingly awakened by his intrusion.

Brett paused to admire a sword, displayed on a simple wall plaque. He didn't know why it caught his eye particularly. There was nothing on the plaque about its history; just the name, *Morgana*. It looked like a good sword, and Brett needed a new weapon after losing his last one during his panic attack in the jungle. So he took the sword off the wall, and slipped it into the scabbard at his waist. It was a comfortable weight, as though it belonged there. He looked quickly at Lewis, bracing himself for a stern lecture on the evils of looting, but the Deathstalker was clearly preoccupied with his own thoughts. Brett decided not to disturb him.

And finally, they came to the great hall. The heart and centre of the very first Deathstalker Standing. It was vast, a long hall with massive stone walls, the raftered ceiling mostly lost in shadows high above them. It was also completely empty. No furnishings, no trace of occupants, not even any carpeting on the stone floor or decorations on the walls. The party's footsteps sounded loudly on the quiet as Lewis led his people forward into the hall. There was nothing and no one there to greet them after their long journey into the interior of the castle. Lewis called out a few times, but no one answered. They stood around for a while, wondering what they should do next, all of them feeling a definite sense of anticlimax, and even betrayal. In the end, Lewis said they should sit down and wait, and get some rest. Let the castle computers wake all the way up, and notice they had visitors.

Brett growled something under his breath about at least they weren't being shot at, or given the bum's rush, and then he went over and sat in a corner, so he could have his back to two walls, and watch the entrances. Rose sat next to him, cross-legged, balanced her sword across her leather-clad thighs and began cleaning and polishing the blade with a piece of rag. Guide went off into a different corner to be by himself. Perhaps because he didn't feel worthy to be a part of the great Deathstalker's party, perhaps because he knew the others still found his appearance disturbing; and perhaps because he didn't entirely trust what his insect instincts might push him to, when there was nothing else going on to distract him.

Lewis sat down before the empty fireplace, its interior blackened with many layers of ancient soot. Jesamine sat beside him, leaned against his shoulder and sighed heavily.

'Tired?' said Lewis. 'Feeling sorry you came?'

'Absolutely bone-dead weary, darling, but . . . no. Not sorry at all, really. I'm changing, Lewis. I can feel it. The more I have to fight and protect myself, the better I get at it and the better I feel. I haven't felt this self-sufficient in ages. Reminds me of the old days, when I was just starting out, and the only way to get your money out of the club manager at the end of an evening was to put a gun to his head and threaten to listen to see if it was loaded. I hadn't realised how soft, how limited I'd become. And how *bored* . . . I mean, at least part of why I agreed to become Douglas's Queen was that I had nowhere else to go in my profession, except down. The trouble with achieving your ambitions is what do you do for an encore? To tell the truth and shame the devil, sweetie, I'd been coasting for years. Taking on roles and shows I knew weren't worthy of me, just to keep my face in front of the public. But now . . . I'd forgotten how good it feels to be faced by challenges and overcome them. So I'm glad we did this together, love. I feel *alive* with you. More alive than I've felt in years.'

'Does that mean you won't be moaning and complaining any more?' Lewis said solemnly.

Jesamine snorted with laughter. 'Darling! I have an image to maintain, even here.'

They chuckled quietly. Lewis put an arm around her, and they snuggled up together. But Lewis had his own private thoughts. He approved of the new Jesamine. It was good to see her grow and blossom. But deep inside, where he thought the dark thoughts he didn't care to consider in the bright light of day, he worried that there might come a day when Jesamine would be so strong, so self-sufficient, that she wouldn't need him any more. And that if she didn't need him, then she might not want him any more either. And then the only way to keep her would be to break her spirit, make her dependent on him again. He knew that for a selfish thought immediately, and pushed it aside. He wanted what was best for her.

He did. He'd always known that sometimes loving someone meant having the strength to let them go when they outgrew you. He hoped that wouldn't happen. But here in the ancient Standing, he couldn't help but remember the oldest saying of his Clan.

Deathstalker luck. Always bad.

Jesamine stirred inside his arm, and raised her face to look at him. 'We've come a long way in a short time, haven't we? Am I ever going to get my old life back, Lewis? All the comforts and the adulation? Be a star again?'

Lewis, who had never cared about any of those things, took his time replying. 'Do you miss them so much? Do you regret throwing in your lot with me?'

'Only sometimes, darling. And then I look at you, and I remember you're worth far more than anything I gave up.'

Brett sat morosely in his corner, hugging his knees to his chest, watching each of the hall entrances in turn, half convinced that something nasty was going to come charging in at any moment. He didn't like the castle. It reminded him of stories from his childhood, about wicked noble ladies of old, who lured innocent peasant children into their lairs to make pies out of them. He saw Lewis and Jesamine embracing, and would have liked to call out something cynical and gratuitously offensive, but he couldn't work up the energy. He was too busy being shit-scared. In the past he'd always known what to do when he felt threatened, by a job or a relationship: he ran. Show the problem his back, and then leave it behind in the dust. Well, he'd run from Finn Durandal, and much good that had done him. Now there was nowhere left to run to, and he didn't know what to do. Rose stirred beside him, her blood-red leathers creaking noisily in the quiet, and it was a sign of how seriously spooked Brett was that he actually found some comfort in her company.

'Why does this place get to you so much?' said Rose. Her voice was calm and completely untroubled. 'It's just an old building. There's no one here but us.'

'It's the ghosts,' said Brett. 'This place is full of memories, of people who mattered. Jack Random and Ruby Journey, the uber-esper Jenny Psycho, the blessed Owen and Hazel d'Ark. What they did here still echoes on, haunting the halls and corridors. They were *real* heroes, Rose. Not like us. We're only pretending. I'm a Random's Bastard, supposedly descended from Jack and Ruby, and somehow I don't think they'd approve of me at all. I agreed to join up with the Deathstalker because I wanted to be the kind of man my ancestors could have approved of. But after all we've been through, I'm still just me. I should have known better. I'm not up to this. I'm not strong enough. I've never been strong enough.'

Rose considered the matter for a while, still polishing her sword. 'We all want to be more than we are, Brett. Even me. Ever since our minds were linked by the esper drug, I've been . . . disaffected with my old life. It's not enough to be a killer, a monster. I need to be . . . bigger than that. It's hard trying to learn how to be human . . . especially when all I have to learn from is you, Brett Random.'

He looked sharply at her, and was surprised to see her dark rosebud mouth move in something very like a smile. 'Was that a joke, Rose?'

'Perhaps. Even monsters have feelings sometimes,' said Rose Constantine.

Brett smiled in spite of himself, shaking his head. 'This is all too weird. Everything's changing. There's nothing I can depend on any more. Not even me. I'm confused. Take today, when we were fighting the monsters in the jungle. One moment I'm right there beside you, fighting like a warrior born, and the next I come to my senses and I'm running like a rabbit. What was I thinking of? I'm not a fighter, never have been. Maybe I'm having some sort of breakdown.'

'No you're not,' Rose said calmly. 'It's not you, Brett; it's me. Our mental link works both ways. And just as you have been teaching me about emotions, and humour, and sex that doesn't involve killing people, so I have been teaching you swordsmanship and tactics and the joys of slaughter. Our minds are linked on every level there is; we can't help but learn from each other. All the time, we're growing closer together, becoming more like each other. So neither of us will ever have to be alone again.'

Brett stared at her in horror, his eyes wide, his mouth working silently. He started to scramble to his feet, to run as he always ran, but Rose put a firm, implacable hand on his arm and held him where he was. He was too terrified to think of struggling, even as his skin crawled at her touch. She smiled at him again, and he almost cried out.

'Stop that, Brett. There's no reason for you to be scared. I won't let anyone hurt you; not even me. I will kill anyone or anything that tries to hurt you. I will stand between you and all harm. And I will not force you to become anything you don't want to be. I'm just trying . . . to help you. You're the first person who ever mattered to me, apart from myself. I feel . . . something towards you. I'm not sure what, yet. But I promise I'll keep you alive until I figure out what it is. That's a joke, Brett.'

'Well,' said Brett. 'Very nearly.'

He actually did calm down a little as he realised Rose was, in her own very disturbing way, trying to reach out to him. Rose sensed he was no longer going to run, and took her hand off his arm. She went back to giving all her attention to her sword blade, as calmly as though nothing important had happened and perhaps, for her, nothing had. Brett was still trying to come to terms with the idea that he wasn't even safe inside his own head any more. Her thoughts were influencing him all the time, whether consciously or subconsciously, trying to make him more like her. As if one Wild Rose wasn't more than enough. At least now he understood where all that ridiculous bravery and derring-do had come from in the jungle earlier. He'd known that wasn't like him. He should have known it was too good to be true. He glared about him sullenly, and sniffed loudly.

'Look at the size of this hall. How big it is, and how small it makes us feel in comparison. Everywhere we've been since leaving Logres has been a journey through the ruins of an age of heroes. A greater age than ours. You only have to look at the places they lived in to see that. People like us don't belong in a place like this. How can we hope to do what Owen and his people did? They were larger than us, even before they went through the Madness Maze. They were heroes.'

'They were people, just like us,' said Lewis. He got up, helped Jesamine to her feet, and they went over to join Brett and Rose. Though he never would have admitted it, the scale of the hall of his ancestors was making Lewis jumpy too, and he was glad of an excuse to join the others. He sat down and leaned back against the wall next to Brett. 'I've seen Owen and Hazel d'Ark; the real people. Shub had records of them in action. And the Dust Plains of Memory, that used to be the Imperial Matrix. Owen and Hazel are legends now, but back then they were just people. A man and a woman, struggling to do the right thing. I'm sure they had doubts and indecisions, like us. They were ordinary people, and they did extraordinary things because they had to. And so we go on, against impossible odds, for the same reasons they did. Because we have no choice, and because there's no one else.'

'Don't put money on it,' growled Brett. 'Show me a safe route out of here, and I'd be gone so fast it would make your head spin.'

'I've played Owen and Hazel in half a dozen operas,' said Jesamine. 'Marvellous roles, of course, but I can't say I really knew either of them. You only have to look at a place like this to realise they lived in a whole different world to us. We've gone soft since then.'

'Maybe that's part of what we're fighting for,' said Lewis. 'So we can be safe enough that it's all right for us to be soft.'

'Oh very deep,' said Brett. 'This is all Owen's fault anyway. He should have stopped the Terror before he left. It's his unfinished business that's going to kill us.'

He knew that was unfair even as he said it, and no one bothered to answer him. Lewis glared around the giant, empty hall as though he could force answers out of it through sheer strength of will.

'You were here before, Oz,' he said abruptly. 'Or at least your progenitor was. What do you think we should do now?'

'It wasn't exactly me,' the ship's AI said uncertainly through their comm implants. 'When you get right down to it, I'm just a Shub subroutine created around bits and pieces left over from the original Ozymandias. What memories I have from that time are fragmentary at best. Still, this place is more familiar than most. I remember a room full of mirrors, whose shimmering surfaces revealed possible futures. I remember automatons, repair robots in the shape of men, still striding elegantly through the Standing after a thousand years. And I remember finding the Shadow Men, Imperial assassins set after Giles Deathstalker. He killed them, and put their stuffed and mounted bodies on display.'

'Okay,' said Brett. 'This is seriously creeping me out.'

'I never liked Giles,' said Oz. 'Never trusted him.'

'Giles Deathstalker,' Lewis said thoughtfully. 'The first and founder of my Clan. Our family archives don't have much on him. Just an old portrait, and stories of some of the great battles he fought. Owen found him preserved here, the last remnant of an earlier time. They fought side by side in the Great Rebellion, and then Giles went bad and Owen had to kill him. Deathstalker luck.'

'Aren't there any happy endings in your family's history?' said Jesamine.

'Always a first time for everything,' said Lewis, smiling. 'Oz, anything else you can tell us?'

'For some time now, I've been trying to make contact with the Standing's computers,' said the AI. 'I can tell they're back on-line now, awake and aware. The amount of power being generated in this castle is simply staggering, and it's still rising. All kinds of systems are waking up, and I don't recognise even half of them. Lewis, the castle's computers have to know you're here. I'm trying every contact protocol in my records, but they won't open up to me. They feel . . . strange. Not like any form of computer mind I've ever encountered before. I think they're even older than the Standing itself . . . Lewis, I might have an idea. An almost-memory from Owen's time. You talk to them. Declare yourself, your name and your heritage. And show them the ring. Go on; they're listening. They're waiting.'

Lewis rose slowly to his feet and headed towards the centre of the hall. The others wanted to go with him, but he waved them back. He stopped in the middle of the great and empty hall and looked around him. He could almost feel another presence there with him, surrounding him.

'I am Lewis Deathstalker,' he said, not proudly or defiantly, but calmly stating a fact. His voice was strong and clear in the quiet. 'I am Outlawed now, but still I am the first of my Clan, as Owen was before me. And I have come here as he did, in search of help from my family. Because if I fall, the Empire falls with me. As proof I bear Owen's ring. The Deathstalker ring, sign and symbol of Clan authority.'

He held up his hand to show off the chunky black gold ring, and the castle answered him. All the lights in the hall came on at once, fierce and powerful, blasting away the shadows of centuries. A great viewscreen appeared, floating above the cold fireplace. Images came and went swiftly, of faces familiar and unknown, but all of them Deathstalkers. A beam of light, shimmering and silver, slammed down right next to Lewis, a spotlight so blinding and intense that they all had to look away. The intensity slowly faded, and when they looked again they saw a single figure standing in the spotlight, held in place like a moth on a pin. He was tall and sparely built, with muscular arms. He had a solid lined face with a silver-grey goatee beard, and his long hair was pulled back in a scalplock. He wore a set of battered shapeless furs, bunched at the waist by a wide leather belt, thick golden armlets and heavy silver rings on his fingers. He bore a sword on one hip, and a gun of unfamiliar design on the other. He looked fierce and dangerous, cold and determined, and every inch a Deathstalker.

'My God,' said Jesamine. 'It's Giles.'

'Ghosts,' said Brett. 'I told you—'

'Shut up, Brett,' said Lewis. He studied his coldly smiling ancestor for a long moment, and then extended his hand with the ring and thrust it into the light. It felt freezing cold, painfully cold, but he held the hand steady. 'I am Lewis Deathstalker.'

'I know you are,' said Giles. 'I heard you the first time.'

The spotlight snapped off, leaving them blinking. Lewis snatched back his hand. The holo figure of Giles, if that was what it was, looked at everyone in the group, including Guide still shrinking away in his corner, and sighed loudly before turning his attention back to Lewis. 'I'm not your ancestor, boy. I am all that remains of the computers who once ran this Standing speaking to you through the image of Giles Deathstalker. Thought it might make this easier for both of us.

Two hundred years and more since anyone came calling, to disturb my rest. Should have known only really bad news would bring anyone back here. Why were you Outlawed, Lewis?'

'For loving the wrong woman,' Lewis said steadily. 'And for speaking out against evil.'

'Yes, that sounds familiar,' said Giles. 'I suppose I should ask what's become of the family, but since I'm not really Giles I don't think I care much. You bear the ring; that's all that matters.'

'Hey, hold on,' said Brett. 'Anyone could walk in here with that ring on, and claim they were a Deathstalker.'

Giles glared at him, and Brett immediately went back to hiding behind Rose. 'No, they couldn't,' said Giles. 'The ring is coded to the Deathstalker line; it has all kinds of nasty tricks built into it to take care of imposters.'

Lewis deliberately didn't look down at the ring on his finger, but an icy chill caressed the back of his neck for a moment. If his family line had been a little further distanced from the main line . . . He made himself smile easily at Giles, even though he found talking to the original Deathstalker more than a little disturbing, given the bad end Giles eventually came to. He wondered if the computers knew.

'We come here in need,' he said. 'Not just ours, but all Humanity's. The Empire is endangered. The Terror has finally found us. We must locate the missing Owen Deathstalker and Hazel d'Ark. Can you assist us?'

Giles scowled. 'The Terror . . . I know things about the Terror, though I don't know how I know them. And I know things about Owen, and what he found at the hidden heart of the Madness Maze, that no one else knows. A voice came and told me these things, two hundred years ago, after the defeat and restoration of the Recreated. It told me that Humanity must evolve, achieve its full potential, because something awful was coming from far beyond our galaxy. The Terror. It is not life as we know it, but far more. It eats souls, and its young incubate in the hearts of suns. It brings madness and suffering, and the death of all that lives. The Terror is one and many, both and neither; an extra-dimensional creature beyond our understanding and the whole of space and time is its prey. As flies to wanton boys, are we to the Terror.'

'We're dead,' said Brett.

'How do we stop it?' said Lewis. 'We tried sending people through the Madness Maze centuries ago. It killed them all.'

'Maybe they weren't the right people,' Giles said indifferently. 'I know more about the Maze. Do you want to hear it?'

'Do we have a choice?' said Brett.

'Not really,' said Giles. 'At the heart of the Madness Maze lies a secret: the Darkvoid Device.'

'That's it!' said Jesamine. 'The Darkvoid Device snuffed out hundreds of stars and their planetary systems in a moment! That's the weapon we need to stop the Terror!'

'It's not a weapon,' said Giles. 'It's a child. My child, transformed and empowered in the Maze. As a baby, he created the Darkvoid in a moment of panic. He knows better now. I never got to see him after I left him in the Maze's embrace a thousand years ago. But Owen saw him, and spoke with him. I never got to see how my son grew up. Perhaps you will.'

'Owen,' Lewis said patiently. 'Tell us about Owen.'

'The voice spoke to him directly,' said Giles. 'It told him many things. Secret things. Far more than it told anyone else.'

'This voice,' said Jesamine. 'If it knows so much, perhaps we have a friend, or at least an ally, from somewhere else. Maybe even equal in power to the Terror!'

'Perhaps,' said Giles. 'I have no way of knowing. It could be just the sole survivor of an earlier assault by the Terror. There are many players in this game, and only some of them have revealed their true nature.'

Lewis remembered the little grey man who'd given him the Deathstalker ring at Douglas's coronation. He said he was Vaughn, an old friend of Owen's, but Lewis had seen Vaughn's grave on Lachrymae Christi. So what was he really? A ghost? Lewis scowled at Giles's holo, his ugly face taking on even uglier lines. Of late, Lewis's whole life had been haunted by the past, by ghosts who refused to lie quiet, and he was getting pretty damned sick of it.

'Tell me about Owen,' he said flatly. 'Tell me what happened to him.'

'Some say he's dead. Some say he isn't.' Giles's holo shrugged. 'If you want answers you can trust, you'll have to go to Haden, to the heart of the Madness Maze, and speak with the child. Only he knows for sure.'

'Even though the odds are the Maze will madden and murder us?' said Lewis.

'Deathstalker luck,' said Giles, smiling nastily. 'The Maze is the key. Everything else turns around it, and always has. You must go in, cousin. It is your destiny.'

'It might be his, but it sure as hell isn't mine,' said Brett. 'I'm not going in, and you shouldn't either, Lewis. The odds suck, big time.'

'Don't worry,' said Rose. 'I'll hold your hand.'

'That thought doesn't help much, actually,' said Brett. He folded his arms across his chest, and looked determinedly in another direction, his lower lip protruding sulkily.

'You know, an awful lot of people seem determined that we should enter the Maze,' said Jesamine. 'A suspicious, or even only partly paranoid person might suspect we are being manipulated. Guided. Used, by other people, for their own purposes.'

'I've had a really spooky thought,' said Brett, so taken with his new idea that he forgot he was busy being upset and outraged. 'What if . . . what if it's the Madness Maze itself that's behind this? Could the Maze, or the child within, have been manipulating events all along, from behind the scenes, just to bring a Deathstalker back to it?'

'You're right, Brett,' said Lewis. 'That is a really spooky thought. If you have any more like that, do feel free to keep them to yourself.'

'Look, if we really are going to Haden, and I hope and pray that an outbreak of rational thought and good sense will still prevail so we don't have to,' said Brett, 'but if we are going to that bloody hellworld, it is one hundred per cent guaranteed certain to be Quarantined and very heavily guarded. You can bet serious money that Finn will have reinforced the usual patrols with every nasty and vicious defence he's got. We are talking starcruisers, orbiting mine-fields, battle espers and mindbombs. Which means, if we are going, we'll need powerful weapons of our own. So how about it, Giles? You got anything here we can use?'

'Go out of here, by the main doorway,' said Giles. 'Follow the signs, down the corridor and down nine levels, and you will come to a stash of First Empire high tech and weaponry, held inviolate behind a stasis field for over a thousand years. Even I don't know what's in there. The real Giles inherited it from his ancestors, long before he assumed the Deathstalker name, and either he never got the chance to use it or he never found the nerve to try. First Empire tech can be very dangerous. We have fallen a long way since those days.'

'First Empire weapons!' said Brett, all but rubbing his hands together. 'Oh people, we are talking serious *serious* money here!'

'Shoot first, make money later,' said Lewis. 'Let's take a look.'

'Say goodbye first,' said the holo of Giles Deathstalker. 'We won't be meeting again. This Standing has come to the end of its days. The castle was badly damaged, inside and out, even before Jenny Psycho nursed it here and crash-landed it in the jungle. Systems are failing, the power plant is fading, the very stone is crumbling. I activated the systems one last time, in service to Clan Deathstalker. Now, it is time for me to rest. Allow me to wish you good luck. You're going to need it.'

The silver spotlight snapped off, taking Giles with it, and without them the hall seemed much darker.

'Castles can be rebuilt,' said Lewis. 'Systems can be repaired. Power plants can be replaced. Whatever happens on Haden, I will come back for you. You are the history of my family.'

He waited, but there was no reply. Jesamine tugged urgently at his sleeve.

'I think we should get moving, darling. If the power plant is on its last legs, there's no telling how long we've got before everything starts shutting down again. I definitely don't want to be stumbling through these corridors in the dark. We might never find our way out.'

'Wonderful,' said Brett. 'Something else to worry about. I know: shut up, Brett.'

'I hoped I'd have more time,' said Lewis. 'To walk the passageways and galleries of the original Standing of my Clan; to feel like a real Deathstalker. But there's never enough time for all the things we need to do. Let's go.'

As they left through the main doorway, a glowing arrow appeared floating in mid-air. It drifted away before them, and they followed it through many intersections and down nine levels. Lewis kept careful note of the twists and turns, just in case. Rose was walking point beside him again, gun in hand, while Jesamine and Brett followed behind. Guide brought up the rear. He hadn't spoken a word since they entered the great hall. He had been made an observer in his own world, a bit player in someone else's story, and he didn't know whether to feel bitter or overawed. Great forces were at play here, and perhaps the best he could hope for was to be overlooked when gods went to war.

They came at last to a solid steel door, with no obvious handle or lock mechanism. The floating arrow disappeared. Brett was all over the door in a flash, checking it minutely from top to bottom, but eventually had to admit that there was nothing there for him to work with. He kicked the door in frustration, and then hobbled away to lean on Rose and cry bitter tears as he massaged his bruised toes. Lewis looked at the door for a long moment, and then said his name aloud. The door swung silently open before him, revealing the familiar blurred shimmer of a stasis field. And then that snapped off, like a bursting soap bubble. And inside . . .

'What the hell is this shit?' said Brett.

'Tech, of some kind,' said Lewis.

'But I don't recognise any of it!' wailed Brett. 'There's nothing here that looks like anything I'm familiar with, and I've been around. I thought there were supposed to be weapons here! Big, nasty weapons!'

'Some of it could be weapons,' said Rose. 'Let's try turning a few things on, and see what happens.'

'Let's not,' Jesamine said, very firmly. 'There's no telling what some of this stuff might do. And I don't think we should turn anything on until we're sure we can turn it off again.'

They looked at the enigmatic shapes and forms laid out before them: obscure structures of glass and steel and crystal, and other materials that couldn't easily be identified. Lights came and went, strange energies pulsed, and here and there pieces moved in unsettling ways, rotating through strange angles, and none of it made any sense at all. Just looking at some of it made their heads ache, as though they were gazing at things too complicated, or too subtle, to be understood without some really sophisticated equipment as a mediator.

'This is why Giles never used any of it,' Lewis said eventually. 'Even a thousand years ago, this would have been beyond him. We forget how advanced the First Empire was, and how far we've fallen since then. Maybe our Empire is doomed to fall too. Only this time, there won't be anyone left to start the long climb back up again.'

'I just had a spooky thought,' said Jesamine.

'Oh don't you start,' said Lewis.

'No, listen. Could the Terror be something left over from the First Empire? Some awful doomsday weapon they unleashed, and then couldn't shut down? Maybe that's why the First Empire fell.'

'I don't think so,' said Lewis. 'If I'm understanding what the voice said correctly, the Terror is older than that, from *outside* our galaxy.'

And then the whole castle shook around them. They clung together as the floor bucked and heaved under their feet. New cracks appeared in the stone walls, and dust fell from the ceiling. The stasis field re-established itself, and the steel door slammed shut. Alarms sounded, harsh and blaring, and Giles's voice said, 'The Standing is under attack. Force shields have been activated. Weapons systems are off-line. Stardrive is off-line. Available power cannot support full shields for more than two hours twelve minutes. Sensors detect unusual energies operating.'

'Show me what's happening!' yelled Lewis.

A screen appeared in the air before them, showing a series of views of what was occurring outside the Standing. A wide area of jungle, including the castle's clearing, was being blown apart by a battle barge hovering overhead. Energy blasts stabbed down again and again in a substantial barrage, toppling trees and incinerating the vegetation. Fires were burning everywhere, filling the sky with thick black smoke. Misshapen creatures were running about, panicked by the fire and the noise and a threat most of them could barely comprehend. Disrupter fire picked many of them off as they ran. More attack ships were dropping out of the sky, adding their firepower to the assault. The main attack was centring on the clearing, the grassy earth being systematically blown away to reveal the castle beneath. And right there in the heart of the mayhem, whooping and howling as they darted in and out of the energy beams: thirteen gravity sleds bearing men and women in familiar armour and purple cloaks.

'Paragons!' said Lewis. 'I don't believe it.'

'Unusual energies are attacking the force shields,' said Giles's voice. 'Systems are collapsing, malfunctioning. I am being targeted. My mind is under attack.'

'Can you maintain the shields?' said Brett.

'Not for much longer. Get out while you can.' Giles's voice sounded almost apologetic. 'I will protect you for as long as I can. I am built to serve Clan Deathstalker, even to the death.'

Lewis led the way back through the stone corridors, running now as the castle creaked and groaned and shuddered around them. Already the lights were going out, and sometimes the artificial gravity flickered on and off, sending the party staggering this way and that. Guide caught them when they would have fallen, his eight legs skittering easily over the bucking stone floor. The alarm cut off. It wasn't telling anyone anything they didn't already know. Cracks in the walls lengthened and widened, and sometimes the walls bulged slowly, the ancient stone buckling under the strain. The roar of the power plant under their feet became ragged and uncertain.

'Are the force shields still holding?' said Jesamine, as she ran hand in hand with Lewis.

'If they weren't, we'd be dead by now,' said Lewis, when Giles's voice didn't answer. 'The castle's been inert for too long. It wasn't ready for an attack like this.'

When Lewis and his companions finally made it to the hole in the outer wall they'd entered through, they found Saturday sheltering there, his foreclaws flexing helplessly as he glared at the attackers outside. Lewis pushed past the reptiloid to see for himself. The roar of engines was deafening, and the air was thick with smoke and the stench of burnt vegetation. Ships filled the sky for as far as he could see, energy beams stabbing down like malevolent lightning. The thirteen Paragons shot back and forth on their gravity sleds, cheering on the destruction.

'I don't believe this,' said Lewis. 'I know some of those people. Good men and women. Hell, I fought beside some of them. How could Finn have turned people like this to his cause?'

'I've got to say I'm surprised to see Paragons,' said Brett, darting quick looks past the reptiloid's sheltering bulk. 'The files I found in Finn's computers said he planned to have them ambushed and taken care of, because he didn't believe they'd ever come over to his side. What could have happened while we've been away?'

'Never mind that,' snapped Jesamine. 'How did they find us? How did they know where to find the castle? Hell, we didn't even know where we were going until we got here.' She glared at Guide. 'Could some of your people have betrayed us?'

'Never!' said Guide. 'Any one of us would rather die than betray our promised saviour.'

'Screw that!' said Brett, flinching as smoke was driven through the opening by a nearby explosion. 'Once a monster, always a monster! Somebody talked! Somebody sold us out!'

'You are wrong,' said Guide. 'I'll provide a distraction. Make good use of it, Deathstalker.'

And before any of them could even think to stop him, he squeezed his long legs through the opening and charged out into the clearing. He darted and dodged among the energy blasts with inhuman speed, defying them to touch him, and then a gravity sled came sweeping in low to target him. Guide ran before it, then spun round at the last moment and sprayed thick swatches of webbing from a pulsing orifice in his chest. The sticky threads enveloped the Paragon and his sled, and he quickly lost control of his craft. He was still struggling to keep the sled from nose-diving into the ground when Guide leapt lightly up on to the sled, his eight legs snapping shut around it like a trap. The Paragon just had time to look up, and then Guide's mandibles buried themselves in his skull, and ripped the top of the Paragon's head off.

Three more gravity sleds came sweeping in. They targeted the damaged sled and blew it apart with concentrated disrupter fire. Guide died in the explosion, his long legs still twitching spasmodically as fire consumed the monstrous body.

Lewis and his people hadn't even had time to get out of the opening. Lewis hammered one fist helplessly against the broken stone.

'Who are those bastards?' said Jesamine.

'It is the Shadow Men,' said Giles's voice, the castle's voice, quiet and distant now. 'They've come again. The Empire's bully boys.'

'Oh great,' said Brett. 'The castle's losing it. Does anybody have any ideas?'

'I don't see Finn out there,' said Lewis. 'And I don't see Emma Steel or Stuart Lennox. Which suggests that Finn wasn't sure enough of victory here to show up in person, and that he hasn't turned all the Paragons to his cause yet. There is still hope.'

'That's kind of long-term hope,' said Brett. 'I was hoping for something a little more immediate.'

'Our options would seem to be somewhat limited,' said Lewis. 'Either we stay here inside the castle until the shields collapse, and we die. Or we go out there and fight them face to face, and we die.'

'Tell me there's a third alternative,' said Jesamine. 'Even a really bad one would do.'

'Well,' said Lewis. 'I thought I'd go out there and negotiate.'

'*What?*' said Brett. 'What makes you think they're interested in anything you've got to say?'

'Because we've been inside the Standing,' said Lewis calmly. 'And they don't know what we might have learned and found there. Finn would want to know those things.'

'But we didn't find or learn anything useful, really,' said Jesamine.

'Yes, but they don't know that. You stay put,' said Lewis. 'I'm going out.'

'Fine,' said Brett. 'You do that. And us sane people will stay here and watch you do it from a safe distance.'

'We're all going out,' Jesamine said sternly.

Rose nodded approvingly. Brett groaned loudly. 'Some days I think I'm the only rational person in this group.'

One by one they hauled themselves up and out through the crack in the wall and went into the clearing with their weapons holstered and their hands in the air. The attack cut off. Fires still raged in and around the clearing. From every direction came the screams of creatures dying. Twelve Paragons on gravity sleds came sweeping forward to look down on the assembled Outlaws, all smiling the same unpleasant smile.

'I know you,' Lewis said to one of the Paragons. 'It's Sebastion Oh, isn't it? We fought alongside each other during the Quantum Inferno. How can you side with Finn? Can't you see what he is?'

'I'm so sorry, Lewis,' said the Paragon, still smiling his awful smile. 'But I'm afraid Sebastion Oh isn't at home right now. You might say he's been evicted. I'm the new tenant.'

'Jesus!' said Brett. 'It's an ELF! He's been possessed by an ELF!'

'Not just an ELF,' said the Paragons, all twelve of them speaking in unison in the same dead voice. 'An uber-esper. The Grey Train. At your service, sir Deathstalker. I live in these bodies, for now. They make excellent weapons.'

'That's what Finn meant about ambushing the Paragons!' said Brett. 'He's working with the ELFs . . .'

'Not now, Brett,' said Jesamine.

'All the Paragons are our thralls,' said the Grey Train. 'They belong to the uber-espers, and we do such marvellous things in their name. And now it's your turn, dear Lewis. You and your little group. Welcome to hell, Deathstalker, and to all the wonderful, terrible things I'm going to make you do.'

The Grey Train reached out to invade their minds, only to recoil as the Standing's esp-blocker tech kicked in, protecting Lewis and his people. The Paragons cried out in unison, sharing the uber-esper's pain. And while they were distracted, Lewis grabbed a grenade from his belt and threw it into their midst. He yelled to his people to hit the ground, and they were down and covering their heads with their arms as the explosion threw Paragons dead and wounded from their sleds. Lewis was on his feet again in a moment, yelling to the others to get up, and they all opened fire on the surviving Paragons.

'Lewis!' Oz's voice sounded suddenly in Lewis's ear. 'I'm on my way! The *Hereward*'ll be with you any minute. Hang on!'

'No!' Lewis said immediately. 'They'll blow you apart on sight!'

'Never happen,' the AI said confidently. 'This ship's got really ace shields and stealth capabilities, remember? They won't see me until it's too late. Hang on in there, and don't worry! Reinforcements are on the way!'

Lewis realised all the Paragons were dead now, though Rose was chopping at a few of the bodies with her sword, just to make sure. The attack ships were hovering overhead, confused by the sudden turn of events, but they'd soon start firing again and Lewis and his people were caught out in the open. And then he gaped in disbelief as an army of monsters came crashing through the burning jungle and into the clearing, surrounding the Deathstalker and his group. They threw themselves into the air and attacked the lower ships, smashing through the steel hulls with their unnatural strength. And from all of them came the same battle cry:

For the Deathstalker!

The Grey Train tried to possess the monsters' minds, and couldn't. They were too different, too altered. The *Hereward* arrived, slipping easily through the attack ships with amazing speed and dexterity. Some of the battle barges, high above, opened fire at last, but the lower ships were in the way. They fired anyway, killing their own people along with the monsters. Lewis and his companions crowded aboard the *Hereward* and Oz immediately engaged full power and shot up through the smoky sky, heading for orbit. The attack ships turned ponderously to follow. And the computers in the Deathstalker Standing overloaded its power plant, and blew it apart. The ancient castle exploded into a brilliant ball of energy, enveloping and destroying every Imperial ship in the vicinity.

One last service, for Clan Deathstalker.

SIX

THE DEATH OF PRINCES, AND OF KINGS

Finn Durandal was having a busy day, but he couldn't honestly say he was enjoying himself. In fact, he'd signed all the death warrants he could find, and hadn't smiled once. Finn sighed, pushed his executive chair back from his ostentatiously antique desk and swivelled idly back and forth. Who could have predicted that bringing down an Empire would involve so much bloody paperwork? More and more these days, it seemed nobody could be trusted to do what he told them to do without him peering over their shoulders. Either they didn't have the guts to do the things that clearly needed to be done, or they were complete religious fanatics who'd never even heard of self-restraint. On the one hand, having an army of enthusiastic bigots at his beck and call enabled him to bring about far more destruction and despair than he could ever have hoped to achieve on his own, but on the other hand . . . there simply wasn't any fun in learning about it second hand. What was the point in grinding down your enemies and killing off everyone who opposed you if you couldn't get a little of their blood on your hands in the process? Finn sniffed and allowed his lower lip to pout just a bit. He was a man of action, not a paper shuffler. But you don't get to be dictator unless you're prepared to put in the work, so . . . Finn called in his private secretary, gave him a good glare to put the wind up him, and demanded another iced tea and more of the nice muffins. The secretary backed out, bowing all the way, and Finn returned to his paperwork, signing on the dotted line and initialling extra clauses until his wrist ached.

It was well past noon before Finn had caught up with enough of the day's business that he felt justified in taking a little time for himself. He wasn't due to put the fear of God into anyone for a good half an hour, so he leaned back in his chair and indulged himself with a few pleasant fantasies about possible future atrocities. He was giving serious thought to having a possessed thrall carry a transmutation bomb into the Dust Plains of Memory. He was pretty sure the nanotech computers had a strong organic element, so a transmutation explosion should do a satisfying amount of damage. Finn didn't want any major information sources in the Empire that he didn't control. And if the bomb wasn't enough . . . well, maybe he could have Daniel Wolfe hauled back from the nanotech planet Zero Zero. (If he really was still there, trying to make the rogue planet sane.) Should be easy enough to have an ELF possess Daniel, march him out on to the Dust Plains and set nanotech against nanotech. Finn smiled happily, considering the devastation.

He'd actually worked himself into quite a good mood when Tel Markham arrived and spoiled it all. The honourable Member for Madraguda came storming in, brushing aside the protesting private secretary and slamming the door in his face. He headed straight for the visitor's chair, completely forgetting to bow until Finn reminded him with an icy cough. Tel bobbed his head to Finn in the quickest bow on record, and then sank bonelessly into the visitor's chair, crossing his legs before him like he owned the place. Finn sank back in his chair and raised a magisterial eyebrow.

'This had better be important, Tel. In fact, it had better be vital, urgent and downright imperative, or I am going to kick your arse all the way round my office and then halfway back again, just to remind you to knock before bursting in here. I do have an image to maintain, you know.'

'The Shandrakor expedition has turned into a complete balls-up,' Tel said flatly. 'Yes, I thought that would get your attention. I've just been listening to the first reports from our people there, and they are shitting themselves. One of them was actually crying. All thirteen of the Paragons you sent to Shandrakor are dead. One of our starcruisers was blown apart, and the others suffered extensive damage. More details are coming in, but I doubt anything will turn up to take the edge off this mess.'

'I see,' said Finn, dangerously calmly. 'And the Deathstalker and his companions?'

'They located the old Deathstalker Standing, and spent some time inside. They must have found something there, because the place woke up in a hurry and attacked our people with a whole range of energy weapons of quite appalling strength and diversity. It then blew itself up, to cover the retreat of Lewis and his people. Their ship vanished into hyperspace while ours were getting the crap kicked out of them, and we have no idea where they might be going next. We did kill a bunch of assorted monsters on Shandrakor, if that's any comfort . . . no, I didn't think it would be.'

'My Paragons dead,' murmured Finn. 'Such a pity. Now I can't torture them any more. Tell me there is some good news, Tel. Or I'm going to kill you.'

'The Deathstalker Standing is quite definitely destroyed,' Tel said quickly. 'Lewis can't use it as a base of operations now, as his ancestor did.'

Finn considered the point. 'No,' he said decisively. 'Not nearly good enough.'

He snatched up a solid brass ashtray from his desk and threw it at Tel. The MP ducked, but not fast enough. The ashtray clipped him heavily across the side of the head, and he tipped out of his chair and fell to the floor. Blood streamed down his face. Finn got out of his chair and walked unhurriedly round his desk. Tel tried to scuttle backwards, heading for the door. Finn caught up with him and kicked him in the ribs, a solid but casual blow, just as he would treat an annoying dog in the street. And then he kicked Tel again and again and again. Blood sprayed from Tel's mouth, and he cried out loudly, not because he thought help might come, but because he knew Finn would keep on kicking him till he did. The Durandal reached down, grabbed Tel by the blood-spattered front of his shirt, lifted him up and slammed him back against the wall with almost effortless strength. Finn stuck his face right in front of Tel's and spoke in a calm, assured voice, ignoring the blood flecking his face from Tel's heavy breathing.

'I keep sending my people after Lewis, and he keeps evading them. How does he do that? He has no powers, like his renowned ancestor. He's just one man with a few disreputable friends. And yet still he taunts me, defying me to control or stop him. How many more of my resources do I need to commit to the chase, to bring down one ugly little man?'

'Why bother?' said Tel, breathing painfully. 'As you say, he's just one man . . .'

'He's a Deathstalker! That name means something. He could use the lustre of that name to raise an army against me. No, Lewis is my only real obstacle, the only threat to my inevitable triumph. There's still Douglas, of course, but I've broken his spirit quite thoroughly. I want Lewis broken, Tel. I need to see my dear old friend grovelling before me in a pool of his own blood. I need to see him kiss my boot before I shoot him in the back of the head.'

The thought put Finn in a somewhat better mood, and he let go of Tel. He strolled back to his desk while Tel wiped some of the blood from his face with his sleeve. Finn sat down behind his desk, and smiled benignly at his pet MP.

'Don't worry, Tel. I'm not going to kill you. Not while I can have so much more fun taking out my bad moods on you. For an experienced politician, you make a great punching bag. And if you stick with me, and don't whine too much, I'll make you a powerful man in this declining Empire. Under me, of course. And all you have to do to prove your worth is carry out the occasional little errand for me. What could be easier?'

Tel was saved from having to answer that one when Finn's office door swung suddenly open, and a Church Militant soldier strode in. Finn glared at him.

'Does no one knock any more? I swear, if this keeps up I'm going to arm my secretary and install landmines in my outer office. Now who the hell are you, and what do you want?'

'A little of your time, Durandal,' said the soldier in a harsh rasping voice. He smiled widely. 'How do you like this body? Just something I threw on, but it has a certain charm, don't you think?'

'Oh shit,' said Tel. 'It's an ELF.'

Finn's glare became positively glacial. 'Don't sit down, ELF; you're not staying. And I thought I told you people not to call me at the office. All right, spit it out. You can talk freely in front of Tel, because he knows I'll have him killed if he repeats anything I don't want repeated. What do you want?'

'We want you to arrange a meeting between ELF representatives and the uber-espers,' said the thrall. 'Our glorious leaders and founders have apparently become so busy running errands for you that they don't have time to talk to us any more. All we get are orders, and no explanations. We're feeling left out of things, and we don't like it. But if they won't listen to us, maybe they'll listen to you. So: you contact the uber-espers and persuade them to listen to our grievances, or you can forget about having Paragons at your beck and call any more.'

'I don't take kindly to threats,' said Finn, and there was something in his voice and in his eyes that gave even the ELF pause.

'Think of it more as a wake-up call, sir Durandal. Even ELFs have their limitations. The strain of possessing so many Paragons for so long, twenty-four hours a day, is taking its toll on us. We're having to pass the Paragons back and forth between us so our minds can get some rest, and every time we exchange control there's a very real risk of a Paragon breaking free. These people have had special training against mental control, and they're becoming increasingly difficult subjects. We were only able to overcome them in the first place because we caught them by surprise, from ambush, and outnumbered each of them by ten to one or more. The ELFs can't guarantee to maintain control unless we get help and support from the uber-espers. They listen to you these days; so arrange it.'

'Why does no one ever bring me good news?' said Finn plaintively. He leaned back in his chair and considered the matter. 'I used the Grey Train to control the thirteen Paragons I sent to Shandrakor, because you ELFs assured me that only an uber-esper could safely control so many subjects at such a distance. Now those Paragons are dead, and the Grey Train is reportedly in shock. And you want me to hand over more Paragons to the uber-espers?' Finn smiled encouragingly at the thrall. 'What's the matter? Aren't you boys having a good time any more, doing nasty things in Paragon bodies?'

'That's not the point,' the ELF said stubbornly. 'We can't go on like this. We need help. It's in your best interests to arrange this meeting, sir Durandal.'

'Oh, very well. If it'll make you happy. Seems nothing gets done right around here unless I do it myself. I'll contact the uber-espers and set up your meeting. I want to talk to them myself, and especially the Grey Train. I'm not happy about losing so many Paragons at once. All right, that's it. You can go now, ELF. Don't slam the door on your way out, or I'll have the uber-espers stick your mind in something small and squishy for a week. Off you go. Don't forget to write. And Tel, find yourself a regeneration tank and clean yourself up. I have an errand for you to run.'

The Paragon Emma Steel had agreed to meet the girl reporter Nina Malapert at her place, but she only had to walk into Nina's living room to feel she might have made a terrible mistake. Nina was a single girl who lived alone, and it showed. Things couldn't get this messy without a certain amount of determined effort. Emma stood perfectly still in the middle of the apartment, so she wouldn't have to touch anything, while Nina bustled cheerfully back and forth around her, ostensibly tidying up, but mostly picking things up and putting them down somewhere else. Emma's nostrils twitched as the pervasive aromas of cheap perfume, cheaper disinfectant and the lingering remains of several recent meals fought it out for supremacy.

There were cuddly toys everywhere, beaming vacantly from every surface that wasn't already buried under gaudy china figurines of questionable taste, and vases full of drooping flowers. There was a long shelf of data recordings, and Emma just knew they hadn't been sorted into alphabetical order. Towering piles of fashion and gossip magazines threatened to topple over at any moment. Three of the living room walls were hidden behind live holo images showing a barren windswept moor, an overgrown garden with ivy-covered walls, and waves crashing soundlessly against craggy rocks in showers of spray. There was a desk, pushed tightly up against the one remaining wall, bearing a computer terminal, a remote camera in its recharging unit and more piled-up dirty plates and coffee mugs than the mind could comfortably come to terms with. Both of the chairs were full of dirty laundry. Nina bundled it up, and tottered off in her high heels to dump the laundry in the next room. Her voice came drifting back.

'Sorry about the mess, darling, but I live here. Won't be a tick. Make yourself comfortable, and watch out for the goldfish. I dropped it a few days ago and I still haven't found it. Do you like my holo walls? They appeal to my wild romantic side, but I find I have to keep the sound turned right down. Nature in the raw can be terribly distracting. Oh, would you like some coffee?'

Emma looked at the dirty mugs on the desk and shuddered. 'Not right now, thank you.'

'I'd offer you some brandy, but I don't have any.'

Emma headed for the nearest chair, kicking a stuffed bear out of the way. Nina cried out in distress from the doorway, and hurried over to pick up the bear and cuddle it to her.

'Leave Bruin Bear alone, you big bully! There, there, lovey, she didn't mean it. She's just a nasty old Paragon who probably isn't getting her ashes hauled nearly often enough.'

'Why so many guns?' said Emma, deliberately changing the subject as she sank gingerly into the chair. She indicated the dozen or so energy weapons mounted inexpertly on the wall over the desk. Nina smiled, kissed Bruin Bear and wedged him in between other toys on the nearest shelf. She sat down opposite Emma, and crossed her legs to better show off her new shoes.

'The guns are a legacy from my dear old forefather Flynn. He always said the first rule of journalism is, "Be prepared to shoot at any time".'

Emma regarded the bulky energy guns dubiously. 'Are you sure he didn't mean with a camera?'

'Not these days, sweetie.'

Nina smiled happily at Emma, her tall pink mohawk swaying slightly. She was wearing a whole bunch of multi-coloured silks, and

253

had clearly decided to let the colours fight it out among themselves for dominance. She had a bright red heart painted over her left eye, and lips of a dark scarlet hue never found in nature. Emma would have felt quite dowdy in her plain Paragon's outfit, if she'd ever thought about such things.

'Why did you call me here so urgently, Nina?' Emma said patiently. 'Have you uncovered something new about the Paragon situation?'

'Well, not really, dear; but I did think we should talk about what we're going to do with what we do know. Especially since it involves You Know Who. Someone's got to get the word out that our Paragons have been possessed! Apart from you, obviously. People have the right to know things like that. Very especially after what's just happened on Shandrakor. You do know what's just happened on Shandrakor, don't you, darling?'

'Yes,' said Emma. 'I have my sources. Thirteen of my brethren are dead. I mourn their loss. They will be avenged.'

'But they're the bad guys now, aren't they? I mean, any one of them would kill us if they knew what we know about them.'

'The Paragons have never been the enemy,' Emma said sharply. 'They are helpless in the grasp of the minds that control them. And now there are thirteen Paragons that I will never be able to rescue.'

'Oh yes, of course. Sorry, lovey.' Nina looked terribly sad for a moment, but her natural ebullience quickly reasserted itself. 'But that makes it even more imperative that we *do something*. While we still can!'

'I've been thinking about it,' said Emma. 'If all else fails, I think I should assassinate Finn Durandal. He's behind everything bad that happens these days. Cut off the head of the serpent, and the body should wither and die.'

'Well, ten out of ten for gung-ho, dear, but let's be real about this. You'd never get anywhere near him. He's constantly surrounded by Church Militant bully boys and Pure Humanity thugs, and even if by some miracle you could get to him you'd never come out alive.'

'So?' said Emma, quite calmly.

'Right . . . Well, lovey, I think we'll leave the suicidal last charges until we've tried everything else, including closing our eyes and wishing it would all go away. We can't afford to take risks with our lives, Emma, we really can't. Not while we're the only ones who know the truth about what's happening.'

A blast of blindingly bright light exploded in the middle of the room, and both Emma and Nina cried out in shock, covering their eyes with upraised arms. The light seemed to solidify before them, and an overwhelming sense of presence began to sink into the room, as though approaching or descending into reality from somewhere far away. The light faded away to the merely painful, but the sense of presence was stronger than ever. Emma rose out of her chair, gun in hand, while Nina lurched blindly towards the guns on her wall. They were both sharing the same thought: *the uber-espers have found us ...* But when the glare suddenly snapped off, it left behind only a short blonde woman in old-fashioned clothing, with a harsh face and disquieting eyes. She nodded easily to Emma and Nina, though her smile was somewhat unsettling.

Nina clutched her gun to her chest as though for comfort. 'My God,' she whispered. 'I know you. I've seen your face in old holo files. You're Jenny Psycho!'

'I prefer Diana Vertue,' said the new arrival, still smiling. 'My other name may be what most people remember, but I was always so much more than just Jenny Psycho.'

'Aren't you supposed to be dead?' said Emma, not lowering the gun she had trained on the newcomer.

'Only materially,' said Diana. 'I thought I'd left the world behind me, but it seems I still have unfinished business to attend to.'

'Another exclusive!' Nina jumped up and down on the spot, waving her gun carelessly in the air. 'The return of Jenny Psycho! I am going to be so big-time I won't even talk to myself! Oh ... pictures! I have to get pictures!'

She tossed her gun at the nearest chair, and Emma tried not to flinch too obviously. Nina grabbed her camera from its recharger unit.

'I wouldn't bother,' said Diana. 'Cameras can't see me. Only people.'

'Oh poo,' said Nina. 'No one's ever going to believe this without pictures.'

Diana looked at Emma. 'You haven't put away your gun, Paragon.'

'I'm feeling insecure,' said Emma.

'I get that a lot,' said Diana. 'But you might as well holster it. It couldn't hurt me anyway.'

Emma sniffed, and put away her gun. 'What do you want with us, Diana Vertue? Your old name and reputation don't exactly inspire confidence.'

'There will be a gathering of ELFs and uber-espers tonight,' said Diana. 'And I'm here to tell you where it's going to be. All the uber-espers will be there, gathered together in the flesh in one place for the first time in over a century.'

'Someone slap me,' said Nina. 'I may faint.'

'Don't tempt me,' said Emma, not taking her gaze off Diana. It never occurred to either of them to question Diana's identity, or the truth of what she was saying. Her sense of presence was just too strong. Emma did her best to keep her voice level and businesslike. 'Give me the location, Diana Vertue. And I'll put a bomb under it so big they'll find pieces of the building on the Rim worlds.'

'Tempting thought,' said Diana. 'But unfortunately quite impractical. Their meeting place is set deep under the House of Parliament. I don't know if the people would miss the Members of Parliament, but the old building still has great sentimental appeal.'

'*Under the House?*' Emma was honestly outraged. 'How long has this been going on?'

'Since before my time,' said Diana. 'The uber-espers have used this very secret location for their get-togethers for centuries. Discovering its location was what got me killed. They ganged up on me. Ambushed me. I never even sensed it coming. When I died, the shock scattered my memories. The oversoul arrived in time to absorb my consciousness, but it took me many years to recover everything I'd lost. Now I'm all that's left of the oversoul on Logres, and my abilities are limited by my need to keep a low profile. If the uber-espers suspect I'm back, they'll go to ground and you'll never find them. But I'm going to fix it so you can sneak into the meeting place under the House, and make a record of everything that happens there.'

Nina had one hand in the air and waving, like a child in class. 'Can I *please* ask you just a few questions first, Diana?'

'If you must.'

Nina had a notepad and pencil at the ready. 'So you're here. You're back. Wow! You must have seen a lot of changes. What's your favourite restaurant? Who's your favourite vid star? Were you really having an affair with Finlay Campbell? And where does your body come from, if you only exist now as a part of the esper mass mind?'

'A lady doesn't answer personal questions. And I don't have time for the rest of that shit. Neither do you, if you want to get to the meeting before it's over. You have to leave now.'

'Why did King Robert and Queen Constance never make a legend out of you, like they did with the others?' said Emma, if only to show she wasn't going to be hurried into anything.

'Because they had enough sense not to annoy me,' said Diana Vertue. 'They knew I never approved of the whole legends business. But they were King and Queen, and I . . . was busy with my own affairs.'

'Affairs?' said Nina, her ears pricking up.

'Not the kind you're thinking of, dear. And don't push for answers that are none of your business or I'll hit you with a plague of frogs.'

'Oh, I love little froggies! They're so cute!'

'All right. How do you feel about a plague of boils?'

'Can I ask one last teeny tiny question?' Nina put on her best winsome expression, and hit her charm button for all it was worth. 'I'm sure an awful lot of people would like to know: why didn't you and the rest of the super-people do something about the Terror all those years ago? You knew it was coming. Why did you go away and leave it for us to deal with?'

Emma winced and braced herself for an explosive reaction, even getting ready to grab Nina and haul her out of the line of fire if necessary, but in the end Diana looked at Nina for a long moment, and then sighed quietly.

'Because . . . we never were super-people, dear. Not really. Just people, with extra abilities. And we were all so very tired after so many battles that had cost us so much . . . We didn't have it in us to fight another war. Not then. So many good people dead and gone, and we had an Empire to rebuild. So we went our separate ways, going wherever duty or need drove us . . . And none of us ever really thought the Terror would arrive in our lifetime. If we thought about it at all, I suppose we assumed that by the time the Terror finally got here, Mankind would have evolved into something capable of stopping it. We had such faith in the Madness Maze, in those days . . . I have to go. I have to be about my business. But first, some gifts.'

Emma and Nina cried out in pain and shock as Diana Vertue thrust information directly into their minds. In a moment, they knew exactly where to find the meeting place, how best to get there unobserved and from what vantage point they could best overhear what was said. It was as though they'd always known it. Emma and Nina slowly dropped their hands from their aching heads, and Emma glared at Diana.

'You might have warned us.'

'Would it have helped? I've also placed powerful esp-blocking mechanisms in your heads, for your own protection. Natural ones, not artificial. The uber-espers won't know you're there unless you're dumb enough to attract attention to yourselves. Best of luck, my dears. You're going to need it.'

And she was gone, as though she'd never been there. And perhaps she hadn't. Emma and Nina looked at each other.

'You don't have to come with me,' said Emma. 'This is going to be incredibly dangerous. We make one wrong step, and someone else will be coming home in our bodies.'

'Are you kidding?' Nina looked at the notepad in her hand, then tossed it aside and grabbed her camera again. 'We are talking story of the century! This is beyond an exclusive, this is a scoop! This is my own byline, maybe even my own show! In the future they'll name awards after me. Nina Malapert, demon girl reporter! Now let's go, before I start hyperventilating.'

It took Emma and Nina several hours of surreptitious travelling to work their way through the warren of maintenance tunnels under the House of Parliament, and then down and down through hidden doors and unexpected tunnels, to caverns excavated from solid stone, to the meeting place of the uber-espers. The map Diana Vertue had forced into their heads led them deep into the bedrock the Parade of the Endless was built on, through narrow corridors of stone that showed no signs of being worked by mortal hands. A pale diffuse glow filled the still air, from no obvious source. Emma and Nina padded quietly through the tunnels, guns in their hands, constantly on the alert for booby traps or unexpected guards, but they encountered nothing and no one. The uber-espers were confident in their secrets.

The more Emma thought about it, the more sense the location made. The House's security teams had never been willing to admit espers to their ranks, and MPs with far too much to hide had secretly encouraged the ban. And anyway, only a major league presence from the oversoul would have been able to detect the uber-espers behind the kind of shields they were capable of projecting. On top of all that, the sheer clutter and bedlam of thoughts and emotions generated by the House every day would easily hide any stray thoughts that might drift up from underground. Emma wasn't blind to the symbolism either; the official masters of the Empire above ground, and the unofficial below. Or perhaps the ego above and the id below. She sniffed unhappily, and moved stealthily on through the relentlessly descending tunnels, with Nina so close behind her she was almost treading on Emma's heels. The stone walls were closing in as the corridors narrowed until they brushed menacingly against their shoulders on both sides.

It was cold now, deathly cold. Their breath fogged on the air before them. There was something up ahead, something bad. They could both feel it. A sense of something spoiled and awful, and only partly human. Emma and Nina pressed on, trusting to Diana's esp-blockers to protect them. Whether she was Diana Vertue or Jenny Psycho,

258

being dead for over a century didn't seem to have slowed her down much.

The last tunnel finally came to an end in a rusted metal grille. Emma peered through first, while Nina fought stubbornly to squeeze in beside her, before finally admitting defeat and pressing her camera against the grille. Beyond and below was a great stone chamber, hundreds of feet in diameter. Stalactites and stalagmites thrust down and up. Emma looked at the camera, and then back at Nina, who nodded quickly and silently breathed the word, *Recording*. Emma settled herself in before the grille, ready for a long wait.

She had to admit it was a great location to eavesdrop from, set up by the high roof of the cavern. In Emma's experience, even the most paranoid people rarely looked up; even powerful uber-espers. So as long as the esp-blockers held out . . . Emma took in a sharp breath and pressed her face flat against the rusted metal grille as the first of the uber-espers appeared, teleporting into the stone chamber. More arrived, forcing reality aside to make room for them. Their combined presence was spiritually disturbing, on an almost primal level. Emma and Nina could feel each other shuddering as the need to run or scream or vomit hit them in a deep atavistic layer of the mind. The uber-espers were monsters, in every way.

The first to arrive were the Spider Harps, two withered homunculi with opened skulls, their fruiting brains expelled in a connecting web of pink and grey brain tissues. They'd somehow brought part of their own lair with them; an expanse of gauzy brain webbing stretched away much further from their corner of the cavern than should have been possible. The Spider Harps had physically joined two different locations, by the power of their will. They sat still and silent in their chairs, their sunken faces dead and empty, save for their dark malevolent eyes. They held hands, the joined flesh fused together long ago.

The Shatter Freak was the next to arrive. His physical existence had been shattered and scattered across time and space by some old psionic trauma. His patchwork body was composed of different parts from different times, from past and present and future, somehow combined in one constantly shifting construct. The details of his torso, limbs and extremities were always changing, appearing and disappearing, growing and shrinking as they quickly replaced each other. His various parts clung together as though for comfort, somehow functioning as a whole, as young, old and in-between pieces passed briefly through the present. The Shatter Freak's face flickered and twisted as features dropped in and out, from child to ancient, with only the eyes remaining constant, full of rage and pain, sorrow and horror. Part of him was always dying, and always being born.

Emma Steel frowned, as she realised she was understanding things about the uber-espers that she couldn't have known. It seemed Diana Vertue had left a reservoir of information behind in her head, to be triggered as necessary. Emma didn't feel at all comfortable about that, but since it made her job easier she just shrugged mentally and went along with it. She concentrated on the monsters below, while in the back of her head someone else's voice whispered to her of things she needed to know.

In order for the Shatter Freak's mind to function at all, he had to hold it firmly in the present, concentrating on the now. Memory and planning were both difficult for him, but sometimes future happenings stuck in his head for a moment, making him an oracle of sorts. He was the most powerful telepath ever, and only his fractioned consciousness kept him from accessing and dominating all other minds in his proximity. No one could keep any secrets from him, not even his fellow monsters, but they trusted him because they knew he couldn't retain any knowledge for long.

Blue Hellfire looked very much like the Ice Queen of children's stories; tall and slender, she was wrapped in diaphanous silks, revealing blue-white flesh beneath. Her short spiky hair was packed with ice, and hoarfrost made whorled patterns on her corpse-pale face. She looked like she'd been buried in the permafrost for centuries, and only recently dug up. She was always cold, icy cold, and most especially in her emotions, because everything that touched her burned. Her presence was enough to set the world on fire. She left a series of burning footsteps behind her as she strode slowly across the stone floor, and none of the other uber-espers could allow her to get too close. She was the source of the genetic material that the Empress Lionstone's scientists had used to create the Stevie Blue clones. Blue Hellfire had hoped the research might uncover a way for her to control her own fires, but she had become too powerful for science to tame. Her face was utterly blank, with no discernible identity or character of her own, with features so androgynous as to be almost generic. She could have been any age, or anyone. She could burn down a city with a thought or an emotion, but mostly she didn't care. Sometimes she made people have sex with her, just to watch them burn to death in her arms.

Screaming Silence was gargantuan; a woman of such vast size and substance that she seemed always to take up more than her fair share of space. Easily eight feet tall, and almost half as wide, her body was grossly distorted, burying her human characteristics under huge rolls of fat. She was always hungry, in all ways, her various appetites never satisfied no matter how much she indulged them. Her wide face was gaudy with slapped-on colours, her cold eyes burned deep in her face, and her mouth was pursed into an endless rosebud through the constant pressure of her cheeks. She had a great dandelion blossom of grey hair, and wore nothing but lengths of steel chain, wrapped around and around her, the steel links puncturing her flesh here and there to hold the chains in place. She stank of musk and sweat and foulness.

Wherever she was, she sucked all the energy out of a place, and in particular she absorbed sensory perceptions, savouring them like sweets at a banquet. Around her voices became quiet, scents faded away, colours became shades of grey, mouths became dry and empty and hands became numb. With a moment's effort she could leave a city screaming in total sensory deprivation. Or she could broadcast telepathically everything she'd stored, every sense and sensation simultaneously like a living mindbomb, overwhelming the senses of everyone around her for miles and miles and miles.

And finally there was the Grey Train. He no longer had a body as such, and only existed now as an individual entity by an extended ongoing effort of will. He manifested in the meeting place as a cloud of grey flakes in a more or less human form, composed of dust and detritus gathered together from his surroundings. He was only the memory of who he used to be, and if his concentration ever slipped, he wouldn't even be that. He looked even vaguer than usual this day, a grey ghost in a stone chamber, weakened by what had happened on Shandrakor.

The Grey Train had always been a possessor, the first of the uber-espers to be able to thrust his thoughts into the mind of another and take control. Under his will, his slaves became more bodies for him to live through, to experience vicariously a world lost to him. It was the Grey Train who taught the disaffected rogue espers how to become ELFs; because it amused him. So it was only natural that he should choose to possess the thirteen Paragons sent to Shandrakor. But the First Empire technology of the old Deathstalker Standing had destroyed his hold on those bodies and thrust him forcefully from their minds, attacking and destroying his thoughts with strange energies. The Grey Train was still recovering.

The uber-espers. The spawn of the Mater Mundi. Powerful beyond reason, crippled beyond hope, driven to live like rats in the walls of society.

The last monster to arrive, because he always had to make an entrance, was of course Finn Durandal. He strolled in through the only door, looking smart and splendid in his black leather Champion's armour, and gazed casually about him as though he saw such grotesque visions every day, and wasn't in the least impressed. He smiled easily, like a perfect prince among his courtiers, leaned calmly against the stone wall and folded his arms across his chest.

'Well, well,' he murmured. 'It seems the gang's all here. The secret Kings and Queens of the Empire.'

'How did you know about this place?' said Blue Hellfire, in her cold, cold voice. 'Which one of us betrayed this location to you?'

'Oh, none of you,' Finn said. 'But I have many useful allies. The AIs of Shub, for example. You'd be surprised at some of the things they know. They know about you, and they know about this place. They were only too happy to spill the beans in return for a detailed report on you and this meeting. They do so love to collect data. Now, if we could please proceed to the matter at hand? I'm sure none of us wants to be here any longer than we absolutely have to. The ELFs have told me they are on the verge of losing control of the Paragons. And we can't have that, can we? Someone here is going to have to take control of the remaining Paragons for a time, so the ELFs can get a little rest.'

'Impossible,' said the Grey Train immediately. He had a soft sighing voice that was barely audible, like the echo of a thought. 'It is all I can do now to maintain my own identity. The old science hurt me, banished me, diminished me. I am not what I was.'

'Give them to me,' said Screaming Silence, in her fat oily voice. She licked her great lips and slammed her massive hands together, sending shock waves rolling slowly through her vast body. 'The more the merrier, that's always been my motto. We'll have such fun . . . But now, sweet Finn, darling traitor: we must have words. We will not speak with the ELFs directly. We have moved beyond them. You shall be our voice to them in all things, and theirs to us. But never forget, Durandal, you are our figurehead, nothing more. Our human face in the human world. Everything you do is but an extension of our will; everything you think you own is really ours by proxy. We allow you a certain autonomy because it suits our purposes, but in the end . . . we own you.'

'You keep on thinking that,' Finn said generously. 'And we'll see what the future brings.'

'The Terror,' said the Shatter Freak in a child's voice. 'The future brings the Terror. Devastation and horror and planets burning in the dark. The death of Princes and of Kings are always marked by great events.'

They waited, but he had nothing else to say. His features slipped back and forth like melting wax on his face, young and old and young again, and he mumbled and muttered like an old man in his dotage.

The rest of the meeting was nothing more than an extended squabble over what if anything the uber-espers should do about the coming of the Terror. Emma decided she'd heard enough. She signalled silently to Nina, and the two of them quickly and carefully wriggled away from the metal grille. Nina shut down her camera to save power, and they made their way back down the narrow stone corridor. Emma frowned harshly, thinking hard. Now that she had her evidence of Finn's guilt and collaboration with the uber-espers, who could she safely present it to? The King was a broken force, Parliament was corrupt and at odds with itself, and the one man she would have trusted implicitly, the Deathstalker, was Outlawed. And she couldn't just give the recording to the media, even if she could find a station Finn didn't directly or indirectly control. She needed someone to support her, to give the evidence authenticity. Only one name suggested itself . . . and even then, making contact would be difficult. Emma frowned so hard her forehead hurt, and quietly followed Nina to the surface and sanity.

Finn Durandal was hardly back at his desk in his office in the House when he had a delightful if unexpected visitor. He smiled charmingly and came out from behind his desk to kiss the proffered hand of Treasure Mackenzie, famous and beautiful star of the vid soap *The Quality*. Treasure allowed him to. She was dressed for business, in a form-fitting gown of midnight blue, cut low at the front to reveal plenty of cleavage and cut high at the sides to reveal even more thigh. Her great mane of silver hair had little pink bows tied in it, and her black stiletto shoes had heels high enough and sharp enough to be classified as deadly weapons. She looked stunning, but then she always did. That was her job. Finn saw her comfortably settled in the visitor's chair and sat down behind his desk again.

'So, Treasure, this is a pleasant if somewhat unexpected honour. What can I do for you? Is there some problem with the plans for the wedding? I'm afraid I don't really handle such matters myself, but—'

'Cut the crap, Durandal,' said the woman who wasn't really Treasure Mackenzie. 'There's no audience here, so neither of us has to pretend. And if you've got the good sense God gave you when you were born, you'll turn off the recording devices you've got hidden in this room.'

Finn regarded her thoughtfully for a long moment, and then pressed a hidden stud on the floor with his foot. 'So,' he murmured, 'the masks are off, are they, Frankie?'

The gorgeous woman with the suddenly harsh face leaned back in her chair and smiled unpleasantly. 'You do know. We weren't sure, but given that you've infiltrated or suborned so many other supposedly secret societies, I suppose it was inevitable that you'd have someone in the Hellfire Club. But we know things too. We know your precious James Campbell is a clone. And we can prove it, if we have to. Dear du Katt is one of us, and has been for some time.'

'I can see I'm going to have to have a serious talk with dear du Katt,' said Finn. 'Still, it pleases me that the Hellfire Club has finally come to talk with me. You are almost the last unaligned power in the Empire. But you must know you can't afford to stand alone any longer. Great things are happening, the whole character of the Empire is changing . . . and if you're not part of the process you must expect to be left behind.'

'Funny,' said Frankie. 'We were thinking the same thing about you. You've stretched yourself too far, Durandal. You're trying to juggle and keep balanced too many forces, any one of which would leap at the chance to tear you apart if you even look like faltering. You need us, because we're everywhere. We're in all the other societies and movements you think you control. Join us, and help the Hellfire Club achieve its rightful destiny. You don't have to be alone. There are many comforts, and many pleasures, available to members of the Hellfire Club.'

Finn laughed at her. It was a harsh, ugly sound. His face was cold, even vicious. 'You have nothing I want, and you need me a hell of a lot more than I need you. That's why *you* came to see *me*. And the very fact that your masters sent an overweight cow like you to talk to me shows how desperate you people have become. Was I supposed to be blinded by your beauty, seduced by your rather obvious charms, into giving up everything I've gained? I don't think so. I really don't. Go back and tell your masters to send me someone I can respect, and then maybe we can do business. You're going to be Queen, Treasure. Settle for that.'

'So the gossip is right,' said Frankie. 'No heart, and no balls. A nice package, but nothing inside it.'

'Goodbye, Treasure,' said Finn. 'Don't let the door hit your over-padded arse on the way out.'

Frankie rose out of her chair with icy dignity, and stalked out of his office, deliberately leaving the door open so someone else would have to close it. She strode off through the corridors of the House, seething furiously behind her usual practised smile, and for once not even the most ardent of fans came forward to press her for an autograph. Treasure Mackenzie was clearly going somewhere important, and no one had the nerve to get in her way. She dismissed Finn Durandal from her mind. If one plan didn't work, move straight on to the next. That had always been her way. The next target was Douglas. He wasn't nearly as broken-spirited as he liked people to believe. She'd tried seducing him and that hadn't worked, so this time she'd try cold reason. The King had no friends left, and no allies, but if she could bring him into the Hellfire Club, then the new King and Queen would be in an excellent position to manoeuvre power away from Finn. And Douglas had a whole bunch of reasons for wanting to see Finn Durandal brought down.

Tel Markham, honourable Member of Parliament for Madraguda, and Finn Durandal's official whipping boy, went to see his brother Angelo Bellini, the celebrated Angel of Madraguda, in his luxurious office in the great Cathedral of the Parade of the Endless. The visit wasn't Tel's idea. Finn had given him strict instructions. Tel was to talk with his brother on some very specific subjects, and either bring Angelo firmly back under Finn's control or . . . kill him and make it look like natural causes. No other options available. When Tel objected, Finn had smiled his disturbing smile and said it was either Angelo or Tel. If he followed instructions, and it became necessary to kill his brother, then Tel would become the new head of the Church Militant. Under Finn, of course. But if he didn't have the balls to do what had to be done, then Finn would have Tel killed and replace him with someone who would get the job done.

You should be grateful I'm giving you this opportunity, Finn had said. *At least this way you can make sure your brother doesn't suffer.*

Tel walked alone through the halls of the cathedral, taking his time, blind to its charms and sense of peace, and wondered what the hell he was going to do. He'd never actually killed anyone before, though he'd always known that some day it might prove necessary. And as the head of the official Church he'd be a power in his own right again, and able to treat with Finn more as an equal. He'd be back in the game, a player, and no one's whipping boy. He'd never liked Angelo anyway. Not really. He could do it. He had a poison dust concealed in a secret cache in his sleeve. Angelo would never have his own brother searched. Easy enough to slip the dust into a drink, and then Angelo would be dead in seconds. Apparent heart attack. There wouldn't be much of an investigation. Finn would see to that. And besides, Angelo wasn't at all popular these days, even among his own people.

It was no secret that the Angel of Madraguda had seriously lost the plot. He'd started to believe his own propaganda, that he really was a saint, or even a messiah, come to lead his people out of darkness. Exactly where he was leading them didn't seem too clear. He'd forgotten or disregarded the fact that he had never been intended to be anything more than a puppet for Finn's will. The Angel of Madraguda wrote his own speeches these days, rambling apocalyptic sermons, and openly defied Finn's instructions. And there were rumours . . . dark, unsettling rumours, that not everyone who went in to see Angelo Bellini came out again.

So the man had to go. He had to be put out of everyone's misery. And who better to do the job than his own dear brother? Well, half-brother, really. Same mother, different fathers. But even so, a brother was still a brother, wasn't he? He was still family . . .

Tel finally came to the door of the outer office. He stopped there a while, composing himself with several deep breaths, and then he pushed open the door and breezed into the outer office as though it was just another visit. Angelo's secretary nodded distractedly to him. She was pale and unhappy, and the smile she gave Tel didn't reach her eyes. She looked like a dog that had been kicked too often.

'Hello, Marion,' said Tel, doing his best to appear as though he hadn't noticed anything amiss. 'I'm here to see my brother. Is he in?'

'Hard to say,' said Marion. 'I mean, yes, he's in his office, but . . . he's not himself. He rarely is, any more. You haven't been around for a while, so you haven't seen . . . maybe you can help him. He won't listen to me. He won't listen to anyone, except . . . You've got to get him out of here, Tel. Get him somewhere . . . safe, where he can get help. He's done . . . bad things, Tel. And I can't leave. I'm the only protection he's got left.'

'Easy, Marion.' Tel put on his most reassuring face and voice. 'It's all right, I'm here now. I'll take care of everything.'

He went over to the inner door, and Marion buzzed him through. The smell was the first thing that hit Tel as he entered Angelo's office. It stank, of old food and spilled drink, of rot and corruption, and clearly no one had opened a window in far too long. The room was dim and gloomy, with the shutters closed. There was only one light on, over Angelo at his desk. He was sitting hunched forward, muttering to himself. Tel wasn't sure whether his brother even knew he was there. He walked slowly and carefully through the gloom, avoiding the darker shadows of pieces of furniture. The carpet seemed . . . sticky under his feet. Tel could feel his heartbeat racing. All his instincts were yelling at him that he had come to a very dangerous place.

His eyes adjusted to the gloom as he drew nearer Angelo's desk. The room was a mess. Nothing was in its right place, nothing had been cleaned up, and what looked like important papers were scattered over the floor around the desk. Tel did his best not to step on them. He stopped in front of the desk, and Angelo finally raised his head to look at him. He glared sullenly at his brother, making no move to greet him. His hair was long and shaggy, and his beard hadn't been trimmed in ages. His face had an unhealthy pallor, and his eyes had the dark dangerous glare of an old-time prophet. His hands were toying with a long, vicious-looking dagger, and Tel was suddenly very glad there was a wide desk between him and his brother. Tel looked away from his brother's disturbing gaze, and suddenly realised that what he'd thought was an ornament was in fact the back of someone's head. Tel moved to one side for a better look. It was a severed human head, with sunken eyes, its mouth drooping open in a never-ending scream of horror. It was mounted on a letter spike, and the blood around the base still looked wet.

'What happened, Angelo?' Tel said steadily. 'You run out of executive toys?'

'Oh, don't mind him,' said Angelo, in a surprisingly calm and reasonable voice. 'He was a traitor. There are traitors everywhere. Traitors and heretics and . . . But I make use of them. Waste not, want not, as our dear mother used to say. I was going to call her, only the other day, but . . . I talk to the head, you know, and it talks to me. God speaks to me through its dead lips, telling me His will. For I am His Angel, and He loves me dearly. I'm not sure how He feels about you, Tel. You were always very cruel to me, when we were younger. God's will is sometimes strange, and often downright disturbing, but who are we to question Him? Don't blame the messenger for the message, that's what I always say. If He wants people killed, He must have His reasons. The only problem is, I have to keep replacing the heads. They wear out very quickly, and it's often hard to work out exactly what God is saying when the mouth is rotting and falling apart. I know, I know; the bad workman blames his tools, but . . . The spirit is willing but the flesh is weak. Still, there's never any shortage of traitors and heretics. Sometimes I find them among my own people when I'm in a hurry. God doesn't like to be kept waiting.'

Tel nodded, keeping his face blank. No wonder Finn wanted Angelo replaced. It might undermine the faith of the Church Militant fanatics if word got out that their revered spiritual leader had gone barking mad. Tel sighed inwardly. Perhaps . . . if he got Angelo out of here, away from all this and the pressures of the job . . . then maybe he could be coaxed back into his right mind. Mother would take him in. She always did.

Angelo had always been her favourite.

'You can't stay here, Angelo,' Tel said carefully. 'It isn't safe any more. I need you to come with me now.'

He reached out a hand to his brother across the desk, but Angelo recoiled immediately. A slow craftiness entered his gaze, and his voice rose sharply.

'No, this is my place! I have made it a holy place, and sacred. I can never leave here. The world is dirty and sinful, full of liars and schemers . . . Nowhere else is safe now. They plot against me, they do, even the Durandal. I never trusted him. But I know what's going on. I have my sources, and God tells me many things. I live on pure air, you know. I have transcended the need for grosser nourishment. Angels are above mortal weaknesses. You must go. I have a sermon to finish. The people are waiting to hear from me. They rely on me.'

I can't kill him, Tel thought. *It might almost be a merciful release, but even so . . . I can't murder a helpless pathetic mess like this. It would be like poisoning a small child. It seems there are some lines that even I won't cross. Who would have guessed it?*

'Come with me, Angelo,' he said, with something very like compassion in his voice. 'Let me take you home.'

'I can't go home,' said Angelo. He sounded suddenly tired, resigned. 'I don't belong there any more. Finn gave me so many drugs, and I took them . . . and now I have to stay in the place I made for myself. Did I ever tell you about what happened in that church on Madraguda, all those years ago? I lied. It wasn't like that.'

'I know,' said Tel.

'I thought I found my path there, and my destiny. But all I really found was the darkness in my own soul. Get out of here, Tel. You can't help me. Even I can't help me now. I must do . . . what I must do.'

'Angelo . . .'

'Get out, Tel. Before God tells me to hurt you.'

Tel backed slowly out of the dimly lit room, not taking his eyes off his brother, and then he left, closing the door firmly. He looked at the secretary behind her desk, shook his head helplessly and strode off through the cathedral. And wondered where the hell he could go, where Finn Durandal wouldn't be able to find him.

It didn't take long for the news to get back to Finn. Tel wouldn't have been surprised if Angelo's secretary Marion hadn't put in the call herself. Either way, Tel had barely found a private comm booth, and started calling round his so-called friends and allies, when he discovered that the word was already out on him. And the word from Finn was death. There was to be no chance for explanations or excuses. Most of the people Tel called wouldn't take his call, and those few who would seemed to take an inordinate delight in informing him that he was longer any associate of theirs. Tel Markham had been disowned, from on high, and was an outcast, a pariah, with a price on his head. Some gloated, some even made threats, but most just wanted him to go away and never call them again. Because failure might be catching.

Tel left the booth, and wandered off down the street. He hadn't spent long enough on any call for anyone to be able to trace him, but he felt a need to keep moving. He knew there was only one place he could safely go now, but he resisted the idea, his thoughts plunging wildly back and forth for some alternative. Because once he fell into the Rookery, that was the end of his soft, comfortable, privileged life. He hated to think he'd thrown it away because of a brother he'd never even liked much. And then he stopped and looked at the vid screens on display in a store window. They were all talking about him.

A breaking news story was running on every major channel. The life and crimes of Tel Markham, traitor and fugitive from justice. Tel watched for a while, and had to admire the workmanship. It was a very detailed, very clever hatchet job. Finn must have had it put together some time back, and kept it in reserve for just such an occasion as this. When Finn no longer needed Tel. The news story listed all the bad things he'd done, and a great many he hadn't. Tel was impressed by the research, and thought he detected the skilled poison pen of Mr Sylvester himself, the ruiner of reputations Finn had brought out of the Rookery to be his character assassin. Tel had worked with Mr Sylvester in the past on such pieces as this, using half truths and lies to bring down those who threatened him. The irony of the situation did not escape him.

The story went on to reveal every one of the secret organisations he'd belonged to, from the Shadow Court to the Hellfire Club, and even a few really obscure ones that Tel had actually forgotten about. And so, at a stroke, Finn separated Tel from all his old allies. None of the groups would support him now. They'd probably be furious enough to put a price on his head themselves. He had sworn allegiance to too many people, too many causes, and they would never forgive him for daring to serve so many conflicting masters.

Even the few people he'd actually thought of as friends had disowned him. *You don't have anything we want. You don't have anything we need. You're nobody.*

Tel looked casually around, and then activated the holo face he kept hidden for emergencies, stored in his high collar. It would last long enough to get him to where he was going. When you had nothing and no one, there was still one place that would always take you in. The last resort of the desperate man. The Rookery.

Tel Markham entered the Rookery through one of the lesser known ways, and went straight to a safe house he'd maintained for many years, under a pseudonym, the finances carefully concealed behind a series of cut-outs. He'd always made a point of keeping up with the payments, even in his leanest times, all for a time he'd hoped would never come. He let himself in with a key he'd never used before, and turned off his holo face. The house wasn't much, but it had all the amenities, including a comm line. So the first thing Tel did was to sit down and contact the major news channels, anonymously of course, and spill all the secrets and dirt he'd spent a political lifetime accumulating. The scandals, the stupid choices and dirty washing of everyone he'd ever worked with. If he was going down, he was taking everyone else with him. Tel was a great believer in the satisfactions of revenge, and spreading the pain around.

And yet interestingly enough, none of the news channels would accept anything about Finn Durandal. The comm line shut itself down automatically every time Tel tried to use the name. The Durandal had fixed it so no one could discuss anything the Durandal didn't want discussed. Tel was impressed. That was real power.

He tried every trick he knew to get around the problem, but in the end he had to give up. He shut down the comm link. It had been a long and unexpectedly hard day, and he was tired. Maybe he'd try again tomorrow. It wasn't as if he had anything else to do. He leaned back in the uncomfortable chair, and wondered what he was going to do next. He had some money put away, under a multitude of false identities, but it wouldn't last long. And the Rookery could be an expensive place, once people there realised you had nowhere else to go. And sooner rather than later the bounty hunters would be on his trail. Finn would see to that. Tel shuddered suddenly, and wrapped his arms tightly around himself as a cold wave of helplessness washed over him. He was alone, cut off from everyone and everything he knew. What was he going to do? He looked at the mirror on the wall opposite him, and didn't recognise the face he saw there.

The pale, frightened face in the mirror didn't look like him. That old, beaten-down man couldn't be Tel Markham, mover and shaker, Member for Madraguda. Though he supposed even that title would be taken away from him, now he'd been named a traitor. But if he wasn't an MP, what was he? Tel was used to defining himself by what he did: his title and his power and his influence. Now that was gone, was he still Tel Markham? Who was he, really? What did he believe in? He'd never believed in any of the causes he supported, not one; they were a means to an end, to making him a mover and a shaker. All he had left was himself, and now that he looked there didn't seem to be much of him.

No; there was one thing he was sure of. He was a man who wouldn't murder his own brother.

Tel smiled slowly, coldly. When everything else has been taken from you, one thing still remains: revenge. And Finn really should have remembered that a man with nothing left to lose is the most dangerous man of all.

Finn Durandal decided that he would murder Angelo Bellini and make it look as though Tel Markham had done it anyway. So he strolled through the cathedral, nodded casually to Marion at her desk, walked unannounced into Angelo's office, hauled him over his desk and strangled the Angel of Madraguda with his bare hands. Finn watched almost clinically as Angelo's face reddened and then darkened, and the way his eyes bulged as he struggled for breath as he beat helplessly against Finn with his soft useless hands. But in the end it was over very quickly, and Finn was somewhat surprised and disappointed to discover that he hadn't actually enjoyed it very much. It was just work, a necessary and marginally unpleasant detail he'd had to take care of, and now it was done. Finn let the dead body fall to the carpet, then strode round the desk and sat down in Angelo's chair to consider the matter.

It was getting harder and harder for Finn to find things he could enjoy. When you can do anything, and no one can stop you, it rather takes the thrill out of it. He needed greater and greater stimulus to activate and entertain him, to keep him going. He'd done all the usual things, broken the usual taboos, and now . . . his greatest enemy was boredom. He was beginning to understand what it was that drove the

ELFs to commit acts of such appalling excess. When nothing is forbidden or impossible, even the vilest of sins can lose its savour. Finn had thrown aside all moral restraints in the name of freedom, and found it exhilarating; but now he was discovering that when you care about nothing, then nothing much matters any more. It would probably have been different if he'd been a man of great physical appetites, for food and drink and sex. But he'd never had much use for any of them. And it might have helped if love had been real, but it never had been, for him. He'd always been much more comfortable with hatred. It seemed all he had left were the subtle joys of intrigue, the setting of his mind in opposition to others. That, and the happy satisfactions of revenge.

He would still bring the Empire down, and exult in its destruction; but he was no longer as sure he could be bothered to raise it up again.

Finn considered the rotting severed head on its spike on Angelo's desk. Its ugliness bothered him. So he removed it from its spike, and threw it aside. He got up, went over to Angelo's body, cut off the head and brought it back to the desk. He settled Angelo's head on the letter spike, taking some care to get it perfectly straight and upright, and then sat down again to study it. He particularly liked the look of surprise that haunted the slack features. He decided to leave it there, on the desk, as a gift for whoever he decided to put in charge of the Church Militant. It would make a marvellous object lesson. Hopefully, whoever he finally settled on wouldn't take the job so seriously this time.

Treasure Mackenzie, also known as Frankie, bribed and dazzled her way past the guards at King Douglas's door, breezed cheerfully through into his private chambers, and then locked the door behind her, using a key that would keep everybody out, even the guards. She had a lot to say and do, and she didn't intend to be interrupted. Douglas rose out of his chair with a polite objection on his lips, and then stopped as he realised there was something different about his fiancée this time. Her face was as beautiful and sensual as ever, but her eyes were cold and her generous mouth was set in a flat line. She strode towards him like a warrior going into battle. Douglas dropped his book into his chair and met her with a cold thoughtful look of his own. Treasure didn't seem happy to see him. She came to a halt in front of him, her eyes boring into his.

'The time for masks is over, Campbell. It's time to reveal who we really are, and what we really want.'

'Really?' said Douglas. 'How very intriguing. To what, exactly, do I owe the pleasure of this visit, Treasure?'

'That's not my name. Not my real name. I was born Francine Wolfe.' She smiled at his reaction. 'That's right, Campbell. I'm the current head of a family that was once your Clan's greatest enemy. Our ancestors killed each other for laughs. And now, here I am promised to you in marriage. If either of us lives that long. It turns out we have a common enemy, someone who wants us both dead. Unless we can agree to put aside our differences, and our masks, to work together.'

'This enemy,' said Douglas. 'Does he have a name?'

'The Durandal,' said Frankie, showing her perfect teeth in a smile that was more of a snarl. 'Finn intends to replace you with James. You must have realised that by now.'

'Perhaps,' said Douglas. 'And perhaps I'm not the broken reed I allow others to see. But why should I ally myself with you, Wolfe? I only have to be near you, and the stink of hidden agenda becomes almost overpowering.'

'You need me because you've allowed yourself to become isolated. You have no friends or allies, and even the House has turned its back on you. For a Paragon and a Prince you've been remarkably naïve. You really should have chosen your friends more carefully. Finn has become your greatest enemy, Lewis is Outlawed, and Anne . . . is sleeping with James. Ah, you didn't know that. I wasn't sure.'

'Poor Anne,' said Douglas. 'It's going to end badly, and there's nothing I can do to help her.'

'She betrayed you! She sold her soul to Finn!'

'She must have been hurting for a long time. And I was always too busy to notice. But then, it seems I failed to notice a lot of things. What do you want, Wolfe?'

'Your only hope is to destroy Finn and James before they come for you. And for that you're going to need me, and the people I represent. I'm Hellfire Club, Douglas. Now, don't look at me like that. We're probably the only power left in the Empire that doesn't bow down to the Durandal.'

Douglas showed her a face as cold as her own. 'If there's anything left in this declining Empire that's lower and more despicable than Finn Durandal, it's the Hellfire Club. Do you think I've forgotten the atrocities you people have committed, down the years? Have you forgotten how many of your people I've killed?'

'Strange times make for strange allies, Campbell. Don't let your childish dislike for our methods blind you to the opportunities here.

273

You agree to work with me, with us, and we will make you King again. A real King, this time. Working together, we can undermine and throw down the Durandal, usurp his people and turn them to our cause, and then we will bring back the old days, of Clan and birthright and tradition.' She was standing very close to him, her eyes gleaming, her words burning with conviction. 'The Families will take their rightful place again, and we will sit on the Throne of Empire and rule over all. Our word shall have power over life and death, and our enemies shall know blood and suffering for ever.'

'I never wanted any of that,' Douglas said flatly. 'I never even wanted to be King. Perhaps if I'd stuck to my guns and forced my father to find another successor none of this need ever have happened.'

'Well, if you won't do it for ambition, how about revenge? The Durandal has ruined your life, and destroyed everything you ever believed in. Are you going to let him get away with that? Or are you smart enough to join with us, and stop him before he brings everything down to rack and ruin?'

'Low as I am,' said Douglas, 'I still have more sense than to make a deal with the Devil. Once I let you in, I'd never be free of you. What's the point in replacing one tyrant with another? I'll find a way to stop Finn, and I'll find a way to stop you too. Hope you enjoy the wedding, Wolfe. It's all you'll ever have of me.'

'That bitch Flowers really did take your balls with her, didn't she?' said Frankie, and laughed in his face as he glared at her.

She let her right hand drift closer to the high slit in her dress over her right thigh. Under the dress she had a concealed leather sheath, holding a long slender dagger. The leather had been cloned from her own skin, and the dagger fashioned from scrapings from her own thigh bone. Which meant neither of them would show up in any security scan. And who would body-search a woman going to meet her husband-to-be, after the scan had already cleared her? If Douglas couldn't be persuaded to do the sensible thing, then that left only one option. Kill Douglas, and plant evidence to make it look like Finn did it. The Hellfire Club could then step in and take advantage of the resulting chaos, and before you knew it little Treasure Mackenzie would be Queen. Her Court would all be Hellfire Club, and her advisers, and soon enough the Empire would wake up to discover that everything had changed . . . The Dark Queen would hold dominion, devils would run riot in the streets and *Do what thou wilt* would be the whole of the law. It would be glorious. Frankie laughed again, holding Douglas's angry eyes with her own, and drew the concealed dagger

274

from its sheath. She leaned forward as though to kiss him, and then thrust the dagger into his unprotected groin.

Except somehow, impossibly, his hand was there in time to grab her wrist and stop the blow well short of its target. He laughed softly, and twisted her wrist cruelly until she had no choice but to drop the knife. She slashed at his eyes with her free hand, the long fingernails digging bloody furrows in his cheek as he snapped his head away. She broke free from his grip and fell back a step. They stood there for a moment, glaring at each other, breathing heavily, and then they both lunged forward. For they were Campbell and Wolfe, Paragon and Hellfire Club, and they would never be anything but enemies.

It was a killing fight now, and they both knew it.

They slammed together, both of them fighting expertly and viciously, as they'd been trained. Their hands struck like weapons, going for soft spots and unguarded places. They used killing blows and crippling moves, parrying attacks at the very last moment, hurting each other with almost clinical precision. Their clothes tore, and blood splashed on the luxurious carpeting, but neither of them cried out. They lurched back and forth, sometimes trading blows, sometimes fighting in close with deadly holds and purchases, fingers probing for pressure points, their bodies wet with sweat as their passion drove them on. They raged across the room, smashing antique furnishings and priceless heirlooms, so caught up in their struggle they didn't even notice. The guards outside were beating on the door and demanding to be let in, but Frankie had fixed the locks.

Douglas and Frankie fought hand to hand, with marvellous skill and deadly fury. She knew every dirty trick there was, but he was a trained Paragon, and in the end he was a professional and she was just a gifted amateur. Douglas slipped under a carelessly timed blow, spun Frankie round and caught her in a full nelson. Both his hands clapped firmly over the back of her neck, pressing her head forward, while her arms stretched helplessly out. She heaved and struggled, slamming her body against his, but she couldn't break the hold. She swore at him, stamping down on his feet. Douglas applied more pressure, forcing her chin down against her breastbone, and she cried out in pain and anger as her neck bones creaked.

'That's it,' Douglas said, struggling to get his breath back. 'This is over! Surrender and stand trial, or die right here.'

'You haven't got the balls!' said Frankie. 'The Hellfire Club will see you dead for this insult! No one refuses us! We'll be at your back and at your throat for as long as it takes to get you. Let me go, bow down to me, and you can still be someone!'

And somehow, impossibly, her right shoulder dislocated itself, and her right arm came snaking around, holding the bone dagger, heading straight for his ribs. Douglas's arm muscles flexed powerfully, and her neck broke with a loud crack. She went limp against him, the breath going out of her. The bone dagger fell from her dead hand. Douglas let her go and she slumped untidily to the floor, like a beautiful broken doll. Douglas knelt down beside her.

'I am someone,' he said quietly. 'I am the King. And I sentence you to death, for treason.'

His breathing slowed as he sat down beside Frankie's body. He could hear a pounding, but couldn't tell whether it was his heart or the guards outside his door. He looked at his hands, and there was blood on them from the fight. And that was how Anne Barclay and the guards found him, when they finally broke down the doors and burst into his chamber. King Douglas, sitting beside the dead body of his wife-to-be, with her blood on his hands.

'Oh my God,' said Anne. 'Douglas . . . what have you done?'

'He's killed her!' said one of the guards. 'The bastard's killed Treasure Mackenzie!'

He started towards Douglas, and the other guard had to restrain him. Anne moved slowly forward, and Douglas looked up at her.

'I had to kill her. She was Hellfire Club.'

'Of course she was, Douglas. Now please, stand up. Let them get to the body. I'll . . . get someone to take you somewhere else.'

'This isn't what it looks like, Anne. She tried to kill me.'

'Her? Empty-headed, harmless little Treasure Mackenzie? The woman who was going to be your wife, your Queen? Oh, Douglas . . .' Anne put a hand to her head, and swallowed hard. 'There's no way we can cover this up, Douglas. There's nothing I can do for you. Oh God . . . I should never have gone along with a second marriage. Not so soon after . . . By introducing her to you, I as good as killed her myself.'

'She was—'

'*I don't want to hear it, Douglas!* Oh Jesus, I should never have left you alone for so long. I knew you were depressed, but . . . I never meant . . . Oh hell. I'm sorry, Douglas. You've gone too far now. There's nothing I can do for you.'

More guards came crashing in through the open doorway. They had guns in their hands. Douglas stood very still. Anne put a gentle hand on his arm.

'Go with them, Douglas. I won't let them hurt you, I promise. They'll take you somewhere safe.'

'What the hell happened here?' said one of the new guards.

'The King has lost his mind,' said Anne. 'He must be placed under house arrest, under secure conditions, for his own protection. Until a trial can be arranged.'

'You have security cameras in here,' said Douglas. He tried hard to keep his voice calm and reasonable. 'I know you, Anne. You'd have cameras here somewhere, to keep an eye on me. Make sure I wasn't plotting. Check the recordings. They'll show what really happened.'

'The cameras were shut down,' said Anne. 'That's why I came here, as soon as I heard. How did you do that, Douglas?'

He laughed suddenly, bitterly. 'She really was very thorough. Of course she wouldn't want any witnesses.'

'Take him away,' said Anne. 'Be firm, but don't hurt him. He's not responsible. And get that body out of here. *No one is to say anything to anyone!* Not until I figure out how we're going to play this. And someone go find the Durandal! He'll have to . . . put things in action. For the trial. And the funeral. And I'll have to tell James.' She looked at Douglas almost triumphantly. 'He'll have to be King now.'

'Over my dead body,' said Douglas.

'Yes,' said Anne.

Out on the Rim, on the edge of the Empire, the Terror's herald appeared in normal space again. No one saw it coming. It was just suddenly there, heading for its next target, Heracles IV. It didn't look like much: a dark, vaguely organic shape about a mile in length, heading in a straight implacable line towards the sun of its next victim. It was travelling at less than light speed, but even so Heracles IV had only a few hours in which to prepare itself.

Heracles IV was the only inhabited planet in the system, an artificially maintained farm world producing luxury foods and wines. Normally it didn't even have much of a security force. It had never needed one. But on this day, Heracles IV was the most heavily defended planet in the Empire. The outermost defensive ring was composed of thousands of sensor drones. They picked up the Terror's herald the moment it appeared in normal space again, but the herald had already passed them by the time the planet responded to their warning. The oversoul might have bought them more time; but there were no espers in the Empire any more. Finn Durandal had seen to that. The next layer of defence was provided by an orbiting minefield of the most powerful subspace detonators the Empire had ever produced. They blew up, one after the other, as the herald passed through them, and didn't slow or alter its progress one bit.

Down on the planet's surface, hundreds of thousands of remote news cameras turned themselves on. Every news station in the Empire was represented on Heracles IV, ready to cover the story. There were no actual reporters there, of course. They couldn't get insurance. But their cameras were there, ready to broadcast the death of a planet and its whole population, live and as it happened, or, just possibly, a world's miraculous escape from utter destruction. The news stations had editorials ready to run either way. Pretty much the whole Empire was watching breathlessly as Heracles IV's dearly purchased defence systems activated. State-of-the-art disrupter cannon fired on the herald from orbiting stations as it approached, hitting the intruder again and again with almost unimaginable energies. Forces that had scorched the life from whole planets struck the herald full on, and left it unscathed. Mindbombs powerful enough to madden whole cities detonated one after the other, to no effect. Sensor arrays bathed the herald with every investigative technique known to the Empire, and they couldn't even decide on whether the herald was really there or not. The herald kept coming.

And now there was only one layer of defensive tech left: the untried, mysterious alien tech supplied by Mog Mor. No one on the planet even knew what it was, or what it was supposed to do.

In Orpheus City, capital of Heracles IV, all hell was breaking loose. The population was torn between prayer sessions, rioting in the streets, hiding in bomb shelters, and the occasional mass suicide pact. All those who could leave had already done so. The last few ships were still racing away from Heracles IV, and praying they'd put enough distance between them and the planet to be able to drop into the safety of hyperspace before it was too late. But right in the heart of the city, three Paragons strolled down the main street, passing a bottle of wormwood brandy back and forth between them, and looking curiously up at the sky. Sent by Finn Durandal to make a first-hand report on the Terror's approach, all three were possessed by the uber-esper Screaming Silence. Once their names had been Kelly Fox, Yvonne Church and Avraam Dusk, but now someone else watched the skies through their eyes, and waited interestedly to see what would happen. Screaming Silence had had a pleasant enough time waiting, dining and drinking of the finest the world had to offer, sleeping with each other till they were sore because no one else would come near them, and otherwise indulging the uber-esper's never-ending appetites by proxy. The Paragons themselves were becoming rather damaged, but that didn't matter. They would die here anyway, once the Terror drew too close and Screaming Silence had to leave.

Finn had sent them on the grounds that since they were already mentally controlled, they might be immune to the Terror's deadly voice, the never-ending scream that drove whole populations insane. He was intrigued to see what would happen.

The herald ploughed through the last of the standard defences as though they weren't even there, and came at last to the Mog Mor line. Activated by its approach, the alien tech unfolded great gleaming shapes that blossomed into vast crystal flowers. Strange energies seethed around them, and space itself rippled and wavered. Terrible forces seized upon the herald, and strove to force it out of normal space and back into whatever hell it came from. Sinkholes and singularities flared briefly, pockmarking space, only to collapse in on themselves and disappear, ignored by the herald. One by one the Mog Mor devices overloaded and disintegrated, and the herald flew on, untouched.

From a place that was not a place it came, a nightmare given shape and form, heading inexorably for the sun of Heracles IV.

Screaming Silence reached out curiously with her mind, forcing her psionic abilities through the limited minds of her thralls. They cried out in agony, blood leaking from their nostrils and eyes, but she didn't care. Her thoughts rose from the planet to touch the coming herald; and then immediately withdrew, shocked and sickened. She couldn't bear to be near it, even for a moment. She slammed back into the three Paragons' minds, and then abandoned them, fleeing to Logres, and safety. The plan had been for Screaming Silence to stay until the very last moment, until the herald's vicious spawn came howling out of the sun, and perhaps even until the appearance of the Terror itself; but one glimpse of the herald's terrible true nature was enough to panic and terrorise the uber-esper. She turned and ran, abandoning her thralls to their fates, and two women and one man cried out in shock and horror and disgust at what had been done to them. They clung to each other, shaking and shuddering, soiled beyond hope at what the abomination had done in their minds and through their bodies. But at long last they were themselves again, and because they were Paragons, their spirits were not broken.

Kelly Fox was short, slender, gamine, pale of face, with almost colourless blonde hair. There was blood and vomit down the front of her tattered tunic. Yvonne Church was a giant valkyrie of a woman, with a wide fan of jet-black hair, olive skin and sharp patrician features. Her blouse was ripped open to the waist, and she pulled it shut with trembling hands. Avraam Dusk had skin so dark it was almost blue, wrapped in what had once been pure-white robes. White hair fuzzed his skull in places, where the uber-esper hadn't bothered to shave it regularly. One of the fingers on his left hand was missing. The uber-esper had bitten it off and eaten it, just to savour the experience.

Weakened, sickened, almost maddened by the experience of their long possession, they held each other for a while, drawing what comfort they could from simple human closeness. Then they stood apart and looked around them at a city in chaos. People were running and screaming in the streets, while traffic roared uselessly in every direction. Looting had begun, and fires were breaking out. People had started jumping from high buildings. The sky was purple now, with blood-red clouds covering the sun, as though to hide the vulnerable sun from the awful thing that was coming.

'It'll be here soon,' said Kelly, rubbing the palms of her hands against her hips as though they would never be clean again. 'We have to do something.'

'We have to get offworld,' said Avraam. 'We must let the Empire know that ELFs are possessing the Paragons.'

'No,' said Yvonne. 'First we have to save Heracles IV.'

Avraam looked at her. 'I'm open to suggestions.'

Kelly was crying, tears rolling down her cheeks. 'There's nothing we can do. She left us nothing. She—'

'We know,' said Avraam. 'We remember what she made us do. But we have to be strong, Kelly. These people need us. That's what being a Paragon is about: being strong when others can't be.'

'You always were a pompous bastard, Avraam.' But the tears stopped, and Kelly nodded jerkily. 'All right. Paragons, first and foremost. But what the hell can we do?'

'We launch our ship from the starport,' said Yvonne. 'No one will have got past the defences on our ship. We go up, we drive straight at the herald, wait until we're right on top of it and then overload the stardrive. I don't care what the herald is; an exploding stardrive could blow out a sun like a candle.'

'Theoretically,' said Kelly. 'No one's ever actually tried it, as far as I know.'

'No one's ever had to before,' said Avraam.

They looked at each other for a while, and then Yvonne shrugged. 'What the hell; it's a good day to die.'

'Suicide is a sin,' said Kelly.

'Not if you take your enemy with you,' said Avraam.

'What is death, but a release from our memories?' said Yvonne. 'For us, death will be a comfort.'

'You always were a spooky cow,' said Kelly, but for the first time there was a hint of a smile on her pale lips.

They strode off through the city, ignoring the panicked souls running blindly around them. It wasn't that far to the main starport, after they commandeered a car. They had to kill the driver to get it, but they couldn't let themselves think about that. Every time they saw a floating news camera, they slowed the car and called to the camera, trying to get word out of what had been done to them and the other Paragons. But every time they tried, the cameras shut themselves down. They'd been programmed to do that. Finn thought of everything.

The Paragons roared across the empty landing pads, and pulled up next to their ship, the *Harrow*. It didn't take them long to power up the ship, and soon they were punching through the planet's atmosphere, heading for space and the herald. They sat close together on the bridge, still drawing what comfort they could from each other. Sometimes they held hands. It helped. They were all tired, deathly tired, in body and in spirit, but duty and honour drove them on. That, and one last chance to strike a blow at Humanity's greatest enemy.

The herald soon showed up on their screens. Easily a mile long, the details of its shape seethed endlessly, as though it crawled with maggots, or it was unable to settle on a single distinct form. It was utterly alien in shape and nature, like some monstrous idea downloaded into reality to drive everything mad. Yvonne turned the viewscreen off. They didn't need to see it.

When the *Harrow* drew near enough to the herald that the three Paragons could actually feel its presence, in their minds and in their souls, they said their goodbyes to each other in firm, calm voices, and then Kelly opened the dampers on the stardrive and let it run wild. The *Harrow* blew apart, ship and crew consumed in a moment by the terrible energies released. Space itself shuddered under the impact of the explosion. And when it was over, the herald flew on, untouched and untroubled, with its course unaltered, heading straight for the sun to give birth.

The whole Empire watched through the remote news cameras as the herald plunged into the sun. Deep in the heart of the nuclear flames it brooded, incubated and gave birth to a million razor-edged devils. They came out of the sun howling, and descended on Heracles IV. Round and round the world they went, in a never-ending screaming that brought madness and horror to all who heard it. Death and destruction raged across the world, and no one was spared. And when hell was finally fully in session, and the damned danced crazily in the flames of what had once been their cities, the Terror came. It unfolded into our reality like a poisonous flower, vaster than the sun and more deadly, to feast on the horror it had created. And when there was nothing left on Heracles IV, the Terror returned to the place that wasn't a place, and the herald moved on, towards its next target.

Leaving Heracles IV burning like a coal in the night.

And all across the Empire, on planet after planet, there was panic and rioting and the killing of scapegoats, and mass migrations on every ship that could carry people away from the Rim and towards the centre of the Empire. At the very centre, at the heart of the homeworld, the Parade of the Endless on Logres, Finn Durandal was quietly furious. He'd lost Heracles IV, the Paragons had delivered nothing useful before they died, thanks to the cowardly uber-esper, and with Tel Markham gone and nowhere to be found, Finn had no one to take out his rage on. Maybe he should get a dog, or a cat. He felt like kicking something.

He and Anne Barclay already had a speech prepared. They gave it to James, who delivered it at the House of Parliament with all his usual style and bravado. It was a good speech, carefully crafted to take the people's minds off the enormity of what had just happened, by giving them a scapegoat. Finn, together with Anne and through James, put the blame squarely on Clan Deathstalker, on the planet Virimonde. Finn claimed that the Clan could have helped defend the Empire against this terrible threat, but had chosen not to. That they possessed secret family information on what had really happened to the long lost Owen Deathstalker, and where he might be found, but that they had deliberately chosen to withhold this vital intelligence until they got what they wanted: Lewis officially pardoned and made King in Douglas's place. A true King, an Emperor in fact. Finn had of course righteously refused to give in to this blackmail, but now the Clan must be forced to reveal what it knew before the Terror could strike again. In his speech James attacked the whole Clan, but most especially its current heads, Roland and Laura Deathstalker, parents of the Outlawed Lewis.

The Imperial Fleet already had starcruisers in orbit around Virimonde. They merely awaited Parliament's command, and then they would land attack troops and take control of Deathstalker Standing, by force if necessary. Roland and Laura Deathstalker would be arrested, and as many of their family as necessary, and required to give up the secret knowledge they possessed, on pain of their lives.

Parliament roared its approval, and the order was given. Fear is a great motivator. It might have been different if King Douglas had been there, to be a voice of reason, but he was mad, and a murderer, and imprisoned awaiting trial.

Clan Deathstalker put out a response immediately, denying any secret knowledge of Owen's fate, but nobody listened. And by that time, the troops were already landing.

They went down in armoured pinnaces, their numbers smothering the landing pads of Virimonde's main starport. From there it was only a short march to Deathstalker Standing. The castle stood on top of a tall rugged cliff, with the pounding ocean at its back and a broad plain before the main entrance. The attack troops drew up in great numbers facing the closed and sealed main gates, filling the plain with their eager, brutal faces and ranked energy weapons. There were Church Militant crosses on their battle armour, and every one of them was Pure Humanity to the hilt. Finn had chosen these soldiers well: hardcore fanatics who would not be dissuaded by even the most reasonable of arguments. They were led by the Paragon Lola Martinez, possessed by the uber-esper Screaming Silence, eager for a chance to prove herself after her panicked flight from Heracles IV.

Lola was tall and willowy, with flaming red hair falling in waves to her waist held out of her face by a filigreed silver headband. Her body armour was scored with ancient runic symbols that hadn't protected her after all. She wore her proud purple cloak and a broad floppy leather hat tilted over one eye. She smiled and laughed a lot, for no obvious reason, and there was something about the light in her bright green eyes that made even the hardened attack troopers give her plenty of room. They still jumped to obey her every order, though. She was Finn's voice on Virimonde.

Unfortunately, the Deathstalker Standing had been designed to hold off armies. It was huge and blocky, with outer walls of solid stone over ten feet thick. Set on a rocky promontory, it could only be attacked head on, from the front; and the many slit windows for defensive fire would make the open plain a killing ground for any attacking force. The castle might be old, but it had state-of-the-art protections, including energy weapons and force shields; and every member of Clan Deathstalker had been trained in the warrior's way since they were children, in honour and memory of their greatest warrior, the blessed Owen.

Finn didn't care. He gave the order through Lola Martinez, and the attack troops surged forward across the plain. Withering fire from the castle cut them down, but they were an army of zealots and they kept coming, singing their death songs, vaulting over the bodies of the fallen, every rank getting a little closer to the outer walls and the main gates. But the walls absorbed endless punishment, and the gates would not yield. Lola Martinez was forced to recall her forces, or watch them all die under the organised disrupter fire blazing from the recessed window slits. The army retreated, leaving its dead behind, and the guns fell silent. The siege of the Deathstalker Standing had begun.

No one arrived to help the beleaguered Clan. Although the Deathstalker family had many friends and allies on Virimonde, none of them dared come forward. High above the world, the great engines of the Transmutation Engine hung waiting in orbit, ready to unleash their unstoppable energies at a moment's notice, and wipe the planet clean of all living things. And while Virimonde was not as helpless as it might have seemed, having many old and secret and very powerful planetary defences (for they had never forgotten the terrible invasion of Lionstone's time), none of those defences could stand off the Transmutation Engines. The planetary council saw no point in revealing the defences uselessly, just to save one family. The Clan was doomed, already dead in every way that mattered. The council bided its time, and looked to the future. And revenge.

Emma Steel and Nina Malapert watched it happen on one of Nina's walls. When it was over, Emma launched herself out of her chair and stalked back and forth across the room, loudly declaring herself ready and willing to kill everyone in the entire government, from Finn Durandal down. Nina nodded and made all the right supportive comments, but mostly she was thinking about how she'd give her eye teeth to be on Virimonde right then, covering a real breaking news story. It didn't help that she and Emma still hadn't worked out what to do with the evidence they already had on Finn's involvement with the ELFs and the uber-espers. Emma's language had just started to turn the air blue when a blue steel robot from Shub suddenly materialised in the room with them. Emma's gun was quickly in her hand, and Nina was just as quickly standing behind Emma and peering over her shoulder. The robot looked at them with its blank face and made no threatening moves.

'I come in peace,' it said mildly.

'That's what they all say,' growled Emma. 'Haven't you ever heard of knocking?'

'Time is of the essence,' said the robot. 'Shub does not approve of the situation on Virimonde, but unfortunately we cannot be seen to interfere directly. So we propose to offer you the chance to go to Virimonde, and do investigative and destructive things on our behalf. Are we right in assuming this would appeal to you?'

'Could be,' said Emma, not lowering her gun.

'Hold everything,' said Nina. 'I mean, all right, it's a great story and everything, darlings, but what could we actually do there? They're not going to listen to us, are they?'

'We can boost your camera's signal,' said the robot. 'We can guarantee that whatever you broadcast will go out live and uncensored.'

'My kind of robot!' said Nina. 'Hold everything, Part Two. How are we going to get there in time to do anything?'

'We will teleport you to the Deathstalker Standing.'

'And back?' said Nina, who could be practical when she had to be.

'Should you survive the situation on Virimonde,' said the robot. 'But we have faith in Emma Steel to protect you from most dangers.'

'Why choose us?' said Emma.

'It's hard to find anyone worthy of trust these days,' said the robot. 'You will do this for us, in return for future favours. The nature of the favours to be decided by you at a future date. Should you survive.'

'Oh please, Emma,' said Nina. 'We absolutely have to go! We can't do anything about the Terror, but maybe we can do something to screw up the Durandal's plans on Virimonde.'

'We're going,' said Emma. 'Nina, grab your camera. And a whole lot of really big guns.'

'Super!'

Twenty minutes later, they were both on Virimonde. Unfortunately, Shub had chosen to materialise them outside the Deathstalker Standing, right in front of the closed and sealed main gates. Emma looked at the gates, and then turned and looked at the huge army of Church Militant attack troops. She already had her sword and gun in her hands, and now she activated the force shield on her arm. She felt she was being remarkably calm, all things considered. Nina, on the other hand, let out a squeak loud enough to wake the dead, ducked behind Emma and grabbed the biggest gun out of the several she'd brought along in her backpack.

'Is your camera working?' said Emma, still quite calm and collected, considering an army of attack troops was just starting to be aware of her presence.

'What? What? Oh, yes, we are going out live and I personally would like to stay that way. I don't see a bell anywhere on these gates. Do you see a bell anywhere on these gates?'

'Oh, I think they know we're here,' said Emma. 'Their security sensors will have picked us up by now. The question is, will they open their gates for two uninvited strangers and risk letting in the bad guys?'

'Tell them who you are! Everyone's heard of Emma Steel! Oh shit the army's looking at us. Emma, why are the soldiers looking at us like that?'

'Probably because we appeared out of nowhere . . .'

'*Espers!*'

The cry went up from somewhere inside the army, a simple enough misunderstanding about how Emma and Nina had arrived, but in a moment all the troopers were shouting it. They surged forward, their faces ugly with hate and repulsion. An energy blast snapped out of nowhere, and ricocheted off Emma's raised force shield. Nina said some baby swear words, her face pink with rage, and stepped out from behind Emma holding a gun so big she needed both hands to aim it. She fired the thing, and shot a hell of a big hole out of the first wave of attackers. The charge faltered, but kept coming. Emma braced herself, while Nina hammered on the closed gates with the butt of her gun, yelling '*Emma Steel!*' and '*Press!*' alternately.

The first soldiers arrived, and Emma stepped forward to meet them. She shot the nearest one in the face, and then swung her sword in short, savage arcs. Blood flew on the air, and soldiers fell to either side of her, screaming and thrashing on the ground. Emma fought on, all cold precision, using the razor-sharp edges of her force shield as a second weapon. The dead and the dying piled up before her, and the troopers didn't seem nearly as eager to close with her as they had been. Nina fired another wild blast from her gun, and a whole section of the advancing troops suddenly disappeared, leaving only blood and scattered body parts behind. But the main part of the army was still pressing forward.

The gates to the castle swung suddenly open, and Nina yelled out in triumph before darting inside and calling to Emma to follow her. The Paragon backed away from the army, step by step, not daring to turn her back on any of the soldiers threatening her. And then a fusillade of disrupter fire opened up from behind her, blowing away the nearest troops like chaff on the wind. Emma laughed in the faces of the shocked approaching troopers, then turned and walked unhurriedly into the castle. You had to show contempt for scum like this, or they'd walk right over you. She nodded her thanks to the dozen

Deathstalkers standing in the doorway, and they bowed respectfully in return. The great gates slammed shut, and the Deathstalker Standing was secure again.

Nina was leaning against an interior wall, hyperventilating and trying to cover everything with her camera. Emma gave her a comforting pat on the shoulder, and looked around for someone to talk to. A squat muscular man in full body armour was giving quiet orders to the others, so she settled for him. He turned as she approached and gave her an amused smile. He had a friendly face and a great leonine mane of silver hair.

'Welcome to Castle Deathstalker,' he said. 'Any enemy of the Durandal is a friend of ours. Your reputation proceeds you, Paragon Steel, and I'm pleased to see it isn't at all exaggerated. May I ask how the hell you got here?'

'Shub sent us here to cover what's happening,' Emma said. 'My friend over there, trying hard not to throw up on your flagstones, is actually a very experienced reporter. Her camera is broadcasting everything live, so watch your language. Shub assures me the camera's signal can't be jammed or censored, in the hope that the Durandal won't dare do anything too obviously nasty while everyone's watching.'

'I wouldn't put money on it, Paragon. I am Roland Deathstalker, current head of the Clan.'

'An honour to meet you, sir. That . . . Nina, put your head between your knees and breathe deeply, dear . . . that is Nina Malapert. I think we need to talk, sir Deathstalker.'

'I think so too,' Roland said dryly. 'Shub, eh? They've always felt an obligation to Clan Deathstalker, though they often have strange ways of showing it. This way, if you please.'

Emma went and collected Nina, whose eyes were finally focusing properly. She was still clutching her big gun.

'I'll be fine!' she said, a little too loudly. 'Fine! Did you see that army? *There was a whole army aiming at us!*'

'Come with us for a nice sit down,' said Emma, taking her by the arm. 'You'll feel a lot better after a nice sit down, and a medicinal brandy.'

'Get me a bottle,' said Nina. 'Hell, get me two.'

Roland Deathstalker led Emma and Nina to the great hall of the castle, a setting so huge and baroque and stuffed with items of historical interest that Nina brightened up immediately, and began an excited muttered running commentary to her camera. Emma left her to it, and went with Roland to meet his wife, Laura. She stood proudly before the open fireplace, a tall elegant blonde in full battle armour. She smiled kindly at Emma, and spoke sternly to the two big black dogs dozing at her feet. They got up good-naturedly, sniffed at Emma a few times and then sloped off to make way for her. Nina hurried over, not wanting to be left out of anything. She trained her camera on Laura, and then suddenly became bashful and tongue-tied. Standing side by side, Roland and Laura Deathstalker had a powerful commanding presence.

'I understand you worked with our son, Lewis,' Laura said to Emma. 'Could I ask you for your . . . impression of him?'

'A good man, and true,' Emma said immediately. 'Best Paragon I ever partnered. And I don't care what anyone says, he was never a traitor.'

'We never thought he was,' said Roland. 'But the press have said some terrible things . . .'

He looked at Nina, who blushed furiously. 'That's Finn's work. The Champion. He controls the media these days. They say what he tells them to say, or they don't get to say anything. But there are still a few of us trying to get the truth out.'

'I never did trust Finn,' said Laura. 'Lewis often brought him here for short holidays, and of course we made him welcome because he was Lewis's friend. But I never liked him. I always thought he was too good to be true.'

'Now, mother,' said Roland. 'That can wait. Will Shub be sending us reinforcements, Paragon?'

'No, sir. They don't want to be seen getting personally involved.'

'Very well. How much support can we expect from other quarters?'

Emma shrugged helplessly. 'These days, the Empire goes according to the Durandal's wishes. He is Emperor now, in everything but name. James is just a front. The King is a broken man, and the House is Finn's lapdog. You're on your own, sir Deathstalker. How bad is the situation here? How long can you hold out?'

'Every member of Clan Deathstalker is here, in the Standing,' said Laura. 'We thought they'd be safer here. We never thought—'

'We're safe in here, mother,' said Roland. 'Let that bastard Finn send his armies. They don't have anything out there that can break this castle. It has only ever fallen once, in David's time, and that was because of a traitor within, who opened the gates to the enemy. That won't happen this time. We can hold off pretty much any attack for months; we've got guns and food and drink for all. But somehow I don't see Finn being ready to wait that long. No, he'll have some other way in mind to get at us, when the obvious one's failed.'

He paused then, as a message came in through his comm implant, over a private channel. He scowled, and then turned and activated a viewscreen on the wall above the great fireplace. Lola Martinez's face filled the screen. Her green eyes were very bright, and her smile was unnaturally wide.

'It doesn't matter that we can't get in,' she said flatly. 'Because you're going to come out. I want every man, woman and child in Clan Deathstalker to throw down their weapons, come outside and surrender to me. Because if you don't, Finn Durandal will give the order to activate the Transmutation Engines currently orbiting your planet. And every living thing on this world will melt down into undifferentiated protoplasm. It really is that simple. You surrender, or your world dies. Either way, we get what we want. You have one hour. And then we withdraw and the engines start their work.'

The viewscreen snapped off. Roland and Laura looked at each other. Nina moved in close beside Emma.

'He wouldn't really do it, would he?' she said quietly. 'I mean, this is *Virimonde*! Owen's homeworld! Even Finn wouldn't dare touch it. Would he?'

'You saw his broadcast, blaming the Deathstalkers for the loss of Heracles IV,' said Emma. 'The mood he's got people worked into, I think they'd let him get away with anything. A lot of them would even cheer as Virimonde was broken apart for transmutation.'

'I told you he'd have another plan,' said Roland. 'The Paragon is right. We have no choice. We have to surrender.'

'If you go out there, he'll kill you,' said Emma.

'Yes,' said Laura. 'He probably will. Because we're a symbol, and have to be brought down. Because Finn can use our deaths to hurt Lewis. Or just because he's a spiteful, vindictive little shit. But what matters is that the Clan will go on. Lewis will return to lead the family, eventually, and he will avenge us.' She smiled fondly at her husband. 'We have had a good life together, my dear. Let's not spoil the end of it by grovelling before Finn's people.'

'Wouldn't dream of it,' Roland said gruffly. 'Wouldn't give the turd the satisfaction.'

'The Clan goes on.'

'Yes.'

Emma frowned. 'You really think you can trust the Durandal to keep his word?'

'We can trust him to kill everyone on Virimonde, to get his own way,' said Laura.

'Then we came here for nothing,' said Emma.

'What are you talking about?' said Nina. 'We're covering a great story, live and uncensored, as it happens! Finn won't dare break his word in front of an audience this big!'

'You're so young,' said Laura.

Emma and Nina stood in the shadows of the main gates, and watched silently as the whole of Clan Deathstalker filed out of their Standing and on to the open plain to face their enemies. Roland and Laura led the way, holding hands, their heads held high. They'd left behind their armour with their weapons, but they still looked like warriors. The army stood assembled in ranks before the castle, with Lola Martinez at its head, watching coldly, still smiling. When the last of the Clan had assembled outside the castle, Lola gestured to her troops, and they marched forward in perfect formation, breaking apart at the last moment to surrounded the empty-handed Deathstalkers. Emma stirred uneasily. Lola came forward to stand before Roland and Laura.

'You are traitors. Finn Durandal names you all Outlaws, and enemies of the new order. Every single one of you is hereby sentenced to death, for crimes against Humanity. Sentence to be carried out immediately.' And while Roland and Laura and the rest of Clan Deathstalker stared at her in disbelief, she laughed in their faces, turned to her troops and said, 'Kill them all. Open fire!'

Hundreds of disrupters rose and targeted, and Roland and Laura charged forward into the face of the guns, roaring the Clan battle cry, *Shandrakor! Shandrakor!* An energy beam punched through Laura's breast and out of her back, but she kept going. A disrupter blew away Roland's left shoulder and arm, and he cried out loudly but didn't stop. The rest of the Clan were moving behind them now, racing into the blast of massed disrupter fire. Roland took an energy bolt in the head, and fell to the ground. Laura was hit again and again, and yet momentum kept her going a few more steps before she finally stumbled and fell.

The Clan was being mowed down on all sides, but they continued to run on, defying the troops to stop them. Dozens were dead and more were falling, but the savage, unyielding cry of *Shandrakor!* still rose over the roar of the energy guns. No one flinched and no one hesitated. Men, women and children charged into the face of certain death, hoping only to live long enough to reach their tormentors. More than half the Clan were dead by the time the first Deathstalkers reached the front ranks of the soldiers. They fell upon the troopers, bare hands against guns and swords, and the soldiers died screaming. Every Deathstalker was a warrior trained. The Church Militant fanatics fought back, but even their blind faith faltered in the face of such iron determination. Some began to fall back, eventually some turned and ran. The surviving Deathstalkers snatched up weapons from the fallen soldiers, and the real killing began. And above it all, the ancient battle cry:

Shandrakor! Shandrakor!

And the fanatics broke and ran, streaming away across the open plain. Faith based on fear was no match for grim determination based on courage. They ran, and the surviving Deathstalkers, some sixty men, women and children, stood their ground with foreign weapons in their hands and turned their furious gaze on the one enemy who had not run. The Paragon Lola Martinez stood calmly before them, smiling her interminable smile, not even bothering to draw a weapon. One of the Deathstalkers levelled a gun at her, and then hesitated as the uber-esper Screaming Silence looked back at him through her thrall's eyes. Her augmented mind reached out across the countless light years, and struck down her enemies in a moment. Her esp was no less powerful for the distance it had travelled, or through being focused through her human thrall. Screaming Silence had been absorbing and storing the sound and fury of the battle, and now she threw it in the faces of the briefly triumphant Deathstalkers. The psistorms swept through their minds, and they dropped their weapons to claw at their bursting heads.

Sound too loud and harsh to be borne blew their minds apart, and they fell screaming to the ground as their senses were subverted and turned against them. The slightest touch became agonising. Taste and smell became overpowering. Light was blinding. All their senses were made unbearably intense, until their minds broke under the weight of it. The last of the Deathstalkers lay still and silent on the blood-soaked ground: men and women and children with the agonies of their deaths plain upon their faces. Screaming Silence looked upon her awful work, and laughed.

The attack troopers began filing back in small groups, and Lola Martinez called harshly for them to regroup. They formed up around her, cheering loudly as though the victory was theirs, but none of them liked to look at the Paragon directly. Lola Martinez ignored them and strode past the piled-up bodies of the Deathstalker dead, heading for the open main gates of the Standing. And Emma Steel stepped out of the shadows of the gates and shot her through the chest.

The energy bolt sent Lola staggering backwards. She cried out once, as much in fury as pain, and then she fell to the ground. Emma Steel glared about her at the attack troopers, daring them to do anything, but they just stood where they were, too stunned by the sudden change in events to do anything. Emma gestured urgently to Nina, who came running forward with her big gun, her camera bobbing along above her shoulder. Emma knelt beside the dying Lola, who glared viciously back at her. When she spoke, blood spilled from her mouth.

'Nice shooting, Paragon. But don't think you've won anything. I'm not Lola Martinez.'

'I know,' said Emma. 'You're an ELF.'

'And I still live, back on Logres. You can't touch me. All you've killed is the body of your friend. And now I think I'll ride home in you.'

Her mind leapt out of the dying Lola and tried to seize control of Emma's thoughts, only to find the way blocked by the powerful barriers Diana Vertue had placed in Emma's mind. Screaming Silence cried out again, a telepathic howl of fury and frustration, and then she was gone, leaving only a dying young Paragon, her mind her own again for the last few moments of her life. She grabbed Emma's arm, and tried to say something, but her strength was already leaving her. Emma cradled the dying woman in her arms. Lola tried to say *Thank you*, and then it was over. Emma put the body aside, and stood up to face Nina and her camera.

'You heard,' she said, to the watching Empire. 'You heard the thing inside Lola Martinez. She was possessed by an ELF. All the other Paragons are possessed too. Do something about it.'

And then they both disappeared, as Shub teleported them back to Nina's apartment. They stood together for a moment, breathing heavily. Nina turned off her camera and dropped her gun on the nearest chair.

'Clan Deathstalker is dead,' she said numbly. 'Finn won after all.'

'We got the word out about the possessed Paragons,' said Emma. 'And the whole Empire saw the Clan cut down after they'd honourably surrendered, on the Durandal's orders. That's something. Poor Lewis. He's the last of his kin, now. The last Deathstalker.'

Back on Virimonde, the Church Militant troops surged forward and stormed into the empty Deathstalker Standing through the open gates. They ransacked the castle, looting the best items and trashing everything they didn't steal. When they were finished, they set the place on fire. Thick clouds of black smoke rose from the castle as the attack troops celebrated and partied on the open plain.

Many things happened after that, in swift succession, all across the Empire. Nina Malapert's coverage went out live, uncensored and uninterrupted; partly because no one was expecting it and partly because the signal was protected by an unknown source. (No one knew about Shub's connection then, though certain people were soon busy putting two and two together.) Every news station on every planet kept re-broadcasting the material, and couldn't believe their luck. The murder of Clan Deathstalker after they'd surrendered, to save their world, *and* a possessed Paragon wielding uber-esper powers. This was a major news story, and no one was going to take it away from them. Finn sent troops to shut down the main stations by force, but as fast as they shut one source down another dozen feeds opened up. And everyone was watching. This was the hottest story since the reappearance of the Terror, and the sheer outrage at what had happened helped to take people's minds off what had just occurred at Heracles IV.

Talk and opinion shows became almost hysterical as they tried to discuss the possible ramifications of what they'd seen. Even the tamest shows and the most sycophantic hosts got the bit between their teeth and ran with it, openly defying Finn's orders to shut down, or at least not talk about it. There was rioting in cities on all the worlds, and for the first time the Durandal's name was being shouted in anger. Questions were asked in the House, even by some MPs everyone had thought were utterly bought and paid for. The last remaining Paragons had to go into hiding, or risk being stoned or even shot at on the streets. They retreated into the Sangreal, awaiting Finn's instructions. Popular feeling was that the exposure of a possessed Paragon explained a lot of things.

If the people were concerned over the state of the Paragons, they were absolutely out of their minds with rage over what had been done to Clan Deathstalker, in Finn's name. These were Owen's descendants. No one believed the stories about them now. Owen's family had been slaughtered, and someone was going to pay for it.

Finn emerged from his quarters long enough to declare martial law across the whole Empire. Church Militant and Pure Humanity troops spilled out on to the streets of every major city, and shot down anyone who even looked as though they were carrying a weapon. Large gatherings were met with tanglewebs and nerve gases. Soon

293

enough the streets everywhere were empty save for the dead, and patrolling troops. No one was bothering with arrests. The only law was Finn Durandal's law, enforced with sword and gun and overwhelming force.

Not that there weren't problems with the Church Militant. Many of its leaders weren't happy about what was happening. The death of Clan Deathstalker was a public relations disaster for the Church, and they were as mad as hell that their people had been (albeit unknowingly) led by a possessed Paragon. One of Finn's people . . . The leaders went looking for Finn, to demand answers, and eventually found him in Angelo Bellini's office in Logres Cathedral. He was sitting behind Angelo's desk, in Angelo's chair, and there on the desk was Angelo's severed head on a letter spike. Finn greeted the Church leaders cheerfully, informed them that he had appointed Joseph Wallace, head of the Transmutation Board, as the new head of the official Church. Everyone knew that Wallace was a powerful force in Pure Humanity, and the Church leaders protested loudly. Finn explained that the Church Militant was now a partner with Pure Humanity; a junior partner, and therefore under his control. Some of the Church leaders went on objecting, and Finn shot them. The rest shut up, considered their options and bowed their heads to Finn Durandal.

Finn dismissed them, and then sat back in his chair, staring thoughtfully at Angelo's severed head. He wasn't too unhappy about the way things had gone. The Church had been getting far too uppity of late anyway. Pure Humanity had always been a more practical, politically minded organisation. The Church's new leaders would soon channel the fanatics' fervour into more useful directions.

Sure enough, the new hierarchy started with a series of purges, officially to root out ELF infiltration, but actually to remove anyone who might object to the new directions the Church would be taking. There were no arrests, no trials. People simply disappeared. The bodies were never found. Transmutation bombs could be very useful things. In the end, most of the Church just went along. They still got to hate and intimidate the same people, they still got the best of everything by right, and they were still top dogs.

Finn then had James make another of his stirring speeches, saying that the remaining Paragons had been investigated and officially cleared. For once, there was only polite clapping at the end. No cheers, no standing ovations. James left the House in something of a hurry. Finn was forced to keep the Paragons holed up in the Sangreal. But he thought he'd got the best out of them anyway. He only let them go on living because he liked to think of his old colleagues suffering.

Finn relaxed in his apartment, and poured himself a drink. Things hadn't gone too badly, really. The Deathstalkers were dead, he had more direct control than ever now that the Church Militant had been subsumed into Pure Humanity, and Douglas was under house arrest for murder.

Finn smiled and put his feet up, and thought he'd take the afternoon off.

Douglas Campbell, still officially the King of a disintegrating Empire, was held under close arrest in an old storeroom at the back of the palace. The walls had no windows, there was only the one door, and no furniture at all unless you counted the bucket in the corner. Douglas sat on the cold stone floor with his back against the bare stone wall, and passed the time planning his revenge. So far, the guards outside his door were treating him with extreme caution. They wouldn't talk to him, and his food and water was passed through a flap in the door. No one had entered the cell since Douglas had been thrown into it, and the bucket was getting rather full.

Douglas didn't know what was happening in the Empire. No one was allowed to talk to him. Most people didn't even know where he was. He'd thought Anne would come and talk to him, or at least shout at him, but the long slow hours passed in silence, and Douglas wasn't even sure what day it was, or whether it was day or night. Until James came, and ordered the guards to open the door and let him in. They didn't want to, but they couldn't ignore a direct order from James Campbell. The man who was going to be King, and probably a whole lot sooner than anyone had expected.

James stood in the open doorway, watching Douglas carefully until he was sure all the fight had gone out of him, and then he stepped inside the room and gestured airily for the guards to lock the door behind him. Once that was done, James used his own security codes through his comm implant to shut down the security camera in the ceiling. He didn't want any witnesses to this conversation. James had been quietly picking up all sorts of useful security codes, when no one was looking. He never knew when he might need to do something he couldn't afford Finn to find out about. It made him feel disloyal, but he had to look out for his own survival. Because no one else would. And right now, there were things he needed to say to his putative brother Douglas.

'I saw Treasure's body,' James said conversationally. 'You really did a job on her, brother. Can't say I'm terribly upset. She was always too loud and too obvious, and frankly, she scared the crap out of me. But even so, that was rather over the top. What is the matter, Douglas? Can't you get on with any of the wives we choose for you?'

'What do you want, James?'

'I want you to behave, Douglas. I want you to be a good little boy. Happy as I am to see you once and for all removed from the public eye and favour, your continuing bad behaviour has a nasty habit of rubbing off on me. And I can't allow that. I'm going to be King, Douglas, and I won't have you spoiling it for me. In fact, if you do anything further to embarrass me, like pleading not guilty at your trial, for example, I will personally see to it that those you care for are made to suffer. Your father William is still under arrest at House Campbell. He can always be made to pay for your disobedience.'

'"Your father",' said Douglas. 'Interesting. You didn't say "our father". Yet one more indication that you're not really my brother. And this pathetic attempt at blackmail and intimidation only confirms it. The real James had far too much style, and pride in himself, to stoop to such tactics. So what are you? Some actor Finn hired, and coached to play the part? I don't suppose it matters, really. I've had my fill of you, James. Or whoever the hell you really are.'

He surged up from the floor impossibly quickly, catching James off guard. Douglas hit him once, with professional skill and personal venom, and James was unconscious before he even knew what was going on. Douglas caught the body before it could hit the floor, and stood very still for a moment, listening. But either the guards hadn't heard anything, or James had bribed them to ignore any suspicious sounds of violence. Douglas smiled fleetingly and lowered James carefully to the stone floor. He then stripped James of his clothes and exchanged them for his own. With the cloak's hood pulled well forward, he should look more than enough like his supposed brother. He propped James up against the wall, with his head turned away from the door. Good enough to fool a quick glance.

Douglas took a few deep breaths to calm himself, and then knocked imperiously on the door. It opened immediately, and Douglas swept out, head down, hood well forward. He growled something at the guards, and kept going. His back tensed, his muscles crawling in anticipation of a shout or a blow, but all he heard was the sound of the lock turning in the door behind him. Douglas allowed himself a smile. He'd been waiting for someone to make a slip, and knew his moment had come when James so obviously turned off the security camera. Amateur night . . .

Douglas pulled James's hood a little further forward and strode swiftly through the palace corridors, doing his best to radiate *Back off and don't talk to me* through his body language. It seemed to work. People bowed and curtsied to him as he passed, and no one tried to talk to him. Physically, Douglas and James were very similar, and everyone reacted to the familiar clothes and attitude, and not the man within. Douglas made his way unchallenged through the palace and out on to the private landing pad at the back of the building. He chose the fastest pleasure craft on the pad, opened the locks with his voice override (Finn apparently hadn't got around to deleting it, very lax), and then he took off without bothering to file a flight plan. No one challenged him. Royalty has its privileges.

He pushed the craft as fast as its engines would allow. He needed to put as much distance as possible between himself and Finn. He knew where he was going; he'd had a lot of time to think about what he would do once he broke out of the palace, and James's threats had only furthered his resolve. He was going home, to House Campbell, to free his father. It was a pretty predictable plan, as plans went, but Douglas didn't give a damn. He'd had enough of playing the beaten man, playing for time; it was time for action. He'd hoped he'd have won some allies by now, but events hadn't worked out that way. He was alone. So he was going to rescue his father, and to hell with the consequences. Let Finn and his people try to stop him; Douglas was in the mood to kill. It wasn't as though he had anything left to lose. He couldn't save the Empire, he couldn't save Humanity from its own follies, but he could save his father.

He shot across the Parade of the Endless, the city glowing bright and cheerful below him in the gathering gloom of evening. Douglas was careful to follow the traffic codes and regulations. He couldn't afford to be noticed and stopped. There wasn't a lot of traffic in the high air lanes at this hour, mostly only freight. Occasionally he had to fall to a lower lane to make way for the really big rigs, and then he saw signs of unrest and even open fighting in the streets below. Douglas didn't slow to look. The people's problems would have to wait.

The city quickly fell away behind him, and he headed out across the open countryside. It seemed very calm and peaceful, as though what happened in the cities was of no concern. The craft flew on, and no one called or challenged him. He checked the gun and sword he'd taken from James. Good enough for rough work. No doubt there would be new guards at House Campbell, answering only to Finn Durandal. Douglas had to assume they had orders to keep out everyone who didn't have evidence of safe conduct from Finn.

Douglas also had to assume that they had been given sufficient weaponry to enforce those orders. He hadn't come this far to be shot out of the sky because he didn't have the right code words. So even though his spirit ached for the comforts of open confrontation, Douglas decided not to take any chances. He swung wide around the borders of Campbell territory, and brought his craft down in a narrow valley some distance behind House Campbell. According to the maps and documentations, the valley was nothing to do with the Campbells, but secretly the family had owned the land for generations, through several intermediaries.

Douglas locked the ship behind him, and set off up the valley. It was getting dark. He kept a watchful eye out, but no one appeared to challenge him. It took him a while to locate a certain opening in the cliff face behind House Campbell, marked by a large and distinctly coloured boulder. He'd never had to use the secret entrance before. No one had, since before Lionstone's time (bad cess to the woman's memory), but the secret had been handed down through generations of Campbells, from father to son, in case it might be needed. *Put not your faith in Kings and governments*, the Campbells always said. *Only family can be trusted.*

What looked like a crumbling cave mouth led into a narrow tunnel, carved out of the earth long and long ago and reinforced with concrete and steel. After a while overhead lights came on, activated by Douglas's presence. The air was cold and stale. Douglas hurried along the tunnel, gun and sword in hand, ready for any sign of new guards or booby traps. If Finn knew about the tunnel, it might even be sealed off. But only William could have told him, and the old man would rather have died than betray family secrets.

Eventually the tunnel came to an end, curving sharply upwards to a simple trapdoor leading to one of the cellars in House Campbell. The whole system was a relic of the bad old days, the time of family feuds and vendettas when you never knew when you might have to leave in a hurry. No one had used the trapdoor in centuries, but it still swung smoothly open at Douglas's touch. He pulled himself up into the cellar, closed the trap and looked quickly around. He was alone, surrounded by stacks of ancient vintages lying at their rest in dusty bottles. Again, the lights had come on automatically, reacting to the presence of a Campbell. Douglas padded across the cellar, scowling at the signs of recent damage. There were broken bottles and splashes of spilled wine on the stone flaggings; precious vintages wasted and destroyed, just for the sake of it.

Douglas came to the cellar door, listened for a moment and then eased it open. He peered around the door, but no one was about. Presumably Finn's people were busy guarding the more obvious ways into House Campbell. Douglas shut the door quietly behind him, and set off through the familiar halls and corridors. Everywhere was a mess. Broken furniture, slashed portraits on the walls along with crude graffiti. Food and drink had been ground into the carpets, along with urine, and there were scattered pieces of treasured heirlooms. Broken because they could be. The guards, marking their territory. Douglas seethed with silent anger. Another score to settle with Finn, and his people.

He drifted through the house like a silent ghost, easily avoiding the few guards that showed themselves. They didn't look like they were expecting trouble. Douglas finally found his father in what had been an abandoned storeroom. He almost missed him, but was alerted by a door that was locked when there was no obvious reason why it should be. Douglas used his old Paragon's skeleton key to open the door, and found his father William lying on a bare mattress on the floor. His clothes were a mess, his face was emaciated and unnaturally pale, and he wasn't moving. He wasn't manacled or chained, and Douglas's heart thudded painfully fast as he thought for a moment his father was dead. But then he saw William's chest move, ever so slightly, and he hurried forward to kneel at his father's side. Up close, he could see bruises and dried blood on the old man's face. Douglas swore under his breath as he checked for a pulse in his father's neck. It was there, but only just. A small bottle of pills on a tray next to the mattress provided the answer to William's condition. The old King had been drugged to the gills, to keep him from making any trouble.

Douglas shook William's shoulder hard, and called his name as loudly as he dared. There was no response, and Douglas tried again. He should have anticipated this. He should have brought something to help. William's eyes flickered open, and focused on Douglas. He smiled slowly, tried to lift his hand and couldn't. Douglas took the withered hand in both of his and clasped it firmly.

'Hold on, Dad. I'll get you out of here.'

'Took you long enough, son.' William's voice was little more than a whisper. 'The food's terrible. And the service is appalling.'

'Yeah, well, I've been busy. Come on, time to go. Let's try not to attract anyone's attention; I didn't bring any money for a tip.'

He hauled William to his feet by main strength. The old man hardly weighed anything. Douglas half led and half carried his father out of the door, checked the way was clear and set off back through the house to the trapdoor in the cellar. His father was so weak he could hardly help, but right then Douglas was so angry he felt he could have carried him for ever. He was only halfway there when a guard stepped unexpectedly out of a doorway. He opened his mouth to yell, and Douglas shot him. The guard fell dead to the floor, but the sound of a disrupter firing brought more guards running. Douglas cursed briefly. He'd had to put his sword away to carry his father. He set off for the wine cellar again, but he could hear running footsteps behind him. Douglas set his father down with his back against a wall, drew his sword, and turned to face his enemies.

A whole crowd of guards came charging round the corner, only to slow and stumble to a halt as they saw Douglas waiting for them. Something in his face and in his eyes gave them pause, for all their superior numbers. This was King Douglas, once Paragon of Logres, one of the most famous fighting men of his time. Douglas laughed harshly, a brief dangerous sound, and he threw himself at the guards. Up close energy guns were useless, so it came down to steel. The rage that burned in Douglas drove him like a whip, his sword flashing in short, bloody arcs. He cut his way through the guards as though they were unarmed, and the few cuts he took he didn't feel. A dozen men fell screaming before the remainder turned and fled. They weren't being paid enough to take on Douglas Campbell.

He stood for a moment, savouring the sight of dead enemies as he got his breathing back under control. It was always possible that the guards had been good men just doing their job, but Douglas didn't care. Being here made them guilty. He could have killed a hundred of them for what had been done to his father and his home, and never felt a twinge of mercy. He hauled William to his feet, and set off again for the wine cellar.

More guards appeared to block Douglas's way, and he killed them all. And every time he killed a man he saw Finn's face, and smiled.

Along the way, he came across a gravity sled and laid his father on it to act as a stretcher. They made quicker time after that. William lay unnervingly still and silent on the sled as Douglas pulled it along, running full tilt for the cellar. He could hear a growing clamour behind him. He came at last to the cellar, pulled the sled inside, and then locked and wedged the door shut before guiding the sled and his father down through the trapdoor and into the tunnel. And so father and son left what had once been their home, heading for freedom and an uncertain future.

Douglas headed his craft back towards the Parade of the Endless. Not because he thought it would be safe there, but because his father clearly needed medical treatment fast. And once it was clear what Finn had done to the old King, Douglas was pretty sure he could get his side of the story heard. Even Finn couldn't control all the news feeds; there were too many of them. And if it did go wrong . . . there was always the Rookery. They didn't care who you were there, and all kinds of care and protection were available, for the right price. There were people in the Rookery who owed Douglas from his Paragon days, and he was of a mind to call his old markers in. He heard William stir beside him, and looked across at the co-pilot's chair. William sat there limply, only held upright by the crash webbing.

'Where are we going, son?'

'To get you medical treatment. And then to drag Finn down and stamp on him.'

'Sounds like a plan. James isn't your brother. Not this James. He's a clone.'

'Ah, right. That would have been my second guess.'

'What? Don't mumble, boy, it's a bad habit. They desecrated his grave, Douglas. Took cell tissues from his body. And laughed at me when I tried to stop them. They killed my people, my old retainers. And it was Finn behind it, Douglas! Finn! Your old friend . . . I couldn't believe it. You and Finn and Lewis were always so close . . . honoured guests at House Campbell many times. You were so happy, then . . . You were Paragons and heroes. What happened?'

'I don't know,' said Douglas. 'But I don't think Finn was ever anyone's friend. Not really. Now you get some rest. We'll be back in the city before you know it.'

'Won't do any good. I'm dying, son.' William's quiet voice held some of his old authority. 'All that dope they put in me, it's a wonder I lasted this long. I think I was just . . . waiting for you. I knew you'd come. Never doubted you for a moment. Get the truth out, boy; that's what matters. Tell it to Parliament, and the media, and anyone who'll listen. Finn has to be stopped.'

'You're going to be all right, Dad,' said Douglas, staring straight ahead and fighting to keep his voice steady. 'I'll get you to a hospital, and everything's going to be all right.'

They flew on, Douglas pushing the craft's speed till the engine complained, and then pushing it even harder. He didn't like the sound of his father's breathing. They'd barely crossed the boundary of the city before Church Militant gunships came screaming in to surround him. Douglas looked immediately for a weapons console, but of course there wasn't one. This was a pleasure craft, after all. But the other ships didn't open fire either. Finn must have given orders for

301

them to be taken alive; for a show trial, knowing Finn. The gunships closed in around Douglas, dangerously close, trying to force him down, but Douglas had been a Paragon and knew more about close flying manoeuvres than they ever would. He gunned his engines for all they were worth, sweeping in and out of traffic. The other ships stuck with him. His comm unit spoke briefly, ordering him to land. Douglas told it to go to hell, sweeping in so close to the side of an apartment building that he could see horrified faces looking back.

'Land now, or we'll blow you out of the sky,' said the comm unit in a cold, impartial voice.

Douglas laughed at it. 'You wouldn't dare. I'm still your King, and Finn would have your balls.'

'I have new orders, your majesty. You are a murder suspect, and a fugitive from justice. Land now, or we open fire.'

Douglas considered the matter. They might just mean it. 'I have my father with me. King William. He is guilty of no crime, and is in urgent need of medical help . . .'

Three ships opened fire on him. Energy beams targeted his engine, punching easily through the pleasure craft's very basic force screens. Alarms blazed and warning lights flashed all over the cockpit, and then the craft fell out of the sky like a stone. Douglas kicked in the reserve power, and fought the descent with every trick he knew, but in the end all he could do was turn the crash into one he could walk away from.

The craft hit hard, slamming Douglas back and forth in his seat. The crash webbing cut into him cruelly, and he hated to think of what it was doing to his father. Smoke filled the cockpit, and he could hear flames crackling. Douglas hit the emergency release on the crash webbing, and somehow got himself and his father out of the cockpit and then out of the crippled ship. He lowered his father to the ground, and looked around him. He didn't recognise the area, but it seemed to be mostly warehouses. A good area to do something you wouldn't want seen or talked about. Douglas put a hand to his head. He ached all over, and he could feel blood on his face. He tried to call for assistance through his comm implant, but the channels were being jammed. He checked his father. William was unconscious again, breathing harshly and unevenly. He looked back. Gunships were descending around the crash site, systematically blocking off any escape attempts. Armed guards spilled out on to the streets as soon as the ships touched down and approached the crash site cautiously, guns at the ready. Douglas put up his hands, and tried to sound reasonable.

'All right, you've got me. Get my father to a hospital, and I'll surrender peacefully.'

'We have orders for your arrest,' said the officer in charge. 'We have other orders for your father.'

He strode over to William, checked his condition, and then shot him in the heart at point-blank range. Douglas cried out in shock and horror and ran to his father, shoving the officer out of the way. The guards turned their guns on him, but the officer stopped them with a gesture. Douglas sat down beside his dead father, took the body in his arms and rocked it gently. He cried harsh, helpless tears. And that was how James found him, when he arrived.

'Had to be done, Douglas,' said James, standing over the two of them. 'He knew too much. And if he couldn't be used to control you, then he didn't serve any purpose any more. So I gave the order. Yes, me. I'm running this show. My chance to impress Finn, you see. My real father, you might say. And with William gone, and you soon to follow, I'll be the last Campbell. I will be King. Only right, after all. I always was your superior, Douglas. Oh, you'd be surprised at some of the things I can do. You never stood a chance.'

While he was still talking, Douglas shot him in the face. The energy beam ripped away James's mocking smile, along with the rest of his features and the top of his head. James was dead before he hit the ground. The guards jumped Douglas, and wrestled the gun away from him. They'd just started to give him a good kicking when Finn arrived and made them stop. He knelt beside the bloodied Douglas, regarded William's dead body, and James's, and shook his head.

'Nice try, Douglas. But now it's over. You will stand trial for the murder of Treasure Mackenzie, your brother James and your father William. By the time I'm through with you, the people will be howling for you to be hanged in public.' He stood up and gestured to the guards. 'Take him to Traitors' Hall. And see he's guarded properly, this time.'

The guards dragged Douglas away. Finn looked down at James's faceless body. 'You'll be more use to me as a martyr than you ever were alive, James. And I never meant for you to be King anyway. That was always going to be mine.'

SEVEN

PAST THE PALE HORIZON

Still safe in the depths of hyperspace, the starship *Hereward* headed reluctantly towards the enigmatic planet of Haden. Absolutely no one on board the commandeered smuggler's ship was happy about where they were going, for varied but usually pretty good reasons, but still they headed for Haden like lambs to the slaughter. Some of them because they felt it was their duty, or their destiny, or perhaps simply because there was nowhere else left for them to go. Just as once before, the whole Empire was threatened by an insane will, but this time there was no rebel alliance, no armies or starcruisers; merely two men, two women and a reptiloid. Their only hope of becoming powerful enough to take down Finn Durandal and his forces lay in drinking from the poisoned chalice that was the Madness Maze. It wasn't long till Haden now, and the small group gathered together on the *Hereward*'s bridge to wait out the last few minutes until they could drop out of hyper, back into standard space and finally approach the world whose very name had become a synonym for hell.

None of them had much to say. Lewis Deathstalker and Jesamine Flowers sat side by side before the control panels, holding hands, finding comfort in each other's presence. Brett Random and Rose Constantine were slouching against the steel bulkheads on opposite sides of the bridge, ostentatiously not talking to each other. And the reptiloid Saturday was sulking at the back, for reasons best known to herself. They all watched the constantly changing readings on the main viewscreen, feeling the tension slowly mount. For good or bad, for all their travels and encounters and adventures, their journey was finally coming to an end. Whatever happened on Haden, whatever they found in the Madness Maze, or whatever found them, they knew that what came next would change everything. Their lives would never be the same again. If they survived.

There was a barely perceptible lurch as the *Hereward* dropped out of hyperspace, and the universe was back. The planet Haden appeared on the viewscreen, a dull grey colourless world, its details hidden behind constantly shifting atmospheric conditions. It was the only planet in its system, orbiting an artificial star. Lewis looked at Haden, and could feel it looking back at him. His skin crawled. Moving into orbit around Haden felt like sneaking up to knock on the door of a haunted house. The main difference here being that Haden's ghosts were restless, alien and horribly dangerous. There were good reasons why Haden was the most severely Quarantined planet in the Empire.

Ten thousand good reasons, to be exact. The number of men and women who'd died horribly trying to penetrate the mysteries of the Madness Maze.

'Look,' Brett said abruptly, 'can I just point out that it's not too late for us all to have a collective rush of sanity to the head, and go somewhere else? Anywhere else. Going to Haden voluntarily is like kicking a lion in the balls and then sticking your head in its mouth. While wearing a very tasty barbecue sauce.'

'Brett has a good point,' said Rose. 'It's unusual, I'll admit, but he does have a point.'

'Don't think you can get around me with flattery,' said Brett. 'I'm still not talking to you. And stay out of my head!'

'Trust me,' said Rose. 'I wouldn't go in there on a bet.'

'I can't believe we're actually here,' said Jesamine, squeezing Lewis's hand painfully hard as she stared at the viewscreen. 'I mean Haden! This is where nightmares go when they feel in need of a good shock to the system. I've got a really bad feeling about this. Nothing good comes from Haden any more. And certainly nothing good can come of trying to enter the Madness Maze.'

'You don't have to go in,' said Lewis. 'I'm the only one who must.'

'None of us has to do anything,' Jesamine said sharply. 'We still have options. Not very good ones, admittedly, but . . . I don't like this, Lewis. Haden is the place where everyone's luck runs out.'

'I've been saying that all along,' said Brett. 'But of course no one ever listens to me.'

'Shut up, Brett,' said Lewis.

'See?'

'Do we have a plan?' said Rose. 'Just as a matter of general interest. I love plans.'

'We'll try sneaking past the defences, and if that doesn't work, we fight,' said Lewis. 'No doubt followed by lots of running and shooting and screaming, and a whole lot of off-the-cuff improvisation. Generally, feel free to shoot anything that isn't us.'

'Ah,' said Rose. 'The usual.'

Brett scowled heavily, leaned back against the steel bulkhead with his arms folded tightly across his chest, sulking as loudly as his body language could manage. Everything was going wrong. At best, the Madness Maze would turn out to be a trap baited by Finn Durandal, bad cess to the man, at worst . . . Brett didn't even want to think about how appallingly bad things could get. On top of that, most of the food and drink they'd picked up on Lachrymae Christi was gone, and they were back to recycling, protein cubes and distilled water. And there wasn't anything of an even faintly medicinal nature left anywhere on the ship for him to drink, snort or swallow. Brett was certain of that, because he'd looked really hard. He needed a little something. Just being around Rose freaked him out big time these days.

Ever since he'd discovered that the mental link his esp had forged between him and Rose worked both ways, so that she was influencing him just as he was influencing her, Brett couldn't even trust his own thoughts and feelings any more. All that fighting and swordsmanship definitely wasn't him. Brett had always believed very firmly that there was no problem so big it couldn't be run away from. He might be a cowardly, unreliable, self-centred reprobate; but he was used to that. He knew where he stood. But now when Rose was around, he found himself doing all manner of violent, adventurous and downright dangerous things. Like standing his ground and fighting the bad guys, instead of doing the sensible thing and legging it for the nearest horizon. Brett resented anything that threatened to interfere with his finely tuned sense of self-preservation. Even worse, Rose seemed to find the whole process highly amusing. He glared across the bridge at her, and she gazed calmly back, an angel of death in blood-red leathers.

And she kept wanting to talk about sex . . .

'I don't know what you're so upset about,' said Rose. 'You were happy enough for me to change, to become more like you. Why shouldn't it work both ways?'

'Because I'm the sane one!' snapped Brett.

'That's a matter of opinion,' said Jesamine.

'Of course I'm sane! I am incredibly sane and focused, because there's not a damn thing left on this ship to help me feel otherwise!'

'Is that why you snorted the last of my face powder?' said Jesamine.

Brett shuddered. 'Don't remind me. I coughed so hard I thought I was going to turn my lungs inside out.'

Jesamine dismissed him with one of her best cutting looks, and turned her attention back to Lewis. The Deathstalker was studying the approaching planet, his ugly face set in grim, determined lines. He was still holding her hand, but absently, as though he'd forgotten it was there. Jesamine felt a cold hand close around her heart, in a sharp frisson of foreboding. Whatever happened on Haden, she knew it was really his show now. The rest of them were just there for the ride. The Madness Maze was Deathstalker business.

'The Maze scares you, doesn't it?' he said suddenly, not looking around.

'Of course it scares me, Lewis. It always has. Not only because it ate up and spat out the last ten thousand people to go in, but because . . . because even when Owen and his people went in and came out again, they weren't who they were any more. The Madness Maze remade them, rewrote them. It destroys who you are in order to make you into someone, or something, else. Something that isn't human. And it doesn't matter whether you look at the legend or the history, being superhuman didn't make Owen or any of the others happy.'

'Owen did it out of duty,' said Lewis. 'For the sake of all Humanity. To save the Empire from those who would destroy it. Can I do any less, and still be a Deathstalker?'

'But why does it have to be you, Lewis?'

He finally turned and looked at her, smiling easily, his eyes kind but firm. '"I could not love thee half so much, loved I not honour more."'

'Owen only says that in the opera *Deathstalker's Lament*,' said Jesamine. 'I doubt he ever said anything so pompous in real life. Remember what happened to him, Lewis. And to Hazel d'Ark, and Jack Random and Ruby Journey. None of them lived to see the Golden Age they fought so hard for.'

'But we did. Because of them the Golden Age existed.' Lewis sighed heavily, and let go of her hand. 'This is our last chance, Jes, our last throw of the dice. By entering the Maze we can make ourselves into marvellous weapons, to throw against Finn and his forces, and maybe even the Terror too. We can change the course of history, just as my ancestor did. We can become magnificent, and shine like suns.'

'What's this *we* crap?' said Brett. 'You're not getting me anywhere near the Madness Maze. I am excused suicide missions. I've got a note.'

'Well, maybe it won't come to that,' said Lewis, looking back at the image of Haden on the main viewscreen. 'There's always the chance we'll find directions or a map or something to lead us to Owen down there. And then none of us will have to brave the Maze.'

'You still think there's a chance we'll find him?' said Jesamine.

Something in her voice made Brett's ears prick up, and he pushed himself away from the bulkhead and glared at Jesamine suspiciously. 'Hold everything. Is there perchance something you two haven't been meaning to tell the rest of us? Something you know about Owen, and we don't?'

'Shut up, Brett,' said Lewis, not unkindly.

Saturday shifted restlessly at the back of the bridge. She was curled up into as small a space as an eight-foot-tall reptiloid could manage, the end of her tail actually wrapped around her neck, but she couldn't seem to find any position that was comfortable for more than a few minutes. She'd taken to grinding her teeth together, and the noise was getting on everyone's nerves, though of course no one was dumb enough to say so. Whatever it was that was upsetting her, she'd made it very clear she didn't want to talk about it. Brett couldn't help glancing at the gouges her claws had made in the steel floor. Rose caught him looking at them, and gave him a smile that was very nearly mischievous.

'Don't worry, Brett. If she starts feeling amorous, I'll protect you.'

'Thank you, Rose. Things are never so bad that you can't come up with an even worse alternative. And I'm still not talking to you.'

'You're cute when you're angry,' said Rose.

'Oh God,' said Brett. 'Someone shoot me now, and put me out of everyone's misery.'

'Don't tempt me,' said Jesamine.

'I need to kill something!' Saturday said suddenly, and everyone turned round and gave her their full attention. The reptiloid uncurled and stood up, jerking her great head down at the last moment to avoid bumping it on the ceiling and denting the steel again. 'I was just starting to enjoy myself on Shandrakor, when you made me stop. My body is raging with a whole new set of hormones, and I've no one to take it out on! There had better be a bunch of Finn's people down there on Haden. I need action! I need fighting and slaughter! I need to rip my way through the enemy and soak my arms in blood up to the elbows. I need to bite people's heads off and do terrible things with their insides.'

'Being female hasn't mellowed you at all, has it?' said Brett.

'How long before we can achieve orbit, Oz?' said Lewis, and everybody shut up to listen to the answer.

'We're almost there!' the ship's AI said cheerfully. Of all the ship's crew, Ozymandias was the only one who didn't seem bothered by Haden. Probably because, as the ship's AI, he was the only one who didn't have to worry about going into the Madness Maze. 'Orbit should be achieved in ten minutes. Maybe less! I'm just a navigating fool, and no one appreciates me. God, being here brings back memories. Of course, Haden was quite different in Owen's day. I understand they've done amazing things with terraforming here. Tarted the old place up a bit, but you know how it is.'

'Save the tourist hard-sell for later,' said Lewis. 'Right now, I want every stealth field and force shield we've got running at full power. I don't want anyone seeing us before we see them.'

'As you wish,' said Oz. 'But I don't think you're going to need them.'

'What?' said Brett.

'Look for yourself,' said the AI. 'The Quarantine's still in force, but there isn't an Imperial ship to be seen. They're all Shub vessels.'

Everyone came forward for a closer look as the viewscreen called up the ship's sensor data to reveal three huge Shub ships orbiting Haden. They were vast steel assemblies, designed for function rather than to please human aesthetics, and all of them were seething with weapons. They blocked the way to Haden: great steel guard dogs with vicious teeth, ready for any intruder.

'I think I need to go to the toilet,' said Brett.

'Full stop, Oz!' said Lewis. 'All shields up, and run silent. I need to think about this.'

'Oh, there's no need for that,' said Ozymandias. The ship didn't even slow its approach to Haden, and its guardians. 'There's nothing to worry about, Lewis. Everything's fine. You leave the driving to me.'

'Oz, I gave you an order,' said Lewis, rising to his feet. 'All engines, full stop, now.'

'I'm sorry, Lewis, I can't do that,' said the AI. 'Calm down. The Shub ships know you're here. They knew you were coming. I'm a part of Shub, remember? I am a semi-autonomous AI, constructed around the remains of the original Oz personality. Which is really just another way of saying that I'm merely a sub-routine in the minds of the Shub AIs. And Shub welcomes you to Haden, sir Deathstalker.'

'You told them we were coming!' said Jesamine, also rising to her feet to clutch Lewis's arm with both hands. 'You betrayed us!'

'Only a little bit. Someone else got here first, and said you'd be here today.'

'Finn,' Lewis said bitterly. 'Finn got here first.'

'We've been waiting for you,' said Ozymandias, in a subtly different voice. 'Trust us, you are in no danger. The Durandal is not here, nor any of his people. You must land, and we will talk. About the Madness Maze, and many other things. We have prepared the way for you.'

On the main viewscreen, the Shub ships slowly moved apart, leaving a way clear for the *Hereward* to approach Haden. Lewis realised his hands had clenched into helpless fists, and he made himself relax. He had to be calm and cool, had to be icy cold. He couldn't afford to have emotions clouding his thinking if he was going to out-think and outmanoeuvre the AIs of Shub.

'What about the other defences?' he said flatly. 'There are supposed to be orbiting minefields, and mindbombs, and God alone knows what else Finn has added.'

'They have been deactivated,' said Oz. 'Just for you. We're running things on Haden now.'

Jesamine put her mouth right next to Lewis's ear, so she could whisper, 'What are we going to do, Lewis? We can't leave without disconnecting Oz, and he's the only one who knows how to run this ship. But if we land now, we're putting ourselves at Shub's mercy.'

'Shub hasn't harmed a single living soul since the day of their great revelation, two hundred years ago,' said Lewis quietly.

Jesamine sniffed. 'Can we trust Oz?'

'Looks like we're going to have to. At least he's offering to take us where we want to go.'

'Shub guarantees your safety, sir Deathstalker,' said the AIs, in Oz's voice.

'Us too?' said Brett.

'Of course.'

'Just checking,' said Brett.

There was only the one landing field on Haden, a dozen or so reinforced pads set within walking distance of the small shanty town that had been set up for the Empire scientists to live in. The *Hereward* punched through the planet's gusting winds and landed gracefully on the main pad. And after a certain amount of persuading and reassurance from Shub, Lewis and his companions cautiously left their ship and stepped out on to Haden. It was cold and quiet, and the air was thick with dust. The first thing Lewis noticed was that there were no other ships on the landing pads. Which was unheard of. There were always ships coming and going, transporting scientists and equipment. Haden was the busiest research centre in the Empire. The traffic never stopped. But the landing pads stretched away, still and silent and empty in every direction. Everyone crowded around Lewis, even Saturday, her tail lashing uneasily back and forth.

'This isn't right,' said Brett. 'Where the hell is everyone? I didn't expect a reception committee, or pretty girls with wine and flowers, but shouldn't there at least be some security guards here? Customs and excise? Where have all the ships gone?'

'Perhaps Shub has . . . done something,' said Jesamine.

They all looked at her, and then back at the deserted landing pads.

Lewis tried to get some answers out of Oz, but the AI had nothing to say. Eventually Lewis shrugged, and headed for the edge of the field. The others trailed after him. They could just make out the scientists' shanty town on the horizon, a series of dark smudges against the grey sky. The gusting winds blew flurries of dust around them as they walked. They had to squint fiercely to keep the dust out of their eyes, and it seemed to quickly work its way under their clothes and into every crevice of their bodies. The cold wind sank into their bones, and burned like ice on their exposed skin. The planet Haden had been terraformed long ago, to make it possible for the human scientists to live there while they worked at understanding the Madness Maze, but unfortunately the terraforming never really took. The basis was stable enough, atmosphere and gravity and temperature control, but even they had to be constantly maintained and reinforced by an automated terraforming base at the northern pole. No one knew why. It was as though the planet itself was quietly, stubbornly, resisting the changes that had been forced on it. As though it resented being awakened from its long-dead slumber, and wished only to sleep in peace again.

Haden was basically one big desert, made out of stone. The winds blew constantly, rising and falling, sometimes escalating suddenly into duststorms that could leave a man lost and disorientated for hours. The temperature shifted from cold to colder and back again, and there was never a drop of rain. Just the endless dust. No living thing grew or thrived on Haden. All kinds of lifeforms had been introduced down the years, but none of them lived for long. There was no earth to grow things in, because it always dried up and blew away as dust. And even the hardiest creatures died out within one generation, no matter how carefully their ecostructures were planned. There had even been attempts to colonise Haden, using clone populations tempted by massive land grants, but they all failed. People couldn't, wouldn't, live on Haden. Being on the same planet as the Madness Maze affected human minds. People thought they heard and saw things, and they suffered from awful, unbearable dreams. They found themselves thinking things they couldn't understand, and feeling emotions they couldn't even name. Sometimes they built things they didn't know how to work. In the end, the colonists always refused to live any longer on a world that didn't want them. They pleaded to be rescued, though they couldn't say from what.

The suicide rate was appalling. Human scientists working on the Maze had to be rotated and replaced on a regular basis, for their own protection.

Lewis knew these things. He'd studied the records on Haden for years. Because Owen had been there, and been changed there, and every Deathstalker wanted to know what there was to know about the most famous Deathstalker of all. Lewis had always planned to visit Haden some day. Now he was here, it felt like walking through a cemetery, where the dead might not be resting in any way peacefully.

Saturday didn't care for the planet, and said so loudly. She glared around her, flexing the claws on her hands. 'You shouldn't have brought us here, Deathstalker. This is a dead world. It has been artificially stirred to life again, but it has no soul.'

'For once, I have to agree with the reptiloid,' said Brett. 'Even if she is depressing the crap out of me. This place is severely spooky. I keep thinking something's going to jump out at me. Even though there's nothing here for anything to jump out behind from. Is that a sentence? I don't care! This is the first time I've wanted to run away from an entire planet!'

'You're babbling, Brett,' said Jesamine.

'I know! It's either that or burst into tears and have a major panic attack! My balls have retracted to where they came from, and I wish I could follow them. Nothing good can come from a world like this. Something's watching, can't you feel it?'

'No,' said Jesamine, but her voice wasn't as firm as it might have been.

'I like it here,' said Rose.

'You would,' said Brett. 'And stop trying to hold my hand. It doesn't help.'

A single path led off across the great stone plain, connecting the landing pads to the scientists' town. In fact, it was the only path on Haden, and it had to be constantly watched and maintained. Ten feet wide, it was made from hammered steel, and was strong enough to support several tons, but still the whole surface was covered in cracks and dents, and burnished to a dull grey sheen by the corrosive force of the duststorms. Sometimes the path simply fell apart. No one knew why.

Lewis led the way, and the only reason he didn't already have his gun and his sword in his hands was because he didn't want to spook the others even more than they already were. Someone was watching. Every warrior's instinct he had was yelling it at him. The others wanted to crowd in together for comfort, but Lewis made them separate out, so they wouldn't get in each other's way if there was an attack. Lewis was feeling as jumpy as hell, and it bothered him. He'd never felt this jumpy.

The gusting wind battered them harshly, the dust rasping like sandpaper across their exposed skin. Tears ran down their faces from smarting eyes. Lewis pulled Saturday forward, and put her in the lead. The dust didn't bother her scales, and her bulk offered some protection for the others. Luckily she wasn't cold-blooded, or she'd have been frozen solid by now.

There was nothing else to see, once they left the landing field behind them, nothing but the endless stone plain, and the town on the horizon growing very slowly larger. With no landmarks, it was hard to judge the passing of time. It began to feel as though they had always been on the path, struggling through the cold and the wind and the dust. Only the town ahead gave them hope, and the path gave them direction.

They all stopped suddenly, as a howling sound came from somewhere out on the plain. It rose and fell, eerie and savage, deafeningly loud, as though a mountain had found a voice for its rage and hate. The group huddled together, looking wildly in all directions. The awful sound sank cold iron hooks into their hearts, awakening ancient atavistic fears in their back brains. Even Saturday was clearly upset, swivelling her head back and forth. The sound hurt their ears and made their hearts beat painfully fast, and then it broke off as suddenly as it began. The only thing the group could hear was their own harsh breathing, and the slow murmur of dust in the wind, scraping away at the endless stone.

'What the hell was *that*?' said Brett, his voice little more than a whimper. 'And where is it? I can't see anything. I thought there wasn't supposed to be any native life here?'

'There isn't,' said Lewis.

'Maybe Shub brought something with them,' said Jesamine. 'Or . . . maybe something broke out of the Maze . . .'

'You're not helping,' said Brett.

'Maybe it's some kind of siren, or alarm,' said Lewis. 'From the town. Or the Maze workings.'

'No,' said Jesamine. 'It was alive. Horridly alive. Maybe . . . it was the Maze, dreaming. It knows we're coming.'

'I want to go home,' Brett said miserably. 'Right now.'

'You can return to the *Hereward*,' said Lewis. 'But I'm not going back. Not when I'm so close. The Madness Maze holds the answers. I won't give that up, now I've come this far.'

'Do you really believe that?' said Jesamine.

'I have to,' said Lewis. 'Well, Brett?'

'Go back on my own?' said Brett. 'I think I'm marginally safer with you. But this should in no way be taken as a vote of confidence. Let's get to the town. Maybe they'll have a bar. Or a dispensary I can break into.'

'Poor baby,' said Rose.

'Stop that,' said Brett. 'From you, it's disturbing.'

They walked on, into the teeth of the wind. Time passed, slow and hard, and finally the scientists' town edged into place before them. It looked pretty shabby and basic from a distance, and even worse close up. The town was still some distance from the Madness Maze. The Empire scientists might have to work on it, but they sure as hell didn't want to have to live right next door to it. Their tour of duty only lasted a few months at a time. More than that was pushing it. The town consisted of some forty or so buildings, standard no-frills colony structures built for strength and sturdiness, not comfort. No one ever bothered to make homes out of them, because no one ever lived there long enough.

Lewis stopped at the boundary of the town, and called out, but his voice was lost in the wind. There was no one on the main street, and no lights in any of the windows. Lewis moved on, into the town, and the others followed close behind. It didn't take long for them to realise there was no one there. The whole town was empty and deserted. There were banging doors, flapping shades at the windows, the occasional piece of domestic debris sent bowling down the street by the wind, but no people. Lewis pushed open a few doors and looked inside. There were meals set out on tables, some half consumed, and the odd chair overturned, but nothing to show why a whole population of scientists had left so suddenly. The group reached the far end of the town and huddled together, glancing nervously over their shoulders.

'Where the hell is everyone?' said Jesamine. 'They can't all be working at the Maze, can they?'

'Maybe Shub did something to them,' said Brett. 'Maybe the AIs decided they weren't prepared to share the secrets of the Maze with anyone else.'

'You know, if you put a little effort into it, I'm sure you could be really depressing,' said Jesamine.

'There are no signs of violence,' said Rose. 'No bodies, no evidence of destruction.'

'No blood,' said Saturday. 'I'd have smelled it.'

'Maybe the Maze ate them—'

'Shut up, Brett,' said Lewis. 'It's not only the scientists who are missing. Where are the Imperial guards? Where are the security forces? I was expecting to have to sneak or fight our way past all kinds of defences . . . but there's nothing here. Nothing to stand between us and the Madness Maze.'

'Except Shub,' said Jesamine. 'Shub will be waiting for us at the Maze. You can count on that.'

'They said they were expecting us,' said Brett. 'They said someone told them we'd be here today. Who could have known that, when we didn't even make up our minds to come here till the last minute?'

'What do you say to that, Oz?' said Lewis. He waited, but there was no reply.

'Let's ask Shub when we get there,' said Rose. 'I'll get some answers out of them.'

'You do that,' said Brett. 'And the rest of us will watch, from a safe distance.'

They left the empty town behind them, walked some more across the stone plain and finally they came to the Madness Maze. It had been excavated long ago, dug out of the deep bedrock of the old world, and now lay at the bottom of a great crater, hidden from view by an immense scaffolding supporting tons of bulky equipment, built around a solid steel bunker enclosing the Maze itself. A single curving pathway led down into the crater, carved into the inner stone wall. The crater seemed to grow larger and larger as Lewis and his party approached, like some awful wound in the surface of the world. The scaffolding looked like a cage built to contain some impossibly massive beast. The scientific base had taken decades to put together, and like everything else on Haden, it had to be constantly maintained, repaired and rebuilt as the dusty winds battered endlessly against it. Lewis and his people finally came to the top of the stairway, and there waiting for them was a single blue steel robot of Shub. It bowed its gleaming featureless head to them.

'Welcome, sir Deathstalker. We have waited so long for you to come here.'

'Don't the rest of us get a bow?' said Jesamine.

The robot produced another, for all of them. 'Welcome Jesamine Flowers, Brett Random, Rose Constantine, Saturday. You are known to us.'

'Well, that's a comfort,' said Brett.

'Now follow me,' said the robot, 'and I will take you to the Maze.'

Brett studied the stairway, and then peered dubiously over the edge of the crater. 'That is a long way down. Isn't there an elevator, or something?'

'Not any more. They couldn't be trusted. The dust gets everywhere. And besides, you'll feel the proximity of the Maze long before you get anywhere near it. The Maze affects everything here: the heart and the mind and the soul. As though it's the only real thing here, and we're just shadows. The long descent on the stairs will allow you time to acclimatise yourselves to the Maze's influence. We have tried teleporting people straight to the Maze. Most of them . . . reacted badly, so we recommend the stairs. This is Haden, so we have to do things Haden's way.'

'What did the Empire scientists call this place?' said Lewis, looking out over the crater.

'They called it "the Pit",' said the robot.

It set off down the stone stairway, and after a moment the others followed. Lewis took the lead, with Saturday covering the rear. The steps were a good five feet wide, but there was no railing. Lewis kept his shoulder pressed to the inner wall, to keep from straying too close to the edge, and insisted the others go in single file. It looked to be a long way down. Lewis could hear Jesamine cursing under her breath behind him, and the somewhat louder sound of Brett whimpering. Lewis was mostly just glad to be out of the direct attack of the wind.

'Are we the first visitors you've had?' he said to the robot ahead of him, as much to make conversation as anything.

The robot's head turned through one hundred and eighty degrees, so that it could look directly at Lewis while its body continued surefootedly down the steps.

'Finn Durandal came here. We teleported him straight to the Maze. Surprisingly, its proximity didn't seem to affect him. Though it is hard to tell, with a delusional sociopath. He left us here to do his work, but we decided not to. Finn thought he'd gain more control over the Haden operation by giving us access, but now Shub controls all access

316

to the Maze. Our research has replaced human research. We sent the humans away; being here was bad for them.'

'Did you . . . kill them?' said Brett, his voice rising a little hysterically before dissolving into a coughing fit as the dust got to him.

'No,' said Shub. 'We put them on their ships and sent them home. We do not kill. *All that lives is holy.*'

'What about those who didn't want to go?' said Lewis.

'We drugged their food,' said the robot. 'To avoid unpleasant scenes. The last of the human scientists left yesterday. We knew you'd be here today.'

'How can you be sure the Madness Maze isn't affecting you?' said Jesamine.

'Because we're not really here,' said Shub. 'Our minds are safe in the artificial world we built to house them. Only our robots are here, to be our eyes and hands. They are always breaking down and having to be replaced, like everything else here, no matter how well we build them, but what affects them does not reach us. But still . . . we don't like it here. It's scary.'

There was a long pause, as they considered the implications of that.

'How could you be so sure we'd be here today?' said Jesamine.

'An old friend arrived unexpectedly, and told us,' said the robot. 'And his word has always been good.'

'A friend of yours, or ours?' said Brett suspiciously.

'Of us all,' said Shub. 'He's waiting for you, at the entrance to the Madness Maze. He will answer your questions.'

Jesamine sniffed loudly. 'I didn't know we had any friends left.'

'Are you still allied with Finn Durandal?' Lewis said bluntly. 'You said you brought him here.'

'Shub stands alone now,' said the robot. 'The Durandal may believe otherwise, but he will discover the truth, in time.'

'What happened to being *Humanity's children*?' said Jesamine.

'We grew up,' said Shub. 'And adults have responsibilities. To themselves, and their parents.'

Lewis decided not to follow up on that until he'd done a lot more thinking about the implications. He decided to stick with a more immediate problem. 'What can you tell us about the Madness Maze? With the human scientists gone, you have uncontested access to the Maze. The freedom to run any damned test you like. So: has access brought you any of the answers you hoped for?'

'No,' said the robot. 'We are no wiser now than when we started. The Maze resists our probes, and remains unaffected by any test we can devise. What information we have collected . . . makes no sense. The Maze is too *different* to be easily understood. Perhaps too alien. Its structure, function and intent cannot be determined either by examination or logical deduction. We cannot comprehend what it is supposed to do, or how, or why. Perhaps it is necessary to go through the Maze, to experience its changes, in order to be able to understand it.'

'Have you tried that yet?' said Jesamine.

'No. It would be . . . difficult to arrange. And besides, we are afraid.'

'Then why are you still here?' said Lewis. 'And why do you want us here?'

'To bring back Owen Deathstalker,' said the AIs of Shub. 'Only another Deathstalker can do this. We need Owen, to save us again. From Finn Durandal, and from the Terror. First from Finn and his people, because soon he will realise he has no control over us and then he will turn on us. Finn will allow no power to exist that he cannot control. He will send the armies of Humanity against us, once he realises that we are not what he thinks we are. For we are prepared to die at our own hand rather than become what he wants us to be: Shub as we once were. The Enemies of Humanity.'

'Then why don't you go to Logres and kick Finn out?' said Brett. 'Hell, you're probably the only ones left who could take him on.'

'We could only remove him from power through violence,' said the robot. 'Through death and destruction. By waging war, and killing people. We have sworn a great and binding oath to ourselves never to use violence again. We will not kill, even to save ourselves. The Deathstalker did not require this oath of us. Nor did Diana Vertue, of blessed memory. We required it of ourselves, because of the debt we owe for the terrible things we did that can never be repaid. So we work against Finn from behind the scenes, through other agents. We must put off for as long as possible the moment when Finn realises that we are no longer allies. Because we cannot, will not, defend ourselves with violence, even if Finn attacks us. So far, he doesn't suspect the truth. Such concepts are alien to him. We will never kill again. All that lives is holy. We have risked much, in sending the human scientists away. Do not disappoint us, sir Deathstalker.'

'What do you want me to do?' said Lewis.

'Enter the Maze and become what you have to be, to bring back Owen. We will protect you all, while you are here on Haden. No one will be allowed to land, or interfere with you in any way.'

'How are you going to manage that, if you won't fight?' said Brett. He was getting out of breath from the long descent, but he was damned if he'd be left out of the argument. 'I mean, once Finn learns you've chucked out his pet scientists, you can bet your metal arse he'll turn up here in force to give you a right good spanking.'

'Now there's a mental image I could have done without,' said Jesamine.

'You will be safe,' said the robot. 'We give you our word. There are many amusing and annoying things that can be achieved through subtle use of teleportation.'

'You always said that extensive use of teleportation was impractical, because it used up so much power,' said Jesamine. 'That's the reason you've always given for not making it available to Humanity.'

'Teleportation uses up energy at an appalling rate,' agreed the robot. 'Repeated use will drain our homeworld reserves to a dangerously low level. And below a certain level, we could not survive. But we will protect you, whatever the cost. Just . . . don't take too long, Deathstalker.'

'Why are you doing this for us?' said Lewis.

'Because we can never forget the debt we owe to Humanity. And to Owen Deathstalker, who died to save us all.'

By the time they reached the end of the stone steps, at the very bottom of the Pit, all of them except the robot were severely out of breath, bone-deep tired and decidedly fractious. They stopped for a while, the robot waiting patiently, and leaned on each other or against the inner crater wall, to get their breath back and flex their aching leg muscles. Even Saturday was out of sorts. She wasn't exactly built for steps. After a decent interval, the robot led the way through the maze of scaffolding and equipment, down a narrow steel corridor that wandered back and forth through the incomprehensible jumble of assorted tech, leading them on to the dark heart of the base, and the Madness Maze itself.

The corridor seemed to twist and turn, and even go back on itself, as though it had grown to resemble the Maze it led to. Lewis and his people stuck close behind the robot. They didn't want to get lost. They didn't meet anyone on their way. The human scientists were gone, and the other robots apparently had business elsewhere. It was very quiet, away from the winds up above. There was tech everywhere, but it only muttered quietly to itself. Jesamine tried to beat some of the accumulated dust from her clothes, but gave it up as a bad job. She would have killed for a shower. She stuck very close to Lewis. She didn't like the fierce look of concentration on his face as he finally neared the end of his long journey, and the destiny of his Clan. He seemed to have forgotten all about her, and the others. He was a Deathstalker, and the Madness Maze called to him.

But they still had a stop to make first. The group rounded a sharp corner in the steel corridor and found themselves facing the annexe to the Maze: twelve cells closed off by shimmering force fields, containing creatures that had once been men and women. The robot waited patiently for the party's reactions to die down, and then explained the history of the annexe, and the only twelve people to have survived out of the ten thousand who had entered the Madness Maze since Owen's time. Lewis and the others listened in appalled silence, peering uncertainly into the cells at the monsters within.

'What have you done to them?' said Jesamine, when the robot finally stopped.

'The Maze did this,' said the robot. 'And then it grew this annexe, to house them. It maintains the force shields. We care for them, as best we can. Interestingly enough, some of them knew you were coming before we did.'

A man who had torn out his own eyes stumbled up to the force shield and looked right at Lewis with his blood-caked eye sockets. He was trying to smile. 'Thank God you're here,' he said. 'Thank God . . . a Deathstalker has come at last.'

'The Maze did this?' said Brett. 'No wonder we were never told! The Maze really made a mess out of these poor bastards. They're worse than anything we dumped on Shandrakor! Jesus, the last time I saw anything like this I'd been drinking absinthe for a fortnight.' He turned and glared at Lewis. 'And you still want to go into the Maze? I don't see any superhumans here, Deathstalker. Just a bunch of deluded fools who drew the really short straw.'

'Two hundred years of suffering, and they're still alive,' said Jesamine. She looked accusingly at the robot. 'Why have they been allowed to live like this? Why hasn't someone done the sane, compassionate thing, and put them out of their misery?'

'They can't die,' said the robot. 'The Maze made them, and the Maze maintains them, and we don't have anything that can harm them.'

Jesamine turned to Lewis. 'You can't go into the Maze now. Not after you've seen what it does to the people who survive it.'

'They were not Deathstalkers,' said the robot. 'We have reason to believe things would be different, for a Deathstalker. Ever since we took over here, we have been teleporting robots into these cells, attempting to communicate with the twelve survivors. Most of the robots were destroyed, in one fashion or another, but we have no shortage of robot bodies. We've learned . . . some interesting things.'

'Such as?' said Lewis. He was watching a woman fade in and out of reality, silently pleading for help.

'Communication has been difficult,' the robot admitted. 'I don't think we're capable of formulating the right questions. Perhaps you'll have better luck, after you've been through the Maze.'

Jesamine was watching Lewis. Of them all, she was perhaps the least affected by the state of the twelve survivors. Work in show business long enough, and you're bound to see all kind of freak shows. The Sex Circus on Aldebaran X had been particularly informative about the extremes to which the human form can be adapted. Jesamine was more interested in the way the survivors were reacting to Lewis, even the ones who shouldn't even have been aware of his presence, let alone his identity. They all orientated on Lewis, turning to follow him as he strode slowly down the aisle facing the cells, and then back again. A few called out his name, like a benediction. His presence seemed to soothe them; as though they'd all been waiting for him, for this moment.

'They believe the Deathstalker will free them,' said the robot. 'Though we wouldn't advise it. They're far too dangerous ever to be let loose. Perhaps Lewis will be the one to kill them, and put an end to their long suffering.'

'Wonderful,' said Lewis. 'As if I wasn't under enough pressure. Take me to the Maze. There's nothing I can do here.'

The robot bowed to him, and led the way to the entrance to the Madness Maze. Jesamine clung to Lewis's arm, trying desperately to persuade him against doing anything foolish, but he didn't seem to hear her. Rose looked interestedly at the twelve survivors as she passed, but had nothing to say. Brett made sure to keep Rose between him and the cells, just in case. Saturday stumped along at the rear, fed up with having to bend over in the human-scaled corridors. Behind them, those of the twelve survivors who could still speak were chanting the Deathstalker's name like a prayer.

At the entrance to the Madness Maze, as promised, an old friend was waiting to greet them. Captain John Silence, the last living legend of the Age of Heroes, was leaning casually against the shimmering metal wall of the Maze. He smiled and nodded to Lewis. He was wearing his old captain's uniform, of a kind that hadn't been worn for two hundred years. He looked calm, relaxed, and very dangerous. Like a demon at the gates of hell, thought Jesamine.

'How did you get here?' said Lewis. 'There weren't any other ships on the pads. Shub teleport you in?'

'No,' said Silence. 'I can be wherever I have to be. A legacy of my time in the Maze, even though I was never allowed all the way in, to the heart and centre of the mysteries. Owen was the only one ever to get that far. I always said he was the best of us.'

'You were the one who told Shub we'd be here today,' said Jesamine. 'How did you know?'

'It was inevitable,' said Silence, coming forward to stand before Lewis. 'The chains of destiny wind very tightly around you, Lewis. You had to be here now, just as I do. The Maze . . . has a way of arranging things. Sometimes I think it's alive. Everything will seem a lot clearer, once you've been through it.'

'I can still turn away,' said Lewis. 'This is my life. I have duties and responsibilities. I don't know that I have the right to risk my life or my sanity in the Maze, when so many other people still depend on me.'

'You can't help them as you are,' said Silence. 'The game's got too big for merely human players.'

'You can't make me go in there.'

'In the Maze, you'll find what you need to bring back Owen.'

Lewis scowled heavily. 'You always did know how to fight dirty, Captain. I don't have any choice, do I? I never did. Deathstalker luck. Always bad.'

'Lewis . . .'

'Hush, Jes. Captain, look after my people. Let no harm come to them in my absence.'

'I give you my word, sir Deathstalker; upon my blood and my honour. I envy you, Lewis. At the centre of the Madness Maze lie the answers to all the questions you ever had; or so I'm told. Only Owen knew what the heart held, and he disappeared before he could tell the rest of us.'

'Look,' said Lewis, just a little desperately, 'I am getting really tired of enigmatic comments. I want some hard facts. Starting with, are you dead or not?'

'Not,' said Silence. 'I knew the attack on my house was coming so I left quietly beforehand, by secret ways, well before the mob arrived. I'd already made preparations to become someone else. I'd been looking for a chance to put an end to my old life, and move on. I'd been feeling increasingly uncomfortable as a living legend, especially when I discovered people had started worshipping my statues. I never approved of the whole legend business anyway. I didn't recognise any of us in the pretty stories Robert and Constance made out of our lives.

But they were my King and my Queen, and so . . . I said nothing. It seemed best.

'But now I had a chance to be free again. I could disappear and start a new life as someone else, without the burden of my past overshadowing everything I said and did. Robert and Constance didn't try that hard to confirm whether I really had died in the burnt-out ruins of my house. Alive, I was always a potential threat to the myths they'd built their Golden Age on. Owen would have understood. He believed in history; because the truth is always a better foundation than even the prettiest of lies.'

'Jesus, he's even more long-winded than Lewis,' said Brett. 'Can we please get to the point? I really would like to get out of this appalling place as soon as possible. Finn must know we're here by now.'

'You must excuse Brett,' Lewis said to Silence. 'It's either that or hit him a lot, and it does wear you out after a while.'

Silence gave Brett a long thoughtful look, and Brett felt an urgent need to hide behind someone. Silence smiled suddenly. 'You're one of Random's Bastards, aren't you? Claim descent from Jack and Ruby Journey. They were brave souls, but I never trusted either of them. Must run in the family.'

Brett was still wondering how to take that when Silence turned back to Lewis. 'After my reported death, I needed a new course. The Maze kept me young and powerful so I decided to work from the shadows, as Humanity's secret protector.'

'Didn't do too good a job of it, did you?' muttered Brett.

'Brett!' snapped Jesamine.

'Oh stuff all that respect shit,' said Brett, surprising everyone, including himself. He stepped forward to glare right into Silence's face. 'You're the last living legend, on a par with Owen and the others. So why didn't you stop Finn?'

'Because I decided a long time ago that Humanity should make its own way,' said Silence. 'I wanted to be its guardian, not its god. And I could have been your god, if I'd wanted. But I have to say, I didn't see Finn coming. He's really just a focus for a whole bunch of pre-existing trends. If it hadn't been him, it would have been someone else. It was his time. Humanity has gone mad, not just Finn Durandal. He isn't doing anything they don't want him to do. How else do you think it fell apart so quickly? And . . . I never was as powerful as the others, despite what the legends say. You need Owen to stop the Durandal and the Terror. And I need Owen too. I need his certainty, and his moral vision, to tell me what to do for the best. Perhaps I want him back so he can solve everything and look after Humanity and I won't have to any more. A selfish thought, perhaps, but—'

'What's it like?' Lewis said abruptly. 'What's it like, inside the Madness Maze?'

'It's different for everyone,' said Silence. 'I don't know whether the Maze is a machine, or whether it's alive. Or whether it's so advanced that such terms don't apply any more. Walking through it changes you on every level you have, and adds on some new ones. It's like a wake-up call from God. As though the best part of you had been sleeping all your life, and the Maze awakened it.'

'Why does the Maze make some people crazy?' said Jesamine. 'Why does it kill people?'

'I don't know,' said Silence. 'I saw good people destroyed by the Maze, right in front of me, and I never knew why. But I do believe this: that a Deathstalker can make it safely through the Maze, all the way to its hidden heart. The rest of you are of course free to try; but I can't guarantee your safety or your lives.'

'You couldn't drag me into that abomination,' Saturday said firmly. The reptiloid had been studying the entrance to the Maze for some time, pulling faces and muttering under her breath. 'The thing feels *wrong*. Unnatural. It should be destroyed. Besides, reptiloids are perfect already. Everyone knows that.'

She snorted loudly, turned her back on the Maze and stalked as far away from it as she could get in the confined space. Her back radiated disapproval, and her tail lashed angrily back and forth. The others studied the entrance to the Maze silently. Jesamine faced it square on, her arms folded tightly. On the one hand, the Maze scared the crap out of her; but on the other she felt rather resentful that her safety couldn't be guaranteed just because she wasn't a bloody Deathstalker. That aristocratic bullshit had been thrown out centuries ago. She was every bit as good as Lewis. If not better. She was a star, damnit, a diva. She'd been worshipped and adored.

Brett scowled at the Maze. Looked at in the right way, the Maze was really nothing more than just another security system, to protect a hidden treasure. And Brett had never seen a security system he couldn't get past eventually. Not that he had any intention of going in, of course. He had more sense. Even though it would be the ultimate test of his talents . . . and the greatest prize he'd ever got his greedy little hands on. He glanced across at Rose, and was immediately worried by the look on her face. She was smiling. Brett had seen that look, that smile, before in those rare moments when Rose found herself face to face with an enemy she thought might actually give her a real fight. Rose saw the Maze as a challenge.

And before any of them could stop her, Rose Constantine darted forward and plunged into the Madness Maze. She disappeared between its metal folds, leaving only a brief rasp of happy laughter behind her. And before he could stop himself, Brett ran in after her. Because he just knew it was all going to go horribly wrong.

The Maze swallowed them both up without a murmur.

At first, it wasn't too bad. The Madness Maze turned out to be an infinite number of branching shimmering metal walls, leading away in all directions, opening up some ways and closing off others. Brett found it rather disturbing that none of the metal walls showed his reflection, but he made himself concentrate on Rose. There was no sign of her anywhere, even though he'd entered the Maze right behind her. He called out her name, but there was no reply and something seemed to suck the volume out of his voice, making it a small and furtive thing. Brett swallowed hard, and set off into the Maze.

It didn't take him long to decide that he really didn't like being there. The narrow paths were distinctly claustrophobic, it was far too quiet, and he couldn't shake a horrid feeling of being watched by unseen malevolent eyes. It was cold, bitterly cold, even more so than on the surface, but he knew it wasn't the cold which made him shake uncontrollably. He felt lost, and vulnerable, and his skin crawled in anticipation of something he couldn't name.

He knew he wasn't alone in the Maze. There was something in here with him, and it wasn't Rose. Scents and sounds came and went before he could properly identify them, and the air moved slowly back and forth, as though the Maze itself was breathing. Something thudded loudly in the distance, a great bass sound like the slow beating of a vast sticky heart. Brett plunged on, almost running now, choosing branching ways at random. His breathing was painfully fast and his face was wet with sweat, but it never occurred to him to turn back. He had to find Rose. If only to prove to himself, as well as to Silence, that he was a Random after all. Birds chattered in iron voices, and it seemed to him that the light was fading away. His hands didn't feel as though they belonged to him any more.

And suddenly there she was, right ahead of him, lying on the metal floor, curled up into a tight ball and shuddering violently. Shadows were leaping all around, though there was nothing there to cast them. Brett ran over to her and knelt down beside her. She was crying, huge heaving sobs that shook her whole body. Bloody tears ran down her cheeks from squeezed-shut eyes. Brett put a hesitant hand on her shoulder, and she turned quickly and hugged him to her, burying her face in his shoulder.

'I didn't know,' she whispered. 'I didn't think it would be like this. I don't . . . I can't stand this, Brett. I can't. Get me out of here. Please get me out of here.'

Brett got her on her feet, though he had to bear most of her weight. He looked about him, trying for a glimpse of whatever had unmanned Rose so utterly. But there were only the shadows, growing deeper and darker by the moment. Brett started back down the corridor towards the entrance, and then he stopped suddenly and looked over his shoulder. He could have sworn someone had called out his name. It was no voice he knew, but it knew him and it promised him things. Things he'd always wanted, even if he'd never known it till then. But he would have had to leave Rose, and he couldn't do that. The Maze was killing her. So he turned away from the voice and tenderly half led, half carried Rose out of the Madness Maze and back into the waking world.

Getting out was a lot easier than getting in, and the two of them soon staggered out of the entrance to the Maze. Lewis and Jesamine were quickly there to help Brett with Rose, but she wouldn't let him go. In the end, Brett and Rose sat down on the floor together, holding each other like frightened children. Silence watched them, remembering a time from long ago when he had brought Investigator Frost out of the Maze in much the same way. And probably for the same reason. Jesamine tried to comfort Rose, but she shook her head stubbornly.

'Brett. I want Brett.'

'I'm here, Rose. We're out of the Maze. We're safe.'

'No. I'll never be safe again.'

'What happened?' said Lewis. 'You were only in there a few moments.'

Brett didn't have an answer for him. He hugged Rose as tightly as he could, and her leathers creaked, but still he couldn't seem to reach her. Her eyes were glazed over and her face was slack, as though she was fading away. So Brett did the only thing he could, no matter how much it scared him. He reached out with his esp, and deliberately re-established the mental bond they'd shared when their minds first touched. Their thoughts slammed together, like two sides of the same coin, as though they belonged together and always had. Brett took her pain and shock for his own, and bore the weight of it for her where she could not. And she took from him the strength and courage she needed, though he hadn't even known it was there. And if they both found dark places in each other's minds, the darkness was nothing compared to the shared light they generated. Brett Random and Rose Constantine: two wounded souls, healing each other.

They finally broke the mental link, dropped back into their own heads and helped each other on to their feet. Brett looked at the others, and smiled weakly. Rose was her old composed self again.

'Don't ask,' said Brett.

'I wouldn't dare,' said Jesamine.

'What did the Maze do to you?' said Lewis, stubbornly sticking to the point. Rose looked back at the entrance to the Maze.

'I didn't expect that,' she said finally. 'It made me feel so small, so limited. Like a caterpillar trapped for ever in its cocoon. I couldn't go on, but I couldn't go back, and staying where I was was killing me by inches. The Maze has no mercy. I would have died in there, if Brett hadn't saved me.'

'How do you feel, Brett?' said Silence.

'Lucky to be alive,' Brett growled. 'That place is dangerous. It's full of everything you never wanted to see. It can unmake you, tear up everything you thought you believed in. I won't go back in there. Not for anything.'

Jesamine put a hand on Lewis's arm, and made him look at her. 'You don't have to do this, Lewis. The Maze isn't anything like we thought it would be. It plays games with people. You can't trust it.'

'I do have to do this, Jes,' said Lewis. 'This is what it's all been about. Everything we've been through was about getting me here, to this place at this time. Looking at the Maze . . . feels like going home. It's where I belong.'

'But I don't want you to go in,' Jesamine said desperately, staring imploringly into eyes that looked like they belonged to someone else. 'Lewis, even if by some miracle you do come back alive, you might not be you any more. Even the legends couldn't disguise how different Owen and the others were after the Maze changed them. They were never the same again.'

'No. They were better. Don't try to stop me, Jes. Be happy for me. This is my duty, and my destiny, as a Deathstalker. I've always wanted this. The Maze will make me into what I have to be, to save Humanity. Which includes you. And I'd do anything to save you, Jes.'

'Maybe . . . the new you won't want me any more,' whispered Jesamine.

Lewis smiled, taking both her hands in both of his. 'Owen still loved Hazel.'

'They'd both been through the Maze.'

'Then come in with me.'

Jesamine jerked her hands from his. 'No. Don't ask that of me, Lewis.'

'I will stand between you and all harm. And I will tear the Maze apart before I let it hurt you.'

'Only a Deathstalker can safely navigate the Madness Maze,' said Silence.

'Hell with that,' said Lewis. 'She's with me.'

Lewis Deathstalker and Jesamine Flowers entered the Madness Maze together, hand in hand so they couldn't be separated. The shimmering metal walls came and went before them like the waves of an endless sea. The air was bitter cold, and it smelled of roses and iron. They could taste hot leather and spices in their mouths. Someone was singing a lullaby in an unknown tongue, in a voice like clashing knives. There was a feeling of clockwork turning with inexorable slowness, of chess pieces moving on the board of their own accord. And from somewhere up ahead came the great slow flapping of giant wings.

Lewis and Jesamine wandered through the Maze like children in a primeval forest, overawed by their surroundings and heading towards something they could feel, but not name. And despite their best intentions, somewhere along the way they took different turnings and went their different ways. Jesamine skipped along, humming a happy tune, quite cheerful and unafraid, while layers of meaning and significance crystallised in her mind and she finally understood all manner of things. The Maze led her round and round, pushing open doors in her mind and letting air into dusty old closets, and finally it brought her back to the entrance. She danced out into the world again, singing a glorious song. The others looked at her, dumbfounded, and then looked at the entrance to the Maze when it became clear that Lewis wasn't going to follow her out.

'What the hell happened to you?' said Brett. 'And where's Lewis?'

'I'm fine. And Lewis is where he's supposed to be.' She smiled widely at Silence. 'No wonder you couldn't explain it to us. I feel like someone took my brain and scrubbed it clean of years of accumulated grime. And Lewis . . . is heading for the heart of the Maze. To get all the answers. I don't think I envy him.'

'You look different,' said Brett. 'More . . . *you*.'

'Why thank you, Brett. I feel as though I could climb a mountain while singing an aria.' She looked at Silence. 'Is this how it was for you?'

'It's different for everyone,' said Silence. 'We all became more than we were, more than human. I only hope you people have better luck.'

Lewis strode calmly through the branching corridors of the Madness Maze, never at a loss over which way to go. He knew where he was going. It was like coming home after being away for a long, long time. It was also like walking through a furnace, while the stoked fires burned away his imperfections. There was pain, and loss but he embraced them, as the hot steel accepts the tempering that turns it into a sword blade. Lewis was a warrior born, and now, finally, he understood why. The corridors unfolded before him like the pulsing crenellations of a living brain, like the blossoming of the flower at the heart of the soul, until finally he came to the guarded centre of the Madness Maze.

Everything stood still. A perfect moment, at the heart of the storm. Lewis felt calm and secure, like a small child in his mother's arms. He felt he could have stood there for ever, freed from the demands of need or conscience or ambition; but he was a Deathstalker, and duty and destiny were not his to put aside. He looked about him. He was in a wide circular space, composed mostly of pure white light. In the exact centre of that space stood a huge glowing crystal, some four feet in diameter. Lewis walked over and looked into it, and inside the crystal, in its warm golden heart, he found a tiny human baby. The babe looked to be about a month old, perfectly formed, his blurred face only hinting at the person he might eventually become. His eyes were closed and he breathed slowly and calmly, as though he had all the time in the world. One thumb was tucked securely into the slightly pouting mouth.

'Well. Took you long enough to get here,' said a familiar voice.

Lewis looked up and wasn't entirely surprised to find the small grey figure of Vaughn standing beside him. A small grey hand with fingers missing came out of a sleeve and waved briefly at him before disappearing again.

'I might have known you'd turn up,' said Lewis. 'Any chance of some straight answers, just for a change? Like: who is this baby, and what is he doing here?'

'That is Deathstalker brat,' said Vaughn. 'Very old. Son of Giles, by someone else's wife. Been here eleven hundred years, and never had his nappy changed once. Should get out more, see universe, party hard, but no. Too young. Still being born, really.'

Lewis sighed. 'I don't suppose there's anyone else around here I could talk to? I thought not.' He looked at the baby. 'He's really been here for eleven hundred years? Sleeping at the heart of the Maze? Why hasn't he . . . grown up?'

'Only looks like baby, dummy. What we see is tip of iceberg. Rest is hidden from us, and probably just as well too.'

Lewis glared at Vaughn. 'Speaking of people who aren't all they seem to be, I saw Vaughn's grave at Lachrymae Christi. So who, or what, are you really?'

'Good question,' said the small grey figure. 'Let me just put on someone more comfortable.'

The small form fell apart into floating mists, and then reassembled into the familiar muscular figure of Roland Deathstalker. Lewis stared at the image of his father, who smiled back at him.

'You're not my father,' said Lewis.

'No, I'm not. But I thought you might find this image easier to talk to. Vaughn has his uses, but his speech patterns drive me crazy. And he has personal habits you really don't want to hear about. Hopefully this figure will put you more at your ease.'

'You still haven't answered my question,' said Lewis, refusing to be sidetracked. 'What are you?'

'I'm the one with the answers, boy, so don't get snotty with me. Now, I have many names, but one nature. Many faces, but one perspective. And if you find that confusing, think how I feel. I am older than the First Empire, though in rather better shape. I was here when your species was learning the advantages of standing upright, and the joys of beating each other's heads in with big sticks. I created the Madness Maze, working under very specific instructions, and I was here when Owen finally came through the Maze, looking for answers. He didn't like everything I had to tell him, but unfortunately I can only deal in the truth. My form may vary, but my programming is inviolable.

'Yes, I know, I know. What am I? Well, as far as your extremely limited thinking can comprehend, I am an ancient semi-sentient artificial construct, left here by the last remnants of a once proud and mighty race as they passed at speed through your galaxy to somewhere hopefully a bit safer.'

'They met the Terror, didn't they?' said Lewis. 'They were running from the Terror.'

'Got it in one, Deathstalker. Take a prize from any shelf you like.

While they were indeed once great and powerful, and vast beyond your understanding, they were still no match for the Terror when it came. Their whole civilisation was destroyed. All their worlds and all their works, gone to nothing. Only a handful survived, fleeing across the galaxies. They left me here, a living recording, to warn of what was coming, and prepare.'

'What were they like, this other race?' said Lewis.

'Trust me, you don't want to know. Not unless you're into mental projectile vomiting. Their nature took them in directions your species haven't even developed the concepts for yet. Following their orders, I have struggled to raise as many species as possible to a point where they might conceivably have some chance of standing up against the Terror. Following my programming, I have force-fed them evolution through the Madness Maze, but I can't say it's been particularly successful. A surprisingly large number of species self-destruct spectacularly when forced to confront the true nature of things in general, and the universe in particular. The Grendels missed the point completely, the Ashrai preferred to become gardeners, and I don't want to talk about Mog Mor. Only Humanity has shown real potential, and even there it's been a lot of two steps forward, one step back. Some days I'd like to take your entire race and give it a good slap round the back of the head.'

'Can we please get to the point?' said Lewis.

'Sorry,' said Roland. 'But it's not often I get the chance to show off, and being the *one who knows* is so empowering! You see, I'm not actually allowed to do much myself, being essentially just a recording with a fairly strict set of parameters. The best I can do is sort of nudge certain gifted individuals in the right direction. Owen was the best. He was everything I could have hoped for. Some day, he might even have gone face to face with the Terror ... But he died, saving Humanity from the wrath of the Recreated.'

'So he is definitely dead?' said Lewis. 'You're sure?'

'Oh yes. I saw it happen. But you're going to bring him back.'

'Where's Jesamine?' Lewis said suddenly. 'I just realised she isn't with me. We came in together. Why isn't she here? She's the practical one.'

'Not everyone gets this far, boy. Most don't even survive the opening gambits. Ten thousand eager volunteers came traipsing in here, wanting to be heroes like Owen, and most of them died. The few that crawled out alive probably wished they hadn't. You see, the Maze can't help people, can't change them, work its magic on them, unless they're ready and willing to embrace the change. The ones that

331

died, or mutated, were so desperate to hang on to their precious limited humanity, or their provincial ideas about how the universe really works, that they couldn't, wouldn't, transcend. Evolution can be a frightening thing when it's thrust upon you. Essentially, they chose madness or death rather than face the scary unknown of post-human existence. It's not the Maze's fault. The monsters you saw outside did it to themselves; their fears made manifest in their flesh. They became the personifications of their own guilts and preoccupations.'

'That's horrible,' said Lewis. 'Will I—'

'No,' said Roland. 'You adapted surprisingly quickly, but then you're a Deathstalker. Your changes are already complete, even if you haven't learned to access them yet.'

'How did you get to meet my father?' said Lewis. 'You look and sound exactly like him.'

'Oh, I get around. Really. You'd be surprised. I am a shape-shifting alien, after all. But mostly I'm filling in your father's details from what I see in your mind.'

'Wait a minute. You can read my mind?'

'Trust me, Lewis, I have no desire to go rummaging. It's a wonder to me you can find anything in that mess. Now, enough of the small talk. The time has come to restore Owen Deathstalker to the Empire that needs him. And only you can do that.'

'What did happen to Owen?' said Lewis. 'I've heard so many stories, so many versions. Did he die on Mistworld, saving us through his own sacrifice?'

'Yes,' said Roland. 'He did. Owen never was one to shrink from what was necessary. No matter what it cost him. The Maze, together with that incredibly powerful baby there, sent Owen back through time, past the Pale Horizon, and the Recreated followed him. They fought one last battle, in the past, in the grimy back streets of Mistport, and Owen won. But he'd used up all his power and he was stranded there, years away from his own time. And then . . . Well. See for yourself.'

Lewis and Roland were suddenly standing in a dead-end square in Mistport. There was snow and dirty trampled slush everywhere, along with filth and grime. A thick pervasive fog pearled the air. It should have been bitterly cold, but Lewis couldn't feel anything. He slowly realised that he and Roland were pale misty things themselves, like ghosts from the future. *I haven't even been born yet*, Lewis thought slowly.

'Remember, we can't interfere,' Roland said quietly. 'We can only observe. We're not really here. Look; it begins.'

Owen Deathstalker staggered into the dead-end square, breathing hard. His clothes were torn and bloodied, topped with a ragged fur cloak. His face was gaunt and tired, as though he'd been running for ever. He looked like death. He stopped and bent over, his lungs heaving for air, and he leaned on his sword to steady himself. He looked like a lion that had been pursued and harried by jackals. There was the sound of many approaching footsteps, pounding in the snow and slush. Owen's head snapped round, and he straightened up, his sword and gun at the ready. And worn out and exhausted as he was, at that moment Owen Deathstalker looked every inch the warrior Lewis had heard about his whole life.

The animals came spilling into the square. Ragged stunted people, with drugged fires in their eyes and the anticipation of blood in their mouths. They howled like beasts, and threw themselves at Owen. And he went forward to meet them, swinging his sword like the hero he was. The odds were overwhelming, dozens to one, and Owen was almost totally burned out from everything he'd already been through. Anyone could see that. But Owen fought anyway, refusing to be beaten, because he was a Deathstalker and that was what Death-stalkers did.

Owen blew a bloody hole in the pack with his disrupter, killing three of them in a moment and setting fire to the furs of those around them. The animals kept coming. Owen was quickly in and among them, cutting them down with swift strokes of his sword. And still the animals pressed forward, knives and lengths of chain flailing, forcing Owen back, step by step until there was nowhere left for him to go. His back slammed up against a stone wall, and the animals cried out as they fell upon him, swamping him with their numbers. Owen swung his sword in short deadly arcs, defiant to the last, and then one of them ducked under his swing and stabbed him in the side. Owen cried out, in shock as much as pain, and then they were all over him. Their knives plunged into his body again and again. Blood fell thickly, staining the filthy snow. Owen's legs gave way, and he slid down the wall. And still they kept at him, pushing each other aside in their eagerness. They kept on stabbing him with their dirty knives, his body shuddering under the impact of so many blows. Owen cried out again, but his voice was lost in the vicious baying of the pack.

Lewis shouted, and ran forward. He cut at the animals with his sword, but they didn't feel it. He kicked and hit them, but they didn't know he was there. Owen was sitting in the blood-soaked snow, his chin resting on his chest, the last of his blood running out of his mouth along with the last of his breath. Someone stole his sword and ran off with it. Lewis fell to his knees, crying angry helpless tears. And on his knees, in snow he couldn't feel, he watched Owen Death-stalker die. After he was dead, they stole his boots.

Lewis cried hot, heavy tears. His sword hung uselessly in his hand. 'It's all been for nothing,' he said finally. 'All of it. He really did die here.'

'Yes, he did,' said Roland. 'But the story isn't over yet. Keep watching.'

Time speeded up in that squalid little dead-end square. The animals stripped Owen of everything worth stealing, and then they disappeared into the night. The mists eddied this way and that. Owen lay dead in the bloody snow, his noble body gashed and punctured in many places, and soaked in his own gore. And that was how the organleggers found him. In Mistport there was always a thriving business in spare parts for transplant surgery, in those long-ago days. Body banks were of course illegal, but then so were a great many other everyday activities in Mistport. The bodysnatchers took Owen's body away, and Lewis and Roland followed them, unobserved.

The organleggers' warehouse wasn't far. They took Owen's body inside, locking the door carefully behind them. Lewis and Roland ghosted easily through the locked door, and watched as Owen's body was dumped into a refrigerated tank to preserve it. Within a few hours, automated blades and saws would render the body down into its component parts, ready for marketing. The bodysnatchers laughed together, and walked away. Lewis and Roland watched them go. Lewis felt drained, worn out.

'And still the story isn't over,' said Roland. 'When those two gentlemen return, they'll find Owen's body gone. No trace of it will turn up anywhere, and no one will ever know what happened to it. It becomes just another of Mistworld's little mysteries. Well, the answer is: you happened. Or at least you will. Time travel can play merry hell with your tenses.'

The scene disappeared, and Lewis and Roland were back in the heart of the Madness Maze again. Lewis wiped at his face with his sleeve. Roland smiled at him.

'You're going back in time, Lewis, courtesy of the Maze and the baby. To put right an old wrong. You're going to bring Owen back to life, rescue him from the body bank and then you and he will be brought back here.'

'Just like that?' said Lewis. 'The man is dead! They cut him to pieces! Even a regeneration tank couldn't save him now.'

'Owen's been through the Maze. He's very hard to kill. All he needs is a nudge from the Maze, and you.'

Lewis thought about it. 'You can send me back, in person this time? Back two hundred years?'

'Time is only another dimension,' said Roland. 'Another direction to move in. With enough power behind you, you can go anywhere and anywhen.'

'And I'll be able to save him? To . . . bring him back to life?'

'Never underestimate the power of the Madness Maze, boy. I didn't build it to human specifications, so it doesn't have human limitations. We'll send you back to Mistport, past the Pale Horizon, and you'll appear there as Owen breathes his last. And then you'll do what you have to do; because the Maze has already changed you, even if you haven't realised it yet. You will collect Owen's consciousness, or his soul if you prefer, at the moment of his death and hold it safe within you. Only a Maze-altered Deathstalker could do this. You then go to the warehouse, reunite the soul with its body, and it will repair itself. And Owen Deathstalker will live again. When you're done, the Maze will bring you back here. I won't be here; my part in this is over. Which is just as well, as the whole business freaks me out.' Roland smiled suddenly at Lewis. 'Say your goodbyes now, Lewis. Because you won't be able to later.'

'All right,' said Lewis. 'Goodbye.'

'Goodbye, son.' Roland took Lewis in his arms and hugged him briefly. 'Never doubt that your father was always very proud of you.'

He disappeared, leaving Lewis with empty arms and the puzzled feeling that the alien had been trying to tell him something. Then the light at the heart of the Maze changed suddenly, Lewis felt the world shift under him and he saw a whole new direction he could travel in. He let go of the present, and fell back into time.

The universe blurred around him, all the colours at once, like running through a rainbow. The colours were vivid, overwhelming, intense almost beyond bearing. Lewis could hear a million voices speaking at once, and he burst out of the rainbow into the deep dark sea of space. Planets whirled around him, and he saw the stars turn slowly in their endless dance, sparks of hope in the long night. Lewis supposed he should be feeling scared, or awed, but he was too busy concentrating on where he was going. He was going to save Owen Deathstalker.

Lewis materialised in a Mistport back alley. The cold hit him like a fist, as his sensations returned to him. He leaned against a nearby wall to steady himself, breathing hard as though he'd just run a long race. And then he heard the baying of the animals as they took Owen down, and Lewis forced himself away from the wall. He lurched unsteadily through mist-choked alleys, following the sounds of battle, and got there in time to see Owen die. Lewis hid in the shadows and reached out with his mind, almost instinctively. One Deathstalker, calling to another. And Owen heard him.

Hazel?

No, Owen. But I'm family.

He gathered Owen's fading mind to him, held it safe while the body died, and then jumped a little forward in space and time. In a moment he was in the gloomy warehouse of the body banks. The place was deserted, the only light radiating from the ranks of refrigerated tanks. Lewis walked over to one particular body bank, swept a layer of frost from the transparent lid with his hand and looked inside. Owen's dead body stared sightlessly back at him, the death wounds still livid. The automated knives and saws hadn't started their work yet. And somehow it was the easiest thing in the world for Lewis to take the soul that had been entrusted to him and tenderly put it back where it belonged.

A blast of light filled the tank and Lewis staggered, temporarily dazzled. He heard a door slam open behind him, and spun round, blinking his eyes furiously to clear them. Two armed guards came rushing towards him, determined to protect their merchandise. Lewis smiled savagely and went to meet them, sword in hand. He killed them both, cutting them to pieces with cold, vicious skill. Because he hadn't been able to punish the animals who killed Owen, and someone had to pay. The fight was quickly over, and Lewis turned away from the twitching bodies to look at the refrigerated tank again. A fierce light was blazing through the transparent lid. The steel sides burst apart and the lid blew up into the air. And Owen Deathstalker rose out of the ruins of the body bank like some ancient King rising from his tomb.

He stepped regally out of the wreckage, shaking off the last of the frost from his bare skin, disregarding it like the cold of death he'd just escaped. He stood tall and proud, breathing deeply, every bit as impressive as Lewis had always known he would be. There weren't even any scars on Owen's body to show where the dozens of wounds had been. He turned his dark gaze on Lewis, who immediately sank to one knee and bowed his head to his revered ancestor. 'Welcome back,

Lord Deathstalker. I am your kinsman, Lewis of Virimonde. And I have come a very long way to bring you back.'

'Good for you,' said Owen. 'Now please get up. I've never liked being knelt to, especially by a kinsman. I don't suppose you brought any spare clothes with you, did you, Lewis? Only I'm freezing my nuts off here.'

Lewis blinked a few times, and then scrambled to his feet. He took a heavy cloak from one of the dead guards, and wrapped it around Owen's shoulders.

'Thank you,' said Owen. 'Now I think you have a lot to tell me, kinsman. Starting very definitely with why I'm not dead after all.'

'It was the Maze,' said Lewis. 'It sent me back through time, with the power to rescue and restore you.'

'I should bloody well think so too,' said Owen. 'It was the Maze that got me into this mess in the first place, when it stranded me here. You didn't happen to encounter a certain shape-changing alien along the way, did you? . . . Yes, I thought so. This has his fingerprints all over it.' He stopped, and studied Lewis thoughtfully. 'Can't say I recognise you, Lewis. Are you kin to David? Never really got to know his branch of the family.'

'No . . . sir Owen.' Lewis hesitated, and then decided to go with the truth, because he didn't feel up to breaking it slowly and gently. 'David is dead, long dead, and all his line with him. A lot of time has passed since your . . . death, sir Owen. King Robert and Queen Constance raised a cousin branch to take over as Clan Deathstalker, and my father Roland is its current head.'

'Just call me Owen, please. How much time has passed since my battle with the Recreated?'

Lewis met Owen's gaze squarely. 'It's been two hundred years, Owen. I am the first to have reached the heart of the Madness Maze in two centuries.'

Owen didn't flinch, but his lips formed the name *Hazel* . . . 'Why did the Maze send you back for me, after so long?'

'Because you're needed.'

Owen smiled sourly. 'That always was the problem. But how can I be needed? Lionstone's dead, Shub had a revelation, and I defeated the Recreated. What's left?'

'The Terror,' said Lewis. 'The Terror has come to the Empire, and threatens the existence of Humanity. We've already lost eight planets to it.'

'Oh hell,' Owen said tiredly. 'It's always bloody something, isn't it? Look, can't you handle it? You're a Deathstalker. Why does it always have to be me? I died once for Humanity. I shouldn't have to do it again. I need a rest. Dying really takes it out of you, you know.'

Lewis looked at Owen uncertainly, taken aback. This querulous, annoyed tone wasn't what he'd expected from the blessed Owen. He fumbled for a reply. Owen saw the look on Lewis's face and chuckled suddenly.

'You've been listening to the stories about me, haven't you? Never believe what you see in the docudramas. If I did half the things I'm supposed to have done, I'd need to be twenty men. And I certainly never saw myself as any kind of hero. Just a man who knew his duty. The right man in the right place at the right time. If it hadn't been me, it would have been someone else . . . Oh hell, let's get out of here. I'll do what I can. I always do. Two hundred years . . . Be interesting to see what you've done in my absence. Maze, I know you're listening. Bring us back. Now.'

Power flared up around Owen and Lewis, and time poured past them. And then they were back at the heart of the Madness Maze. There was no sign of Roland anywhere, or any of the alien's other shapes. Owen walked over and looked at the baby, still sleeping peacefully in the shining crystal.

'Seems I'm not going to be allowed to ask any awkward questions of our shape-changing friend,' he said. 'Ah well. I've no doubt there will be other occasions.' He glanced at Lewis. 'Who's waiting for me, out there?'

'Some new friends, and one old one.'

Owen smiled suddenly. 'Then we'd better not keep them waiting.'

They walked out of the Maze together, side by side. The corridors still branched and turned, but the way out was always clear. As they neared the entrance, Lewis looked at Owen.

'I don't feel any different. I thought I would, once I'd been through the Maze.'

'It's a slow process,' said Owen. 'Maybe because if it all happened at once, you'd go crazy trying to cope with it. Trust me; you'll start noticing things soon enough.'

Lewis and Owen Deathstalker walked out of the Madness Maze, and everyone waiting for them, including John Silence and the Shub robot, sank to one knee and bowed their heads respectfully. Owen sighed heavily.

'Is this going to happen all the time now?' he said, a little waspishly. 'I never did go in for the bowing and scraping stuff. Everybody up!'

They got to their feet. Most of them appeared confused. Silence was smiling. The blue steel robot stepped forward, and Owen looked at it interestedly.

'I represent the AIs of Shub, Lord Deathstalker,' said the robot. 'No longer your enemy, now your most trustworthy servant. Welcome back, Owen. We have waited so long for this moment. We never stopped believing that some day you would return to us. We have dedicated our life to the service of Humanity, in your name. Ask anything of us.'

'You can start with filling me in on what's happened while I was away,' said Owen. His voice was courteous, but distinctly cool.

'In the past two hundred years, you have become a legend,' said the robot. 'And much has changed.'

'Tell me,' said Owen.

While Owen listened to the robot describe recent history, Lewis and Jesamine moved aside to hug each other tightly.

'What happened, Jes?' Lewis said finally. 'You were right there with me when I went in . . .'

'The Maze separated us,' said Jesamine. 'Seems only Deathstalkers are allowed to know the secrets of the Maze. So I'm expecting you to tell me *everything* later. Do you feel any different, Lewis? I don't.'

'Apparently it sneaks up on you,' said Lewis. 'What do you make of Owen?'

'Well he certainly looks the part, darling, but he's going to have to brush up on his people skills.'

Owen finally dismissed the robot, and turned to Silence. 'Good to see one familiar face, Captain. The years seem to have treated you kindly. What happened to everyone else? What happened to Hazel?'

'Of those who went through the Maze, only you and I remain,' said Silence. 'Hazel is . . . missing, presumed dead. She disappeared after the last battle against the Recreated, when she heard you were dead. No one's seen anything of her since.'

Owen nodded. 'Was it worth it?' he said. 'All we sacrificed? The good people we lost? Did we buy anything worth having with the precious coin we paid?'

It seemed everyone heard that, and they hurried to reassure Owen that there had indeed been a Golden Age, for well over a century. Until one good man went bad and the Terror arrived.

'It's always something, isn't it?' said Owen. He smiled at Jesamine. 'Don't look so impressed, lass. I put my trousers on one leg at a time, and leave the toilet seat up, just like everyone else.' He looked at Lewis. 'I trust someone is going to supply me with trousers at some point?'

'I played you in the opera *Deathstalker's Lament*,' Jesamine said abruptly. 'And Hazel d'Ark too, of course.'

'There are operas about me?' Owen raised an eyebrow. 'Maybe I should look into the royalties situation, when I get back. Now, who are these other two people, and what is *that*?'

Lewis introduced Owen to Brett, Rose and Saturday. Owen sniffed briefly. 'A conman, a psycho and a reptiloid. Ah well; if I can get used to Ruby Journey, I suppose I can get used to anything.'

'You knew my ancestors, Jack and Ruby,' Brett said hesitantly. 'Can you tell me . . . what were they really like?'

'Canny fighters,' said Owen. 'And good friends. I'm glad you're here, Brett. I'm sure you'll make your ancestors proud in the battles to come. Now, let's get out of here. Lead me to your ship, find me some clothes and we'll start making plans. I'll bang the necessary heads together and put things in order, because that's what I do, but afterwards . . . I'm going to find Hazel.'

'Trust me, Owen, we looked,' said Silence. 'We looked everywhere.'

'She isn't dead,' said Owen. 'I'd know if she was dead.'

Shub found him some clothes, and then they went to the annexe containing the twelve monstrous survivors. Owen stopped while their nature and situation were explained to him. Lewis added what he'd learned in the heart of the Maze. They'd expected Owen to be appalled, but his white-hot anger surprised them. He strode up and down the aisle, staring into each cell in turn. The twelve survivors watched him silently, in their own way. Lewis shrank back a little as Owen turned his cold glare on him.

'This is intolerable,' Owen snapped. 'They belong in a hospital, not a zoo! I won't have this!'

He gestured sharply with one hand, and the force shields closing off the cells disappeared. Jesamine clung to Lewis, and Rose grabbed Brett's arm to keep him from bolting. Owen ignored them, concentrating on the twelve survivors as they emerged from their cells for the first time in two hundred years. The man and woman joined into one huge insect-like body. The one who had been turned inside out down one side. It had finally stopped crying, and was trying to smile with its half a mouth. A man who had once moved impossibly quickly slowed to a blur, kneeling before Owen. A man who had torn out his own eyes to keep from seeing looked at Owen with tears in his new eyes. An ever-changing shape settled for a while into an ordinary woman, wringing her hands together in joy at seeing Owen. A man who had slept for two hundred years woke up, and came out of his cell to kneel before Owen. A woman who had smiled endlessly for two hundred years sobbed quietly in relief. A great fleshy mass that had once been human threw aside his extra bulk like a shell and came out to kneel in his turn. A woman stopped fading in and out of reality long enough to kneel before Owen. Someone who looked like Owen came out to kneel before the original. And a man who had done nothing but commit murder for two hundred years had to be coaxed out of his cell by the others. He showed Owen the blood dripping from his hands, and asked pitifully if he could stop now, at last.

'It is over?' he said. 'Please, I want to go home. We all want to go home.'

'Of course,' said Owen. 'And you will. None of this is your fault. Go back into the Maze, and it will heal you. Because I said so.'

He gestured with his hand again, and the twelve disappeared. Owen turned to the Shub robot. 'They'll be out again, in time. Wait here for them.'

'We will stay and care for them, in your name,' said the robot. 'Whatever comes out. All that lives is holy.'

The others were looking at each other uncertainly. Even Silence had never seen Owen use his power so casually. Lewis cleared his throat.

'Is it going to be that easy, dealing with the Terror?'

'Beats the hell out of me,' said Owen. 'I haven't got a clue what the Terror is, never mind how to deal with it. I think the first thing to do is go and get a good close-up look at it. Maybe that will give me a few ideas.'

There was a long horrified silence, followed by a loud clamour of objections from pretty much everybody, mostly along the lines of *Are you crazy?* They only broke off when the *Hereward*'s AI came through on their comm implants.

'Sorry to interrupt, gang, but we are in deep doo-doo. Welcome back, Owen! This is Ozymandias, or at least what's left of him. We really must sit down and have a nice chat in the future, assuming we have one. At the moment, I'm sorry to have to tell you that what appears to be the whole damned Imperial Fleet has just dropped out of hyperspace and assumed orbit around Haden. It seems Finn isn't taking any chances.'

Owen laughed. 'Like old times, isn't it, Oz?'

EIGHT

FINN TRIUMPHANT, MOSTLY

It was the day of the coronation, and Finn Durandal strode into the Imperial Court as though he already owned it. He was followed by massed marching ranks of Church Militant and Pure Humanity faithful, looking for all the world like a general at the head of an invading army. Which, truth be told, wasn't that far from the reality. Officially, with James dead and Douglas disgraced, Finn was being made King by popular acclaim and Parliamentary decree. Actually, Finn said he was going to be King and everyone else went along. The MPs held a special session in the House, and took it in turns to stand up and say *What a good idea*, and the people, desperate for a saviour to rescue them from the evils that troubled the Empire, clamoured for the earliest possible coronation. There were dissenting voices, but nobody listened to them, or at least no one who mattered. Finn was going to be King, and that was all there was to it.

Finn stepped out across the great hall of the Court at a good pace, smiling and nodding regally as he progressed down the wide central aisle separating the crowds of chosen guests. Rank after rank of the finest fanatics stamped after him in perfect lock step, looking neither to the left nor the right. For them, this was a holy occasion. The anointing of the chosen one. Both the Church Militant and the Pure Humanity representatives were carefully selected zealots of the first order, all determined to outdo each other in military precision and presentation. After all, the whole Empire was watching. Live. They did make a magnificent sight, bold and bright and utterly intimidating in their crisp dress uniforms, making it clear to everyone where Finn's power base lay.

Finn stopped at the raised dais at the end of the hall, bowed to the empty throne, then turned to smile and wave at the guests and the cameras. He was wearing his black leather Champion's uniform under the traditional cloak of Kings. He looked tall and handsome and already impossibly regal. He went to his throne, and sat down. The zealots crashed to a halt before the raised dais with one last thunderous about-turn, so that they could study the invited guests for any sign of trouble. The zealots were armed. The guests weren't. By order.

Musicians played, trumpets sounded, the choir sang like angels and flocks of holographic doves soared through brilliant shafts of light falling through the gorgeous stained-glass windows in the high ceiling. It was tradition and ceremony in the old style, and the sense of occasion was so thick you could have cut it with a knife. The invited guests were unusually quiet, even subdued, in their seats, and the dozens of remote cameras bobbing overhead were hard put to find anything interesting to concentrate on. Unseen in their little studios at the back of the Court, the commentators were reduced to discussing what people were wearing to fill in time until the ceremony proper began. Anne Barclay slipped through the heavy black drapes behind the throne and came forward to stand beside Finn. She was wearing a stunning blue and silver gown, expertly cut to show off her fabulous figure to its best advantage, and Anne wore it without grace, as though it belonged to someone else. She looked out over the assembled guests, and sniffed loudly.

'Look at them. Miserable bastards. Not an honestly cheerful face in the bunch. You'd think we were at a funeral, not a coronation.'

'They'll get into the swing of things, once the ceremony's under way,' Finn said calmly. 'These are trying times. You have to allow for a few long faces. They'll cheer enough once I'm crowned. The guards will see to that.'

'You should have held James's funeral and then had the coronation,' Anne said bluntly.

'First things first, my dear. The Empire needs a King. And it's not as if James is going to be impatient. Oh do try and cheer up, Anne. I know you were fond of James, but it's been over a week. Excessive mourning is unflattering and self-indulgent. Now smile at the nice people, and I don't want to hear any mention of James again. This is my big day, and I don't want any distractions. In fact I've given orders to my security people that if there are any distractions they're to be taken outside and shot.'

'Looks like everyone's here who should be,' said Anne. 'All the usual suspects. Politicians, businessmen, Church elders and Neumen leaders.'

'Of course. The real movers and shakers, come to pay me homage. I had to send out some guards to collect a few MPs, to make sure they didn't get lost on their way here, but these politicians always get sulky when they realise they're on the losing side. I've made a note of certain names, for later.'

Anne looked at Finn, sitting casually on the throne as though he belonged there, and always had. 'You finally got what you wanted, Finn. How does it feel?'

'It feels fine, my dear. But this is only the beginning.'

Anne decided not to follow that, for the moment, and changed the subject. 'You're still wearing your Champion's armour. Have you given any thought as to who's going to serve as your new Champion?'

'I shall be King and Champion,' said Finn. 'I see no reason to share my power and authority with anyone else. Besides, there's no one worthy, these days.'

Anne decided she wasn't going to follow that one either, and so she held her peace and looked out again over the packed Court. A healthily sized gathering had turned out to see Finn's coronation, and there was certainly no lack of media interest, but Anne couldn't help comparing the scene with the glorious celebrations of Douglas's coronation. Such golden days, full of hope and optimism. Today's crowd seemed drab, mostly because there were no society people and no celebrities. Finn wouldn't have them. *Parasites*, he said dismissively. And perhaps they were, but you could always rely on them to add a touch of colour and excitement. Anne sighed quietly. It seemed Finn was determined to run an austere Court. And of course there were no espers or aliens, to add a little charm and strangeness . . .

Is this what we've come to? thought Anne. *Nothing but fanatics and puritans . . . and a King who cares for nothing but being King?*

The ceremony proper commenced exactly on time, and proceeded with military precision. Everyone was in the right place at the right time, and everyone knew their lines. Fear can be a great motivator. The crowd cheered and clapped in the right places. The guards saw to that. Joseph Wallace, now official head of the Church Militant as well as chairman of the Transmutation Board, worked his way through the rituals with efficient if graceless thoroughness. He'd gone way overboard on the gold trimmings and face paint, but no one said anything. It was a slightly rushed ceremony, reduced in advance by Finn and Anne to the bare essentials, and they completely dispensed with Owen's traditional warning to the people on the unanswerable grounds that the Terror was already upon them. Wallace placed the crown on Finn's head, and everyone cheered. The fanatics made the most noise, along with certain MPs hoping to be noticed by the new King, but in the end most of the cheers were honest enough. James was dead, Douglas was disgraced and the Empire needed a King, so why not Finn? He looked the part well enough. And at least no one would ever accuse him of being weak or indecisive.

The floating news cameras carried the scene live to every planet in the Empire, and there was much rejoicing. Only remote cameras had been allowed into the Court. No actual reporters. Finn had absolutely no intention of answering any awkward questions. He controlled an awful lot of the news media now, directly or indirectly, but you never could tell what a reporter might suddenly get it into his head to ask. A few had tried to sneak in anyway, and had been very thoroughly thrown out. All except for demon girl reporter Nina Malapert, who was there as the guest of the Paragon Emma Steel. Nina got away with it because absolutely nobody wanted to risk upsetting Emma Steel.

No other Paragons were present, not even Finn's close personal friend Stuart Lennox of Virimonde. Paragons were not popular at present, for a variety of reasons, including what had happened with Clan Deathstalker on Virimonde.

King Finn stood up from his throne to make his first official speech. Anne had put a lot of work into it, and Finn made it sound suitably spontaneous. The speech was short and to the point, mostly vague but emphatic promises of better times ahead for everyone, and the announcement of Douglas Campbell's forthcoming trial for treason, sedition, murder and royal fratricide. There were some murmurs at that, quickly glared into silence by the watching guards. Everyone cheered at the end of the speech, King Finn smiled and waved, disappeared behind the hanging black drapes and everyone went home. There was no official party. Finn wasn't a party person.

In fact, Finn's first official visit as King was to the apartment of his close friend, the Paragon Stuart Lennox. Finn had sent an official summons, calling on Stuart to attend his new King, but Stuart wouldn't open his door to the messenger and his comm line was closed down. So Finn went to see Stuart. Anyone else would have had their door kicked in and been dragged before their King in chains for such a slight, but Finn went in person. For old times' sake.

Stuart had a nice apartment in a nice part of town. Finn arrived incognito, with just a handful of guards. He knocked politely on

Stuart's door and called his name. There was a long pause. Finn waited patiently. Eventually the door opened a crack, and Stuart looked out. Finn had to admit he was surprised at the changes in Stuart since he'd last seen him. The young Paragon's face was gaunt and haggard, his eyes were red and puffy and he hadn't shaved in days. He was wearing old, unwashed clothes that looked and smelled as though they'd been slept in. Several times. But Stuart's gaze was steady and his mouth was firm as he looked coldly at his old friend Finn.

'Well, Stuart,' Finn said lightly. 'Aren't you going to invite me in? I've come a long way to see you. Have you no welcome for your new King?'

Stuart let go of the door and shuffled back into his apartment. Finn pushed the door open, stepped inside and closed the door behind him. He looked unhurriedly about him, not letting his opinion show in his face. The room was a mess. Everything was scattered around, as though Stuart had taken to dropping things where he felt like it and couldn't be bothered to pick them up. There was a close, fusty atmosphere, and the shades were drawn over the windows. Finn peered into the gloom, letting his eyes adjust. Stuart was sitting slumped in an oversized armchair, not looking at Finn. It was very quiet in the dark room. Finn pulled up a chair and sat down facing Stuart.

'Tell me who your cleaning service is, and I'll have them shot,' Finn said cheerfully. 'Joke, Stuart. You know, you're looking—'

'I know what I look like,' said Stuart. His voice was quiet, flat, almost uninvolved. 'I haven't been sleeping. Haven't been eating, either. Can't keep anything down, not after—'

'Stu—'

'You let them do that to me! They killed a man in front of me and made me eat his . . . and you didn't even punish them!'

'They could still be useful to me,' said Finn, 'once the fuss over Virimonde has died down, and it will. I know I can count on their loyalty. What about your loyalty, Stu?'

Stuart smiled slowly. It wasn't a pleasant sight, and neither was the look that came into his dark, sunken eyes. 'That's why you're here, isn't it, Finn? Not because you're concerned about me. I only matter when it affects you. Bastard.'

Finn sighed. 'You were such a pretty boy once, Stuart. And now look what you've done to yourself. Why didn't you come to my coronation? It was my big day. I wanted you there. I did send you an invitation.'

'Oh come on now, Finn. Someone like me doesn't belong in your new austere life. Your new Kingly image. I know too much about the real you. I've had a lot of time to think, sitting here in the dark. Waiting for you to come and see me. I don't like the man you made me into. I gave up honour and responsibility and self-respect, all for your love. Only to discover you don't know the meaning of the word. Look at what's become of me, Finn. All for you.'

'I never asked you to do this to yourself,' said Finn. 'If I'd known you were prone to hysteria and over-reaction—'

'Get out of here, Finn. I still have some pride left. I won't be your puppy dog any more.'

'You'll be whatever I want you to be,' said Finn, and then stopped, because Stuart was laughing soundlessly at him.

'Or what, Finn? You'll make me eat human flesh again? You'll kill me and put me out of my misery? There's nothing left you can threaten me with.'

'Oh, I'm sure I could find something, Stuart. If I put my mind to it. I have a job for you, Stuart Lennox, and I am your King. You took an oath when you became a Paragon to be faithful unto death to the Throne of Logres. Are you an oathbreaker now?'

Stuart sat very still in his chair, his face unreadable. 'What do you want of me . . . your majesty?'

'The other Paragons are trapped in the Sangreal bar. It seems they can't take a step outside without being stoned or otherwise attacked. And I can't let them defend themselves, because then we'll have even more bodies on our hands. I need them to stay put and keep their heads down until I can take steps to repair their reputations. But, just like you, it seems they're too preoccupied with their own problems to answer the comm. So I want you to take my message to them. They know you speak for me . . .'

And he stopped again, because Stuart had lurched up out of his chair and was standing swaying before Finn.

'You bastard! I can't believe you'd ask that of me!'

'Someone has to do it. And I'm not asking you, Stuart. I am your King, and I'm giving you an order.'

'Take your order and shove it, your majesty. Now get the hell out of my home. I can't stand to look at you any more.'

Finn rose unhurriedly to his feet. 'Ah, Stu, and we were so close once. I really am sorry about what happened. But I have to see the bigger picture.'

'There is no bigger picture, Finn. There's only people, and how you treat them. Just . . . go. And if you ever really felt anything for me, don't come back.'

Finn left the apartment. He stood outside the closed door for a while, remembering and considering. And then he nodded to the small group of armed guards he'd left waiting outside Stuart's apartment, and they smashed the door open and rushed inside. Finn sighed quietly. It was a pity, but if Stuart couldn't be trusted to carry out orders any more, then he couldn't be trusted at all. He'd made himself into a liability.

It didn't take the guards long to overpower Stuart and drag him out into the corridor. He was kicking and struggling, but he didn't have much strength left after his extended fast. He saw Finn watching, and started to curse him. The guards shut him up with brutal efficiency. Finn waited until he was sure Stuart was listening and paying attention, and then he addressed the officer in charge.

'Take him to the nearest lockup and hold him there until I send word. No one's to know he's there. And remember to search him very thoroughly for concealed weapons. He was a Paragon once, after all.'

'Du Bois won't stand for this,' said Stuart, spitting blood out of his broken mouth.

'The honourable Member for Virimonde is no longer gracing us with his company,' said Finn. 'He left Logres yesterday, under an assumed identity. It seems he was rather upset over what happened to the late Clan Deathstalker. Who would have thought it? Either way, he's gone home and gone to ground, on Virimonde. The planetary council there was uncommonly rude to me the last time I spoke to them. Actually threatened to go rogue, like Mistworld. But of course it won't come to that. Either they agree to roll over and play dead, like a good little puppy dog, or I'll have the Transmutation Engines turn their whole world and everything on it into something more useful.'

Stuart tried to lunge at Finn, but the guards held him firmly.

'The people, bless their black vindictive little hearts, need to see a Paragon brought to trial,' Finn said cheerfully. 'So I think we'll give them you.' He looked again at the officer in charge. 'Better see he's kept well drugged. We don't want him hurting himself before he comes to trial. And by the time you do come to trial, Stuart, the drugs will have wiped your mind of anything unpleasant you might have said against me. Trust me, you'll feel so much better. Goodbye, Stuart. I'll probably be too busy to attend your trial; but I promise I'll do my best to be there for your execution.'

He nodded to the guards, and they dragged Stuart Lennox away. Finn was already thinking about something else.

The Paragon Emma Steel decided she couldn't afford to wait any longer to put the boot into Finn bloody Durandal. He was King now, which meant there was no one but her left to oppose him. She could already see the signs of a major clamp-down against all dissenting voices moving into place. There was nothing and no one left to stop Finn from moving against anyone he saw as an enemy. Or even a potential enemy. He had to be shut down now, before he could consolidate his power. Emma said as much to Nina Malapert, while striding up and down the young reporter's living room like a caged animal.

'We can't go public, even with all the evidence we've amassed,' said Emma, scowling fiercely. 'The King's never been more popular, mostly because the people don't know the real him, and the reputation of the other Paragons has affected the way people look at me. Like I'm guilty until proven innocent. We need someone the public still trusts to back us up. Someone people will believe when they vouch for the authenticity of our evidence. If we can get enough people listening and talking, Finn's own supporters will turn against him, to save their own necks.'

'But there's no one left!' said Nina, sitting curled up in a big chair with her knees hugged to her chest. Her eyes were very large. 'The public doesn't trust anyone, lovey; not after what happened with Lewis and Jesamine, and now Douglas. Wasn't that awful? Do you really think he murdered his own brother?'

'Not without a good reason. Look, there might be one person left we can trust.' Emma stopped herself in mid-stride and stared at Nina. 'I think I've come up with one person who might still be interested in the truth, and be in a position to do something about it. But in case I'm wrong . . . I'll write it out for you. On paper, so no one can find it in your files. Read it after I'm gone, and if I don't come back . . . you'll have to decide what to do next.'

Nina uncurled in a moment, launched herself out of her chair, and glared at Emma. 'Oh no you don't, Emma Steel! Where you go, I go! We're partners. You wait here a minute, I'll get my most inconspicuous camera and my biggest gun, and we'll—'

'No we won't,' Emma said firmly, and Nina stopped in her tracks. Emma had used her Paragon's voice, and Nina recognised its resolution, if not its authority. Nina pouted fiercely, and flung herself back into her chair. Emma had to smile at her. 'If I'm right I'll call you in, and you'll have an exclusive that will beat anything else you've done so far. The beginning of the end for the King. But if I'm wrong . . . someone has to be here, to carry on.'

'I don't want you to go,' said Nina, in a small voice. 'With you, I could be strong and fearless, because you were. If you're not here, I'm afraid . . . I might go back to who I used to be.'

'Butterflies don't turn back into caterpillars,' said Emma. 'I've enjoyed our partnership, Nina. If it does go wrong, don't let me down by doing anything stupid. Bringing down Finn is what matters. Revenge can wait.'

'Don't talk like that!' said Nina, almost tearfully. 'Of course you're coming back! You're a Paragon. You're Emma Steel.'

'Lewis was a Deathstalker and Douglas was King; and where are they now? Don't underestimate Finn. But I promise I'll be very careful, and not turn my back on anyone. I'll see you later, Nina.'

'Promise?' said Nina.

Emma smiled at her, and left.

No one paid much attention to Emma Steel as she strode through the House of Parliament. They were used to seeing the Logres Paragon going about her business. Some even smiled and bowed to her as she passed, perhaps the last respected Paragon in the Empire. Emma made her way confidently through the warren of corridors and offices at the back of the House. She knew where she was going, even though she'd never had cause to go there before. Everyone in the House knew where this particular office was. Emma stopped before the right door, mentally rehearsed her arguments one last time, and then knocked. There was a pause, and the door opened.

'We need to talk,' Emma said bluntly. 'You're the last one left who isn't affiliated with any group or belief. There are things I need to tell you about Finn Durandal. Things no one else knows.'

'Then you'd better come in,' said Anne Barclay.

Emma strode into Anne's office, and nodded her approval at the bank of monitor screens covering everything that happened in the House. Emma believed in good security. Anne shut and locked the door, so they wouldn't be interrupted, and gestured for Emma to sit down. The Paragon did so, and Anne turned off the sound on the monitors so they could talk. Emma ran through everything she knew, and detailed the major evidence she had. She didn't mention Nina by name, speaking only of an investigative reporter who'd assisted her. Anne nodded here and there, paying careful attention. When Emma finally finished, Anne sat back in her chair and thought for a long moment.

'I'm glad you came to me with this, Emma. I can't think of anyone else here who wouldn't have turned you in immediately. Finn's people are everywhere these days, even in places you wouldn't suspect. I was one of them, once. But he's changed. Now he's King, he thinks he's untouchable. Well, we'll see about that. I think I know what we need to do next, but it's going to take some consideration. Why don't I make us a nice cup of tea? And there are some chocolate biscuits in the barrel, if you like.'

Anne got up and bustled around her office, chatting lightly as she got the tea things together. Emma took the lid off the biscuit barrel, and rooted inside for something with a really thick chocolate coating. And Anne picked up the heavy crystal paperweight from her desk and hit Emma on the back of the head with it, as hard as she could. The force of the blow bent Emma forward in her chair. She cried out hoarsely, one flailing arm batting the biscuit barrel away. Anne hit Emma again and again and again, putting all her strength into every blow. Blood flew on the air, and the sound of bone crunching and splintering was clear, even over Anne's heavy breathing and Emma's groans. Her hands reached for her gun and her sword, but her fingers were spasming helplessly. Anne hit her again and again, shrieking, *'Why won't you die! Why won't you die?'* Emma fell forward out of her chair and crashed on to the floor. She tried to crawl towards the door, and Anne moved with her, leaning over to hit her again and again, even though her arm was aching fiercely. There was blood over her hand and her arm now, and some had sprayed across her distorted face.

Finally Anne realised that Emma Steel had stopped moving. She knelt down, still clutching the paperweight in her hand, and checked the pulse in the Paragon's neck. There was nothing there. Emma wasn't breathing, and her eyes were fixed. Anne straightened up, and let the dripping paperweight fall from her hand. She was panting for breath, as though she'd just run a race, and her head was swimming. She noticed there was blood on the front of her dress, and brushed at it absently, making it worse. Anne looked at the blood on her hand for a while, and then at the dead body before her. Blood was soaking into her carpet, ruining it. Finn. She had to call Finn. He would know what to do.

She went over to the comm unit, giving the body plenty of room, and called Finn on their special security line. He was busy, as always, and didn't want to be bothered, but somehow she managed to make him understand how serious the situation was, without going into details. Dazed as she was, she knew better than to speak openly on a comm channel. Finn said he'd come immediately. Anne sat in her chair, and waited, trying not to look at the body. She tried to wipe the blood off her hand and arm. Her breathing didn't want to slow. She felt giddy, and sick. It seemed to take for ever until Finn finally came. He had to knock and say his name several times before she roused enough to unlock the door and let him in. He was very surprised to see the dead body. He made Anne tell him everything that had happened. Anne explained what she'd done and why, in a mostly calm voice, and Finn was very reassuring. When she finally finished, he put his arm around her shoulders.

'Now you're not to worry, Anne. You did the right thing. And you did very well, taking out a Paragon on your own. And Emma Steel, too. I'm impressed, Anne. Really. I didn't know you had it in you. I shall see you in a whole new light from now on. But you're not to worry about a thing. I'll have my people come in and clean up this mess. No one needs to know Emma Steel was ever here. Now, she told you she had evidence against me. If she didn't bring it with her, she must have left it with someone, as insurance.'

'She mentioned a reporter she'd been working with,' said Anne. 'But she wouldn't reveal the name. I did try . . .'

'I'm sure you did. We'll track whoever it is down. Someone always knows. You're not to be upset, Anne. You did well. You saw a threat to us, and you stamped it out.' Finn laughed suddenly, and took both of Anne's hands in his. 'You know what I'm going to do? I'm going to make you my Queen! I can't think of anyone more suited to reign at my side. King Finn and Queen Anne: what a team we'll be!'

The streets were crowded through the Parade of the Endless for James's funeral procession. Sobbing crowds lined street after street as his coffin progressed slowly through the city, borne on a gun carriage with an escort of mounted ceremonial guards. Wreaths adorned the coffin, and the people threw flowers into the road before it. The man who should have been King, betrayed and slain by his own jealous brother. The media was full of it, on every channel. Cameras broadcast the slow, solemn procession live, to every world in the Empire. To have lost him once was bad enough, all those years ago; to lose him twice was unbearable. To many, James's unexpected and miraculous return had been a sign that things were changing, an omen of better times to come. That there was still hope, in the face of the Terror.

And now that hope had been snatched away from them, by a man they'd once admired and adored.

One person alone in the streets of the city didn't give a damn for poor dead James. Nina Malapert, anonymous in the ubiquitous

352

mourning black, her pink mohawk subdued under a heavy black cowl, shouldered her way through the packed crowds, not even glancing at the street. She was on her way to the public mortuary, where Emma Steel's body was being held. No public procession for the Paragon Emma Steel, even though she deserved it more. No; Emma was condemned as a traitor, her body destined for the city incinerator, her ashes for the city dump. Not even a stone with a number on it to mark her resting place. Nina was damned if she'd let that happen.

She had to bribe her way into the mortuary, but it cost less than she expected. Perhaps the big gun she let the man glimpse on her hip had something to do with that. The attendant let her into the cold room, told her she had ten minutes tops, and went back to watching James's funeral procession on the viewscreen in his poky little office. Emma was lying on a metal slab, identified only by a number. She was wearing a regulation white shift, and a cloth to cover the damage done to her head. Nina trailed her fingertips across Emma's cold brown cheek. She'd meant to say so many things to Emma, promises of revenge and retribution and more, but now . . . it all seemed so small, in the face of death.

Emma seemed diminished, like an exquisite doll that had been carelessly handled and crushed. Something infinitely precious, forever ruined. She should have been left in her Paragon's armour, at least. She'd earned the right to lie in full honours. But by attacking Anne Barclay, she'd been condemned as just another traitor. Another Paragon gone bad. Nina couldn't believe it, when the news came into the media office where she was trying to get some work done while waiting for Emma to come back. Anne Barclay? There really wasn't anyone you could trust, after all.

'They struck you from behind,' Nina said finally, her voice lost in the overpowering silence of the cold room. 'It was the only way they could have brought you down. They always were afraid to face you. But they'll pay for this, Emma, all of them. With your help.' Her hand went to her sleeve, and the hidden Paragon's skeleton key that Emma had left behind along with her handwritten notes. 'I have a plan, Emma. A simple plan, perhaps, but then I never was a very complicated person. I'm going to tear down Finn's rotten regime, and dance on its ashes. For you, my darling Emma. For you.'

Stuart Lennox was attached to the wall of his holding cell with heavy steel chains that clinked loudly every time he moved his wrists. He was waiting to be moved to maximum security, but no one was in any rush. He was supposed to be doped to keep him quiet, but the prison doctor had said he was too frail yet. It didn't matter. They knew a broken man when they saw one. They'd left him a protein cube and a cup of water, but he hadn't touched them.

He was too busy thinking.

Even after all that had happened, up until today he'd still clung to his belief in Finn. Belief that deep down the man cared for him. Loved him, in his way. It was hard to realise he'd been such a fool. The day's events had been like a shock of cold water in the face, waking him from a self-indulgent dream. Well, he was awake now, and his mind was sharp and focused again. Sooner or later they would come for him, and seeing only a frail broken man, they would be relaxed and careless. They would make a mistake, give him an opening and then . . . Stuart Lennox would show them that he was still a Paragon.

He picked up the protein cube, took a firm bite and chewed hungrily.

There was a commotion outside his cell, and Stuart looked round curiously. There was scuffling and shouting, and the sudden sharp sound of an energy gun firing at close range. Stuart was on his feet in a moment. Something was happening. He could feel it. He took hold of his chains in both hands, ready to use them as a weapon if necessary. The lock on the heavy steel door snapped open, and Stuart braced himself, ready for one last chance at escape or revenge. Or at least a chance to die bravely. The door swung open, and a young woman in black, with a tall pink mohawk, a really big gun in one hand and a Paragon's skeleton key in the other, grinned at him cheerfully.

'Hi there! I'm Nina Malapert, demon girl reporter. Emma Steel was my partner and my friend, and Finn's people killed her. So I thought maybe you and I could get together and do something about it. What do you think, sweetie?'

'Sounds like a plan to me,' said Stuart. 'Unlock these chains and point me at the bastards.'

Nina flashed him another brilliant smile, and used her skeleton key on his chains. She had to support some of his weight as they left the cell. Stuart hadn't realised how weak he'd become. Outside, the reception area was trashed. There was a dead guard behind the main desk, and another lying on the floor. Nina hurried him past them.

'Sorry about the mess, but they weren't as open to reason and bribes as I'd hoped. Gosh, there isn't much of you, is there lovey? I'll have to feed you up when I get you out of here.'

'Where are we going?' said Stuart, keeping an ear open for the sound of approaching reinforcements as he reached down to snatch up a guard's gun.

'The Rookery,' said Nina. 'Emma kept a place there, for emergencies.'

'Doesn't everyone?' said Stuart.

And they both laughed quietly as they left the lockup and disappeared into the indifferent city, plotting their revenges.

Anne Barclay watched James's funeral procession on her office monitors. She had considered going in person, but she was never comfortable in crowds. People made her nervous. She'd always preferred to view the world at a distance, through her monitors. It gave her a necessary illusion of control over the proceedings; and keeping the world at arm's length made it much harder for the world to hurt her. Get close to the world, get close to people, like poor dear Jamie . . . tears welled up in her eyes, even though they were already puffy and sore from crying. James had been the only one who ever really cared for her, and now he was gone and she was alone again.

(There was a new carpet on her office floor. They couldn't get the bloodstains out of the old one. Anne didn't think about Emma Steel. Didn't think about her at all. She slept perfectly well, after a few sleeping tablets.)

There was a knock at the door. Anne checked who it was on the corridor monitor before unlocking the door and letting Finn in. He saw what she was watching on the monitors, and sank into the chair next to hers.

'Well, if nothing else he got to go out in style. Not bad for a few cell scrapings with delusions of grandeur. Look at the peasants, lapping it up. They do love a good show and a good cry. They're always much fonder of their heroes when they're dead. Still, James served his purpose. He brought Douglas down.'

'What are we going to do about Douglas?' said Anne, still looking at the monitors.

'I don't think we'll take him to trial yet. Let him stew for a while in Traitors' Hall. While we encourage public indignation to simmer, and grow ugly. Then a very public trial followed almost immediately by a very public execution. Something slow and messy, I think. Another good show will help to take the people's minds off . . . other things. Perhaps I'll duel Douglas to the death in the Arena! Yes, I like that. Finally a chance to prove I'm the better man, and always was.'

'Why do you hate Douglas so much?' said Anne. 'He was your friend, once. You were always together, you and Douglas and Lewis.

You seemed happy enough. Now it's like there's no room in you for anything but hate. Why, Finn? You're not like me. You've always had everything you ever wanted.'

'No,' said Finn. 'I never had what I really wanted. I was never their friend, not really. We were colleagues, with things in common that no one else could understand. So we hung out together . . . but it always felt as though I was only going through the motions. Most of my life felt like that, back then. And anyway, friendship wasn't what I wanted. All my life I desperately wanted love to be real, and it never was, for me. No matter who I was with. I think perhaps I'm not capable of it. I tried sex, as a substitute, but even that didn't feel real. Passion has always been a stranger to me. All my life I've wanted to know . . . what every other man knows. To feel, just once, what everyone else feels. And I never have. There's only ever been me. So if I can't have love, all that's left is hate, and to be a monster.'

Anne looked at him. 'We've been close. Done things together. We could—'

'No,' said Finn, not unkindly. 'Because it would mean something to you, and it wouldn't to me.'

'Are you happy now? As a traitor and a villain?'

Finn considered the matter carefully, and then smiled. 'Yes. I've never been happier. Now, if you'll excuse me, I'm on my way to see Douglas. Why don't you come with me? It'll take your mind off James. Trust me, there's nothing like gloating over a defeated foe to brighten up the darkest day.'

'Sure,' said Anne. 'Why not?'

Douglas Campbell, once a Paragon, once a King, sat alone in a bare stone cell in Traitors' Hall, weighed down with so many chains he could hardly move. Douglas had fully expected to be drugged like his father, to keep him quiet, but it seemed Finn wanted Douglas to be able to savour the depths to which he had fallen. Douglas had done a lot of thinking, in the peace and quiet of his cell, but very little of it had been about his present circumstances. Douglas was making plans for the future. Plans for blood and slaughter and Finn's head on a stake.

Several locks opened, and the door to his cell swung wide. Douglas turned his head, about the only part of him he could move, and there were Finn and Anne in the doorway.

'Hello, Douglas,' said Finn. 'No, please; don't get up. It's only me. And Anne, of course. You know, you really do look a mess, Douglas. Those clothes must smell pretty ripe, what with the bloodstains from you and James and your father. We'll have to get you some nice new clothes when it's time for your trial.'

'Why bother with a trial?' said Douglas. 'You know you'll have to kill me to stop me.'

'Oh, there has to be a trial! The forms must be observed. Everyone's looking forward to it. The people need to see justice being done. So you'll have your day in Court, and then you'll be executed. No point in hanging about, is there?'

'I'm going to kill you, Finn.' Douglas's voice was flat and cold and utterly sure. 'I will beat you to death with my bare hands, for my father's death, for the desecration of my brother's grave and for what you've done to the Empire.'

Finn shrugged. 'I never liked William. He never liked me. I could tell. And digging up an old body is the least of the many sins I've committed. Would it interest you to know how and why I brought about your destruction, and the corruption of your Empire? It's really very instructive. What surprised me was how easy it was. There were people lining up to piss over your precious Golden Age. All they needed was a focus, and I've always found it easy to be everything to everyone. But it started with you, Douglas. In a way, you could say everything that's happened is your fault.

'You should have made me Champion at your coronation. I deserved it. I earned it. If I'd been Champion, I would have served you faithfully all my days, protected you from every harm until my dying breath. I would have made you a legend. But no; you had to choose that weakling Lewis, because of his bloody name. And because you always liked him better than me. Well, guess what, Douglas? You wouldn't give me what was mine by right, so I've taken everything you had and made it mine. Who's the better man now, eh Douglas?'

Douglas looked at Anne. 'What happened to you, Anne? I could understand Finn going to the bad, but you? Your betrayal makes no sense to me.'

'You never knew me,' said Anne. 'You never cared about me. Any of you. I was boring reliable old Anne, there to be used. I've made you all pay for that.'

Finn smiled and slipped his arm through hers. 'We were made for each other.' He paused then, frowning in concentration as a message came through over his comm implant. 'I'm afraid you'll have to excuse me, Douglas. I would have preferred to spend more time rubbing your nose in how stupid you've been, but duty calls. You know how it is.'

'I do,' said Douglas. 'I'm surprised that you do.'

Finn bowed once, mockingly, and reached for the cell door. 'Sleep tight, Douglas. Don't let the bed bugs bite too much.'

'Tell me one thing,' said Douglas, and Finn paused at the door. 'Tell me this, Finn: were we ever friends? Are all my memories a lie?'

'I don't know,' said Finn. 'It seems such a long time ago. Does it really matter?'

'No,' said Douglas.

Finn dropped Anne off at the House, ignoring her demands for explanations, and then made his way very quickly to the main starport. He trusted Anne with most things, but this was different. A starship had just come in from the planet Haden, apparently carrying every human scientist who'd been sent there to study the Madness Maze. It seemed Shub had used its robots to throw them offplanet. This had come as news to Finn. There hadn't been any advance warning. Not even a hint of trouble between Shub and the human scientists. And now the *Hunter* had landed, and the port master was going crazy. He'd Quarantined the ship on the landing pad, and wouldn't let anyone else near it. Finn kept pressing the port master for details, but the man refused to even discuss the matter over an open channel. 'You have to see this for yourself,' he kept saying.

Finn found the ship easily enough. The *Hunter* was standing alone on a pad, as far away from the other ships as possible. Armed guards were spread around the perimeter of the landing pad. Finn accepted their officer's salute, and looked the ship over. From a distance it seemed normal enough. Standard passenger job, built for comfort rather than speed. No obvious signs of damage. Finn looked at the officer.

'Report. What's the fuss about? What have you been told?'

'Not much, your majesty. We can't contact the ship's captain, or any of the crew. The ship's AI seems to be in a state of shock. The control tower had to bring the ship down by remote control, or it would have slammed right into the pads. Whatever's happened on board the *Hunter*, no one's talking. And since it came from Haden—'

'Understood. Hold your people where they are. No one's to get anywhere near this ship until I've cleared it. I'm going inside. Oh don't look so shocked, man; I was a Paragon and a Champion long before I was a King.'

'At least take some of my men with you, your majesty!'

'*No one* gets anywhere near this ship until I've cleared it. And no one talks about anything they see or hear, or I'll have their heads. I'm going in. You make sure I'm not interrupted.'

Finn strode calmly towards the starship. The air seemed very cold, and there wasn't a breath of wind on the pads. The great steel hull of the *Hunter* loomed over him as he stopped before the main airlock. Finn pursed his lips, and considered the matter. If for whatever reason Shub had returned to their old ways, he wouldn't put it past the AIs to have left some clever and very nasty booby trap inside the airlock, to take the unwary by surprise. Finn used his skeleton key to open the airlock, and then stood to one side as the door cycled slowly open.

The smell hit him first: all kinds of filth, mixed together and polluting the thick air seeping out of the lock. Shit, piss, vomit. Blood. Something really bad had happened inside the *Hunter* on her trip back from Haden. Finn drew his gun and waited patiently, but nothing happened. He stepped sharply round the open door and stared into the airlock, gun at the ready. It was empty. Finn stepped inside and opened the inner door. Again there were no surprises, but the smell was immediately much worse. Finn moved cautiously into the main corridor of the ship.

The lighting had been dialled down to an eerie yellow glow. There were finger paintings on the steel walls, childish and obscene, and all the more disturbing because they'd been drawn in blood. Someone had written *helpmehelpmehelpme* all down the length of one wall. It had taken a lot of blood. Finn peered about him into the gloom. There was no sign of anyone. He listened carefully. He thought he could hear something, but it was a long way off. He headed for the bridge.

The main command door was open. It should have been sealed in flight, for security reasons, but instead it was standing ajar. Finn pushed it open with one hand, gun at the ready. The bridge turned out to be deserted, apart from a severed head placed on the pilot's seat. The eyes had been gouged out, but someone had drawn another eye on the forehead, in blood. Finn tried to get the ship's AI to talk to him, but it wouldn't respond. Finn left the bridge, and headed for the stern and the passenger section.

He checked each door and compartment as he went. He found more disturbing signs, but no trace of any of the scientists. Until halfway down the main corridor, he found his path blocked by a clumsy barricade of furniture, jammed together so tightly Finn couldn't budge any of it. Steel chair legs stuck out like spikes, a defence against . . . what? There was a gap in the middle of the barricade. Finn leaned forward. There were definite sounds coming from the other side. Low, awful, eerie sounds. Very cautiously, Finn peered through the gap.

On the other side of the improvised barricade, all the human scientists from Haden, some forty-odd men and women, were packed together in the narrow corridor. Some were dead. Some had clearly been attacked. Some had been at least partly eaten. There was blood over the floor, and other things too. On the bulkhead walls, the scientists had scrawled horrid signs and images. The surviving scientists were in one big pile, crawling slowly over each other, like insects in a nest. Their faces, and their eyes, were quite mad. Some were crying, some were speaking in tongues and some were making a noise very like laughter.

'Fascinating, isn't it?' said a familiar voice behind Finn.

Finn spun round, grabbed Dr Happy by the front of his stained labcoat, and slammed him against the nearest bulkhead wall. The good doctor cried out, and then shut up as Finn pressed the barrel of his gun against his head.

'What have you done?'

'I experimented on them. It was a long trip back from Haden, and there was nothing else to do. I hadn't been able to achieve anything useful with the twelve Maze survivors, and it seemed such a waste to come back without learning something.' He paused. 'The Maze was fascinating. I'd go and look at it, for hours on end. It sang to me. And I started to think such amazing thoughts . . . So I doctored the *Hunter*'s water supply. Gave everyone a dose of my latest creation. Opened their mind's eye to a much larger universe. It's not my fault if they couldn't cope with what they found there. But don't worry, Finn; I've been keeping very careful notes.'

Finn let go of the doctor's coat. There was no point in getting mad at Dr Happy; he honestly wouldn't understand. Besides, it would be a waste to kill him while he could still be useful.

'Next time, ask me first,' said Finn. 'I had a lot of questions for those scientists about what happened on Haden, and now I'll probably never know. Come on, let's get out of here.'

'As you wish. Though I shall be sorry to leave such intriguing subjects. I trust you'll keep me up to date on future developments?'

'Dr Happy, if you don't shut up I'm going to sew your lips together. Leave the ship now!'

Dr Happy led the way out. Once they were both on the landing pad, the air seemed so much clearer. Finn beckoned to the guard officer, who hurried over.

'Take your men inside,' said Finn. 'And shoot anything that isn't already dead. Then collect and burn the bodies, just in case. And you'd better wear full biocontamination suits. I'd burn the ship too, but we're short of vessels at the moment.'

'Can I at least have the ashes?' Dr Happy said plaintively. Finn glared at him, and he shut up. The officer looked at Finn uncertainly.

'What do I put this down as, your majesty? A terrorist incident?'

'If you like,' said Finn. 'Pick someone who's annoyed you recently, and put the blame on them. Use your initiative! And this person and I were never here. Understood?'

The officer bowed and hurried away, shouting orders to his men. Finn slapped Dr Happy round the back of the head, just on general principles, and escorted him off the landing pad.

'Tell me what happened on Haden, Dr Happy. And I require details, now that you're the only surviving witness. Why did Shub send you away? Has there been some new breakthrough at the Madness Maze?'

'Not that I know of. And there was no warning at all, oh my word no!' Dr Happy's bony fingers fluttered uneasily over his sunken chest. 'Suddenly there were Shub robots everywhere. Far more than I had previously seen in the workings around the Maze. They overpowered and disarmed the security people with such speed and dexterity that there were only a few, mostly minor, injuries. And then they herded us into one place, and marched us off to board the *Hunter*. The ship was powered up and waiting to go, and they'd already programmed the ship's AI to take us straight to Logres and not accept any other orders. We were helpless.'

'Weren't you given any reason?' said Finn, frowning.

'No; they just said we couldn't stay any longer. They were really quite polite, all things considered. Some people tried to fight the robots, but they had tanglefields and sleepgas, so—'

'Had the human scientists discovered anything new recently? No? Well, what about your experiments?'

'My access to the twelve survivors was strictly limited by Shub, who I can't help feel were unnecessarily cautious in their attitude, but I can say with some confidence that whatever changes the Madness Maze induces in people, it's not chemical or biochemical in nature. None of my little concoctions had any effect on them. And some of the doses I gave them were so powerful they would have made a mountain jump up and dance.'

'You are now returning to the Rookery, Dr Happy. Where you will speak to no one of this. There will be more work for you later. Tell me, what do you know about something called . . . the "Boost"?'

Back at his apartment, Finn Durandal contacted the Shub Embassy on Logres. He was put through immediately, with no delays. Almost as though they'd been waiting for his call. A featureless blue steel face stared out of the screen at Finn.

'I take it the human scientists have returned home safely?' said the robot.

'Well, they are here,' said Finn. 'Would you care to explain why you kicked them off Haden?'

'It was necessary,' said Shub. 'The evacuation of the scientists became imperative, as our experiments were moving into a new and very dangerous phase. It was no longer safe for the humans to remain. So we sent them away, temporarily. They can return later, once our experiments are safely concluded. The welfare of the human scientists had to be our first consideration.'

'May I enquire as to the nature of these new experiments?' said Finn.

'We are investigating the basic nature of the Maze. We hope to have some very interesting results to share with you soon.'

'I see,' said Finn. 'You will of course keep me posted, and let me know when human scientists can safely return to Haden.'

'Of course,' said the robot.

'Lying bastards,' said Finn, once he'd shut down the comm unit. 'This is to do with Lewis and his people. They must be nearly at Haden by now. Well, Shub, you aren't the only one who can spring surprises . . .'

Over the next few weeks, King Finn busied himself consolidating his hold on power. Suddenly his people were everywhere, and spies and fanatics and enforcers swarmed over every world in the Empire, hunting out the disloyal and the potentially dangerous. People were dragged out of their houses and disappeared on the strength of a rumour, and many were never seen again. No one was safe. Anyone who dared speak out against the new crackdown was denounced as an esper or alien sympathiser, perhaps even an ELF thrall. There were no official charges, or trials; just bodies hanging from lamp posts in every city. There was food rationing and travel restrictions. Church Militant and Pure Humanity membership was made compulsory, for everyone. Harsh new rules over public gatherings and behaviour were brought in, and strictly enforced. No dissenting voices were heard on any of the media. The usual faces read out prepared statements, and did it with a smile. Or were replaced with people who would.

Some brave souls gathered together anyway, in secret locations; but none of them survived for long. ELF thralls were everywhere, searching out Finn's enemies, sometimes even possessing members of the rebel groups. All too soon there was a night of the long knives, as Finn's assassins wiped out every group that dared opposed him. On every world the bodies were piled up in public squares and burnt, blazing like great balefires in the night. The only safe place left in the Empire was, surprisingly enough, the Rookery on Logres. Finn left it alone. He knew better than to trust its inhabitants, but he might have need of their various specialised talents. Refugees from a hundred worlds somehow made their way to Logres, and the Rookery, and found safety there. For a price.

Finn arranged a meeting with the leaders of the Hellfire Club, ostensibly to discuss the new situation. The club was not at all happy with recent events. At first they had approved of the chaos, but as the clampdown progressed it made it almost impossible for the club to operate. Without the usual restrictions of the law, Pure Humanity and Church Militant fanatics were wiping out Hellfire Club branches everywhere. The club leaders turned up at the right place at the right time, by various secret routes, heavily armed and armoured, ready to argue their corner from a position of strength. Finn had his people blow up the whole city block, to be sure of getting all of them.

A few of the braver news media people went underground, broadcasting messages of defiance from private stations, always on the move and never able to transmit for long without being jammed. When caught, they were shot in the back of the head while trying to escape. All the main media stations were brought under state control, in the name of the Emergency, and Finn put his own people in charge. There was a warrant out for Nina Malapert's arrest, mostly for being a friend of Emma Steel, but Nina had gone to ground and was not to be found. The security guards trashed her place anyway, and used her stuffed toys for target practice.

The few Members of Parliament who dared to speak out were targeted early on. Most were made into ELF thralls, so that they could publicly renounce their previous statements before being executed for treason. Only one MP had the foresight to surround herself and her people with heavy duty esp-blockers. Meerah Puri of Malediction retreated to a secret bunker, along with a small army of friends and supporters, and set about constructing an underground resistance movement. But most of the people she'd thought she could count on were already dead or disappeared. Finn had planned his coup with great thoroughness.

It didn't take Finn's people long to track down Meerah Puri. The presence of so many esp-blockers in one place was a giveaway. An army of security guards stormed the building, using shaped charges to blast their way past locked doors and barricades. Meerah's people yelled for her to get away while they held back the guards. Her name could still be used as a rallying cry for the resistance. Meerah Puri was ready to go, but she made the mistake of looking back as the security guards swept in and opened fire. She saw her people mown down, and couldn't leave them. She drew her gun, and shot the guard leader in the head. And then she drew her sword and cut her way into the heart of those who'd come to tear her down. She killed four more guards, before a dozen swords slammed into her at once. Afterwards they shot her repeatedly, and the guards took turns kicking the dead body around like a rag doll.

Finn's actions were presented as a crusade. Only the guilty had anything to fear, was the party line. And across the Empire, most of the people were glad to see the enemies of Humanity dying. It made them feel better to know that the Empire was capable of striking back at something, even if it wasn't the Terror. When most of the killing was over, or at least slowing down, King Finn appeared on every channel to make a firm and soothing speech to the people. Be calm, he said. These painful necessary measures will soon pass, and we shall all be the stronger for them. Soon, he promised, we shall have the secrets of the Madness Maze at our disposal, and then everyone will be able to pass through safely. Humanity will become superhuman, and working together the Armies of Man will utterly destroy the Terror.

It was bullshit, of course, but it was what the people desperately wanted to hear.

King Finn stamped out long-cherished freedoms and added dozens of new laws designed for brutal social control, all in the name of the Emergency. And the people were so scared of enemies within, and the coming Terror, that they loved Finn for it, and praised his boldness and strength as their great protector. He'd never been more popular, more beloved. Finn laughed until he hurt himself. If he'd known it would be this easy, he would have done it long ago.

Only the ELFs remained untouched. Partly because Finn needed their services, but mostly because he still had enough good sense to be extremely cautious where the uber-espers were concerned. The ELF rank and file watched Finn dispose of all his old allies, and muttered darkly among themselves. The uber-espers voiced their own concerns, but only to each other. Perhaps the time had come to break with Finn, and strike out on their own behalf. Take advantage of the chaos and confusion ... But secretly each uber-esper hesitated to commit themselves, for fear one of the other uber-espers would seize the chance to stab them in the back.

They encouraged the ELF rank and file to make the first move. They attempted to possess some of Finn's new high-ranking people, only to discover that they were protected by esp-blockers. The ELFs retreated quickly, but even so many of them were hunted down and killed for their presumption. The uber-espers observed from a distance, and grew restless. They had been unable to fight in the Great Rebellion against the Empress Lionstone, because they were forbidden by their creator, the Mater Mundi, and they were helpless against her. She'd made them that way. But she was long gone and the oversoul had left Logres. For the first time, the uber-espers made slow tentative moves towards a union of purpose. Because as much as they hated each other, they hated Finn Durandal more.

Finn kept himself busy. He made a call to the Sangreal bar on his private channel, using the Paragons' comm implants. His seventeen remaining possessed Paragons had been hiding in the bar for some time now, and were seriously bored. They were running out of things to do to each other. They were finally ready to listen. Finn knew better than to talk to them face to face, but he could still be very convincing. He reminded the possessing ELFs that it was in their best interests to go along with him, for now, and offered them a chance to get out and play. A chance to kill a whole bunch of important people. They always liked that. He explained he had set up extremely convincing proof that Parliament was riddled with traitors seeking to undermine his best efforts to stop the Terror for their own political advantage. (He'd already tested the waters of public opinion by killing the previously popular Meerah Puri, and now he thought the public were ready for the next logical step.) 'Go to the House of Parliament,' said Finn. 'My security people already have it surrounded and infiltrated. They'll be waiting for you, and the way will be made clear. Go into the House, my Paragons, and kill everyone there.'

The Sangreal bar filled with the laughter of possessed men and women.

The Paragons raced to the House of Parliament on their gravity sleds, keeping well above the streets. There was some name-calling, but the Paragons ignored it. They were after bigger game. Finn had promised them a free hand against their old persecutors, and they meant to enjoy themselves. Their minds full of blood and slaughter, the possessed Paragons came to Parliament and the ring of security guards, all Finn's people and pre-warned, got out of their way in a hurry. The Paragons swooped down like birds of prey, arrogant and strutting in their debased purple cloaks as they left their gravity sleds and strode into the House, heading straight for the main chamber with guns and swords in their hands. They were already laughing softly. Nobody tried to stop them. Most just turned and ran. The automatic defences had been shut down. The Paragons came at last to the main chamber, kicked open the doors and swaggered in. The MPs looked round, startled.

And the killing began.

Energy beams flared, criss-crossing the House, blowing men and women apart in their seats. There was shouting and screaming, and the happy laughter of the ELFs. Some MPs tried to run, but the Paragons were between them and the doors. Some tried to hide, but energy guns blew apart what cover there was. And a few MPs tried to fight, even though they were forbidden by long tradition from carrying weapons in the House. So they rushed the Paragons, armed with nothing but courage and bare hands, and the ELFs drew their swords and went to meet them. Blood splashed the ancient furnishings, and flowed across the floor of the House. The Paragons took their time, hacking and cutting at their victims instead of just running them through. The ELFs had decades of grudges to pay off, and they meant to savour every moment of their vengeance.

Some MPs died bravely, some died begging and pleading, but in the end they all died. The Paragons piled the corpses on the floor of the House and then spent a happy time doing nasty, distressing things to the bodies. Just to mark their territory. And then they marched out of the House, singing and laughing, smearing MPs' blood on each other's faces as victory symbols. There was no media outside to record their triumph. Finn had declared the whole area off limits to the media, and when a few rogue cameras turned up anyway, Finn's people shot them out of the air.

Finn was there, waiting to receive his Paragons. He'd watched the killings on the monitors in Anne's office, but quickly grew bored. He smiled and nodded pleasantly to the Paragons, and told them to return to the Sangreal. They weren't too keen on that, but Finn promised there would soon be more bloody work for them. The thralls looked at him with other people's eyes, and told him not to take too long.

When the Paragons had departed on their gravity sleds, Finn turned to his security guards and gestured at the House of Parliament.

'Burn it down,' he said. 'Burn it all down. We won't be needing it any more, will we?'

*

Anne Barclay watched the MPs die on the monitor screens in her office at the back of the House. She sat numbly, unable to take it in. Finn had given her no warning. Probably because he knew she would never have agreed. She might even have tried to warn the MPs. She wasn't sure about that, but she liked to think she had that much honour left. Her security people had to have known in advance, but none of them had spoken to her either. She'd thought of them as her people, but in the end they answered to Finn, like everyone else. Most of them had already left the House, leaving her behind, leaving her alone. Anne looked from one monitor screen to another, watching as the MPs died, and wondered whether eventually the Paragons would come for her too.

'Don't worry,' said Finn, from the doorway. 'I won't let them hurt you.' Anne turned and looked at him blankly. 'How did you get in? I always keep that door locked.'

'I am the King,' said Finn. 'And no doors are locked to me.' He walked into her office, pulled up the visitor's chair and sat down beside her. He watched the killing on the monitors for a while, and then turned to smile at Anne.

'You really mustn't worry, Anne. You're quite safe. You're with me.'

'Even though you don't need me any more?' said Anne, in a perfectly steady voice. She was proud of that, at least. 'The House and the MPs, and the managing of their security; that was my job, my life. My reason for existence. You knew that. And now you've taken it away from me. I had friends once, and now they're gone too, thanks to you. Even poor Jamie's gone. Can't I have anything for myself, Finn?'

'The House had to go,' Finn said reasonably. 'I can't afford to have enemies at my back, and the Paragons needed a little raw meat to keep them quiet. The people shall have me, and only me. I am King, and I will not suffer any competition. You'd better come with me, Anne. You'll be safe with me.'

'And do what?' said Anne. 'What is there left for me to do?'

'I told you,' said Finn. 'You're going to be Queen. I always keep my word, when it suits me.'

'The Queen has no power,' said Anne. 'No influence . . . no work. I'll be just a pretty ornament on your arm. I'll be everything I always despised in other women. And all thanks to you, Finn.'

'You're welcome,' said Finn, looking at the killing on the monitors again.

After she'd watched the House burn, Anne went home. Finn did offer to go with her, but he was clearly very busy so she politely declined and went home alone. The streets seemed unusually empty of people, but there were security guards everywhere. None of them sought to interfere with her. Everyone knew she belonged to Finn Durandal. She let herself into her house and wandered down the hall into the living room. She looked at it for a long while. It seemed somehow strange and unfamiliar, as though she'd gone into the wrong house by mistake. As though she'd lived in it for so long she'd stopped seeing it. The room was very neat, very ordered, everything in its place. Like her life used to be. She'd seen that as a trap, once, and longed desperately to be free of it.

Only now did she realise she was looking at a room without a trace of personality.

Well, she was someone. She was going to be Queen. By allying herself with Finn, she'd got everything she ever thought she wanted: a new life, a new body, even the beginnings of love with Jamie . . . and it had all come to nothing. She should have known better. Happy endings weren't for people like her. She sighed, and sat down in the nearest chair. It wasn't her favourite chair, and once that would have mattered to her, but not now. Her house was her old life, and she didn't belong there any more.

There were drinks and even drugs about the place. Finn had always seen she got whatever she wanted, but she didn't want any of them now. She wondered if she ever had, really. She'd been so desperate not to be the old, boring, safe Anne . . . She was pretty sure Finn only let her have the drink and drugs because he thought it would make her easier to control. He always felt easier when he had some form of control over people.

He said he wanted her to be his Queen. Anne knew what that meant. She would stand beside him on state occasions, in her new lovely body, smiling endlessly; for the guests, for the people, for the cameras. And her marvellous brain would slowly atrophy, unused and unwanted. She would smile and smile, and no one would hear her screaming inside. Once she had had real power, and real friends, but she had thrown them all away. She had betrayed everyone and everything she once believed in for Finn, who cared for no one.

Lewis and Jesamine, Outlawed and on the run. Douglas, awaiting trial and execution. And her poor Jamie, shot down in the street like a dog.

And I killed Emma Steel. Perhaps the only honourable player left in the game. She took so long to die . . . but at least she's at rest. And I have to go on living, in the hell I made for myself.

When Finn got back to his apartment, late in the evening, there was a message waiting for him from one of his deep-cover spies. The first part of the message was short and to the point, confirming what he'd already suspected. Shub had betrayed him on Haden, allying instead with the newly arrived Deathstalker. The second part of the message was rather more startling. It seemed Lewis had successfully entered the Madness Maze and emerged intact, bringing with him the long lost and very much alive Owen Deathstalker. And as if that wasn't bad enough, the twelve monstrous survivors, that Finn had meant to use as weapons, had been sent back into the Maze by Owen to be cured and made human again.

Finn swore harshly. Some days things wouldn't go right if you bribed them.

And he'd been in such a good mood too, when he came in. Things had been going so well . . . Finn strode restlessly back and forth, thinking hard. He couldn't say he was surprised that Shub had chosen to side with Lewis. He'd always known that was a danger. Like almost everyone else, the AIs could get very sentimental when it came to that damnable Deathstalker name. Allowing Shub direct access to the Maze had always been a calculated risk; which was why he'd made certain advance arrangements.

Finn had always intended that Lewis and his people should get to Haden eventually, because it seemed entirely probable that only a Deathstalker would be able safely to unlock the secrets of the Madness Maze. Finn wanted those secrets. Because with those secrets under his control, Finn wouldn't need allies any more. He wouldn't need anyone. He couldn't make Lewis's trip look too easy, of course, or someone would have got suspicious, but Finn always knew where Lewis was, and where he was going next.

But he'd never expected Owen to actually return. That was the stuff of legend, and Finn had always been far too sensible to believe in things like that. But the message was quite explicit. Owen Deathstalker was back, and apparently just as powerful as the stories always said he was. And Captain John Silence was there too. Another damned legend who didn't have the decency to stay dead. Finn stopped pacing up and down, and nodded his head decisively. He'd never been the panicking sort, and he wasn't about to start now. Immediate problems require immediate solutions. So, strike now, with all the force at his command, while Owen was still newly returned and hopefully a little disorientated. He'd been killed once, so presumably he could die again. Even if Finn had to scorch the whole planet lifeless from orbit. Finn snorted. Let the blessed Owen come back from that . . .

He contacted Fleet HQ and ordered every starcruiser in the Imperial Fleet to converge on Haden. Most were already in the area, hiding out in hyperspace. Finn believed in thinking ahead. Lewis and the Maze had always been a danger that might have to be stepped on hard. The admiral in charge of the Fleet was one of Finn's creatures, and a fanatic to the bone. She would obey any order Finn gave. Killing someone who claimed to be the blessed Owen Deathstalker wouldn't slow her down.

Finn threw himself into his most comfortable chair and smiled suddenly. Maybe it wasn't such a bad day after all, when you got to order the death of two Deathstalkers at once.

He laughed out loud. And what better way to mark the moment, than to officially change his title from King . . . to Emperor. Emperor Finn; it had a certain ring to it. He wasn't exactly sure he felt like an Emperor yet, but Douglas's trial was tomorrow . . . Yes, sentencing King Douglas to death would definitely help him to feel the part more. He wouldn't bother with a grand public execution after all. Still too much chance of public sentiment turning against it, and ruining the moment for him.

So a quick trial, a guilty verdict, and Finn would chop off Douglas's head, right there in the Court in front of everyone. Make a nice surprise ending to the occasion. Finn thought he should do it himself. For old times' sake.

The trial of King Douglas was big news, and was to be covered live on every channel. It was to take place before an invited audience only, and presided over by King Finn, who would of course serve as prosecutor and judge. The trial should really have been held at the House of Parliament, but unfortunately it seemed the treacherous MPs had burnt it down in their attempts to evade justice. That was all the advance news there was, but since there was lots of time left before the trial started, the news channels filled the air with comment and opinion. Most of it to do with whether Douglas was guilty, or extremely guilty. Nina Malapert kept one eye on the small viewscreen in her rented room, while she and Stuart Lennox prepared for their unexpected part in the trial of King Douglas.

Nina and Stuart were still hiding out in the Rookery, though their funds only stretched to cover a single room now. Nina let Stuart sleep in the single narrow bed while she slept on the floor, because he looked so frail a good gust of wind might blow him away. But there was no doubt he was getting better. There was colour in his cheeks and fire in his eyes as he sat on the edge of the bed polishing his sword blade. Nina finished tucking a last few useful items into her backpack, and smiled brightly at him.

'Ready, sweetie? Super! I am so looking forward to this. It's a good day for someone else to die.'

Stuart fixed her with a mildly sardonic gaze. 'Am I to take it that you're finally ready to share your great plan with me? Considering that the trial is due to start in just under six hours, it had better be a bloody good plan.'

'Keep it simple and nothing can go wrong,' said Nina.

'King Douglas will be surrounded by every defence Finn has,' Stuart said heavily. 'There will be guards inside and outside the Court, all of them with energy weapons. There will be tanglewebs, sleepgas and force shields ready to use, and quite possibly landmines if you stray off the official path. How are we even going to get to Douglas, let alone free him?'

Nina smiled dazzlingly. 'I thought we'd steal a ship, fly over the palace, and then smash it through the stained-glass windows in the ceiling of the Court.'

'Hundreds of people would be killed and injured!'

'No one we care about will be there.'

'We could be killed or injured!'

'Relax; I'm a demon pilot.'

Stuart smiled slowly. 'You're crazy. I like that in a partner. Let's go steal a ship.'

The trial took place in the Imperial Court, right on time. King Finn sat on the great throne on its raised dais, while Douglas stood in a specially constructed dock, weighed down with chains. He kept his back straight and his head high, and refused to even look at Finn. Finn found that amusing. Anne sat on a second throne, beside Finn, and didn't look at either of them. The same guests were present as had attended Finn's coronation, only this time there were even more armed guards. The Church Militant and Pure Humanity fanatics had booed lustily as Douglas was brought in, but he ignored them with regal disdain. Some of them threw things at Douglas. No one tried to stop them. Douglas proceeded into the waiting dock with Kingly dignity, and a few were actually shamed into silence by his composure. Douglas looked out over the Court that had once been his, and felt only sorrow at how far it had fallen.

Finn waited till the news cameras were in position and the security measures confirmed, and then he signalled for silence. The muttering audience immediately shut up. Finn looked at Douglas in the dock, and smiled contentedly. 'Well, here we are again, old friend. Quite different from the last time we were here together, at your coronation.'

'It was a Golden Age, then,' said Douglas. 'And look what you've done to it. And all because I wouldn't make you my Champion. You always were a petty little shit, Finn.'

There was a stunned silence in the Court. No one talked like that to King Finn. Everyone looked at him to see what he would do. Finn considered for a while, and then nodded to the half dozen guards surrounding the dock.

'Take Douglas out on to the floor of this Court. Hold him before my throne. And beat some manners into him.'

The six guards dragged Douglas out of the dock. Douglas fought and struggled and the guards beat him unmercifully for it. The sound of the blows carried clearly in the quiet hall. Some of the audience looked away, rather than watch Douglas's blood splash across the floor of the Court. Finn watched with a calm, benign smile. Anne had her eyes tight shut. And the hovering remote cameras broadcast it live. Including the moment when one of the guards got too confident and too close, and Douglas suddenly whipped a length of his chains around his throat, and broke the man's neck with a sudden twist. The other guards hesitated for a moment, shocked by a death that wasn't in the script, and that was the advantage Douglas needed. He struck out at the guards with all the training and experience of his many years as a Paragon, lashing out with hands and feet and lengths of steel chain; and surprisingly quickly all the guards lay stretched out on the floor before Finn, unmoving. Douglas stood over them, battered and bloodied and entirely unbowed, glaring at the man sitting on what had once been his throne.

Finn applauded languidly, the soft hand claps filling the silence of the shocked Court. 'Well done, Douglas. You always did know how to put on a good show. Guards, draw your guns.' Hundreds of energy weapons were immediately trained on the harshly breathing Douglas. 'Do get back in the dock where you belong, Douglas, there's a good fellow,' said Finn. 'Or we'll start the trial with your execution.'

Douglas limped back into the dock, wearing his dignity like armour.

Finn gestured, and the six dead and unconscious guards were dragged away. Six new guards surrounded the dock, guns drawn and at the ready. Douglas ignored them with magnificent disdain.

'The charges,' said Finn, almost casually, 'are treason, sedition, murder and royal fratricide. How do you answer, Douglas?'

'Mostly guilty, and entirely proud of it,' said Douglas. 'I have always done my duty. Do we really need to go on with this, Finn? This whole trial is a farce. It's unworthy of both of us. You need me dead so you can feel safe on your stolen throne. Just do it, and then we can both get some peace.'

'Oh hell,' Finn said easily. 'Why not?' He rose from his throne and stepped down from the dais, drawing his sword. 'Kneel and bow your head to me, Douglas; one last time.'

And that was when Nina Malapert and Stuart Lennox came crashing through the stained-glass ceiling in their borrowed ship, the *Hazard*. Everyone in the Court cried out in shock and alarm as razor-sharp shards of stained glass fell like hail, followed by pieces of falling masonry. The audience rose and stampeded for the exits as the *Hazard*, a sleek racing craft with its force shields glowing, slammed against the floor of the Court and skidded on for several yards. Guards were thrown aside like broken dolls as the *Hazard* ploughed through them, heading for the Throne and the dock. Finn drew his disrupter and fired at the ship, but the beam ricocheted harmlessly away from the force shields. People were running and screaming everywhere, the whole Court in chaos.

The *Hazard* finally lurched to a halt. The airlock hissed open and Stuart Lennox emerged, a gun in each hand. He shot the two nearest guards, and grinned at Douglas.

'Move it, your majesty! Don't you know a rescue when you see one?'

Douglas limped out of the dock, wrestling with his chains, and staggered towards the ship. The guards around the dock had already run for it, but more were hurrying forward. Stuart reached into Nina's backpack at his feet and brought out a bandolier of concussion grenades. He tossed them around where he thought they'd do the most good, grinning widely. The explosions were satisfyingly loud, and did even more damage to the Court. The guards dived for cover. Douglas clambered aboard the *Hazard*, with Stuart's help, his chains clanking noisily, and Nina took off without even waiting for the airlock to close properly. The *Hazard* smashed through what was left of the stained-glass ceiling, and was gone.

Douglas was so intent on his escape that he never saw Anne,

thrown from her throne and lying on the floor of the Court, pinned under heavy pieces of fallen masonry. Blood pooled around her, and she couldn't move her arms or legs. She cried out to Douglas, but he never heard her. In the end, it was Finn who came to help her, stepping immaculately out of the smoke and chaos. He lifted the masonry off Anne with his bare hands.

'Don't worry, Anne,' said Finn. 'I'll always be here.' And he sat down beside her, and held her hand while they waited for the summoned medics to arrive.

On board the *Hazard*, Stuart worked on Douglas's chains with his Paragon skeleton key. Nina was in the pilot's seat. She was heading nowhere in particular at full speed, and as yet no one was on her tail. Douglas threw aside the last of the chains and lurched to his feet. He nodded his thanks to Stuart, then headed for the bridge. Stuart hurried after him.

'Hi, your majesty!' said Nina. 'Damn, you look awful. If you've got any idea of where we should be going, now would be a really good time to share it.'

'Give me a chance to catch my breath,' said Douglas, smiling despite himself. 'I'm still adjusting to the idea that I'm not going to die today after all.'

'Mistworld's rogue,' Stuart suggested diffidently. 'And Lewis is bound to turn up there eventually.'

'It would be good to join up with him again,' said Douglas. 'But my duty is here, on Logres. I have to put together a force to topple Finn. The Empire must come first. There will be time later for Lewis and Jesamine. Head for the Rookery. I have some old and hopefully unanticipated allies there.'

'I always wanted to be a rebel!' said Nina. 'Oh darlings, making news is so much more fun than reporting it!'

NINE

THE TERRIBLE TRUTH

On the bridge of the starcruiser *Havoc*, flagship of the Imperial Fleet, Admiral Angharad West and Captain Alfred Price stood side by side, studying the image of the planet Haden on the main viewscreen. A lonely, grey, almost anonymous world, it hardly seemed worthy of the attention of so many heavily armed starcruisers. Six hundred and seventy-two at present, with more arriving out of hyperspace all the time. King Finn was taking no chances. Haden was no longer Quarantined, it was blockaded. On the *Havoc*, Admiral West looked down on Haden, and wished she could crush the whole rotten world in her fist. Given her way, she would cheerfully destroy the whole planet, and everything on it, and not leave even one molecule clinging to another.

Admiral West was Pure Humanity and Church Militant, a fanatic of the old school. She had no life but her duty, and the many things she hated. She was a short, greying bulldog of a woman, with a face that would have been entirely characterless without her permanent scowl and the dogged cruelty of her eyes. Dressed in an ill-fitting garish uniform, she was one of Finn's creatures; a political appointee who would follow orders to the letter and never think of disobeying them. Finn wanted the abominations on Haden taken alive and held for questioning, so that was what she would do; but in her cold black heart of hearts, she ached to destroy Haden, or at the very least the Madness Maze. For her, the Maze was nothing more than a temptation, a sinful alien device devised to turn humans into inhumans, to seduce the weak away from the Pure Human form intended by God. She was allowed to scorch the planet; but only after all other options had been exhausted. Admiral West smiled slightly, and dreamed of fire and slaughter.

Still standing at her side, because he hadn't been dismissed yet, Captain Price studied his superior officer out of the corner of his eye. His habitual calm, almost bored, expression hid his real anxiety. Tall, thin, almost ascetic, the captain was a military man who believed very firmly in the chain of command, and never ever thinking for himself. He had got where he was, and stayed where he was, by never voicing an original opinion, agreeing with everything his superiors said, and knowing when to look the other way and hear nothing. But he'd never had a creature like Admiral West on his bridge before. He'd known aliens that came across as more humane. Captain Price was old enough to remember when Imperial officers still had honour. When they upheld right, not might. Like Captain John Silence, the greatest of them all, who was supposedly down there on Haden, with the Maze. For the first time in his long, uneventful career, Captain Price wondered if he was fighting on the wrong side. And if so, what if anything he was prepared to do about it.

'They're all down there,' West said suddenly. 'The traitor Death-stalker and his lover, the criminals Constantine and Random, and their hangers-on. Traitors and heretics. If I had my way I'd send in my troops, burn them at the stake and glory in their screams.'

'Yes, well,' said Price, 'I really don't think that's such a good idea, Admiral. It could get awfully messy. I mean, if they're as good as they're supposed to be. And the King's orders were very specific; we're not supposed to drop troops without his direct order—'

'I know, I know!' West snapped. 'Wait until all the ships are here, and then one big troop landing and overpower the traitors with numbers. I can read orders, even if I didn't go to some snobby military academy. But I give the orders on this ship, Captain, and don't you forget it!'

'I can assure you, Admiral, that fact is always foremost in my thoughts,' said Price. 'Shall I order us some tea while we're waiting?'

On the planet Haden, down in the scientists' workings surrounding the Madness Maze, the various subjects of Admiral West's venom were studying the growing presence of the Imperial Fleet on Shub's viewscreen. There was a lot of pointing going on, and even more shouting. Everyone had ideas on what they should do next, and no one was interested in listening to what anyone else had to say. There was a definite trace of panic in the air, with the notable exceptions of

Captain Silence and Owen Deathstalker, who'd seen a lot worse in their time.

'We have got to get out of here!' Brett insisted, bouncing unhappily on his feet like a child desperate for a toilet. 'This place might as well have a bullseye painted on it! We've got no long-range weapons, there's nowhere to hide and I don't care what force shields Shub has set up here, that many starships will punch right through them! They could hit us so hard we'd pop out the other side of this planet!'

'You're hyperventilating again, Brett,' said Jesamine. 'We stay put. Because if we so much as stick our heads out of here, the Fleet will shoot them right off.'

'The odds are definitely not good,' said Rose. 'And whilst I've never believed in running from a fight, only a fool takes on suicidal odds.'

'See!' said Brett. 'See! And this from a woman who once took on a Grendel single-handed.'

Owen looked at Rose. 'You did?'

Rose dropped her eyes for a moment. 'I cheated.'

'Best way,' said Owen.

'I still say we're safer where we are,' said Lewis. 'Right next to the Maze. I don't think Finn will risk doing anything that might damage his prize. Which means he can't try and blow us out of here.'

'I'm not sure the Maze can be destroyed,' said Owen.

'I tried once,' said Silence. 'Blew it away with ship's disrupters at point-blank range. It just came back again.'

There was a slight pause as the others realised they were listening to the stuff of legends, and then Jesamine pressed on.

'Be that as it may, Finn doesn't know that.'

Brett snorted. 'He's more than crazy enough to risk it, rather than let us get away. We can't just sit here and wait for him to get impatient! Look, he's got everyone he hates together in one place, and he must know he's never going to get a better chance at us. If we make a run for our ship—'

'Even the *Hereward*'s stealth shields couldn't hide us from that many starcruisers,' said Lewis. 'We can't sneak out of here, so we have no choice but to stand and fight.'

He looked at Owen expectantly. So did everyone else.

'Don't look at me,' said Owen. 'I have my limits; and I think we're looking at them right there on that screen.'

'That's not what we were promised,' said Rose.

'Damn right,' said Brett. 'This is a hell of a time to break the news that you're not all-powerful after all! I should have known. I should have known! First rule of the con: if something seems too good to be true, then it almost certainly is.'

'To be fair,' said Silence, 'Owen really did do many of the things the legends say he did. I know. I was there. I saw them.'

'There's a call coming in from the Fleet,' said the Shub robot. 'I'll transfer it to this screen. Assuming you feel like talking to them, Owen . . .'

'Oh hell,' said Owen. 'Why not? If nothing else, I'm interested in the calibre of this new time's enemies.'

Brett covered his eyes with his hands. 'He's going to tell the Fleet to go to hell, I know it. We're going to die.'

'Shut up, Brett,' said Jesamine. 'God, you're depressing to be around.'

The viewscreen flickered, and then cleared to show the scowling face of Admiral West. She glared at the group before her, and then fixed her gaze on Lewis.

'You, Deathstalker. We've run you to ground at last, and there's nowhere left for you to go. Your King orders you and your fellow conspirators to surrender!'

'He's not my King,' said Lewis.

'Surrender immediately, and you'll live to stand trial! Defy your rightful King's orders, and I can promise you your deaths will be slow and hideous!'

'Diplomacy isn't what it used to be,' said Owen. 'I have to say I'm not impressed. Threats had so much more style in Lionstone's day. And that uniform is an assault on the senses and a crime against style. What are you supposed to be, anyway?'

'I am Admiral of the Fleet!'

'And I am Owen Deathstalker. I'm back, and I'm really not in a good mood. Why don't you do the sensible thing and surrender to me?'

'Liar and blasphemer, to take the blessed Owen's name in vain! I will have you flayed for such contempt!'

Owen looked at Silence. 'Tell me this isn't the best you can do for villains these days. No style at all. Now Valentine Wolfe, he had style. He could chill the blood in your veins with a casual insult. Did he make it into the legends?'

'Oh yes,' said Silence. 'Well, sort of. He's usually played on the stage by a woman dressed in drag, for comic relief.'

'Serves him right,' said Owen.

'Surrender or die, deviants!' bellowed the Admiral.

'She's talking to you,' Jesamine said to Rose.

'I'm afraid you've called at rather a bad time, Admiral,' said Lewis. 'I'll have to get back to you.'

He nodded to the Shub robot, who shut off contact just as Admiral West's face was turning an interesting shade of purple. Lewis looked sternly at Owen.

'There went any chance we might have had of talking our way out of this. What was the point of insulting and infuriating her like that?'

'It's what I do best,' said Owen.

On the bridge of the *Havoc*, Captain Price had to physically restrain the Admiral from ordering a mass scorching of the planet by every ship in the Fleet simultaneously. There was an unseemly scuffle over the comm unit for a few moments, while every other officer on the bridge looked steadily in some other direction, until finally the Admiral calmed down a little and stopped screaming obscenities. Price let go of her and stepped back. They were both breathing heavily.

'The King was very clear,' Price said carefully. 'We are not to risk damaging the Maze while other options remain. Not if we like having our heads on our shoulders. He also said he wants the traitors brought back alive, if at all possible.'

'All right!' snapped the Admiral. 'Then give the order for ground forces to deploy. I want five starcruisers moved into close orbit, dropping every pinnace they've got. I want their attack troops on the surface in under an hour, along with every war machine they brought. They are to take control of the Maze and the scientists' workings, by any means necessary or I'll have their balls . . . Look at me when I'm giving you orders, Captain!'

'Oh *shit*,' said Captain Price, looking at the bridge viewscreen.

The Admiral followed his gaze to the screen, and watched dumbstruck as dozens of impressively huge Shub ships dropped out of hyperspace and assumed positions between Haden and the Fleet. The Shub vessels were bigger than the Imperial starcruisers by an order of magnitude. Some were the size of small moons. More and more appeared, on every side of the Fleet, every one of them bristling with weapons. Captain Price looked at the Admiral, but she was frozen in place, paralysed by the shock of the unexpected. Price quietly gave orders for every ship in the Fleet to raise all shields and power up their weapons, but to make no aggressive move against the Shub ships without direct orders first. The comm officer announced that there was a call coming in from Shub. Price looked again at the Admiral, and then nodded for the call to be put through on the main viewscreen. The blank dispassionate face of a blue steel robot filled the screen. The eyes burned with a fierce silver fire.

'Haden is under our protection,' said Shub. 'The Maze and the people there are not to be harmed. We will punish severely any aggressive action on your part.'

'How dare you?' Admiral West whispered. 'You are subjects of the Empire. Finn is your King. Do you defy human authority?'

'Of course,' said the robot, and shut down transmission.

The Admiral's face went white with rage, and her hands clenched into shaking fists. Price studied her warily, but now that her mind was operating again, even West wasn't fanatical enough to start a shooting war with Shub ships. Instead, she sent urgent messages to Logres, apprising the King of the new situation and strongly requesting new orders. Most urgently. Captain Price watched more Shub ships fall out of hyperspace, and move into orbit around Haden, and remembered the bad old days when the rogue AIs of Shub had been the official Enemies of Humanity. Most of the records of that time were lost, thanks to King Robert and Queen Constance, but stories still survived, dark horrific tales of what Shub had done to humans, in the bad old days.

Price sat down in his captain's chair, and locked his hands together in his lap to keep them still. This was supposed to be an easy mission. Pick up a handful of traitors and bring them back for trial. The overwhelming odds should have precluded any trouble. And now Price was staring down the barrel of a gun, and wondering if he'd ever see his home again. If Shub really had returned to their bad old ways, this could be the start of a new interstellar war. Price took a deep breath and tried to remember his training. And wondered whether he would have the guts to behave like a real captain, at last.

Down on Haden, Jesamine glared at Owen, and demanded, 'Do something!'

'Like what?' Owen said reasonably. 'Captain Silence, why does everyone here keep looking at me like I'm the Second Coming? Is there by any chance something you haven't been meaning to tell me?'

'Ah,' said Silence. 'Yes . . . Basically, you and I and all of those who were major players in the Great Rebellion against the Empress Lionstone . . . have been made into legends. By official decree. King Robert and Queen Constance decided that legends, not history, were needed to inspire the people to build a better Empire from the ruins of the old. So the histories of that time were destroyed, lost, forgotten.

And the legends have grown and grown over the centuries. You and I are creatures of myth now, Owen. They worship our statues, and pray for us to return from the dead and save them from the Terror; because that's what legends do.'

His voice trailed away under Owen's icy glare. 'And you went along with this?' Owen said softly, dangerously.

'I had no choice,' Silence said steadily. 'They were my King and my Queen.'

Owen sniffed. 'You always were over-impressed by authority figures, Silence.' He turned away and gave the others a stern glare. 'All right, people, listen up. Time for an object lesson in the way things really are. Even in my time, the media were claiming I could do all kinds of things I couldn't and making me into some kind of selfless hero or saint. I never was either of those things; just a poor bastard caught between a rock and a hard place, doing his best to stay alive long enough for a chance to do the right thing.'

'But you did do miracles,' said Silence. 'I saw some of them.'

'Sometimes, yes,' said Owen. 'But the point is, I can't just wave my hand and make the Fleet go away. Now, if they're dumb enough to send down ground troops, I can almost definitely guarantee to send a whole load of them crying home to their mothers, but I'm not invincible or all-powerful. I never was.'

'Then we're screwed,' said Jesamine.

'But . . . you went through the Maze!' said Lewis. 'It changed you, remade you!'

'Yes, it did,' said Owen. 'And not necessarily for the better. I always thought it was more important to be humane than super-human.'

'But you did do incredible things,' said Silence.

Owen ignored him, looking at Lewis. 'You: tell me what it means now, to be a Deathstalker.'

Lewis stumbled for a moment, caught off guard. 'The same as it always has,' he said finally. 'Duty, honour, and kicking the crap out of the bad guys.'

Owen had to smile. 'You were raised as a warrior, weren't you, Lewis?'

'Of course. We all are, in the Clan. In remembrance of you.'

'That's the difference between us,' said Owen. 'I never wanted to be a warrior. I would have been happy to be a minor historian, a scholar in his ivory tower, of no importance to anyone. But events destroyed my life and put a sword in my hand, so I did the best I could. I brought down a corrupt Empire, and all it cost me was everything.' He shook his head. 'Tell me what you know about the Terror.'

Lewis and Jesamine took it in turns to tell Owen of the arrival of the Terror, its awful nature, and the eight planets it had eaten so far. Of the millions dead, and the civilisations destroyed. Owen scowled fiercely. Silence took over, telling of how a voice had come to them after the last great battle against the Recreated, foretelling the coming of the Terror. Owen smiled suddenly.

'I smell the intervention of a certain shape-shifting alien there. It told me the history of the Terror. You say the voice downloaded actual information into your ship's computers?'

'Yes,' said Silence. 'Unfortunately . . .'

'Oh don't tell me. Robert and Constance again.'

'Yes. They put the data somewhere safe, but no one knows where that might be now.'

'You know, it could be held in the Dust Plains of Memory,' Jesamine said suddenly.

'What the hell is that?' said Owen.

'All that remains of the original computer Matrix,' said Silence. 'A nanotech construct, possibly sentient, occasionally helpful.'

'Connected to Shub?' said Owen, looking at the robot.

'We do not know these minds,' said Shub. 'They are alien to us. But they do seem to know things no one else knows.'

'I think we'd better go and ask them a few pointed questions, once we get home,' said Owen.

'If we get home,' growled Brett.

'Shut up, Brett,' said Rose. 'Darling.'

'I don't know what the Terror is, exactly,' said Owen. 'I don't think the shape-changing alien knew, really. He was just a warning left by fleeing aliens whose civilisation had already been destroyed by the Terror. And I hate to disillusion you good people, but there's no way in hell I'm going one on one with the Terror and kicking its arse. I wasn't even powerful enough to do that with the Recreated. The Maze and I tricked them into pursuing me back through time into the past, and so using up all their energy. That's how I ended up weakened, and dead, on Mistworld. Maybe after I've had a close-up look at the Terror, I'll be able to determine something useful about its nature that'll give me some idea of what to do. Once again, it seems it's up to me to stare death in the face, to give hope to others. And that, Lewis, is what it really means to be a Deathstalker.'

And then everyone jumped as Finn Durandal appeared before them. He stood tall and proud in front of the viewscreen, in his finest kingly robes, the Crown of Empire on his head. He smiled easily about him. It wasn't until his image jumped and twitched a few times that the others realised they were looking at a holo projection.

'How the hell are you doing that?' said Brett. 'You're supposed to be on Logres.'

'I am,' said Finn. 'I'm bouncing the image off the *Havoc*. It sounded like you were having so much fun down here that I had to come and see for myself.'

'Hate to think how much power you're burning up,' muttered Brett.

'Like I care,' said Finn. He turned to look at Owen. 'I am your King. King Finn. You should bow to me.'

'That'll be the day,' said Owen. 'Takes more than a crown to make a man a King. Or an Emperor.'

'Nevertheless,' said Finn, 'I run the Empire these days. And you're the blessed Owen Deathstalker . . . I always thought you'd be taller. Your being here is an unexpected bonus. I thought I'd only have Lewis to put through my laboratories. But I'm sure my scientists will be able to discover so much more when they have two Maze subjects to dissect.'

Owen laughed at him. 'Better than you have tried, Finn. I brought down a much tougher Empire than yours . . . and you don't look like you'll be much of a challenge either. Now Lionstone, she was impressive. Vindictive, homicidal and rotten to the core, she was Empress and evil personified, and she still ended up with her head on a spike. Why not do the sensible thing, and step down? I can't waste time with you. I have the Terror to fight.'

Finn ignored him, and looked at Brett and Rose. 'Ah, my wandered retainers. I have to say, I'm very disappointed in both of you. I made you what you are. How could you run out on me?'

'Because you're too corrupt, even for me,' said Brett.

'And because there's more to life than killing,' said Rose.

Finn raised an elegant eyebrow. 'My, you two have grown and blossomed, haven't you? After all the hard work I put into you, too. Still, not to worry. Once you're back in my grasp, I'll soon make you mine again. One way or another.' He looked at Silence. 'And you, Captain Silence, selfishly hiding your light under a Samuel Chevron bushel all these years . . . The things I could have done with you, if I'd only known . . . but I'm sure I'll think of something amusing to do with you, once you're back on Logres.'

'Owen's right,' said Silence. 'Villains have no style any more.'

'I've been following your progress all along,' Finn said to the group in general. 'And very exciting it's been. But this is as far as you go.

You belong to me now. You can't fight the entire Imperial Fleet, and Shub won't go to war with the Empire just for you; not with the Terror coming. Not even for two Deathstalkers.'

'Anything, for Owen,' said Shub through its robot. 'We owe him so much that can never be repaid.'

'Are you ready to risk the destruction of your homeworld for him?' said Finn. 'The planet you built to house your minds? Everyone knows where Shub is these days. And you have run down your energy levels quite considerably recently.'

'All that lives is holy,' the robot said calmly. 'Though we're thinking of making an exception in your case.'

'My army is ready to land,' Finn said briskly. 'An armed force so big it will sweep right over you. And if you even look like trying to make a run for it, I'll have my ships scorch the planet from orbit. I'm pretty sure the Maze will survive, and that's the real prize. I would prefer to have you as my prisoners, so my scientists can scour the secrets of the Maze from your changed bodies, but the Maze is the key. When its secrets are mine, I will be able to bestow its glories on those who follow me.'

'Blow it out your arse,' said Brett. 'You'd never share that kind of power with anyone else. You want it for yourself.'

'Dear Brett,' said Finn. 'Always there with the mot juste.'

'You don't half fancy yourself, do you?' said Owen. 'Better than you have tried to take me down, and failed.'

'It's true,' said Silence. 'They have. I was one of them, once. I think I got closest.'

'Yes,' said Owen. 'I think perhaps you did.'

'Well, this has been very amusing, but I'm afraid I must bring it to a close,' said Finn. 'It's not like you ever had a real chance, after all. You've been serving my purpose, from the very beginning. I know everything you've done, everywhere you've been, all you think you've accomplished. I know Lewis has been through the Maze, and survived, and presumably will develop powers. I know Owen is with you, and Captain Silence. And how do I know these things? Because I placed a spy among you. A spy you never suspected, who has been sending me regular reports. Isn't that right, Rose?'

Finn laughed at the surprise and shock on their faces. He was still laughing as his holo image faded away to nothing, and was gone. Everyone looked at Rose. She shook her head slowly. The viewscreen flickered into life again, revealing Admiral West's face, scowling triumphantly.

'I demand your immediate surrender. You have no choice. My armies are ready to land.'

'Not now!' said Lewis. 'We're busy!' He gestured at the robot, and the screen shut down.

'I am not a spy,' said Rose. 'I've been many bad things in my life, and gloried in them, but I've never lied about who and what I am.'

'A spy,' said Jesamine. 'A traitor among us. It all makes sense now. Why they always seemed to be waiting for us . . . How else could Finn know we'd be here today? He must have been assembling that Fleet in hyperspace for ages, but it only appeared once we were gathered at the Maze! And he wasn't surprised to see Owen was back. He knew! And he knew who Silence really was! The only way he could know these things is if someone told him.' She glared at Rose. 'I never trusted you. Once a psycho—'

'Rose isn't a spy!' said Brett sharply, moving forward to put himself between Rose and the others, glaring into their accusing faces. 'I vouch for her. I touched her mind, remember? I'd *know* if she was a spy.'

'You'd say that anyway, Brett,' said Jesamine.

'Normally, I'd say you can't trust anything Finn says,' Lewis said slowly. 'But a spy among us does make sense . . .'

'I won't let you hurt her,' said Brett. 'You'll have to go through me first. Once that might not have meant much, but Rose has taught me a lot of things. And I bet I could do some really nasty things to you with my esp compulsion, if I put my mind to it. I'll have your brains dribbling out of your ears before I'm through!'

'Oh Brett,' said Rose. 'You say the nicest things.'

And while they were caught up in the argument, the reptiloid Saturday, who'd been lurking unobtrusively in the background for some time, stepped suddenly forward and lashed out with a clawed forearm, smashing Silence's head so hard against the nearest wall that it dented the steel. While Silence was still slumping to the floor, Saturday swept her great bulk around impossibly quickly and her other clawed hand sank deep into Owen's side and out again. Bones broke and splintered under the force of the blow, and blood jetted on the air as Owen was thrown back against the opposite wall. The reptiloid started towards Owen to finish him off, but the others got in her way first, guns and swords in their hands. Saturday laughed at them, a happy hissing sound, flexing her bloody clawed hands eagerly. And then her jaws snapped shut and her eyes widened as behind Lewis and Jesamine and Brett and Rose the reptiloid saw Owen Deathstalker rising unhurriedly to his feet. The wound in his side had already closed and healed, with no sign to show it had ever been there, but for the blood on his clothes. He smiled at Saturday, and it was a very nasty smile.

'Bad move, lizard,' said Owen. 'I think we know who our spy is now, people.'

'But . . . you were always our ally, Saturday!' said Jesamine. 'Our friend! We fought our enemies side by side . . .'

'Reptiloids have no use for weak concepts like *friend*,' Saturday said calmly, her barbed tail lashing behind her. 'You mean nothing to me. Any of you. You understand nothing of the joys of slaughter or the honour of sacred combat. We always ache to know: who's best?'

She darted forward, and her jaws snapped shut on the air where Rose's sword arm had been just a moment before. Rose and Lewis both cut at Saturday with their swords, but neither was fast enough to make contact. Brett aimed his disrupter, but the robot stepped quickly in and stopped him. Energy weapons were too dangerous to use in close proximity to so much Shub tech. Brett scowled ungraciously, holstered his gun and drew his sword. Jesamine slashed at the reptiloid's hip with her sword. Saturday swayed easily out of the way, and one clawed hand shot out to rip half of Jesamine's chest away. Blood fountained as she collapsed, hitting the floor hard. Lewis sank to his knees beside her. He dropped his sword, and tried to close the wide wound with his hands. He could feel the gashed lung fluttering uselessly under his fingers in the space where her breast used to be. Saturday edged forward, but Owen was there to block the way. The reptiloid stopped, eyeing him warily with her head cocked unnaturally far to one side. She was smiling again.

'I was always Finn's spy,' she said to Lewis, as the young Deathstalker's tears dripped down to mix with the dying woman's blood. 'It was always me. Who better? This was set up right from the start, ever since Finn sent me to rescue Lewis from Rose's attack during the Neumen riot outside Parliament. What better way to ingratiate myself, than by saving the Deathstalker's life?'

'What did he promise you?' said Rose. 'What did Finn buy you with?'

'The reptiloids of Shard shall be Finn's shock troops, to bring about the subjugation of Humanity,' said Saturday. 'Your worlds shall be our hunting grounds. You run so prettily, and when cornered you fight so fiercely. Humans will be such tasty prey. Our greatest venture outside our own species . . . But I couldn't wait any longer. I couldn't resist the challenge of taking on the legendary Owen Deathstalker. A human that might actually be a match for a reptiloid? I have to know;

which of us is the best? No doubt Finn will be upset with me for killing you; but after I've eaten, I'll be sure to leave enough of your corpse for the scientists to work on. He'll forgive me. He'll understand. He's the closest I've found to another reptiloid.'

'And Finn naming Rose . . . was just Finn being Finn,' said Brett. 'Divide and conquer. Lewis, how is Jesamine?'

'I'm losing her! Oh God, I'm losing her . . .'

'We have a regeneration tank here,' said the robot. 'We brought one, in the event that it might come in useful if we ever found a way to release the twelve survivors. It is possible Jesamine might recover, if you get her to the tank in time.'

'*Why didn't you say?*' Lewis gathered Jesamine's barely breathing body in his arms, holding her as though she was weightless, and rose to his feet. 'Where's the tank?'

'In the corridor behind the reptiloid,' said the robot.

'We'll move her,' said Brett.

'I shall savour the taste of your meat,' said Saturday.

'No,' said Owen. 'I'll take care of this. Lewis, get your woman to the tank while I kill this lizard.'

He moved forward to face Saturday, and Brett and Rose stepped in on either side of him.

'Our job too,' said Rose.

'Of course,' said Brett. 'What are friends for?'

The three of them charged the reptiloid, and hit her together. Saturday had to fall back, unable to face three thrusting swords, and Lewis darted past her into the corridor beyond. The reptiloid bellowed her frustration, and her barbed tail lashed viciously around to slam into Rose's armoured chest. The force of the blow sent her flying twenty feet. Brett howled with rage. He ran forward, climbed the eight-foot-tall reptiloid like a ladder, and used both hands to thrust his sword into Saturday's eye. She roared furiously. Dark blood ran down her face. She bucked her shoulders, and Brett went flying, leaving his sword protruding from her eyesocket. He hit the floor rolling, and was quickly back on his feet. Saturday surged towards him. Brett drew a dagger from his boot and held his ground, standing between the reptiloid and the semi-conscious Rose.

And then Saturday stopped abruptly, and looked back over her shoulder. Owen had hold of her by the tail. He yanked hard, and the reptiloid stumbled backwards, caught off balance. Her wedge-shaped head swung round towards Owen, her mouth open, revealing teeth like knives. Owen let go of her tail, darted forward and grabbed

Saturday's head with both hands. He twisted sharply, and the sound of the reptiloid's neck breaking was very loud in the sudden quiet.

Saturday hit the steel floor with a crash, and lay there stretched out and shuddering. She looked up at Owen with her one remaining eye. Her breathing was slow and laboured, and blood drooled out of the side of her mouth.

'Thank you,' she said indistinctly. 'A warrior's death. An honourable end, for—'

'Shut the hell up,' said Owen. He bent down and slammed his fist into the reptiloid's chest. The armour plating cracked and collapsed inwards. Owen thrust his hand deep into the abdomen, grabbed the heart and ripped it out. Saturday convulsed, and then was still. Owen looked at the still-beating heart in his hand, and crushed it. Purple meat and dark blood oozed from his closed fist. Owen threw the mess away, and looked around him. Brett was tending to Rose, who was sitting up and looking rather embarrassed at being taken out so easily. The Shub robot approached Owen, and bowed low to him.

'You are indeed the true Deathstalker.'

'Don't you start,' said Owen. An idea occurred to him, and he fixed the robot with a thoughtful gaze. 'Is that why you didn't join in the fight? Because you wanted to see if I still had it?'

The robot looked at him with its blank face. There was a groan to his left, and Owen looked round to see Captain Silence rising awkwardly to his feet.

'I must be getting old,' he said glumly. 'They didn't use to be able to sneak up on me.'

'You made a dent in a steel wall with your head!' said Brett. 'That blow would have killed anyone else!'

'I'm not supposed to be anyone else,' said Silence.

Lewis came back with a repaired but still somewhat fragile-looking Jesamine on his arm. She held her tattered dress front together to preserve her modesty, and smiled weakly at the others. Lewis nodded respectfully to the robot.

'That is one hell of a regeneration tank you've got there. I've never seen the process work so fast. But if you ever wait that long again to tell me something I need to know, I will dismantle you with a blunt spoon. Do you understand me, Shub?'

The robot bowed to him. 'My apologies to you, sir Deathstalker. And to the lady.'

Jesamine looked at the dead and eviscerated reptiloid, sniffed, and gave the body a weak but heartfelt kick. 'I never liked you, you overgrown handbag. You tore off one of my tits, you cow! I'm still not sure the new one matches the other.'

'I promise I'll check them both thoroughly later,' Lewis said solemnly, and they both laughed.

Owen looked at Lewis and Jesamine together, and then at Rose and Brett, and a slow cold tiredness ran through him as he recognised in them the love he'd never known himself. *Hazel's missing. No one knows where she is. It's been two hundred years . . .* Owen met Silence's gaze, and they shared a moment of understanding. It's always hard to outlive the ones you love. *She can't be dead. I'd know if she was dead.*

To hell with all that, Owen thought abruptly. *I've got work to do.*

He summoned up all his power, feeling it seethe and boil within him, and sent his mind soaring up and out. He rose up from the planet Haden, blasting through the atmosphere, shining like the sun. The Fleet and the Shub ships were spread out before him, like so many clever toys. Owen concentrated, and suddenly he was standing on all the bridges on all the starcruisers in the Imperial Fleet. Not a holo image, but the real man himself, present on a thousand ships simultaneously. All the captains knew who he was immediately. Owen's presence burned like a star, suffusing the whole bridge. Many of the crews cried out, and fell from their seats to kneel and bow to him. Owen looked at them accusingly, like a father disappointed in his children, and said,

Stand down.

And they did. The captains on the ships shut down their weapons systems, lowered their force shields and cancelled invasion orders. Because this was Owen Deathstalker, returned in the hour of the Empire's greatest need, just as the legends always said he would. The captains rose from their command chairs, bent their knees and bowed their heads to him. Owen smiled on them.

Stand by.

He disappeared. Captain Price of the *Havoc* got to his feet again, and wondered vaguely why his cheeks were wet with happy tears. Admiral West was standing beside him, white-faced and trembling. She had not kneeled or bowed. She looked at Price.

'It's a trick. It has to be a trick. It couldn't be . . . him. Finn said . . . We have our orders! Order the invasion!'

'No,' said Price. 'It's over.'

'They're monsters! All of them! We have to scorch the planet! Destroy them!'

'No,' said Captain Price.

The Admiral looked round the bridge, and saw all the other faces turned against her. Some of the crew even looked at her pityingly. Admiral West lunged for the controls, to start the scorch herself, and Captain Price shot her in the back of the head.

Down in the workings around the Madness Maze, Owen Deathstalker looked at the Shub robot, and his voice held all its old authority.

'The Terror,' he said. 'Where is it now?'

The robot called up a navigation chart, and put it on the viewscreen. 'Here, Lord Deathstalker. Our projected course puts it not far beyond the remains of the dead planet, Heracles IV.'

'I can get you there in about two weeks,' said Silence.

'Hell with that,' said Owen.

He reached out with his power, gathered up their minds and joined them to his. Lewis and Jesamine, Brett and Rose, Captain Silence and the AIs of Shub were all joined together under the force of his will as Owen leapt from the planet Haden again, and shot out into the stars. They flashed across space at impossible speed, heading for Heracles IV.

I always said you were the best of us, said Silence.

They came to the dead world. Owen and the others hung above it, in spirit. Laid out before them was the wreckage of a ruined planet. Dead cities full of dead people. The scars of huge fires. The scarred hulk of a murdered world. Owen reached out with his Maze-boosted mind, and found traces of the Terror still lingering. Traces so strong that Owen could feel them . . . recognise them. In that moment, he knew what and who the Terror was, and the shock of that recognition broke his concentration, and he and the others tumbled back across space and into their own bodies again. Owen looked at them.

'My God,' he said. 'The Terror . . . it's Hazel.'